The *Whisper* of REASON

Harry J. Connolly III

First Edition

PAGE PUBLISHING, INC.
New York, NY

First originally published by Page Publishing, Inc. 2018

ISBN 978-1-64138-800-9 (Paperback)
ISBN 978-1-64138-801-6 (Digital)

Printed in the United States of America

Wisps of sand driven by wind slithered like snakes across the hard-packed beach at low tide. Tourists frolicked in the warm green translucent ocean waters that gently lapped on the wide beaches. Teenagers flew stunt kites, while children played at the water's edge, building sandcastles, soon to be flooded by the incoming tide. People strolled or rode bicycles on the beach of the sub-tropical paradise known as Hilton Head Island, South Carolina. The month was August, and the year was 1992.

A twenty-seven-year-old man named Ray Bangor stood at the water's edge. This was the start of the turnaround, the time when the tides reverse direction. Ray knew from experience that the turnaround produced perfect conditions for surf fishing. Where he stood right now would be covered in six to eight feet of seawater in another six hours. The afternoon sun began its descent in the cloudless sky. There would be perhaps two more hours of daylight left. Plenty of time to catch dinner.

Ray walked his surf rod out into the ocean and made a twenty-five-yard cast with the spinning reel. Using frozen cut mullet on a double leader, Ray was hoping to hook into a school of bluefish, which made for excellent eating. He placed his rod in the rod holder and waited. If something didn't bite within the next five minutes, the baits had been nibbled off the hooks by crabs. But it was not even one minute before the eight-foot surf rod bent in a sweeping arc. Whatever was on the other end was a powerful swimmer.

Grabbing the rod out of its holder, Ray walked out into the ocean and began to reel in his fish. It was strong and tried to pull the rod out of Ray's hands. Soon there was an ever-increasing number of tourists gathering on the shoreline, hence the reason Ray walked out into the water in the first place. He came to this beach to commune with nature, not discuss saltwater fishing with some tourist from the mid-west. The fish on the end of his line had stamina, and it swam back and forth through the gentle waves.

The crowd of tourists had grown to probably fifty people by the time Ray landed his played-out fish. It was a stingray, about eighteen inches across tip to tip. Ray never even pulled the fish out of the water. He flipped the exhausted fish on its back, causing tonic immobility or temporary paralysis. In the shallow water close to the shoreline, Ray removed a towel from around his neck and threw it over the fish's belly, thereby holding it in place.

Ray reached into his back pocket and produced a pair of needle-nosed pliers, which he used to collapse the barb on the hook. He then easily extricated the hook, grabbed the angry fish with the towel, and flipped it over on its belly. The stingray, sensing that its harrowing ordeal was over, swam off into the deeper water. Ray packed up his gear and headed back to his villa. He'd had a hard day at work, and he really did not feel like talking to people right now.

Early the next morning, Ray would drive over the state line into Georgia for a day of offshore fishing with his coworker buddy Max and Max's sexy girlfriend Gina. On the long drive out on Highway 80, they blasted rock music and smoked weed. It was going to be a great day, thought Ray. Max and Gina were good people. They were both funny and knew how to have fun. Max had an old twenty-six-foot center console, which he had personally wired with a powerful stereo sound system.

Their destination that day was the Savannah River Shipping Channel. Huge containerships from all over the world made their passage into and out of the Port of Savannah. Max expertly piloted the tiny twenty-six footer between lanes of shipping traffic. It was a ballsy move. An enormous ship with Chinese symbols painted on its faded and rusting hull blasted its powerful ship's horn at the tiny fishing boat, just to let them know that tonnage has the right of way.

On the bridge of the huge containership, the pilot turned to the ship's captain and said, "These crazy American motherfuckers!"

Ray had always made the argument that the loud rock music would scare the fish away. Max dared Ray to dive into the water of the shipping lanes. Max blasted his boat's stereo while Ray dove into the ocean. It didn't take Ray but a second to realize that the music was all but drowned out by the rumbling engines on the huge container ships. Quickly, Ray climbed back aboard Max's fishing boat, aptly named *The REEL BITCH*. Max had proved his point.

Now it was time for Max to fuck with his crewmates. "I can't start the engines, the stereo must have killed the batteries, we're going to get annihilated by a containership out here!"

"You … you fucker-head Max! Your stupidity is gonna get us all killed!" Gina screamed and began to hyperventilate.

"Heh, heh … heh!" laughed Max as he turned over the ignitions and the engines roared to life. He pushed the throttles forward and maneuvered *The REEL BITCH* out of the shipping lanes headed north to the southern end of Hilton Head Island.

"You are a fucking asshole, Max!" Gina yelled. "One of these days … all the stupid shit that you do is gonna come right back around on you!"

"Relax, Gina … ," said Ray. "Everyone knows Max is a fucking asshole … he doesn't need to prove it to us!"

A couple seconds passed before all three began laughing hysterically. It was time to fish, damn it! Also, it was time to crack open that all-important first beer of the day! It was 10:00 a.m. Max sat at the helm. Gina guzzled cold beers, while catching some rays in her bikini. It would not be long before she became the drunkest, most misbehaved girl on the boat! Ray stayed busy baiting the hooks with deboned bluefish. With the spine removed with a coring tool, the dead fish appeared to "swim" as they trolled over the ocean swells at high idle. Ray had just popped his second beer when one of the bait caster reels began to zing. Gina immediately jumped up and grabbed the second rod and furiously began to reel it in. Whatever was on the other end of the first rod was a big, powerful, lightning-fast swimmer.

Ray tried to set the hook, but in doing so made a crucial mistake. Whatever it was, it must have either stopped or did a complete 180-degree turn. The line on the large reel had "bird-nested."

"Oh … fuck!" yelled Ray.

"Gimme that fucking thing!" demanded Gina. She grabbed the rod and began to wind in the line over the top of the tangled mess.

Ray grabbed his beer and now both men watched Gina as if she had something to prove. But Gina was no amateur at landing large saltwater fish. She took her time winding in the reel inch by inch. She knew that eventually this thing was going to wear itself out, and as in most things, she was usually right. This was going to take a while.

Max used the break in the action to have a serious conversation with his friend Ray. "My old man just passed away," Max said somberly.

"Man … I'm so sorry for your loss … ," lamented Ray.

"It was all real sudden … I had to go to Charleston for the funeral."

Ray had never met Max's father, and he felt bad about it. Now he would never get the chance.

"Yeah … he was a good guy," said Max. "He left me something special, he left me something that he didn't want anyone else to have … it's a 1985 forty-six-foot convertible sport fisher with twin 671 engines. Free and clear."

"That's fantastic!" Ray exclaimed.

"That isn't even the best part … how would you like to quit your job as a diesel mechanic and go into business with me, charter sport fishing?" Max asked, grinning from ear to ear.

"Well … fuck yeah, dude! That's the best thing I've ever heard in my life … bro!"

"When you two fuckwads come back to earth … I could use a hand over here!" Gina sniped. Miraculously, she had wound a hundred yards of line over the bird's nest of tangles. Now the large fish was rolling on its side, completely played out. It was a shark and a pretty good-sized one at that. "It's either a blacktip or a spinner … I can't tell yet. Get ready, Max … you idiot!" she yelled.

Max very calmly reached into the console compartment and produced a .357 caliber revolver. He sat on the gunwale and yelled at Gina. "Get it in closer!" Gina pulled the rod tip straight up. Max leaned over the side and blasted the shark right between the eyes. "Help me gaff this bitch, Ray!"

"Man … I can't believe you just shot that shark," said Ray, completely perplexed.

"Are you gonna help … or are you just gonna sit there?" Max asked sarcastically.

Once aboard, the shark was in fact identified as a blacktip, and every bit of five and a half feet. And it had some girth, apparently it had been eating well. The three friends decided that it would be shark steaks on the grill tonight, a delicacy when prepared properly. It was Max who expertly beheaded, gutted, and skinned the shark, and now the "keeper cooler" was loaded with shark fillets and ice. It was now a little after noon. Time for lunch, time for a cold one, and time for a good smoke. Afterwards, it was time to begin the journey back to the Lazaretto Creek Landing. Ray and Gina took turns at the wheel as Max barked precise navigational instructions. There was no doubt in anyone's mind that day that Max was an expert boat captain.

Not much was said on the way home. It had been a good day, and it was going to be a good night! Everyone was tired and stoned, and once again, they blasted rock music as they rode. On the long drive back to Max's house, they stopped in a particularly rough section of Savannah to pick up more beer and ice. Locals were loitering in the area and seemed to be sizing up the three friends. Were they an easy mark? It was Max who would ultimately answer their question with a bold gesture. As he stepped out of the truck, he handed Ray, still seated in the backseat, the .357 revolver in plain view of everyone in the immediate area.

Gina said to Ray, just loud enough for all to hear, "There's another gun under the passenger seat … a .45 semiauto, chambered and ready to fire."

Max and Gina disappeared into the store under the cold stares from the locals. When they returned with a couple more cases of beer and 20 lbs. of ice, Ray was indeed relieved.

"Anything happen out here?" asked Max.

"Nap!" said Ray.

Max took a look around and said, "I didn't think anything would!"

Max was a true bad-ass! Most people spent their whole lives avoiding hostile situations. Max seemed to enjoy seeking them out. He was someone you would want to have on your side in a nasty bar fight.

His level of confidence and natural leadership skills would make him a fine charter boat captain, Ray was sure! What Ray needed right now was to talk about it more with Max. But there was no way Ray was going to bring up the subject in front of Gina. She seemed real negative about it all day. Ray couldn't understand her reasoning. She was a bad-ass chick and an expert fisherman. She would be perfect for the crew of Max's recently acquired sport fisher.

Ray would have his chance soon enough. When they arrived at Max's house, Gina would prepare dinner, and Max and Ray would off-load, clean *The REEL BITCH*, and run freshwater through her engines, all while drinking beer and smoking weed. Gina called over a friend to help her and join them for dinner. This was great! That other chick would keep Gina occupied all night, leaving the two men to handle the details of their new business venture.

"So did you offer Gina a position on your new crew?" Ray asked nervously.

"Yeah, I did, and she respectfully declined. Full-time sport fishing is just not her thing. She only does it on the weekends to make guys like you look like chumps!" Max said laughing.

Ray had to laugh at that one too. "Well, I think she's making a mistake, she's a pro!"

"Nah, man … it'll be cool just you and I … we can handle this! Besides, it'll be better this way, now I don't have to hire a third hand, and both of us make all the money!" Max said confidently.

A hot-rodded seventies muscle car pulled into the driveway. It looked and sounded pretty damn good! A very sexy, full-figured blonde shut off the engine and stepped out of the car.

"Damn!" said Ray, "That girl is hot as hell!"

"Yes … she is. She's Gina's friend Amy. Her husband is serving in the Middle East."

"That is too sad. I don't think I could marry a woman like that and serve in the military," Ray said respectfully.

The two women were good friends and very happy to see one another, even though they were neighbors and saw each other almost every day. The two women headed into the house. Soon there were the sounds of a blender crushing ice, then hysterical laughing, and then loud dance music. Amy, it seemed, was a partier. She would fit in nicely.

"Son of a bitch!" Max shouted as he grabbed his .357 and began firing in the direction on the house.

"What the fuck, man, who are you shooting at"? Ray asked nervously.

"Neighbor's dogs in the garbage … Don't worry, I was firing just over their heads … just barely over their heads, mind you!"

"Hey, Amy," Max yelled at the house. "Y'all don't own a big white dog, do you?"

The girls obviously could not have heard this over the music, so the two men walked into Max's house. In the living room, the stereo blasted techno funk music so loud that the bass frequencies made the whole house vibrate. Gina and Amy were "freak dancing" to the trance-inducing electronic music. Max and Ray took seats on a couch, and just sat there, watching these two very hot women "turn out" on each other. This was better than any strip club. This was real! One thing was certain. No strip club would ever allow the raunchy antics that Gina and Amy displayed while they danced.

Over dinner, everyone was extremely drunk or high or both. The dinner itself was a gourmet feast. Gina had expertly prepared the shark fillets by marinating them in whole milk in order to reduce the gamey flavor of shark meat. With butter, lemon, salt and pepper, grilled perfectly on each side, it was delicious! Amy was the life of the party now. She had only begun to party in the last couple of hours, whereas the other three had been at it since 6:00 a.m. and they were annihilated.

"So … y'all killed this thing today?" asked Amy in her sexy southern drawl.

"We took turns ... Ray hooks it, fucks up the reel, I reel it in ... and then Max shoots it in the head!" Gina giggled.

"Sounds like a fun time for y'all," Amy agreed.

It was getting late now. Max was chasing Gina around the house.

"I gotta go," said Amy.

"Are you all right to drive?" asked Ray.

"We just live across the road ... I'll be all right. It was nice meeting you, Ray," said Amy.

"Likewise," said Ray, trying to act cool, but he knew he was a drunk, incoherent idiot, right about now. In less than two minutes, he would be passed out on the sofa. At age twenty-seven, Ray Bangor was a functioning, hard-core alcoholic.

The following Monday found Ray transporting his mechanics tools from his former employer over the state line into South Carolina to a waiting storage facility. He would then concentrate the collection into a single chest to be loaded and stowed aboard *The REEL OPPORTUNITY*, the boat Max was about to inherit. They were heading to Charleston Wednesday morning and Ray couldn't wait. It was a whole complete lifestyle change for him, and he was looking forward to it greatly.

And so it came, Wednesday morning at last! Papers were signed. The complete ownership of the sport fishing vessel *The REEL OPPORTUNITY* was signed over to Max. They headed directly to the marina. The dock master directed them to pier number 4. It was there, all the way at the end of the pier, that they found *The REEL OPPORTUNITY*. It just looked just plain awesome!

"I wanna ride with you guys on that thing back to Hilton Head!" Gina said when she saw it for the first time.

"We agreed that you were going to drive my truck to Hilton Head Island ... baby," said Max.

"Yeah, well, I changed my mind!" Gina said excitedly. "We can leave your truck here ... and come back later to get it ... on that thing!"

Max could swear that Gina was getting wet, eye-fucking *The REEL OPPORTUNITY*. He never saw this coming. He hadn't counted on Gina being so visually affected by it size and sleek lines.

And it was beautiful! Gina walked over to it. She could not take her eyes off of this thing. Taking a deep breath, she turned toward the two men. "I wanna drive it!" Gina said.

"Slooooooooooow down, cowgirl!" said Max.

Gina had by now already boarded. "Open the door already!" she barked.

Max fumbled with his key ring. Gina bounced up and down on the balls of her feet excitedly. Max unlocked and opened the deck house door. Gina flew past him. "This thing is fucking awesome!" she screamed from inside the salon. A moment later, she was planting a kiss on Max. She even kissed Ray for good measure. There were tears in her eyes. She was so happy as of this moment.

The three set about the task of provisioning *The REEL OPPORTUNITY* with endless trips pushing dock carts back and forth from Max's truck to the end of pier no. 4. It was time-consuming, tiresome work. But all three adults were excited and highly motivated and the effort required was well worth it, they all knew. To think that the passing of one man, so greatly affecting all of them, was overwhelming. He had just completely altered the lives of three young adults and he had never lived to see it.

They popped corks and toasted their newfound freedom from the everyday world. They were set to embark early tomorrow. They set about to exploring the new vessel. Max sat up on the bridge. Ray poked around in the engine room. Gina went below and fell backward onto the master stateroom bed. She lit up a joint and stared in disbelief at the new world surrounding her. It was a moment she would remember for the rest of her life. They spent the night aboard the vessel moored at end of pier no. 4.

"Wake up, fucker-head!" Gina teased Ray at six the next morning.

Ray opened his eyes and, realizing where he was, smiled inwardly. The air inside the cabin was filled with the aroma of fresh brewed coffee and fried bacon and eggs. This vessel was really starting to feel like home already. They sat at the mess table and ate their breakfast. It went perfectly with the extra spicy Bloody Mary's Gina had prepared. They just could not wait to get under way.

"Listen, you two … ," Max said directly to Gina and Ray. "There is no time limit on this mission … we get to Hilton Head whenever we get there. We can stop anywhere along the way. This is our newfound freedom! All hands prepare to get under way!"

Max started the engines from the bridge, then visually scanned the Ashly River. As the engines warmed up, anything that could come loose or roll around was made fast. Ray jumped onto the pier and untied the mooring lines. He hopped back aboard. Gina was now up on the bridge with Max, sitting on his lap. They were under way! Max engaged the screws and eased the throttles forward. As it turned out, this was not his first time piloting *The REEL OPPORTUNITY.* He knew the boat's handling characteristics pretty well. He headed the boat slowly east by southeast down the Ashley River, eventually passing between Fort Sumter National Monument and Sullivan's Island, and from there, out into the Atlantic Ocean.

Ray was down in the engine room, and even though he was wearing hearing protection, the 671s were deafening. They sounded good to Ray and they were clean. It was obvious that Max's father had taken very good care of this sport fishing vessel. The 671's were common truck and generator engines, and Ray knew them well, having worked on many.

He knew them to be notoriously reliable as well. He had a good feeling about the boat!

Several miles out into the open ocean, Max changed the heading to south by southwest, eventually passing Folly Beach and later the upscale Kiawah Island. They had been cruising for hours. Gina had learned a great deal about *The REEL OPPORTUNITY,* its controls, its electronics, and its two-way radio. She had piloted the boat from the time they had entered the open ocean, and it was a total rush for her. To be sitting on the top of this massive fishing boat, but not only that, to be controlling its every move, was mind-blowing! What a sense of power! And there was no doubt, in her mind now, that this vessel was, in fact, designed to handle the open ocean.

"Get us in about one half mile off Kiawah Island," Max ordered Gina.

Gina reduced speed. The upscale barrier island loomed ahead as Gina, steering the vessel with her feet, picked an anchoring spot. When she felt satisfied with their position, she reduced the engines to low idle and turned to face Max, sitting next to her, scanning the island with binoculars. Max turned to Gina, smiled, and ordered to everyone, "Drop anchor … all hands … prepare to party!"

After ten minutes of Max making sure they weren't dragging the anchor, the three friends met in the lounge, and Gina began making cocktails for everyone. Max and Ray both twisted up doobies and set them ablaze. The only sounds were of wind, the Atlantic Ocean lapping at the hull, and noisy seabirds screeching, waiting for something to be tossed over the side. They sat in silence, enjoying their cocktails and smoke. They were all relaxed, it having been a day of little physical effort.

It was Gina who finally broke the extended silence by saying, "It's been such a great day … really! I want to fuck you guys … both of you … at the same time, like right now!"

Max turned to face Gina and just stared, and continued staring. He always knew that Gina was wild. He figured she might propose something like this at some point. The circumstances of being right here and right now led him to one conclusion. Wild girls like Gina are addicted to sex. If they don't get it, they definitely will get it from someone else, and that someone might be someone you don't like. That left Max with one choice, he turned to face Ray.

"Well … how about it now, cowboy? Wanna take her for a ride?"

Ray was blown away. This caught him completely off guard and he never imagined it. He felt extremely awkward. He knew that his reaction right now could change everything, and not for the better. Gina was sexy, all right. And there was no doubt in his mind that she was totally capable of making a man or men, in this particular case, feel real, real good! There was probably nothing this chick wouldn't do. There could be only one answer.

"I'm … flattered … I really, really am!" Ray said nervously, looking at them both. "But I have to be honest with you both. If we did this, it will change everything. I'm a pretty emotional guy. I would always be thinking about this, and I mean always! And there is no way I could stop thinking about it! This would totally fuck me up! I would never be able to look at both of you the same way ever again. We gotta good thing going on here … us three. Let's just keep it going!"

It was now Max and Gina staring at Ray as though he were some type of space alien. "What a disappointment you turned out to be, dude!" Gina said while standing up. She threw a beach towel in Ray's face. "I'm going below to lie down."

"Relax, man … it's all good!" Max said to Ray. "Things like this happen every day … no worries, mate!" And with that, Max stood up, stretched, and headed below into the master stateroom with Gina.

Ray stood, he felt weird. He could hear Max and Gina below decks, talking in hushed tones.

"Did it ever occur to you that maybe he's not ready for something like this?" Max could be heard asking Gina. "Cruise ain't over yet … baby, maybe he'll change his mind later … just to please you!"

Suddenly, Ray didn't feel so bad anymore. He fired up the boat's generator. He put on some spacey, classic British rock and turned it up. This way, he wouldn't have to listen Max and Gina fuck, again. He remembered that Max's father had a small arsenal on board. He decided to check it out. There he found a semiauto AR15, a 12 ga pump shotgun, and even a semiauto 30 06, an extremely powerful and uncommon rifle. There were several handguns as well. One was an old .44 magnum with a six-inch barrel. It came with a black leather shoulder holster. How cool is this thing? Ray adjusted the straps on the holster to fit him. He flipped the cylinder open and loaded six shells.

Ray felt like a real bad-ass as he climbed on up to the bridge to stand watch, even though the captain had not ordered so. Ray figured that he wouldn't mind. There could be some real knuckleheads out here tonight, he thought as he took a deep drink of liquor. And damn if he wasn't right! Here they were, a half mile or so offshore, with miles of empty ocean everywhere, and here was some other powerboat a mere fifty yards away. And they just had to anchor right next to us, thought Ray.

Later, when Max and Gina finally woke up, the party resumed, and to Ray's relief, everyone acted as though the previous conversation never took place. Gina mixed up more liquor drinks before heading down into the small galley to start making dinner. Max and Ray sat on the rear deck, watching this other powerboat lower a small tender into the water with a deck crane. Two men and two women boarded the small tender, and they pushed off and headed directly toward Kiawah Island.

"Rich socialites," Max guessed. "They anchored right next to us because they think that we are rich millionaires like them. They're probably visiting rich friends on Kiawah. They will probably be attending some wild sex party tonight … millionaires sometimes do that; you know … because they can. And the whole time, not one of them will be thinking about the safety or security of their really expensive pleasure craft, because they anchored next to us thinking that we're rich, and that we will not only not fuck with their boat, we'll keep an eye on it for them!"

"Man … wouldn't it be cool if we were rich and did not have a care in the world?" Ray pondered.

"Maybe … someday," Max said. Then he broke into laughter. "Man, I hope so, bro!"

Over dinner, pasta with meat sauce and a garden salad, they talked of getting up early again tomorrow. They talked of everything necessary to get this charter fishing service started and running now that they had acquired the vessel they would need to do so. Operating this business was going to take money, so they all agreed that they would take every charter that they could, every day of the week, weather permitting. After the fine meal, Max offered take the first watch. Ray would relieve him in four hours.

Once again, Ray decided to sleep on the sofa bed in the salon, preferring it to the somewhat cramped bunks right outside the master stateroom. Max was up on the bridge with Gina, talking to other boat captains on the two-way. They all said they were staying in tomorrow, the forecast for the next twenty-four hours was nasty. Lots of rain. It was Max who decided that they would need to learn to handle all types of weather. They would leave early tomorrow morning as planned.

Ray couldn't sleep. Despite the smoking and the drinking, he was wired. The generator was shut down for the night, so there was no light, he couldn't read. Sometimes being out on the ocean was boring. The thought had never occurred to him. He heard someone climbing down from the bridge. It was Gina on her way to the master stateroom, or so he thought. Pretending to be asleep, he was shocked to find her getting into bed with him. Snuggling up against Ray, she couldn't help but notice his full-blown erection.

"I can help you with that!" she purred in his ear, half licking, half whispering.

Before he could object, he could not object! The launch codes had already been entered!

He tried thinking of baseball, surfing, riding a motorcycle, anything so that he would not have to think about what was happening right now. It was a losing battle, he knew, but he would not give up hope. He wanted to make this moment last forever. He thought of the proposition she made earlier. The nerve! The last thing Ray wanted to see while having intimate relations with a woman was another naked man. She was going to have to pay for that. He was going to have to give it to her.

They were really going at it, like all hot and sweaty like! Gina was having difficulty repressing noise she usually makes at times such as this. Finally, she said to Ray, "Okay… I think I've had enough."

"What? Like hell you have! Now you're really gonna get it!"

"Oh no!" thought Gina aloud.

It was midnight. Max came into the salon to wake up Ray. Sleeping next to Ray was Gina. She was snoring. "Dude … it's your shift," Max said, just barely loud enough for Ray to hear.

Max headed back up to the bridge. Ray got dressed and met him up there. The two men sat together. It was Ray who spoke first. "Man … I didn't do anything!"

"A beautiful girl gets in the bed with you … and you didn't do anything?" Max asked, unconvinced.

"That's right … I didn't do anything!"

"Then … you're an idiot!" Max said sternly. He could not hold it in any longer, and he burst out laughing.

Max was having way too much fun at Ray's expense. Ray couldn't help but laugh as well. "You are one crazy motherfucker!" he said.

"I noticed that you seemed to like that .44 hoarse cannon … ," Max said to Ray. "Keep it, man … take it home with you."

"Thanks, bro … that's the nicest thing anyone has ever done for me … well … almost the nicest thing!"

It began to rain. Lightning flashed to the west, followed by ear-splitting thunderclaps. Wind gusts whistled through the outriggers and antennae array. The damn thing is heading right for us, thought Ray as he sat up on the bridge alone now. It was time for him to get below. It was 3:00 a.m. He was still on watch. Peering through the salon windows, he watched the storm intensify. Out on the ocean, the thunder was deafening, as there was no land mass to absorb the sound waves. Ray grabbed a beer from the cooler. It tasted so good, he had another. By now, it was a torrential summer night's storm. Ray did not bother waking Max for his shift at 4:00 a.m.

The rain was still going at it pretty good, but the wind and lightning had dissipated by 6:00 a.m. Ray called down to Max and Gina in the stateroom to wake them up. They were still half asleep, sitting in the salon in their underwear, staring at the raging storm outside the windows. Gina stood and left for the galley below to make breakfast for everyone. Max twisted up a joint and fired it up. He pulled deeply on the smoke before passing it to Ray. Ray took some puffs, then brought it down below to Gina, who accepted it graciously.

"Thanks for taking the rest of my shift, buddy!" Max said sincerely. "You didn't have to do that."

"You folks have been so good to me … I figured it was the least I could do," Ray said.

"We're gonna play hell today, buddy! This storm is a bitch, we're gonna have to man up! Why don't you drink a couple beers, get some rest, and we'll see you in four hours from now. Gina and I got this covered. She needs the experience anyway."

"Hey, man … I'm here for one reason … to help you guys any way that I can, in furtherance of monetary gains." Ray laughed out loud.

No one said a word during breakfast. Now, it was time to weigh anchor and prepare to get under way. Gina and Max got dressed and donned their wet weather gear. Ray went below to wash the breakfast dishes. He could hear the engines rumble to life one at a time. He felt the deck beneath him move as soon as the anchor let go of its hold on the sandy ocean bottom. They headed southwest along the coast, five miles or so offshore.

Up on the bridge, Max was giving precise direction to Gina about low visibility navigation.

The bridge was equipped with two radar screens set to two different scales. The plastic windshield made outside visibility next to useless in these conditions. The trick was alternating between the radar, compass heading, and outside visual, never staring at anything one thing for too long. They made slow progress past Edisto Island and much later Hunting Island.

Ray put on his wet weather gear and joined Max and Gina on the bridge.

"Gina, Ray is your relief, you can go below and relax, baby," Max offered.

"No way, buddy … I wanna stay up here with you guys!" she protested.

That would be just fine with both men, Gina was good company, and a valuable third set of eyes. They passed Fripp Island, then later Pritchard's Island. The rain had slacked off considerably since early this morning, but the sea and sky remained a solid slate gray. They crossed the Port Royal Sound onward toward Hilton Head Island.

The tranquil passage so far was suddenly shattered by the depth finder audio and visual alarms. "Oh fuck!" yelled Max. "We are in less than five feet of water, throttle back the engines!"

The REEL OPPORTUNITY had a draft of about three feet, and they were well offshore. As the outside visibility was still poor, the three young adults had been neglecting the radar and compass headings, a bad, bad rookie mistake.

"We're up on the Joyner Banks," Max determined. "It's a sandbar that sticks out for a couple miles on the northern end of the island then curves southwest. Here we are, right where it makes the curve," Max pointed out. "Head 90 degrees to port at low idle. Keep an eye on the depth finder!" Max instructed Gina.

"Uh … Max, what in the hell is that thing?" Ray asked, looking to the starboard in the direction of the sandbar.

"It's … it's a wreck," exclaimed Max. He found the binoculars in the compartment and focused in on the beached craft a hundred yards away. "It's a sailboat, mast severely damaged, lying on its side, well up on the Joyner Banks, at low tide."

"Lemme see!" said Gina, taking the binoculars. "That is so … creepy!" She handed the glasses to Ray.

"That's probably a 50 footer. There is a New Zealand flag on the stern post," Ray observed. "Definitely an oceangoing sailing vessel."

Max reached overhead to grab the two-way radio mic. Just as he was about to key up the mic, Ray grabbed his arm. "Wait a second, dude. Let's not give our position away just yet."

"Why the hell not … it's a vessel in distress!"

"Looks more like an abandoned wreck to me … ," said Ray.

"Looks scary," said Gina.

"What are you trying to say, man?" Max snapped back.

"Let's see what's on it first, then make the call!"

"You are a crazy motherfucker, Ray!" Max dropped the anchor, and shut down the engines. "Now, go up on the forward deck and unlash the dinghy. I'll be up there directly to help you get it in the water. You can paddle over and check it out!"

Ray climbed over the stern and into the small dinghy. Gina and Max began handing him tools, a flashlight, a crowbar, and a small handheld two-way radio. He pushed off and stroked over in the direction of the sandbar. The current was strong and the rowing was difficult. It took much longer and required much more effort than he had anticipated. When he finally did reach the bar, he was exhausted from the effort. After beaching the dinghy, Ray walked over to the wreck.

A storm-battered flag of New Zealand hung from the stern rail post. Faded lettering on the stern revealed the vessel's name. Its owner had named it *Winsor2.* Its mast was broken off at the cabin top. The sails and the rigging lay all about. Ray climbed into the cockpit and switched on the flashlight, shining it in through the open cabin doors. She was full of water. Ray descended down into the cabin and was very fortunate having avoided serious injury in doing so. He stood in water, maybe a couple feet deep. He shone the flashlight all around the salon as he made his way forward, sloshing through water and floating debris.

This had once been a world-class ocean-sailing vessel, and here she was, seemingly damaged beyond repair. Not much in the way of salvage here. That's too bad. Someone had spent a lot of money on this thing, and now she was ruined. He now stood in a forward passageway, crew bunks on either side. On a top bunk, port side, something heavy leaned out into the passageway straining against heavy nylon mesh netting. Whatever it was, it was too massive and heavy to be a body.

Ray took his knife and cut at the netting before pulling out a tightly wrapped packet. He cut through several layers of plastic wrap, and then finally paper, and found a dense white power that glittered in the strong flashlight beam. "I fucking knew it!" Ray shouted out loud to no one but himself. It was coke, pure fucking coke, and there were hundreds and hundreds of these things. The starboard side bunk was loaded as well. Ray realized that his hands were shaking.

"Baby Bird to Momma Bird. The elephant is in the doghouse!" Ray shouted into the small radio.

"Rodger that, Baby Bird. Can you shoot it, and bring it out with you?"

"Affirmative … I mean negative … oh … never mind! There is something you just have to see for yourselves!" Back aboard *The REEL OPPORTUNITY*, Ray was still shaking as Max and Gina helped him out of the dinghy.

"You don't look so good, bro … something scare you?" Max asked.

"Check this out!" Ray fished the packet out of his wet weather gear and placed it on the mess table.

"Ray … what the fuck? Is that what I think it is?"

"You can bet that it is! And there are hundreds of these things over there!"

"Say what?" asked Gina

"Fucking hundreds of these things … there is like a zillion dollars over there! And no one else knows about it but us!"

"What about the previous sailors … Ray?" inquired Max.

"The survival raft is missing, they probably ditched. They probably don't even know where this vessel is right now." exclaimed Ray.

"We don't know that for sure!"

"Well … there is no one out here but us on this nasty day!"

Max went up to the bridge to have a look at the radar. Two minutes later, he was back in the salon with Gina and Ray. "You … got a plan?"

"Yes, I do, actually!" said Ray. "But it's not going to be easy!"

It was a simple plan, but not easily executed. Ray would take the dinghy with a towline attached back over to the *Winsor2*. He would bring a gas-powered, one-inch centrifugal pump and hoses and use them to pump out the water in the hold. The incoming tide would be approximately six feet higher than it was right now. With a towline attached to the *Winsor2*, they could pull it off the sandbar and pull it out to sea. There, they would tie the two vessels alongside each other, and transfer the coke onto *The REEL OPPORTUNITY*, then scuttle the *Winsor2*. There was only one problem with the plan. They didn't have enough diesel to take it very far offshore. Max proposed they could sink her in the deepest part of the Port Royal Sound. That sounded just fine to Gina and Ray.

It was pure adrenaline now giving Ray the energy required to perform his mission. On the stern of *The REEL OPPORTUNITY*, Max paid out the heavy nylon towline attached to the dinghy, aboard which Ray stroked like it was his very last act on earth, which it could very well be, should something go wrong. Ray pulled the dinghy up to the crest of the sandbar and tied it off to the wreck, keenly aware that the tide was advancing. First, he made fast the towrope to a bow cleat on the *Winsor2*. He then climbed aboard and made his way around the cabin while carrying the fifteen-foot-long, one-inch suction hose with a foot valve. Halfway around, he busted through a cabin window with the crowbar, then lowered the hose down into the hold and down into the water there.

He next used a bucket of seawater to fill the suspended hose and attach it to the pump, positioning it so that the discharged water would flow over the side and down the port side hull. After several pulls on the recoil starter, the little pump fired off and Ray opened the choke slowly, until it was running full speed. Once the water started flowing over the side, Ray went back down into the hold with his flashlight. After a mere fifteen minutes, the little pump had dewatered the hold low enough so that Ray could pull the engine hatch. The engine compartment was still half full of water. Ray wriggled down into it and grabbed the engine crankshaft pulley with both hands. It would not turn, the little diesel engine was locked up!

It all began to make sense to Ray now how the tragedy may have occurred. The *Winsor2* may have caught a rogue wave which rolled her, breaking the aluminum mast. Seawater entered the hold and flooded the engine, killing it for good. With no power and no sail, the crew abandoned the sailboat in an inflatable survival raft, which self-inflates with the pull of a rip cord. Ray imagined that he would have done the same in similar circumstances.

After just thirty minutes, the hold was nearly emptied. Ray calculated that over a thousand gallons of seawater had been pumped out. Ray climbed out of the hold to find the dinghy afloat beside the sailboat straining to escape its mooring line against the incoming tide. There was no sandbar remaining. It was on now. Waves were splashing against the port side hull, and for the first time, he felt the vessel move beneath him. This is actually going to work! This has to work!

"Baby Bird to Momma Bird, the doghouse just moved! Time to take up the slack," Ray yelled into the little handheld radio.

"Rodger that, Baby Bird, understood!"

A few seconds later, a female voice came over the air. "You rock, dude!"

Oh yeah, baby, this is it, thought Ray. He could feel the hull moving now with each incoming wave. The tide waits for no man! Ray used the time to further search for treasure in the hold. There he found two AK-47 rifles with long banana clips fully loaded. In a wooden crate in the aft stateroom, there was an opened wooden crate with five more AKs packed for transit. There were a bunch of extra high-capacity magazines in a smaller crate, and yet another crate loaded with ammunition. The previous sailors could have easily thwarted almost any act of piracy.

The *Winsor2* was still at a list, but there were still twenty minutes remaining until the tide was full.

"Baby Bird to Momma Bird … we're getting close."

"We can see that, Baby Bird!" came a female voice.

Ray stood at the ship's wheel in the cockpit. *The REEL OPPORTUNITY* was now pointed out in the direction of the open sea, the towline now taunt. After the remaining twenty minutes had elapsed, Ray called into the handheld, "Go for it, Momma!"

"Rodger," came the reply.

Ray could feel the hull lurch beneath him as the sport fisher's powerful engines were engaged. And with that, the wrecked sailboat was sitting upright in the water and moving for the first time in who knows how long? After ten minutes, Max pulled the sport fisher's throttles back to idle. Gina was on the stern, signaling to cut the towline which Ray accomplished with a machete. The sport fisher motored around in a big slow circle while Gina pulled in the towrope. It came alongside the sailboat and the two vessels were tied together.

"How about that now!" yelled Ray exuberantly.

"You are the man!" Max yelled back.

"You're both my heroes!" yelled Gina, filled with excitement.

It was time to get to work. The three descended into the cabin and formed a human chain, with Ray removing the packages from their respective locations and pitching them one at time to Gina, who pitched them to Max, who pitched them up and out of the cabin and into the cockpit. It seemed to take forever, and it did. Up until this moment, the three had never imagined that smuggling was so laborious. About halfway through, they were in the cockpit pitching the packages over the rail onto the rear deck of the sport fisher. Then back down into the cabin to repeat the whole thing again. This was going to take all night.

The adrenaline still flowed as the three concentrated their efforts on removing the weapons, ammunition, and anything else of value to them. There were a couple ponds of pot, probably personal, nice! There were even more weapons, better! There was even a ship's log, unbelievable! Now they could read about what happened. It was Gina who found perhaps the most surprising items yet. All four former crew had left their IDs behind in their hasty effort to abandon ship.

The sport fisher was now underway, pulling the sailboat out into the Port Royal Sound. Max was watching the depth finder. "Right here is a good spot, get ready!" Gina cut the towline, and Max motored the sport fisher around in a big slow circle, coming up alongside the sailboat.

Ray, still in his wet weather gear, now donned safety glasses and hearing protection. He hopped over the rail onto the sailboat. Max grabbed one of the AKs, the only one with a rifle sling, and tossed it through the air to Ray who caught it with both hands. Ray slung the rifle over his shoulder then went below into the cabin. He removed the clip, locked the bolt open, and checked the barrel bore for obstructions. He reinserted the clip, chambered one of the heavy rounds, shouldered the weapon, and emptied the entire magazine with one pull of the trigger, sending shards of fiberglass everywhere. He next emptied two additional thirty-round magazines in similar fashion. Ray climbed the stairs out of the cabin as seawater seeped into the hull, through ninety holes in a tight cluster below the water line.

The three were exhausted, but stayed to watch the *Winsor2* for nearly an hour until the decks were awash, and she was headed to the bottom of Port Royal Sound, never to be seen again. It was time to move on to plan B, which involved heading to an alternate, closer marina; they were that low on fuel by now. Through the Port Royal Sound, they motored until finally docking at a marina in Skull Creek. Max docked his sport fisher right at the fuel dock. A man emerged from the dock house and met them at the fuel pumps. It was 7:00 a.m.

"Fuel emergency, fill 'er up, mister," said Max to the man. Max peeled off a wad of one hundred dollar bills and handed them to the man. "Keep the change."

"Thank you, sir!" the man said, counting the bills.

In the salon, the three discussed their next move. It was decided they would motor back out to the ocean and anchor offshore, get some rest, and decide their next move. They were exhausted from their ordeal, yet they were still full of nervous energy. The events of yesterday had forever changed the course of their lives. They sat at the mess table deciding what to do next. It's amazing how just a series of events in the proper order can determine success or failure. They had all been damn lucky so far and they knew it. One wrong move now could spell disaster. It was Gina who finally made the suggestion.

"Let's try some of this stuff," she said, while pulling out the first kilo Ray brought aboard.

They chopped. They snorted. They got high, really high.

"Put that on the top shelf, baby!" Gina said while her brain froze. The two men agreed, nodding their heads.

"Do you even know anyone who can help us with our problem, Ray?" Max said now accusingly.

"I do, as a matter of fact. I know some bikers upstate who would love to get their hands on this!"

"Really now?"

"Really!"

And so they hatched a plan. Max would have to cancel his non-refundable dock reservation.

They would stay anchored offshore a day or so just to calm down and get some much-needed rest. They would drop Ray off on the island where he could get a cab, rent a car, and find a suitable private dock owner sympathetic to their cause, then move the product to a suitable safe house, then meet up with those bikers, take them a sample, and see if they like it. All bets were that they would. At any rate, Max, Gina, and Ray were pretty jacked up on pure coke right about now.

"Sounds to me like you have this all figured out, smart guy!" Max said condescendingly.

"You don't have to be an asshole about it!" said Ray.

The coke was pushing them over the edge. The two men stood and faced each other.

Gina sensed what was about to happen. "Guys, please … what do I need to do to stop this from happening?"

Both men turned to face Gina now.

"What would you suggest, baby?" said Max.

"I think we should all cool out and relax, use the nervous energy we all feel right now in a positive way. I think you guys need to spit-roast me … like right now already!"

"She's always right," Max pointed out.

"I'm finding that out," added Ray.

This time around, Ray did not hesitate to accept Gina's offer.

The next morning, they weighed anchor and headed for Harbor Town. Ray took a cab to the airport where he rented a car. He then drove to his own villa. He ate, drank beer, and fell into a deep restful sleep. He woke again after midnight and turned on some late-night scary movie on cable. He opened his suitcase that he had brought with him on *The REEL OPPORTUNITY*. It contained all the parts with which one could assemble into a complete full-auto AK-47, which he did. It also contained one dozen kilos. The next time he woke, his phone was ringing. He screened the call with the answering machine.

"Hey … Ray, this is Lester Price … I, uh, think I've got a highly motivated buyer who is interested in buying the villa you're living in now … so … I'm sending over an appraiser, they will be able to let themselves in to do the appraisal. And don't worry, buddy, we'll find you another place to live … you like oceanfront … I think we can get you into an oceanfront for just a little more than you're paying now and—"

Ray shut off the machine. He hated listening to long phone messages. He began to make breakfast, but was interrupted by a knock on the door. Who in the hell could it be at ten in the morning on a weekday, when he was supposed to be at work? Taking a look through the door peephole, he was very surprised to see an attractive brunette wearing sunglasses. As he continued looking, he could hear a key in the lock turning the tumbler. The door opened and was pushed into a surprised Ray Bangor. "Just a second … I was about to let you in and …"

In walked the very hot real estate appraiser Lester had mentioned on the phone, smartly dressed in a tight-fitting skirt and equally tight-fitting top, and she was a knockout. A little fat in the backside, but Ray liked it that way. Ray figured she was probably 5'2", but with her heels and big hair, she was every bit of 6 foot. She took off her sunglasses and made eye contact. She was hot as hell.

"Mmmm … smell good in here," the woman said in a very thick Spanish accent. "I'm Marcella De Silva, real estate appraiser … theeese your place, no?"

"Actually, no … I'm renting it … I'm Ray, nice to meet you," he said a little awkwardly.

"Nice to meet chu, Ray … I do queeckly … okay?"

"Huh?" said Ray. "Oh … yeah … the appraisal."

"Done chu worry, I do queeck … then I leave you, okay?"

"Please don't rush yourself on my account."

She walked into the kitchen first. "Chur pancake burning, no?"

"Oh, yeah, thank you. I'll take care of that."

Marcella next walked into the dining room which opened up to the living room, making notes on a clipboard. She pulled back the drapes and looked through the sliding glass door. Ray was watching her every move from the kitchen. She just oozed sexuality. She disappeared into the guest bedroom, then master. Ray just realized what she might see in there, but it was too late. She came back into the living room. Her pleasant demeanor had disappeared completely. She made eye contact with Ray, wearing a nasty frown.

Ray tried to defuse the situation. "Would you care for some breakfast and coffee, Marcella?"

"We have a problemo, Ray … chu have illegal coke and a macheene gun in your room … chu are a keengpin, no?"

"Illegal coke? Versus legal coke?" Ray tried humoring her, but it clearly was not working.

"Chu gotta problem, man, someone need to call police, no?

"Listen, Marcella … I'm going to tell you a story, please, please listen to what I have to say. Are you sure you don't want any coffee?"

"Just a leeettle cup please."

"Please, have a seat, Marcella. Would you like a little dessert liquor in your coffee?" Ray asked, showing her the bottle.

"Maybe, just a leeettle." Marcella smoothed her skirt beneath her backside as she sat down at the dining room table.

Ray poured the coffee with a little splash of liquor in each cup. "You have to swear to me you won't tell anyone what I'm about to tell you, okay."

"I no swear!"

"Whatever …"

Ray began to tell this complete stranger everything that had happened, starting with picking up the sport fisher in Charleston to finding the wreck on the Joyner Banks, right up until the present moment. Gauging by her initial reaction, Ray felt he was slowly chipping away at the ice surrounding Marcella De Silva. It was an unbelievable story, he knew, but he had to do everything he could think of to make it not only believable, but undeniable. It seemed to be working, he could sense that she was a little bit more relaxed now.

Ray looked deep into her dark eyes. "Surely there must be something we can do to make this all work out for both of us."

"Actually … ," she hesitated. "There eeeze … come on, I show you."

Marcella rose from the table and Ray followed her to his front door, and then outside into the blinding sunlight. "Right there." She pointed with her index finger to a very clean, very shiny, and very new black Corvette. "I trade you theese car for one of chur packages."

"Let us go back inside and discuss this a little more … shall we?" said Ray, again looking straight into her eyes.

Seated at Ray's dinner table again, he asked her if she had a clear title for the vehicle. She said that she did, and then went on to add that she hated the car because it was a gift to her from her now ex-husband. Ray asked her if she would like some more coffee and liquor. She did. Now we are getting somewhere, he thought. He went back into the master and returned with a single unopened kilo. Ray took a razor blade and made a small incision in the package and spilled out a couple grams onto a mirror. He turned off the overhead lights and shined a flashlight onto the coke. It glistened under the light. He went on to explain that it was pure. Marcella, not taking Ray's word for it, had to find out for herself, which she did with a couple lines. She seemed to perk up immediately. Ray attempted to explain that the original wholesale buyer probably paid about five thousand dollars for this package, but that would have been in its country of origin, somewhere down in South America, he figured. Here in the States, with the potency reduced by half and sold at street level, it could fetch 2 million dollars!

Marcella's reply was basically she already knew all that stuff. Was Raymond interested in the car or not? That's all she cared about. It was a good deal she was giving him, the car was less than a year old and in perfect condition. It was a showroom model that she had literally driven right out the front door.

Her asshole ex-husband paid a lot of money for it. It was just a good deal for Raymond, the car for the package, and the promise that she would keep her mouth shut about the whole deal.

Ray knew that he was taking a huge chance with this woman who, less than an hour earlier, had been a complete stranger. But there was something about her. Head to toe, she was the most unbelievably sexy woman he had ever met. He not only wanted her, he wanted to marry her. Everything about her, her eyes, her face, her beautiful full figure, her sexy accent, and the funny way she spoke of things, made Marcella De Silva the most desirable woman on the planet right now to Raymond Bangor.

Yeah, sure, she played mind games with him, but didn't all women? The way she brazenly accused him of being a kingpin, for example. If she actually believed that he was a kingpin, would she have been so sassy and disrespectful to him? He didn't think so! She knew exactly that type of man he was and she played him. Threatening to call the police, really, Marcella? Would you have stood outside and watch the police haul me away in handcuffs? thought Ray. Then pose for a picture in the local paper under the headline, "Island Woman Brings Down Drug Kingpin!"

Then it occurred to Ray the sorry-ass truth of the matter. He was on his way to becoming a drug kingpin, he was just getting started and, having no previous experience, was not very good at it. That's precisely what that woman saw today. Boy, do you feel like a dork or what? Because you are fool! If he stood any chance at all with this woman, he was going to have to prove himself worthy. He really wanted to believe this was possible but he wasn't sure just yet.

Ray turned to face Marcella De Silva. "I'm a busy man, if our business here is completed … might I make a suggestion?"

"And what would that be, Raymundo?" Marcella asked, blinking her incredibly long eyelashes at him.

Ray's mind went completely blank, staring into her dark, moist eyes. He had to catch himself. "Oh yeah … well, I'll tell you what. You bring me the title to the Vette and sign it over to me. There is a white convertible out front. It's a rental. You take this car for the day, do whatever you need to do. Then this evening … meet me for dinner."

"What if I say no?" Marcella asked very seriously.

"Then I will feel really low in myself!"

"Then I say yes, Raymundo!"

This was turning out to be the best day ever. They made dinner plans. Now came the all-important task of securing a place to land the load and somewhere to take it without raising suspicion. This was turning out to be a challenge, and Ray liked a challenge. And he had an idea. He put on a cool outfit, one that looked like he just stepped off a crime fiction movie set in South Florida. Satisfied with his appearance, he stepped outside into the hot, midday sunshine. He put on his cool shades.

He got into the black Corvette and started the engine. He liked the way it sounded. But a Corvette is not like a normal car.

It's more like sitting in an aircraft cockpit. It would definitely take a little time getting used to it. Ray decided there was only one thing he needed to do right now, and that was to make this car his bitch. He drove it from his villa into South Sea Pines. He pulled up to a beautiful, huge, expensive home. Last week he had attended a house party there. The owners were in Europe, and Ray hoped they still would be.

He rang the doorbell. A dog started barking. Moments later, an attractive young woman in her early twenties answered the door. She was the daughter of the couple who owned this house. Ray explained to the young woman who he was. She vaguely remembered him, if only because he didn't start any trouble at the party. He explained that he had a business proposition for her. Now, for a girl that comes from money, money was not even an option. It might even serve to make her more suspicious of him than she already was. But Ray was a keen observer of human behavior. This attractive young woman was a regular in the nightclub scene.

The last time he saw her, she was exiting the ladies' room at a club, popular with young adults. She was sniffling a lot, which was a tell-tale sign that she was a cokehead. Ray tried to break the ice by describing how much he enjoyed her party, the alcohol, the music, the friends, the drugs in particular. How it was just a shame that some people couldn't handle themselves and caused some trouble that night. Oh yeah, she remembered all right!

It was time to put it all on the table. He showed her a nice sample of what he had to offer. She invited him to come inside. They both sampled the sample. Ray explained to her what he needed from her, the use of the deep water dock behind her house. For her trouble, he would give her one kilo of pure product in advance. How far in advance? How about right now? He went out and retrieved it from the car. She agreed readily. They had a deal. They exchanged phone numbers.

Later that afternoon, he met his partners aboard *The REEL OPPORTUNITY* at yet another marina at a prearranged time. They were all very happy to see one another, they were, after all, partners in this. Ray explained the plan to off-load. Max and Gina were pleased,

Ray had done his homework and they were impressed, Max in particular. If Ray was correct on this one, it sounded like the absolute perfect place he could have chosen.

What about the safe house? Ray explained they would have to take it to Max's house in Georgia. Max became furious. He did not want it at his house in Georgia. Ray explained that it was a temporary solution, and not only that, the safest one as well. No one else on the planet would know where it was. Not only that, it was the perfect place, out in the middle of nowhere. Max was heavily armed. All he had to do was just sit on it a few days. If they wanted to become rich, which they all obviously did, this had to be the safest bet. Gina thought it was a good idea also. Max reluctantly agreed.

The plan was in place. Tomorrow morning, they would all meet where they were right now. Ray would navigate them directly to the deep water dock. What could possibly go wrong? Well, everything imaginable. All they had to do was do everything right, and everything would be fine. There had to be zero margin for error here. Otherwise, the odds of failure would grow exponentially. So that was to be that. Would Ray care to join them for dinner? He could not, he had a date. Really?

Really!

Ray was a little bit late meeting Marcella for dinner and he apologized. Marcella wore a dark blue dinner dress and she looked spectacular, so much so that one of the other restaurant patrons walked into a plate glass door, he was paying so much attention to her instead of where he was going. Smooth move, moron, thought Ray. They ordered drinks, and they ordered their meals.

"So how was chur day, Raymundo?"

"Fine, it was busy!"

"So, I was theenking Raymundo, that package chu gave me this morning, I have a lot of friends who like to party and … chu have more of those, no?"

Ray wasn't expecting a business meeting during dinner, but hey, he could smell another opportunity brewing. "Yes, actually … I do. Ten grand per. Those are preferred client prices, actually."

"I like the price … actually," Marcella purred. "Chu have five more, no?"

"That would be fifty … cash."

"I have with me now, no?"

Damn, thought Ray, he hasn't been the only busy little beaver. "Yeah … we can do that … after dinner; my place."

"That would be so nice!" she purred.

Marcella followed Ray back to his villa after dinner. Once inside, he retrieved five packages from the back bedroom. He placed them on the coffee table in front of Marcella, now seated on the sofa. There was a fat stack of hundreds on the table, neatly placed there by Marcella. It would be a total mood killer for Ray to count it right now.

"Would you like a margarita, Marcella?"

"I love it!"

"Great, I'll make some."

From the kitchen, Ray watched Marcella pull a disk out of her purse, walk over to the stereo, and put it in. Seconds later, the room was filled with funky Latin dance music. Ray liked it. He watched Marcella kick off her high heels and begin to dance, really shaking it. Ray could not believe what he was seeing. The good life had just gotten that much better, the most amazing part being the fact that Marcella was a spectacular dancer. She had the moves and the body to go with it. It was as if the most beautiful woman on the planet had decided that she would entertain him with a performance that he was sure to remember for the rest of his life.

Ray walked into the living room carrying two glasses and a pitcher of margaritas. He sat on the sofa. He could not take his eyes off the beautiful woman dancing in his living room, just for him no less. It was as if she was trying her hardest to impress him, and she was of course, but it was not necessary. He was already addicted to her, like a drug, he wanted her so badly right now. Watching Marcella De Silva was the most hypnotic and erotic experience he had ever known in his life. It was as if she were pulling him into her world with just her eyes, as she moved to the wild music, never taking her eyes off of his. The front doorbell rang.

Motherfucker! thought Ray. Someone always has to spoil the special moments in life. Who in the hell could be at my door, this late at night? Ray was pissed. As he got up from the sofa and walked to the front door, the doorbell rang two more times. Now he was really, really pissed. He looked through the peephole. It was a dude, actually two dudes. And they looked like dorks. Ray unlocked the front door, pulled it open quickly, and leveled the .44 right in the face of the man standing in front of him.

"Why in the fuck are you clowns knocking on my door?" Ray hissed at both of them.

"What … what, what's with the gun, man?"

"What do you guys want?" Ray snapped back and cocked the hammer.

"We don't want any trouble!" the man said, now visibly shaken. "We're staying in the condo upstairs … we were like wondering if you could turn down the music … a little bit … maybe?" The man's hands were shaking. Clearly he was ill-prepared to deal with the situation.

"I'll tell you what, motherfucker! I'll make a deal with you two! I'll turn down the music, but I don't ever want to be bothered by either of you, ever again, do we have a deal then?"

The two stunned men nervously looked at each other, then back to Ray.

"Yes …"

"Thank you and good night!" Ray kicked the door shut.

He turned to find Marcella had been standing right behind him the whole time, watching the whole thing.

"Chu are a brave man, Raymundo!"

"It's easy to be brave with a loaded gun in your hand, Marcella."

"What if they call police? That could be trouble, no?"

The thought had never even occurred to Ray, and he kicked himself. "There's no law that says you cannot brandish a weapon at someone who is invading your personal residence, baby!"

"I no understand what chu say, but chu sound like chu know what chu are talking about."

"Where were we … ah yes, margaritas?"

"Yes … I love one!"

Ray put on soft music, then headed over back to the couch and sat with Marcella. What about the police? he thought. This could very well be a problem. He had to think about it fast. This could bust the whole thing open wide. The cops would do some sniffing around, and bam! They'd be in prison directly, for life, probably.

"Hey, Marcella, I have an idea. Let's go ahead and put that product in the trunk of the convertible. If the police come, that car wouldn't be readily traceable to us."

"Okay."

Ray handed her a shopping bag. "Put those five packages in here, I'll front you another three, you can pay me later."

"I like your style, Raymundo, and chu smart too!"

Marcella put the stash in the back of the convertible, just as Ray put the cash, the AK, and the remaining unsold package in the Corvette. They went back inside. They sat. Now, they could relax. They talked about life. They talked about people, family, and friends. Ray told her he could not wait to introduce her to Gina and Max. They drank margaritas until after 2:00 a.m. Ray excused himself and went to the guest bathroom. We he returned, he found Marcella sleeping. That was fine with Ray, he was pretty buzzed by now anyway. He had a heavy day tomorrow.

At 7:00 a.m., Ray gently woke Marcella, who smiled when she recognized him.

"Who put theeese blanket on me?" she asked, in a momentary state of confusion.

"It was the boogie man."

"Huh?"

"Never mind, listen, I've got someplace important I need to go this morning, it's still early. You can stay here if you like. Just lock both locks when you leave, there's a key on the coffee table. Please, come back here early tonight? We can talk some more, I'll make you dinner."

"That would be peeerfect, Raymundo!" she said as she snuggled back down into the soft pit sofa, smiling.

Ray boarded *The REEL OPPORTUNITY* at about 7:30 a.m. a little ahead of schedule. He knocked on the cabin door and was glad to see Gina and Max dressed and ready for the day. They made small talk about Ray's date last night, but Max was getting impatient. Apparently, live-aboard life was not for him. He began complaining about this, that, pretty much everything. When he got to finances and dock fees, Ray cut him short.

"Here's 50K, big guy!" he said while handing Max the stack of hundreds. "Got another thirty coming!"

Max fanned the money under his nose, smelling it. "You're the man, Ray!"

"Are you guys ready to fuck this pig?"

"What?" snapped Gina.

"It's just an expression, Gina! Are you two ready to find the dock with me, I've never been there coming from the water."

"We'll find it just fine, man, I have complete and total faith in you!"

Now, that was a real compliment coming from Max. They made loose from the dock and were on their way south on the Intracoastal Waterway. Gina took the opportunity to explain to Ray that with all the time she had available over the last couple of days, she took the time to read the ship's log that was taken off the *Winsor2*. It seems that the yacht belonged to a wealthy New Zealand couple who sailed her all over the world. The very last entry was made after they landed in Miami, Florida, over one year ago. Conclusion, the vessel was either sold or stolen shortly after the last log entry. Interesting.

Ray excused himself and climbed up to the bridge with Max, they should be coming up on their destination soon. Max took the opportunity to thank Ray for all he had accomplished over the last couple of days. Ray was distracted by the conversation, he was too busy searching the port side of Broad Creek. Hadn't he already told his partners he'd never be there from the waterside? It would be easy to miss and motor right past it.

"There it is!" said Ray excitedly. "I remember the flagpole in the neighbor's backyard."

It was a cross-shaped flagpole bearing three flags.

"No worries, mate!" Max approached the dock slowly, *The REEL OPPORTUNITY* did not have thrusters and was not an easy vessel to dock. Max made it look easy, having had a lot of very recent practice.

The 46' sport fisher barely nudged against the pilings as Ray clamored to secure the bow line, while Gina made fast the stern. Ray walked around to the front of the house and rang the doorbell. There was no answer. Positive they were in the correct location, Ray suggested they just wait on the boat, burn a couple joints. It would give them time to talk of logistics. Gina suggested they start ledgering everything to keep track of the money flow. Everyone was in agreement on that one.

A sliver Mercedes-Benz pulled up in the driveway, it was the owner's daughter. She waved. She made her way along the stone walkway, past the swimming pool, and onto the dock. She greeted the three friends warmly. She offered Max and Gina the use of the swimming pool and other amenities, like the barbeque pit, while she drove Ray to the truck rental place. They would probably be back in a couple hours. Rather than a cargo van, Ray chose a cube truck, figuring that it would offer more security for the product and look less suspicious. Back at the house, they found Max and Gina smoking joints and pounding beers. The four young adults hung around all afternoon together, eating, drinking, swimming, and even playing badminton. So much fun was to be had that Ray almost forgot about his date with Marcella. He begged the hostess to give him a ride back to the marina where he left his car. She was pretty high, but agreed, on the condition that she not have to leave her residence again. Agreed.

It was Max who wanted to know more about Ray's friend. Why was he bringing her here, and could she be trusted? Ray told him it that it was Marcella who came up with the 50K he'd handed over this morning. Besides, she was his date. Besides that, he really, really liked her. Somehow he just knew that Max and Gina were going to like her also. What was not to like about Marcella De Silva? Ray reasoned. Marcella, under the impression that she was going to be home alone with Ray all night, had dressed for such an occasion. She wore a short, very tight purple dress and high-wedge cork sandals with matching purple straps. Ray thought she looked fabulous. She wasn't exactly happy about the change of plans though. She wouldn't have to do any of the off-loading, Ray explained to her, she could just supervise.

Max and Gina were sitting around the pool when a black Corvette pulled up in the driveway. They were both stunned to see Ray get out and walk around to the passenger side door and open it for his date. Out into the sunset stepped Marcella De Silva. Max and Gina stared and just kept staring at this woman in the purple dress. Their faces conveyed total and complete shock. Nothing could have prepared them for the entrance of Marcella De Silva into their lives!

"Chu must be Max? And chu must be Gina?" Marcella gave both a big hug and a kiss.

Ray felt weird for a moment. He was about to introduce her, and here she was giving hugs and kisses to total strangers, as if she had known them all their lives. He hadn't even been given any hugs or kisses yet. He felt cheated. That's the weed talking, he told himself.

Marcella was a business associate, he just wished she were his girlfriend. He had to remain cool, professional, relaxed.

They all went aboard *The REEL OPPORTUNITY*, and Marcella was impressed to say the least, not having set foot on any other sport fishing boat. Max put on some cool music. Gina had been tipped off ahead of time that Ray's date enjoyed margaritas, so Gina blended some. There was a pile of coke on the mess table for the taking, and from which they all took. Max was distracted by Ray's date and couldn't keep his eyes off of her, which did not go unnoticed by Gina.

It was getting dark. Ray explained that the rental truck was approximately eight feet wide. The dock was ten feet wide. He could back the truck all the way to the end of the dock, he really had done his homework. It was time to apply insect repellent and get to work. Ray personally made sure Marcella was adequately protected. After spraying her upper body, he even got down on one knee to make sure her legs and feet weren't bitten as well. What a kind gesture!

They started pitching the product out and off of the sport fisher, then into the rental truck, all the while knowing this was going to take a while. Marcella was a good sport. She sat in a lawn chair on the dock, next to a cooler. She offered bottled ice water and even words of encouragement. The physical effort was considerable, and the three friends were sweating profusely. Max and Gina could not help but crack up every time Marcella had something to say.

"Awe … chu look so tired, Raymundo … chu need to keep working now, okay, baby!"

When the product was fully loaded, it was determined that the *Winsor2* had been transporting six hundred kilos. They sat in the salon and discussed tomorrow's plan. Max would take his boat back to Charleston, get his personal truck, and drive it back to his house in Georgia. Ray and Gina would drive the rental truck to Max's house under the guise of being a young couple moving. They would then unload the product into Max's basement, which was easily accessible from the back of his house. Marcella, for her part, was to drive the Corvette back home with her tonight. Ray would grab a few kilos and head back to Hilton Head to return the rental truck. Ray would see her tomorrow night. Gina would then wait for Max to return from Charleston.

It was a simple plan, they all agreed.

They all spent the night aboard *The REEL OPPORTUNITY*. Max and Gina in the master, and Ray and Marcella on the couch in the salon. The air conditioning felt good. It was actually a little too cold. Marcella snuggled up against Ray under the soft blanket. Finally, they were at least sleeping in the same place, thought Ray happily. All he knew right now was that she felt so good against his body.

The sport fisher's engines were running when Ray and Marcella woke at 6:00 a.m. They all had another heavy day ahead of them, they would need an early start. Marcella said goodbye to Ray, she even gave him a kiss. He was greatly looking forward to seeing her again tonight. Gina and Ray said goodbye to Max and wished him luck. Max now had the unenviable job of piloting the boat all the way to Charleston by himself. But it was Ray and Gina who now set off in the rental truck loaded with enough drugs to send them to prison for life.

In those days, there was no one on the roads this early in the morning. Ray did the driving and it was Gina's job to keep him awake. She went into her purse and found the four IDs left behind by the previous sailors of the *Winsor2*. She read the names and addresses aloud. Two of the names, a forty-year-old man and a thirty-eight-year-old woman, had separate addresses in New York City. The other two names, a thirty-five-year-old man and a twenty-six-year-old woman, shared the same address in Ocean City, Maryland.

They drove to Max's house without ever stopping. When they arrived, Gina volunteered to make breakfast, they were both starving. Next came the very boring and repetitive task of moving all those packages again. This was getting old. While they worked, Gina asked Ray a lot of questions about Marcella—had they done it yet? Ray told her a gentleman never tells and it was none of her damn business anyway. Then that pretty much means no, Gina guessed.

Ray filled up the fuel tank on the rental truck and returned it, asking the rental agent to please call him a taxi. Back at his villa, Ray checked his phone messages, ate lunch, and took a shower. He next did the one thing he had been avoiding up to this point. He made the call to Ronald "Wolf" Zeigler, president of the Ingrate Order, Motorcycle Club. Ronny owned a small trucking company way out in the South Carolina countryside. Ray had done some freelance engine work on Ronny's tractors. Ronny trusted Ray. Ray thought Ronny was a decent enough guy, a real hard-dog. Ray had no issues with Ronny, but such was not the case with some of the other members of the Ingrate Order MC. They never seemed to trust Ray, if only because he wasn't one of them.

"Zeigler Trucking," a female voice with a deep Southern drawl said after the fifth ring.

"Yes, good afternoon, I need to speak with Wolf, please.

"Can I tell him who is calling?"

"Ray Bangor."

"Just a moment."

After a minute or so, Ronny picked up. "Ray, how you doing, man?" he said in his unmistakably raspy voice.

"I'm good, thanks … Ronny, I've got something you should look at, you think we could meet?"

"Sure, how about tomorrow? I'll be around all day. You still remember how to get here?"

"Yeah, man, I do, see you around noon, I guess."

"All right!"

This was a huge risk Ray was taking. The Ingrates pretty much hated everyone and pretty much everyone hated them. They were all outcasts for the most part, ex-military, ex-police, ex-firefighters, ex-gainfully employed. They all loved to party and they loved wild women. Ray would have to play this hand carefully. One wrong move could be fatal around these dudes. All he had to do was to avoid that mistake which might cost him his life. No pressure here!

Ray sat down on the couch and blew some hits through his water-pipe. Now relaxed and in a much better mood, he decided to take a long walk on the beach. It was late August, and the beaches were crowded with tourists. It was low tide. Out in the ocean, off in the distance, he could see the Joyner Banks. Ray paused for a moment to consider the fact that out of the billions of other humans on the planet, only three others knew the truth about what had happened out there that stormy day.

Marcella arrived at his place at around 6:00 p.m., just as they had planned. She wore a skin-tight black body suit and she looked stunning, as always. She greeted Ray warmly. He offered her a glass of wine. They stood in the kitchen while Ray prepared dinner and talked about the day's events. He even went on to describe his brief conversation with Ronny Zeigler and his plans to meet with him tomorrow. Marcella did not like the sound of that at all. Ray assured her that he knew and trusted this man. Everything would be just fine. Still she was not convinced.

Over dinner, Ray went on to describe how Ronny and his gang were the key to moving the product. Ronny, Ray knew, had a vast network of associates all over the country. The fact that he owned a trucking company was paramount. Ronny could easily move just about anything almost anywhere. Marcella was still not sure this was a good idea for Ray. He would be going there alone, and these men were known to be extremely dangerous.

They sat down at the dining room table. The dinner Ray had prepared was restaurant quality, chicken, steak, and shrimp over linguini with white sauce. Marcella was impressed and asked Ray where he learned to cook. His ex-wife was an executive chef, he explained. Marcella wanted to know why they were no longer married. Ray told her that he worked during the day, and his ex-wife worked at night. They rarely saw each other. They grew apart. It was sad, really.

Ray asked Marcella about her ex-husband. Was he dangerous? wondered Ray. Marcella's mood changed abruptly. She went on to explain that her ex-husband was a fucking asshole. Period! Bad subject. Ray offered that her ex-husband really must have been a screw-up to lose a beautiful woman like her. Oh yes, he was!

They sat on the couch. Marcella turned to Ray and related how she was so shaken up by her bad marriage, she had all but sworn off men and had become a full-fledged lesbian. She let that sink in. Bummer! Ray felt like he had been cock-punched. Those damn lesbians are ruining everything for him. The fucking bitches!

"I just keeeding … Raymundo!"

Marcella climbed on top of Ray, rubbing her ample cleavage in his face. Ray could feel his heart about to explode through his chest. They kissed passionately. She tasted like wine, she tasted good. Lips still together, she pulled him up off the couch by his shirt collar. Ray fumbled with the zipper, in furtherance of helping Marcella out of her body suit, pulling it down to her feet so she could step out.

She stood there in front of him, completely naked. Nothing in this world could have prepared Ray for this moment. Staring at her beautiful naked body, he began to question himself. Would he be able to handle this without having a coronary? He was young and healthy, he decided. Even if he did stroke out, wouldn't this be the perfect way to die?

Hooking his arm around the back of her neck, he kissed her as he gently laid her down on the pit sofa. Starting at her neck, he very slowly planted kisses all the way down her body, stopping at her breasts, and continuing down to her belly button. Marcella was receptive, but vey ticklish, and she writhed in pleasure as Ray finally made his way down to her hips. His technique was gentle, but intensely focused. Years of practice, on his ex-wife, had taught him the methods he now employed with great success. Apparently, this would-be lesbian had never known the likes of Ray Bangor before.

Marcella couldn't stand it any longer and succumbed to an orgasm that washed over her like a rolling ocean wave. Ray wouldn't stop. He kept at it until she climaxed again and again. They did not teach you that in lesbian school, did they Marcella? wondered Ray. Marcella couldn't handle any more, she was becoming too sensitive. She had, by now, decided that Ray needed to take his clothes off. He was too slow and clumsy, she had to help him. She knelt in front of him and began to fellate him. Now it was time for Ray to get a hold of his senses. Is this really happening? Is this just a dream? He just couldn't believe this moment was real. He began to back away. She began to follow on her knees, hooking her arm around him, never taking him out of her mouth.

In the master bedroom, Ray gently grabbed her shoulders and extricated himself. Marcella climbed onto bed. Ray entered her and began the slow rhythmic motion that intensified with every thrust.

Right outside the sliding glass door was a swimming pool. People could be heard laughing and enjoying themselves in the early evening. To think that just a pane of glass and a plastic window blind was all that separated them from the outside world was somehow funny to Ray. Marcella was well aware of the people right outside and had to forcibly suppress her groans of pleasure.

Unable to control herself any longer, Marcella dug her fingernails into Ray's back. The sensation of pain only served to make Ray push harder and deeper. Marcella was intent upon making Ray forget about every woman he had ever known, and she was succeeding. She grabbed Ray around the waist, and together they rolled over with Marcella now on top. She would now decide how deep and how intense their experience would be. Ray lay rigid, as Marcella ground herself against him. Ray wanted to make this last as long as possible, but he now realized that it was not up to him anymore.

They lay next to each other now, catching their breath. It was an amazing experience either one would ever forget. They looked into each other's eyes. They both smiled at each other. It was right then that they both realized they were meant to be together. And they made a handsome couple too! All was bliss as they stared at the ceiling fan. Marcella grabbed Ray's elbow and asked if he were ready to go again. He said yes, and that was a good thing. That would be just fine with Ray.

Ray made breakfast while Marcella was in the shower. She came in the dining room wearing Ray's bathrobe. As they sat and had breakfast, Marcella begged Ray to take her with him today. Ray told her no way, it was way too dangerous. Marcella wouldn't let it go. She pleaded with Ray. This wasn't her first rodeo, if anything bad went down, they could handle it together. She just needed to stop by her place to get into some different clothes. Ray wasn't having any part of it. It just wasn't going to happen.

One hour later, Ray was standing in the living room of Marcella's villa, waiting for her to get ready. When she finally did emerge, Ray regretted having ever changed his mind. She was wearing a short black faux leather dress and spikey high-heeled boots. It was the sexiest outfit she had worn for him so far. This was bound to make some kind of impression upon Ronny and his gang of malefactors.

"How do I look?" Marcella asked, twirling around so that Ray could see her from every angle.

"You look like a bitching biker slut!" Ray said, half-jokingly, half-seriously.

"Peeerfect!"

They had a couple of hours' drive ahead of them. Ray used the opportunity to ask Marcella about her family. She told him that her dad was from Cuba and that her mom was from Brazil. She had three sisters. Growing up, her father always spoke to them in Spanish, her mother always spoke Portuguese. They grew up in Brazil, before moving to the States, when she was sixteen years old. The family moved to Florida, then to South Carolina a couple of years later.

They drove for miles on scenic back country roads. Marcella asked Ray about his family and growing up. Not much to tell really, one brother living in the Midwest, both parents still married, living there as well. Everything was fine right up until high school, where he developed an insatiable appetite for marijuana. He bailed out of college after a couple of years. It interfered with his partying, and in the back of his mind, he knew that the ways of the world and of success, for him anyway, would not be learned in any college lecture hall.

So busy was Ray, going on about his formative years, that he almost drove right past their destination. It was easily missed from the main road. Ray stopped short and turned right onto a road surface made of crushed stone, just wide enough for two vehicles to pass each other with extreme caution. They came to an electric gate with an electronic keypad. Ray exited the vehicle and walked over to the keypad, which was mounted next to a two-way intercom.

"Ray Bangor … here to see Wolf … I have an appointment."

There was silence for the next few seconds. The gate began to rattle as it rolled open behind the eight-foot-high chain link fence. The only other sounds were of cicadas in the trees. They drove back to a warehouse terminal where there were ten bays for big rigs to back into. They drove on past a mechanic's garage and past that to a small office building. There were about a dozen bikes parked out front in a neat row. They stepped out into the midday heat. It was probably one hundred degrees or so.

Ray held the door open for Marcella, and she stepped into nice, cool air conditioning. Ray followed her inside and felt a big hairy male hand stop his forward progress, while the other hand reached for the butt of Ray's .44 caliber Smith and Wesson.. Oh shit, thought Ray. He wasn't even one whole step inside and already this was turning out to be a problem. Son of a bitch!

"It's all right, Buzz … he's cool!" Wolf said to his sergeant at arms, who begrudgingly took his hand away from the handle of Ray's gun.

"Hey, how ya doing, Ray?" The two men shook hands. "Who's the beautiful lady with you?"

"That would be my girlfriend and associate, Marcella. Marcella, meet my friend Wolf." Marcella shook hands with the big, heavily tattooed club president.

From the outside, what appeared to be an office building was in fact a biker clubhouse, with all the trappings, pool tables, a jukebox, a bar, neon beer signs, and even a small stage. Almost every square inch of every wall was covered with framed pictures of men and women standing next to or seated on motorcycles and choppers. Dusty bikers sat at the bar sipping cold beers. Four men sat at a corner table playing poker. There was a substantial amount of money on the table as well as watches, rings, a switchblade knife, and a small handgun. Someone is going to win big. Hope there's no sore losers here today.

But the attention of everyone present was on the ever-beautiful Marcella. The normally cool and funny Marcella, now sensing that it was she who was the cause of the momentary lapse in everyone's conversation, stood very close to Ray, nervously so. Ceiling fans whirled overhead. Old school country played softly over the jukebox. Ray could not help but notice that every woman present was also staring at Marcella.

"Janie … where's your manners … offer my friends a cool drink on a hot day," rasped Wolf.

"Sorry," a young tattooed woman said as she got up from a couch and stepped behind the bar.

"What can I get for y'all?"

Marcella had a diet soda and Ray had a beer. Wolf invited them into his office behind the bar.

There were very beautiful paintings of nude women hanging on the walls. Ray was pretty sure Wolf didn't buy them at an art auction. On one corner of Wolf's huge oak desk was what appeared to be a very old human skull. Marcella stared at it, smiling nervously. She was visibly uncomfortable.

"Anyone I know?" Ray said as he motioned with his eyes toward the skull.

"Naw … that thing is probably two hundred years old. My granddaddy found it on his property when I was a kid. Probably an early settler. Now what can I do for you folks today?"

Ray gently nudged Marcella out of her momentary stupor. She reached into her purse and produced a package, laying it gently on the desk in front of Wolf. His eyebrows raised as he looked at the package before picking it up. This is it, thought Ray. Everything that happens from here on starts right now.

Wolf pushed the button on the intercom on his desk. "Janie … I need you back here."

A second later, the young tattooed bartender stepped into the office. "Janie here is our resident chemist," Wolf explained.

Wolf stabbed the package with a double-edged knife, carefully spilling some of the contents onto his glass desktop. Janie, for her part, picked up a magnifying glass out of the pencil holder and studied the sample closely. She smiled wide. She chopped the sample into two lines and snorted both. She released her breath and tilted her head backwards sniffling deeply as she did so.

"That's good coke!" she said. "Good and pure!"

Wolf picked up the package and held it in his hand feeling its weight. "How much for this?'

"Ten thousand, cash."

"Worth every penny!" Janie advised Wolf.

"Ten Gs, huh? Janie … take care of that, would you?"

The skinny little biker chick disappeared out the door. She came back with a cigar box full of Ben Franklins. She counted out one hundred of them before placing them on the desk in front of Ray.

Janie stood next to the desk waiting to be excused. Wolf removed several grams with his knife blade and dumped it into a plastic bag, before handing it to Janie. Consultation fee.

"There is more where that came from!" Ray advised. "Just let me know if you guys like the product!"

"More, you say? I'll be in touch."

Wolf stood, as did Marcella and Ray. The two men shook hands. They walked out into the clubhouse, only now, no one seemed to be paying any attention to them. Ray opened the passenger side door for Marcella, who climbed in and fastened her seatbelt. They drove off headed home, back to Hilton Head Island. Marcella was pissed. How could Ray take her to such a place that creeped her out so badly? Ray recalled that he had warned her against it, but she insisted. Still, knowing the type of people who would be there, how could Ray do such a thing? Ray explained that he really was sorry he had taken her there. She did not have to see that. He told her she would never have to come back there ever again. Marcella was just fine with that.

That skull on Wolf's desk, for example. What was Ray thinking? She said that the whole time they were sitting in Wolf's office that thing was giving her "the eye!" But it's just a skull, it doesn't have eyes. But it used to! They sat in creepy silence as they both pondered what's going to happen the next time Ray has to meet with these men. He didn't have to wait long. The very next day there was a message from Wolf on Ray's answering machine. Ray called him back. Wolf said he could really use another ten at ten per. That was fine with Ray, although he dreaded the long drive out there again, this time with no company, and who knows what was waiting for him on the other end. There was a lot of money at stake here.

The next day, Ray made the same drive, only this time he had a lot of time to think about everything. In the rear cargo space were ten of the twenty packages he had brought back with him from *The REEL OPPORTUNITY* when she was docked in South Sea Pines. It seemed like a long time ago, and in a different world. It's all good. This was just the hassle of doing business. Wolf and his boys, well, they were good boys. They would probably want to do a little celebrating when it was all said and done.

Ray pulled up to the clubhouse. Today, there were thirty or so bikes parked out front. Maybe they were having a party? Ray stepped through the clubhouse door and was immediately relieved of his .44 caliber. Two strong dudes held his arms while a third continued searching him, also relieving him of a .40 semiauto in a waistband holster, and a .25 semiauto in an ankle holster. A hot prickly flash of adrenaline swept over Ray as he knew his death could come at any second.

"He's clean," said Buzz, the sergeant at arms.

"We'll see about that!" barked Wolf.

"Wolf!" Ray screamed, "I thought we had a deal!"

"That's the trouble with thinking. For example, my sergeant at arms here, Buzz … well … he thinks you might be working for the police."

"Wouldn't they be in here right now, busting your sorry asses if that were the case?"

Wolf and his sergeant at arms looked at each other.

"Let go of him!"

The two mammoth goons released their tight grip on Ray's arms.

"All right then, dude, just relax, we need to make sure you're not wearing a wire."

There was a click. One of the Ingrates had just pulled the hammer back on the .44 caliber and was now aiming it at Ray's head. Janie and another girl stepped forward. They stood on either side of Ray and began taking off his clothes. A third chick went through the discarded clothing as it was removed. Ray now stood completely naked. One of the girls wet her finger and shoved it up his ass. Ray had never in his life felt more violated and vulnerable.

"He's clean!" she said smiling.

"Well then … give him his clothes back."

The girls tried to help him, but he shook them off, fucking bitches! He fumbled to get dressed while sixty or so people watched him. Fully clothed now, he felt anger like he had never felt before in his life. He wanted to kill every motherfucker in the room. Veins were popping out of his temples and his face was dark red. "What kind of paranoid shit was that?" he yelled to all present, but especially to Wolf and Buzz.

"Just one more thing, man … where did you get this coke?" Wolf asked point blank.

The dude holding Ray's gun waved it in his face, meaning it's time to start talking, buddy.

"My friends and I, we found it! We took it off an abandoned wreck on the Joyner Banks off of Hilton Head Island!"

Suddenly, the entire scene shifted. Everyone went about talking and doing whatever it was they were doing before his entrance. Someone handed him a double shot of whiskey and a cold beer. His hands were still shaking. And he was still pissed, swearing to himself if he makes it out of this one, he's going to come back here with two fully auto AKs and mow every last one of these motherfuckers down.

"You did all right, son! Welcome to the party!" said Wolf.

"Motherfucker!" said Ray. "Here I am helping you assholes get rich, and you jokers are jerking me around like a bitch boy!"

"I'll bet you could use a good smoke right now, calm your ass down a little! Step into my office."

They sat in Wolf's office. Janie came through the door and placed another whiskey and another long neck in front of Ray. She sat and rolled joints, handing each one to each man before sparking one up herself. They puffed on the joints. They drank their drinks, everyone a little bit more relaxed now.

"If it's any consolation to you, it wasn't my idea. The VP and the sergeant at arms were convinced you were a narc. You are just too polished, too educated for these people."

"Then why as club president didn't you stop them?"

"Because … it was the only way I could convince them. Feel better now, man? Janie here would like to give you something!"

Janie got up from her chair and knelt down in front of Ray. "You got some balls on you, honey! I love to give a man with balls a good suck!" She began to loosen Ray's belt.

"No … not just no … fuck no!"

"What is your problem, dude?" asked Janie.

"Yeah, what is your problem?" added Wolf.

"I have a girlfriend, it wouldn't be fair to her! Let's just do this fucking deal so I can get the fuck up outta here!"

"Suit yourself then, righteous dude!"

Ray drove through the night back to Hilton Head Island. His backpack that formerly held ten kilos now held one hundred thousand dollars. He drove straight to Marcella's villa. Ray let himself in with the extra key she had given him. Finding her asleep in her bed, he lay down beside her. He was glad to be alive, right here, right now, right next to his Marcella. Marcella had a thousand questions over breakfast. How did his clothing get torn? What in the hell happed to him last night? Ray told her the whole story. Marcella was visibly affected. She put her hand over her mouth. There were tears in her eyes. She was in shock. Those motherfuckers!

A little while later, after calming down, she had something important to ask Ray. She wanted to know if Ray would kill her ex-husband. He was a fucking asshole, and he was harassing and humiliating her all over town. Restraining order, fuck that, the guy just needed to die. Would Ray do this for her and make the world a better place?

No, he would not. But he knew some guys who would. Besides, they owed him a huge favor, he figured. Now they all knew for sure that he wasn't a narc. This was official underworld business. They could do this easily. Marcella and Ray would have to have rock-solid alibis. How bad could this guy be, anyhow?

It was noon when Ray said goodbye to Marcella. He drove straight on through the day to Max's house in Georgia. Max had just arrived from Charleston where he left his boat and picked up his personal truck. Max and Gina were glad to see Ray. They cracked open some beers and celebrated.

Ray placed stacks of money in front of Gina as she accounted for every single package sold so far. Gina counted money all afternoon, giving Max and Ray a chance to talk.

Ray told him in detail about his dealings thus far with the Ingrates. Max was visibly affected. There was no laughter, no poking fun, not a word from Max, for he now knew that everything was going to hell after those bikers got involved. Their whole sorry world was going under. Max was pissed. They were Ray's stupid-ass friends anyway. But they just made two hundred and one thousand dollars in just one week. That was a cool seventy thousand apiece. Ray was getting results no one was expecting. And without getting Max and Gina involved in the messy end of things. Ray was to be congratulated.

Back in Hilton Head a couple hours later, Ray was picking up some office supplies Gina had requested. Upon returning to his car, he found a dark metallic blue Dodge Viper parked right up against his Corvette. If the two cars were any closer, they would be touching. All these empty parking spaces and this asshole was parked right up against him. Ray could feel the hairs on the back of his neck standing up.

"Hey, asshole … hey you? Where did you get that car?" said the man sitting in the Viper and now getting out of the car to face Ray. "Where does a lowlife like you come up with a car like that?"

"I have a clear title on this car, purchased from one Miss Marcella De Silva!"

The man winced, as though her name were an icepick in his ear.

Ray went on. "How do you know that I'm not a sociopathic murderer, getting ready to go over the edge, and all I need is a push?"

The man produced a gun from a waistband holster and stuck the barrel up under Ray's ribcage.

"I have a license to carry this!" the man hissed. "And this is how I deal with sociopathic murderers!'

"I'm not saying that I am … I'm saying what if I were? You wouldn't know that! And now you're gonna shoot me, an unarmed man, in front of witnesses no less. Soon as you fire that gun, everyone's going to be looking in your general direction. You didn't even pick an inconspicuous getaway car!" Ray paused to let it sink in.

Marcella's ex-husband holstered the weapon. "I'll be seeing you around!"

"I hope so!" said Ray.

This was the second time in twenty-four hours that people have tried to screw and fuck with Ray. There would not be a third. Now this guy here, he just needs killing, some people just need that. Unfortunately, in this world, there are people who deserve it, but never get it. That's probably the case most of the time. This asshole was going to pay, and pay dearly. Ray decided he was going to take immediate action.

One hour later, he was in his car taking the long drive out to the Ingrate Order MC compound.

In Wolf's office, Ray produced a picture of Marcella's ex and placed it on the desk in front of Wolf who neither touched it nor looked at it. Wolf explained to Ray that they don't, as an organization, do that sort of thing. However, he might know someone who might take the job, but it was to be between individuals.

A prospect of the Ingrate Order MC now sat across from Ray in a corner of the nearly empty clubhouse. His name was Rooster and aptly so, he was sporting a high red Mohawk. He was out to make a name for himself, not being a full patch member yet. He was a scary-looking dude all right. He would do just fine, Ray figured. Now the question was price. Rooster wanted ten thousand cash, firm. That was twice the going rate for professional hitmen. Ray reluctantly agreed. He wanted Marcella's ex-husband dead. Marcella wanted him dead. It was well worth it. They made plans.

It was going to be a fun thing for Ray and Marcella anyhow. They checked into a nice hotel in downtown Savannah, Georgia. They had hotel room sex. Then it was time to get ready for a night on the town. They had dinner in a nice restaurant. They walked down River Street and had drinks in a little bar on Bay Street. Ray saved all the receipts. Then, it was back to the hotel for more drunken sex. It really was fun.

By 3:00 p.m. they were back on Hilton Head at Ray's place. He checked his phone messages. There was a message from his landlord Lester Price, wanting to know how if Ray could move out by the end of the month. Lester said he had an oceanfront for Ray to move into for just two hundred more a month. Then there was the message he drove all the way back from Savannah to hear. Except it wasn't the good news he was expecting. Son of a bitch! Ray called Wolf and was told to come out to the compound now. Ray told him there was no fucking way he was coming out there now. He would be there later tonight, they would just have to deal with his busy schedule, which included sex with Marcella and a long nap. When self-employed, it's easy to make one's own rules. The stress over the last couple of days was taking its toll. Ray decided right now he just needed to relax, and he did just that.

Marcella went ballistic when she found out there was a problem. How could they possibly mess this up? All they had to do was kill one man. Ray explained to her that there was no "they" involved. He had made the deal with a prospect, an individual, man to man. The Ingrate Order MC was not to be involved. Somehow, this rookie wannabe bad-ass fucked things up badly, and now the Ingrate Order MC was involved. Probably, a lot of bad feelings were going around right now. Tough shit, thought Ray. He loaded the Vette with weapons and ammunition. He wasn't going to let anyone disarm him this time around. Marcella insisted on going with him. It was, after all, her ex-husband. Ray explained to her that this was very likely going to be ugly, no lady should have to see that. She didn't care, she just wanted to set things straight. It was personal now. They sat in complete silence on the long drive out into the countryside at night.

When they arrived at the compound, they could hear gunshots and revving motorcycle engines. Every single overhead lamp inside the perimeter was on. Ray entered the code and the electronic gate rolled open. Slowly, they drove past the terminal, past the garage, on towards the clubhouse on the back of the property. It was a full house tonight! Everyone was outside. There were bikers and their women all over the compound. They were all armed heavily. Anyone who decided to crash this party would be making a huge mistake.

It was in front of the clubhouse that Ray and Marcella found Wolf, Ace the club VP, and the asshole sergeant at arms Buzz having a serious conversation. Ray interrupted them. Probably not the best move under the circumstances. The three club leaders turned their attention to Ray and Marcella. "You asked me to come out here … here I am … with my girlfriend," Ray explained. "Now I know what you're thinking … you're thinking … this is all my fault. I had an agreement with your guy, and this … whatever the hell is going on right here, right now, wasn't part of the plan!"

Wolf folded his arms and squinted at Ray. "No shit!"

Now seated around a table in the deserted clubhouse were Ray, Marcella, and the three top dogs of the Ingrate Order MC. The only other person in the room was Janie, standing behind the bar. Wolf began to explain that this wasn't all about them, rules had been broken. There were going to be severe penalties for those involved. This had become official Ingrate Order MC business. Wolf had something to show them. Would they please follow him outside? On the side of the clubhouse were two men and one woman stripped down to their underwear, their outstretched arms and legs chained to eyebolts, anchored in the cinder block wall. There in front of them were Marcella's ex-husband, an unknown woman, and the prospect, Rooster. Two biker chicks were taking turns swatting mosquitoes off the three helpless victims chained to the wall. All three were covered with welts from the grimy fly swatters.

Marcella went berserk. She began punching and kicking her defenseless ex-husband, while screaming at the top of her lungs. Ray slipped his arm around her waist and pulled her away, only to have her wriggle free and resume the beating. Ray grabbed her with both arms this time and pulled her backward as she continued kicking and screaming. It was hard to watch. Marcella would just not calm down. The mere sight of her ex-husband had set her into a boiling rage that just would not subside. She began cursing and spitting on her former husband as amused bystanders looked on.

"Damn, son! She's speaking in tongues," observed Buzz.

"Naw, man! That's Spanish," said Ace.

"You're both wrong … it's Portuguese," said Ray, as he still struggled to hold on to Marcella.

"Wolf, you need to tell me what this is all about!"

"Everyone calm the fuck down!" shouted Wolf. "That goes for you too Chiquita!" he barked at Marcella.

Wolf laid it all out. The original agreement between Ray and Rooster was now null and void. Rooster had brought his woman along with him to do the hit for Ray. It was supposed to be a home invasion gone bad, but Marcella's ex-husband pleaded for his life, telling them he was worth so much more alive than dead. So these two geniuses took him hostage, but they made the fatal mistake of bringing him here. This simple act of blatant stupidity would not be tolerated in the Ingrate Order MC. The penalty for Rooster, death! For her part, Rooster's woman, was to service the Ingrate Order MC. As for Marcella's ex-husband, if they wanted him dead, they were going to have to do it themselves. Buzz handed Marcella a nightstick and told her to go for it.

Marcela grabbed the nightstick and went ape-shit on her ex, beating his entire body as hard as she could! Hardened, full patch members had to look away, it was so revolting. She broke ribs, arms, and legs.

More than one onlooker vomited profusely at the horrid display of violence. Ray grabbed his .44,and held it high over his head and fired it into the air. The deafening crack brought everyone to attention and, in Marcella's case, back to temporary sanity. Her ex, beaten unconscious, hung limp on his outstretched arms. Ray now leveled the gun and, taking aim, fired it at the head of Marcella's ex-husband, blowing it apart. Ray stood there, looking at the mess he had just created. He had never killed anyone before. One thing was certain, that guy would have died anyway from the beating he received from Marcella.

Wolf, Ace, and Buzz now stood between Ray and Marcella and their car. Ray holstered the heavy weapon. He put his arm around Marcella. They walked ten feet or so, now standing directly in front of the three large men. On each side of the couple were full patch members, everyone's ears still ringing from the gunshots. "You said that if we wanted him dead, we'd have to kill him ourselves … well we wanted him dead!"

"Yeah," Wolf said, "I think you got him." And with that, he stepped aside, as did everyone else. Ray helped Marcella to their car. They drove in silence the first hour or so.

"Thank you for killing David," she finally said.

"Huh?"

"My ex-husband, David."

Ray wanted to know why she hated that man so much. A person has to have real hatred in their heart to try and beat someone to death with a nightstick. Marcella told Ray that David was fucking her younger sisters. She just couldn't take it. For him to do that to her was the ultimate sign of disrespect. They continued driving in silence the rest of the way. When they finally reached Ray's villa, they went straight to bed, they were exhausted.

They had yet another heavy day ahead of them. They were supposed to meet one of Marcella's "friends" who wanted to meet Ray in person. On the deck of his enormous pleasure yacht *PRINCESS*, the man introduced himself as Diego Ortiz. Over lunch, Diego wanted to know if it was possible to do a deal, one hundred kilos. This guy Ortiz must be some kind of heavy hitter, thought Ray. He made Ray feel uncomfortable. One hundred kilos were difficult for Ray at this time, he explained. Perhaps they could do a smaller deal, say fifty. What Ray was not telling Ortiz was the fact that fifty kilos were much easier and far less conspicuous to transfer. They could just do a follow-up deal. Ortiz told Ray there was a time limit. In two days, Ortiz would be leaving the island. That would be cutting it too close.

That left Ray with a difficult decision. He would do the deal, one hundred kilos for one million dollars, on the condition that Ray's three business partners were present to assist. That would be Marcella and another man and another woman. They would assist in bringing the product onto Ortiz's yacht. Ortiz wasn't comfortable allowing total strangers onto his yacht. Ray pointed out that up until one hour ago, he was a total stranger to Ortiz. The only reason Ortiz met with Ray today was that they had a common associate, Marcella, whom Ortiz trusted completely. Ortiz asked Marcella in Spanish if she had ever met Ray's other partners. Marcella explained that not only had she met them, she stayed overnight on their pleasure yacht with Ray. With that said, Ortiz agreed. The deal would take place tomorrow night.

Ray made the call to Max. He knew Max would not be pleased with being involved, but these circumstances required special arrangements. There was, after all, one million dollars to be made on just this one deal. Ray could not do it with just Marcella, he would need Max and Gina's help. There was no other way. They had to do this. Max reluctantly agreed, figuring the sooner they get rid of all the product, the better. He instructed Ray to meet him at his house the following day.

Marcella made the long drive out to Max's house while Ray reclined in the passenger seat.

There was something about this Ortiz fellow that bothered him, he didn't quite know what it was. He just didn't like or trust the guy. Unable to contain his suspicions any longer, he asked Marcella, point blank, how it was that she knew this guy. Marcella cleared her throat and shifted in in her seat. Ray could sense that he had broached an unpleasant subject.

Ortiz was a businessman and had known Marcella since she was eighteen. The smooth-talking Ortiz offered her a job with an escort service he ran, explaining to her that there was huge income potential in this line of work. It wasn't Marcella's ideal career choice, but being young, the lure of easy money and the chance to strike out on her own were too much to pass up. The problem for Marcella was, there was nothing easy about it. The rules of the game were simple enough. The client could not, under any circumstance, penetrate the escort. But not all of the girls followed the rules. If a client could convince them he was not a cop, it was pretty much anything goes, for the right price of course.

Marcella restricted herself to giving massages and hand jobs to mostly married men. It was not something she was particularly proud of. Nevertheless, she did it for about a year and, in doing so, completely won the trust of Diego Ortiz, who by now was just getting started in the cocaine business. Her business relationship with him has continued right up to this day. If Ray didn't like Ortiz before, he really didn't like him now.

They arrived at Max's house ahead of schedule. Max and Gina had already loaded the packages into old suitcases, eight old suitcases, and they didn't even match. Ray didn't like it. But there was no other choice. It was too late in the day to buy matching sets. They went over the plans again. Max and Gina would drive Max's truck loaded with the product. Ray and Marcella would follow them in the Vette.

Max had a surprise. He showed Ray a ten-shot .22 semiauto pistol, its barrel drilled and tapped for a homemade silencer. Max demonstrated by firing a round into a tree trunk. It was unmistakably the sound of a gunshot, only greatly muffled. Max went on to explain that he'd made good use of his free time over the last few days to build these silencers from scratch in his workshop, knowing that they could come in handy one day. Max handed one of the modified weapons to Ray and another to Gina. Marcella, Max knew, didn't like guns.

It was just getting dark when they arrived at the marina. They made their way past throngs of summer tourists. They arrived at the *PRINCESS* to find Ortiz sitting on the rear deck, smoking a cigar. With him were four body-guards, all packing side-arms. They exchanged greetings. Ray could not help but notice that all four goons were fixated on Marcella and her sexy outfit. Looking down over their sunglasses, so as to have a better look, the four men admired the shapely Latina standing before them. What kind of idiots wear sunglasses at night? thought Ray.

Ortiz wanted to know if everything was in order. Ray told him they should wait until dark, then transport the product from their vehicle to the *PRINCESS*. They would need help carrying the suitcases, explained Ray. Ortiz said that would be no problem at all. The four body-guards, meanwhile, seemed oblivious to the conversation, focusing their attention instead on the beautiful Marcella.

One of the senior goons asked her in Spanish where she was from. How unprofessional, thought Ray. These guys really were idiots who probably regarded Max, Gina, and himself as dumb American rednecks.

Ortiz invited everyone inside the spacious salon aboard the *PRINCESS*. It was huge and very nicely furnished, with soft white leather sofas on which they all sat. The hired help remained standing, still preoccupied with Marcella as she sat with her legs crossed, fanning herself. Ortiz asked if anyone would like something to drink, motioning to the bar in the corner. They respectfully declined. Ray told Ortiz that before they made the switch, he would like to see the money. Ortiz laughed, but nevertheless produced a flight case which he now set down on the coffee table. He opened it to allow Ray to examine the contents.

Ray picked up one of the packets of neatly wrapped one-hundred-dollar bills and fanned it. He removed a single bill and held it up to the light so as to see the watermarks. All of this served to annoy Ortiz, who appeared agitated by the gesture. Having recently handled over two hundred thousand dollars in cash, it occurred to Ray that even if this flight case was loaded with hundreds, there was no way in hell there was one million dollars there. It was probably more like half a million.

Ray surmised that Ortiz must have regarded him as an idiot, who wouldn't know one million dollars in cash if he saw it. Ray had a difficult decision to make and only a few seconds to make it final.

He looked at Max and Gina. He looked at Marcella. He next looked down at the money stacked inside the flight case. "It's all good!"

That was their prearranged code for "Abort mission, this is a drug burn, kill everyone on board!"

Max and Gina pulled their weapons and began firing at the four goons who never saw it coming. Unfortunately for them, Max and Gina were both good shots, and each of the .22 caliber rounds found their mark. Ray pulled his weapon and fired it into the forehead of Diego Ortiz, killing him instantly. The criminal mastermind and his four bodyguards now lay dead, having seriously underestimated their adversaries.

Ray closed the flight case and stood to face Marcella. "I'm sorry about this," he lamented.

"I never like heem anyway!" was her response.

There was no way of knowing if anyone outside the yacht heard the gunshots. They would exit like nothing ever happened. They casually walked down the aluminum gangway onto a gravel walkway. Miraculously, no one seemed to be paying any attention to them. They split up, only to meet at Max's truck a few minutes later. Ray handed the case to Max. Ray and Marcella got into the Vette and followed Max's truck out of the marina parking lot, right past three sheriff deputies speeding in the opposite direction, lights flashing, sirens silent.

The two vehicles rendezvoused at Ray's villa where, once inside, Ray switched on his police scanner. They all sat in the living room now, smoking pot, drinking shots of whiskey and cold beers, listening to the chatter on the police radio frequencies. A perimeter had been established. Road blocks were being set up. Suspicious vehicles were being pulled over. Everyone in the room let out a sigh of relief when it was announced over the airwaves that the authorities were looking for a mini-van. Probably half the vehicles driving around the island were mini-vans.

Convinced they were in the clear, for now anyway, Max and Gina took the guest bedroom, Ray and Marcella retired to the master bedroom. They could not sleep. They made wild, passionate love that did not go unnoticed by Max and Gina in the next room, doing the same thing. Sleep became much easier for them afterwards. What a day it had been for all of them, certainly not what they had expected.

Ray woke to the sound of his doorbell. Walking to the front door past the guest room, he noticed that Max and Gina had already left with the cash and the unsold product. At Ray's front door were the movers. Fuck, thought Ray, he had forgotten all about it. They spent the rest of the morning moving into Ray's new one-bedroom oceanfront villa just a few blocks away. Marcella fell in love with the view.

Ray asked Marcella if she would be interested in moving in with him. That would be just fine with Marcella.

The next morning, Ray and Marcella were awakened by the ringing telephone. The answering machine began to record the incoming message, but was cancelled by Ray as soon as he heard the raspy voice of Ronny "Wolf" Zeigler. Ray picked up the handset still half asleep. Wolf explained that he would need twenty packages today, the sooner the better. Ray told him that he was all over it. He called Max across the state line and told him to expect them in a couple of hours. When asked if she had a problem accompanying Ray to the biker compound again, Marcella explained that those folks didn't scare her anymore.

At Max's house, Gina had something to show Ray and Marcella. She handed them a New York State driver's license. Ray handed it back to her, saying it looked like a big, fat stupid fuck with a mustache. Gina held the license directly in front of Ray's face and said it looked exactly like one of the men they killed the night before last. Ray examined it more closely and thought it did bear a striking resemblance to the senior goon that was bothering Marcella. It could have been his twin brother or other close family member.

Ray brushed it off, saying that it was just a mere coincidence. Gina was not so easily convinced. She would not let it drop, saying that she had a bad, creepy feeling about this. She showed the license to Marcella, who agreed, yes, it did look just like the man Gina had shot in the face.

Ray told Gina he did not have time for this nonsense, he had a load to deliver, for fuck's sake.

In the basement, Ray found Max in the process of completely disassembling, cleaning, and removing surface rust off of the Chinese-made AK-47s they took off the *Winsor2*. Also on his work bench were the three .22s used to kill Ortiz and his henchmen. Max had altered the rifling characteristics with a special knurling tool he had fabricated. He even went so far as to alter the machined surfaces of the firing pins and shell ejectors. There was no way, Max explained, that these weapons could be traced to the murders.

As far as the murders were concerned, Ray had been dead nuts on about the amount of cash they took off Ortiz's yacht. It was in fact four hundred and ninety thousand dollars, all in hundreds. So far in their criminal enterprise, they had taken in almost seven hundred thousand dollars in less than two weeks. Gina made entries in the ledger as Ray removed twenty packages from the storage closet in the basement. He jokingly asked Gina if he needed to sign for these. Gina was not amused and stormed out of the basement muttering profanities.

Out at the Ingrate Order MC compound, it was just another hot, sunny afternoon, but the place was busy. There were a couple of big rigs backed up to the terminal warehouse. The mechanic's garage was busy as well, the sounds of impact wrenches disturbing the otherwise peaceful surroundings. Ray and Marcella entered the cool air-conditioned clubhouse and walked over to the bar past grizzled full patch members who paid them no mind.

They found Janie sitting on a barstool, painting her toenails. Upon seeing the couple, she immediately took her post behind the bar and popped the tops off a long-neck beer and a diet soda. As she set the drinks in front of the couple, she made brief eye contact with Ray. Ray took a long pull off the cold beer and asked Janie where Wolf could be found. She told him Wolf could be found working in the garage. Ray grabbed his beer and, with Marcella, headed out into bright afternoon sunshine, not a cloud in the sky.

Wolf greeted the couple warmly, but did not offer to shake hands. His huge hands, as well as his huge tattooed forearms, were covered with grease. He was in the process of removing the cylinder head from an old in-line six-cylinder truck engine. Wolf's trusted Ray Bangor so much so by now that he went on to explain that this engine, with the pistons and connecting rods removed, would be used to transport the twenty kilos Ray had brought with him up the East Coast to Baltimore.

Setting his impact wrench down on a work table, Wolf excused himself to wash up, explaining that he needed a break anyway. As they walked to the rear of the complex to the clubhouse, Wolf stopped, saying he had something to show Ray. The north wall of the clubhouse, where Ray had shot Marcella's ex-husband, had been freshly painted. Even the eyebolts had been removed and the anchors patched over. There, Wolf pointed with a big fat finger to a particular spot on the wall.

Unsure of where this was going, Ray asked Wolf what exactly he was pointing to. Wolf again pointed to a particular cinder block, explaining that the .44 caliber round Ray had fired through the skull of Marcella's ex-husband had not only penetrated the cinder block wall, it also damaged an expensive painting. Ray said he was sorry about the collateral damages, but he did compliment the expert repair job. Wolf told him that his sergeant at arms Buzz was their resident brick mason. It was Buzz who chiseled out the damaged blocks and mudded in the replacements. Ray was impressed. Buzz had done such an expert job that the damaged portion of the wall was indistinguishable from the rest. Ray asked Wolf what they did to Rooster. Wolf just shook his head saying Ray and Marcella really didn't want to know about that.

Sitting at a table now in the cool clubhouse, Janie brought over a fresh round. Wolf hoisted the 12 oz. beer bottle and drained it, motioning for Janie to bring another. Wolf offered a joint to Ray as he lit one himself. Blowing a huge cloud of smoke out through his nostrils, Wolf began to lay out his business plan. Baltimore was in the midst of a huge crack epidemic. The product Ray was offering was in high demand in that region of the country. Wolf went on to say he would expect that demand to increase in the coming months.

This was good news, indeed. The sooner they got rid of all the coke, the sooner they could all retire, comfortably so. Max and Gina would be thrilled when told there was light at the end of the tunnel. Ray was hoping he could talk Marcella into moving to some obscure place in the world, far from the memories of the evil acts they had committed so far. Marcella was a strong woman, he knew, but she was becoming increasingly affected by the events that had taken place over the last two weeks. Ray had become affected also. He would kill anyone that stood in their way. He never imagined he would become the type of human being he was now.

Wolf excused himself saying that he had to have this shipment ready pronto. He had a driver standing by, and he wanted to get this man on the road as soon as possible. As Wolf left the clubhouse, other full patch members started filing in. It was happy hour. Not only that, there was a big party planned for that night. It was the club VP Ace's birthday today. There was going to be a stripper and a live band. It was time for Ray and Marcella to leave anyway before things got too crazy.

On the balcony of their new villa, Ray and Marcella sipped cocktails and snorted rails. A thousand stars glittered in the night sky over the ocean. Life was good. They talked about the future. They talked about where they wanted to be, say, a year from now. But the topic always came back to now and, inevitably, tomorrow. They were still sitting on more than a half ton of product. The prospect of getting rid of all of it seemed distant.

The next morning, the ringing telephone jarred them from sleep for the second day in a row.

Ray let the answering service take it. It was Lester Price, his landlord. Lester said that overnight someone had kicked in the front door of Ray's old villa, the one that he just moved out of a couple of days ago. Lester wanted to know if Ray knew who would be capable of doing such a thing. There was, after all, nothing to steal.

The sorry truth was Ray had no idea who may have perpetrated the crime, and it scared him.

All his known enemies were dead. But what about unknown enemies? Was Diego Ortiz so connected that people were seeking revenge? The thought turned his stomach into a knot. Marcella, who heard the entire message, now became visibly upset. Ray resumed his composure and told her to relax.

No one, except for Lester Price, knew that they had moved and to where. Their new villa complex offered gated security, as well as 24-7 armed security guards.

One thing did stand out in the mind of Ray right now. He had to get rid of the black Vette, too many people knew that he had it. Reluctantly, he drove with Marcella to the dealership where they were immediately greeted by a salesman as soon as they entered the showroom. Ray politely explained that he had a special trade, and he was in the market for two vehicles, one for Marcella, one for himself. He would need to speak to the sales manager personally.

The sales manager greeted them and told them in his deep Southern drawl that he would work with them any way he could to make sure they left this dealership today as satisfied customers who would recommend it to their friends. We'll just see about that! Ray asked him point blank if people ever paid cash for their purchases here. The manager laughed as he said, "This is Hilton Head, old buddy, people here do that all the time. No one who could afford to wanted to pay for unnecessary financing."

Impressed with their trade-in, which was in impeccable condition, the sales manager wanted to know what types of vehicles they were interested in purchasing. It was all Marcella's show now, she loved car shopping, if only because she would be picking the car she wanted for the first time. Ray, on the other hand, hated car shopping and wanted to get the whole thing over with as soon as possible, so he could go home and get drunk and stoned.

Three hours later, they were still in the dealership. Marcella wanted to see everything they had. Ray had to remind her that they did have a budget and there was no wavering on that. When Marcella climbed into a car, she had to check out everything, starting with the vanity mirrors. No vanity mirrors were an instant disqualification. At least that narrowed the field by a whopping five percent, thought an increasingly restless Ray Bangor.

When they finally agreed on two vehicles they wished to purchase, Marcella took control over the negotiations. She struck model poses. She leaned back against the car she wanted with her outstretched arms. She bent over the hood to closely examine a tiny scratch, commenting that there was significant depreciation in value with this one. They finally left the dealership late in the afternoon with Marcella driving a lightly used Cadillac and Ray driving a lightly used Lincoln. The best part being they came in ten grand under budget, thanks in whole to Marcella's impressive negotiation skills and her great ass. They would celebrate their newly acquired purchases with dinner at a nice restaurant.

Eager to road-test his new wheels, Ray called Wolf to ask if he needed anything. It was Janie who answered the phone and, recognizing Ray's voice and manner of speaking, somberly told him Wolf was dead. Ray could not believe what he was hearing. He felt his heart skip a beat. This can't be! What on earth could possibly kill the "Big Bad Wolf" before his time?

The answer, ironically, was a deer. Two nights ago, leaving Ace's birthday party, a huge twelve-point collided with Wolf's Road King as he drove it home. He struck the deer with such force that it sent him over the handlebars and onto the road surface, breaking his neck. Last night, the Ingrate Order MC cremated his body right on the compound premises. Ray was in a state of shock. Why had no one called him, they were old friends? The answer, Ray knew, was that no one other than Wolf knew how to reach him. Bummer!

This changed everything. The next morning, Ray drove his Lincoln out to the compound. He first paid his respects to Wolf. Ray placed a glass vase full of black roses right next to the pile of bones and ashes, which were still smoldering from the all-night burning. Full patch members who saw him do this took off their hats and bowed their heads in honor of their fallen leader. Even Buzz came forward and put his arm around Ray's shoulders in an uncommon display of emotion. There were tears in his eyes. Ray didn't think a tough guy like Buzz was even capable of crying. Soon he was crying also, he was so overcome with emotion.

Buzz invited him inside the clubhouse for a drink. The clubhouse was unusually dark and quiet, no music played. Ray sat down at a table with Buzz and Ace. Janie brought them shots and beers. They toasted the memory of Ronald "Wolf" Zeigler. There was a painting of Wolf mounted on an easel surrounded by flowers. All around them were passed-out full patch members, still grieving in their unconsciousness.

They drank, they smoked, they told funny stories about Wolf when he was alive. They recalled the time when Wolf responded to a classified advertisement in the newspaper, only to find that the motorcycle offered for sale had been stolen from Wolf a few months earlier. The seller had rebuilt the engine and transmission and was expecting to make a substantial profit. Wolf threatened to beat the man to death upon discovering that the bike was the same one Wolf had owned previously. The seller offered Wolf five hundred dollars not to beat him up, and Wolf took possession of the stolen bike in better condition than before it was stolen.

Buzz excused himself, he could no longer talk of his friend in the past tense. Ray now sat alone with Ace. Ace was now club president and wasn't taking it so well. He confided in Ray that Buzz would make a more effective club president. Ray didn't know how to respond to that, he didn't know either man that well. But Ray used the opportunity to try and change subjects. He told Ace that Wolf's death placed him in a really bad position. He asked the drunken Ace if he knew about Wolf's business contact in Baltimore. He did not, but knew someone who did.

Ray approached Janie with extreme caution. It was Janie who handled all Wolf's business affairs. Ray asked if he could speak with her in private. Janie led him back to Wolf's office. Rather than sit behind the desk, out of respect Janie sat in a chair in front of the desk and invited Ray to do the same. When he sat down, Janie leaned back and propped her feet up on Ray's knees. She held a cigarette in her teeth and asked Ray for a light. Janie took a deep drag and blew smoke rings.

Janie was intent on letting Ray know that she owned the situation. If she were to divulge the requested information, it was going to cost him. Janie went on to explain that she was the only other person on the planet other than Wolf who knew of his business dealings. The problem for her now was that Wolf handled the nuts and bolts of the operation, and he was meticulous about it. She couldn't bring herself to trust anyone else. It was just too risky. Mistakes would be made, and ultimately, there would be dire consequences.

There was another aspect as well. This business associate was a scary dude who Wolf was not the least bit afraid of. But practically everyone who either knew or crossed paths with this man was scared to death of him, and for good reason. Janie didn't want the hassle that came along with doing business with this individual. She didn't even like talking with this dude on the phone. If she were to give this information to Ray, she would need fifty thousand up front and ten percent of every deal. Ray told her he would have to discuss these terms with his associates and get back to her.

Absolutely not, was Max and Gina's response. Ray had a difficult case to prove. With Marcella's contact dead and now Wolf, there was no one else he knew that could move the product, and he reminded them both they were still sitting on a half-ton. That product was not going to get rid of itself. Max wanted to know if this was the same woman who offered to suck his dick. Ray said that yeah, she was, but their cultural norms weren't the same as everyone else's, and that shouldn't even matter right now, this was business.

Ray tried a different angle. "Imagine that we're a long-distance phone company, paying other carriers to use their fiber optic cables, it's kind of the same thing, it's just the cost of doing business. Everything has a price! No one is going to do this out of the goodness of their heart! Everyone wants to get paid, that's the way the world works!" Ray wished that he knew of an alternative but he didn't. Max and Gina agreed, on the condition that they personally had to meet this "Janie." Ray thought that wouldn't be a good idea. These folks didn't exactly warm up to strangers. He would have to call her first. He would do his best to explain to Janie that his associates had a huge personal stake in the matter and they just wanted to meet her. He would make the call tomorrow.

Marcella understood the situation, but there was something about Janie that Marcella didn't like.

Ray hoped that Marcella would never suspect the obvious, Janie was toying with him. Ray had played it cool by rejecting Janie's advances so far, he knew he could continue to do so. The wild card was Janie herself, she was totally unpredictable. There was no telling what this girl might say or do in front of his associates. But Ray knew that Janie's real motivation was financial, a very strong motivator indeed.

The next morning, Ray and Marcella woke to the sound of rolling thunder. He walked to the living room and stared outside at the pouring rain. Marcella came up behind him and rubbed his shoulders. The storm outside made him recall the day they found the *Winsor2* on the Joyner Banks. Now, he wished he'd never suggested to Max that they check it out. If he had just let Max report the wrecked sailboat, they wouldn't be in the fucked-up situation they were now. This whole mess was all his fault. It's not what a person does with their life that really matters. It's what that person does, and how it affects others.

Ray sat down on the sofa and lit up a joint. He had been dreading this moment since yesterday. He picked up the phone and dialed Zeigler Trucking, expecting Janie to answer when she got around to it. Instead, he got an annoying message informing him the number he was dialing was no longer in service. That's weird! He dialed the number again and received the same message. Maybe the storm had damaged the telephone cables? But there was something in the back of his mind telling him something was terribly wrong.

He called Max and explained the situation. Max didn't like the sound of that at all. The two men discussed possible courses of action. The first option was to wait, call again later or even tomorrow. Maybe they hadn't paid the phone bill. Ray doubted that. The next option, wait for Janie to call him. She knew how to reach him. But what if she never did, then what? That left only one other option, they ride out there and see what's going on. They decided they would do it that evening.

The two men rode in silence out to the Ingrate Order MC compound. Ray passed it without knowing it, and when he no longer recognized any landmarks, he made a three-point turn. The reason he had passed right by it the first time was because the whole compound was completely dark. It was as if the power had been cut to the whole property. They parked on the side of the road next to an empty field. It began to rain as soon as they stepped out of the car. They put on ponchos and grabbed weapons and flashlights.

As they approached the compound gate, there it was, removing any doubt in anyone's mind as to what had happened. There was plastic yellow tape reading, "POLICE LINE DO NOT CROSS." The Ingrate Order MC had been busted. For what was anyone's guess. Max shined his flashlight into the compound through the chain link fence. He asked Ray if they really were going to do this. Ray told him they had made the long trip out here, they at least had to check it out. Ray produced a lock-picking gun and began manipulating the padlock tumblers until it finally snapped open. They pushed the gate open slightly, just enough for both men to squeeze through. They pushed the gate shut and dummy-locked the padlock.

The place was deserted. All the darkened buildings were locked up tight, and all had the yellow police tape stretched across the doors. They would start with the clubhouse. Ray pick-gunned the padlock and pushed open the door. The place was trashed. It smelled dank. All the tables and chairs lay strewn about. Broken glass crunched under their boots as they walked back to the office behind the bar. There they found the office door severely damaged, most likely from a police battering ram.

Inside the office, it appeared as though a bomb had detonated. Filing cabinets had been emptied of their contents and turned on their sides. The oak desk had been ransacked. Missing were the beautiful French paintings that previously hung on the walls. If there was anything of value to Ray and Max, it would not be found in this room. Ray smacked the padlock shut with the palm of his hand locking the clubhouse door as they left, like they had never been there at all. Next, they investigated the mechanic's garage. Tools were strewn everywhere, tool cabinets had been knocked over. There was a small office Ray hadn't noticed before. It also had been thoroughly ransacked. Ray noticed that the in-line six-cylinder diesel engine used to smuggle the coke was missing. Ray wondered if it ever reached its intended destination. Oh, how he wished he knew where that was.

Inside the warehouse terminal, once again they found everything in disarray. Shipping crates were opened and their contents strewn about, mostly engine parts and the like. There was yet another office in the warehouse. It too had been trashed. Ray's heart sunk in his chest, now realizing they had wasted their time. He now motioned to Max that it was time to leave this place. It was near the front door that Ray stopped, bent down, and picked up a single piece of paper. It was a yellow carbon copy of a shipping order. On it was a shipping address in Baltimore. Items to be shipped: one Caterpillar 3406 diesel engine! What were the odds of Ray finding this single piece of paper among many strewn about the warehouse floor? This was what they had been searching for all along.

Ray could not believe their stroke of luck. Max asked him what made him pick up that particular shipping order among the dozens littering the floor. Ray didn't have an answer for that. All he knew was that it caught his eye, and he picked it up. Max had a hard time swallowing that, it was just too coincidental. Ray agreed.

They pulled into Max's driveway and went into his house, finding Gina asleep on the couch in the living room. She had obviously been waiting for Max to return from their covert mission. The television set was still on. Max and Ray sat at the kitchen table and poured glasses of whiskey. They talked in hushed tones so as not to disturb Gina, but to no avail. Soon, Gina was sitting at the table with them wanting to know what had happened that night. They examined the document Ray had found and came up with an intended receiver's name. That would be one Mr. Otis Williams. Ray spent the remainder of the night at Max and Gina's house.

First thing the next morning, Ray called Marcella, just to let her know he was alright, and that they had found what they were looking for. Marcella was happy for him and explained that she was going back to sleep. Ray next called the phone number on the shipping order and asked to speak with Mr. Otis Williams. Ray was told by an unknown female on the other end that there was no Otis Williams who worked there. That left Ray but one choice. He was going to Baltimore. Marcella didn't like the idea. She didn't want Ray going by himself, but she didn't want to go with him either. She didn't like big cities, but then again, neither did Ray. But he had to do this. It was their only means to find a buyer for the cocaine. Eventually, she agreed to make the trip with Ray. He would need her help. Ray picked up the phone and dialed information. Next, he was making hotel reservations at a posh hotel in downtown Baltimore.

After informing Max and Gina of their travel plans, they packed and started the long drive up the East Coast. They dressed casually so as not to draw attention to themselves, but as always, Marcella was the focus of every male's attention everywhere they stopped along the way. Ray was becoming increasingly annoyed by the attention she received once they got into major population centers. Total strangers would hit on her with Ray standing right beside her. At one point, after crossing the Virginia state line into Maryland, they stopped for gas only to have some idiot start hitting on Marcella while seated in Ray's car. Ray approached the passenger side to confront this fool who was in the process of asking Marcella if she were willing to "dump the chump" she was with and "take up with a real man."

Ray casually asked the man, "Who was the real chump? Was it the man who would go home and whack his wee wee, or the man who was going to bury this woman's face in a pillow later on?"

It was on now! The idiot stranger threw an awkward roundhouse that Ray easily sidestepped, as he brought the right heel of his cowboy boot down onto the left toe of the tennis shoe worn by the other man. The man winced in pain, realizing that bones in his foot were broken. Ray then delivered a right elbow just below the ribcage up into the chest, followed by a right back-fist to the face. The man staggered and appeared dazed.

It's not over yet, thought Ray, as he sent a right elbow to the face, immediately followed by a right back-fist, immediately followed by a left jab and a left elbow to the side of the face. In the span of two seconds, the opponent had received four blows to the face and was down for the count. An onlooker asked Ray where he learned how to fight. "Martial arts movies made in the Philippines," replied Ray, which actually was the sorry truth.

Looking down at his fallen opponent, Ray stomped on the man's left forearm then right forearm, breaking both. The seriously injured opponent started going into shock, as Ray replaced the gas nozzle, took his receipt, and got behind the wheel of his Lincoln. He was getting sick of this shit. Everywhere they went, it seemed, someone was trying to hit on Marcella. He maneuvered his vehicle out of the gas station, onto the on-ramp, and onto Interstate 95 North. He lit a joint with the electric cigarette lighter and tried to calm himself down.

What if there were surveillance cameras, Marcella wanted to know. All they would see is a man defending his woman and his honor, Ray rationalized. Marcella warned him that his out-of-control temper was going to land him in big trouble one of these days. Ray didn't care about that one bit.

He was getting sick and tired of other men who didn't know how to conduct themselves in public.

That guy back there, lying on the ground, just found that out the hard way.

It was nightfall when they finally exited onto 395 North into Charm City. At first glance, Ray could not get over how big Baltimore was compared to Savannah. This was not going to be easy. This city was huge and anything could be waiting for them when they arrived. Fortunately for them, it was a friendly and very professional bellhop who met them in the fire lane as they pulled up in front of the hotel. The bellhop opened the door for Marcella allowing her to step out, then immediately began loading the luggage onto a cart. In less than one minute, Ray was handing the keys and a twenty-dollar bill to the valet.

Up in their room near the top floor, Marcella marveled at the view of the city below and all around. People on the sidewalks far below looked like tiny specks. Ray produced a bottle of vodka from his luggage and poured a glass for each of them. They sipped on their drinks as they unpacked, then headed to the hotel restaurant for a fine evening meal. Then it was back to the room for drunken hotel room sex. They ordered room service breakfast. Ray told Marcella that she should not leave the hotel under any circumstances. She could go anywhere in the hotel, just don't go outside. Marcella was disappointed, she wanted to go sightseeing. Ray told her that big cities like Baltimore were dangerous. There were a lot of flimflam in places such as this, purse snatchers, pickpockets, and the like. She would be much safer if she just stayed in the hotel.

Ray purchased a city map in the hotel gift shop and asked the concierge about the neighborhood he was trying to find. He was told that it was an industrial park, and not in a particularly good part of town. Ray sat in the hotel coffee shop, studied the map, and planned his route. The valet had his car ready in less than five minutes. He pulled out of the hotel's main entrance and into busy city traffic. It was total culture shock for Ray now as he drove through the city, trying to take it all in.

There were people shouting at each other from the opposite sides of four lane streets in apparently normal everyday conversation. Construction workers whistled and shouted at pretty office workers as they walked briskly on the busy sidewalks. The city streets were heavy congested with vehicular traffic of all kinds. Kids and even full-grown adults washed windshields at the countless intersections trying to earn tips. Everywhere there were panhandlers trying to bum money. Ray decided he could never live in such a place. They couldn't pay him to do so.

Finally arriving at his destination, Ray stepped out into the summer heat and made his way to the main entrance. He approached a pretty black receptionist and introduced himself as Ronald Zeigler. He produced a copy of the shipping order and explained that he just had to get in touch with Otis Williams. There was a problem with the shipment, and he had traveled all the way from South Carolina to straighten it out. The receptionist told him she would find someone who could help him, as she punched an extension and told Ray to help himself to coffee and doughnuts.

A few minutes later, a tall well-dressed black man in his forties came out and introduced himself as the shipping and receiving manager. Again, Ray introduced himself as Ronald Zeigler and explained his dilemma. The man invited him back to his office. Holding the shipping order in his hand, the manager punched information into a desktop computer. He found the order and the date and time it was received at the warehouse. He also found a contact name and a street address. He gave the computer a command to print a copy and handed it to Ray.

Ray briefly read the document and shook hands with the shipping and receiving manager, thanking him for his help in this matter. Out in the parking lot in his car, Ray studied the document more thoroughly and found that the name of the person who signed for the order was definitely not the mysterious Otis Williams he was looking for. Both the signature and the printed name were all but illegible. Ray studied the city map, only to find that the contact address was all the way on the other side of town in North Baltimore.

Great, though Ray. Fighting his way through heavy traffic, he observed even more bizarre human behaviors, drug deals made out in the open, people talking to themselves, men and even women urinating in alleyways. Street-level drug dealers, junkies, winos, and street gangs ruled the wasteland known as Charm City. He got more than a few cold stares from the local population who probably thought he was a G-Man on his way to a stakeout. That was fine with Ray, let them keep on thinking that.

It then occurred to Ray that these people were victims of the society that spawned them. No one, he imagined, grew up wanting to be a wino or a junkie. It's just what happens to people living in a place such as this. Had he been born here, he'd be right out there with them. Inwardly, he felt sorry for them, right up until someone threw a brick at the passenger side door of his car. He pulled to the curb and stopped. He saw a young black male running away. His first instinct was to chase this individual and blow his ass to kingdom come. Then he thought better of it and continued driving.

When he arrived at the street address he was searching for, it turned out to be a rundown building with a garage door. The windows on the first floor were bricked over and a door made of steel bars blocked access to the front entrance. It appeared to be deserted, abandoned. What a bummer, thought Ray. By all outward appearances, this building looked as though it had not been used in decades. This was a dead-end, or was it? He had no way of knowing. He made his way back to the hotel to plan his next move.

In the hotel room, he found Marcella and an unknown adult Hispanic female having a party. There were empty bottles of champagne everywhere, and they were snorting coke. Marcella introduced her new intoxicated friend as Isabella. They had met in one of the hotel shops and struck up a conversation in Spanish. As it turns out, Isabella's husband was here on business also and had also instructed his wife not to leave the hotel for safety reasons. Ray sat down, poured a double shot of vodka, and began rolling joints. He tossed one to each of the women and fired one himself, he was done chasing leads for today. There was always tomorrow. He had booked the room for a week. The trouble was that when he did resume, he had no idea where to start. He invited Marcella and her new friend to lunch. They graciously accepted.

Over lunch, Isabella told Ray that her husband was a criminal defense attorney and was representing a client in a murder trial. The client, she explained, was a wealthy underworld crime boss, who had used her husband's services many times in the past, with great success. She suggested that they all meet for dinner so that she could introduce him to Ray and Marcella. Perhaps Isabella had pegged Ray as someone who could use her husband's legal expertise in the future.

They all met in the hotel restaurant at 6:00 p.m. Introductions were made and Ray was impressed with Isabella's husband, Jeff. He just seemed like a highly intelligent man who was direct and to the point when he spoke. Ray knew better than to ask Jeff about the case he was working on. Instead he asked Jeff about Baltimore. How well did he know Baltimore City? The answer was basically, very well indeed. Most of Jeff's clients were from Baltimore and he had spent a lot of time in the city over the years. Jeff went on to say that they lived in Annapolis, Maryland, the state capital. They always stayed at this particular hotel when representing his clients in the city. After a few cocktails, Jeff started to loosen up a little, and appear more relaxed and informal.

Ray used the opportunity to ask Jeff if he knew a man named Otis Williams. Jeff's demeanor changed abruptly. Explaining that he knew of Otis Williams, but did not know him personally, Jeff was now highly suspicious of Ray's motives. Otis Williams had a fierce reputation, and it was unusual for anyone to go around asking questions about this man that so many people considered unpredictable and dangerous. Otis Williams was well-known and feared by just about all who knew him. Jeff wanted to know why Ray would ask him about this man who Ray had obviously never met. Ray explained that Mr. Williams and himself had a common associate in South Carolina who was recently killed in a motorcycle accident. Ray wished to meet Otis Williams, express his condolences, and handle a business matter that the deceased man was working on immediately prior to his death. The subject matter was highly sensitive, and only to be discussed face-to-face with Mr. Williams. But unfortunately, Ray did not know how to go about contacting him.

Jeff told Ray that Williams was a major player in the criminal underworld here in the city. There weren't many illegal activities that Williams wasn't involved in. Williams owned many businesses that were used to launder money. If Ray really wanted to meet this man, his best chance was to find him at an after-hours club that he owned called Felicia's. Jeff cautioned Ray that he had a zero probability of being admitted into Felicia's without a date, preferably an attractive black one.

Ray thanked Jeff for his help, and Jeff responded by handing Ray one of his business cards, figuring he might need it one day, if he lived long enough. After dinner, Ray and Marcella retired to their room. He explained to Marcella that he was going out later to meet this Otis Williams. She didn't need to worry, everything would be fine. Marcella was tired after a full day of partying with Isabella. Soon she was fast asleep. Ray also went to sleep, but set the alarm for 12:30 a.m.

By 1:00 a.m. Ray was in his car, cruising an area frequented by prostitutes, information he obtained from the concierge after slipping the man a one-hundred-dollar bill. Ray immediately found what he was looking for. He pulled his Lincoln to the curb and was almost immediately approached by a good-looking black female in a tight leather mini-skirt. Ray introduced himself and asked the woman how much it would be for all night. That would be five hundred, she explained, and worth every penny. Ray asked her if she had a friend. That would be an additional five hundred. Ray agreed.

The two women climbed into the car with Ray and sat in the front seat with him. They immediately asked him if he was working for law enforcement. Ray told the women he hated cops, he could never live on a cop's salary. Besides, would a cop go around carrying something like this? He pulled a bag of cocaine out of his sport coat pocket. The woman sitting next to him, still leery of his intentions, dipped into the bag with a long pinkie fingernail and held the coke up under Ray's nose. He snorted deeply. It was time to party, the two hookers, now disarmed by Ray's partaking of the cocaine, helped themselves to the coke. Ray cautioned them about the potency. They were both well aware of that after the first snort.

They wanted to know exactly what Ray was into. It was very simple, he explained, they just needed to look pretty. He was taking them to Felicia's, and all they had to do was pretend to be his girlfriends for the night. He handed the woman sitting next to him a thousand dollars. She handed five hundred to her friend. They were excited, but cautioned Ray that he would probably be the only white man who ever set foot in Felicia's. They asked if he was packing heat. He told them that he was. They told him he would have to check his weapon at the door, just like everyone else.

They drove past Felicia's and Ray was disheartened to see a line that went around the block. The woman sitting in the passenger seat told him that wouldn't be a problem, one of the doormen was her cousin. How cool is that? thought Ray. They parked and walked a block or so to the entrance of Felicia's. Ray felt like a million dollars, arm in arm with the two gorgeous women. Ray avoided eye contact with everyone as they passed. Practically everyone in line studied them closely as they walked right up to the main entrance. One of the doormen, upon recognizing his cousin, gave her a big hug and admitted them inside without hassle. Just inside the front door were two men with metal-detecting wands. They motioned to a counter where Ray carefully placed an N-Frame revolver, a pocket semiauto, and a switchblade. The woman at the counter took the weapons and placed them in a pigeonhole cabinet. She handed Ray a ticket and told him not to lose it. Lose the ticket, lose the weapons.

Inside the club, it was loud, so loud that normal conversation was next to impossible. Otis Williams had seemingly spared no expense in creating a nightclub experience with no rival. There was a huge dance floor and spectacular lighting effects. The bass frequencies in the dance music literally made the floor vibrate. There were hundreds of people drinking, drugging, and dancing. Ray led his dates to an empty table where a cocktail waitress soon appeared to take their drink orders. When she returned with the drinks, Ray slipped her a hundred and told her he was here to see Otis. She told Ray that Otis could be found in his office upstairs.

Ray excused himself and headed to the staircase, which was guarded by two huge men on either side. The stopped him and asked what was his purpose. Ray told them he had traveled all the way from South Carolina to straighten out a business matter involving Mr. Williams. Ray produced a copy of the shipping order and handed it to one of the men, who looked at it closely. He handed the paper back and motioned for Ray to follow him upstairs.

Upstairs there was a private party already in progress. People were having sex all around him. Ray was told to wait, which he did, trying not to pay any attention to the spectacle all around him. A few minutes later, he was told he could meet with Mr. Williams. Ray slipped his handler a hundred. The man nodded in appreciation and opened the door to Otis Williams's office. There, he found Otis Williams seated behind his desk which was covered with firearms and stacks of money. A woman climbed out from under the desk and excused herself, while Otis zipped up his fly. He motioned for Ray to take a seat. The floor shook from the vibrations from the dance party down below. Otis made eye contact with Ray studying him intently.

"Who are you?" Otis finally asked.

"My name is Ray Bangor, from Hilton Head Island, South Carolina. It seems that we have a common associate."

"And who might that be?"

"Ronald 'Wolf' Zeigler."

"How is Ziggy doing these days?"

"With all due respect, Mr. Williams, Ronald Zeigler is dead, killed while riding his motorcycle a few days ago."

Otis Williams stared at Ray for a few moments. He stood and removed a framed black-and-white photograph from the wall behind his desk. He walked around the desk and handed the picture to Ray. There looking back at him through the picture glass were two shirtless men, standing in front of a helicopter. The two men had served together in the Vietnam War twenty-five years earlier. Ray studied the picture. Wolf looked like an all-American young man, minus all the tattoos. Otis still looked about the same, only much younger and much thinner. Ray respectfully handed the framed picture back to Otis.

"I'm sorry, Mr. Williams."

Otis walked back around the desk and placed the portrait back on the wall. It was obvious that he was deeply affected. Ray imagined that the two men had shared many life-or-death experiences together. Their hellish experience in the war had bonded the two men. Now, one of them was dead. Otis sat behind his desk and continued staring at Ray, making him feel even more uncomfortable than he already was, if that was even possible.

"So … ," Otis now said, "what can I do for you, Ray Bangor?"

Ray produced the shipping order and placed it on the desk. "I think I can help you with this."

Otis picked up the paper, put on his reading glasses, and read the document. He placed it back on his desk smiling at Ray. Just then, the phone on the desk began to ring. Otis picked it up and hollered into the handset that he was in a meeting right now. He listened intently to the voice on the other end. "Bring her in!" he said into the handset before hanging up.

Moments later, the office door opened and two large men dragged a kicking and screaming young woman in a short leopard print dress into the room. The two men held the woman by the arms. She shook them off defiantly. She leered at Otis, sitting behind his desk. One of the men came forward and placed what appeared to be a sophisticated pipe bomb, with a motion-sensing triggering device on the desk in front of Otis. Otis picked up the bomb and examined it more closely. Placing the bomb back down on his desk, he stood and walked around it to face the woman.

In the blink of an eye, Otis had both hands around her neck and proceeded to strangle her to death. Ray stood up and backed away as the kicking and clawing woman fought for her life. Her eyes bulged from their sockets and saliva ran down the corners of her mouth as the life drained from her body. Otis pulled her in closer until they were literally eye to eye. He shook her like a rag doll as he continued choking her.

Ray could not believe what he was seeing. He felt sick to his stomach as he continued watching Otis kill this beautiful young woman. Ray desperately wanted to stop what was happening, but he knew that would be a fatal mistake. Besides, it was too late anyway. By now the young woman was dead. Otis released his grip and she crumpled to the floor, her dead eyes now staring at the ceiling. The men who had brought the woman into the office now picked her up by the arms and legs and carried her out. Otis calmly sat down at his desk.

"Now … where were we?" he asked Ray.

Ray was shaking. He sat back down and avoided eye contact. He had to pull himself together and try to forget what he had just seen. He had come a long way, and their business here was not yet concluded. Taking a deep breath, he now faced Otis and laid out his plan to continue smuggling coke, concealed in old engine blocks up the East Coast, in tractor trailers. Ray could tell from Otis's demeanor that he liked what he was hearing.

Back at his hotel now, Ray tried not to disturb his sleeping girlfriend as he picked up the bottle of vodka and began guzzling. His hands were still shaking. He kept replaying the scene over and over again in his mind. He could not believe he had just witnessed the murder of a beautiful young black woman. One thing was certain. Otis Williams was every bit as dangerous as everyone made him out to be. Ray just figured incorrectly that he would never have to see it firsthand.

They had a long drive ahead of them, and Marcella was taking forever getting packed. Ray could not wait to leave this city. He sat at the table in the room and puffed on a joint as Marcella stood in front of the bathroom mirror, brushing her long black hair and applying makeup. Finally, she picked up her purse, indicating she was ready. When the valet opened the passenger side door for her, she asked Ray what had happened. Ray wasn't sure what she was talking about until he remembered the dent caused by the thrown brick. He promised he would tell her everything once they were on the road. Well, maybe not everything.

They drove straight on through the day, stopping only for fuel, restroom breaks, and meals. It was almost midnight when Ray pulled into his parking space in front of his villa. He grabbed Marcella's luggage before heading inside. His could wait. He figured Max and Gina would be asleep by now, but he called them anyway and left a message saying that Operation "Big B" was a success. He then proceeded to get shit-faced drunk. He climbed into bed and curled up with Marcella, glad to be home.

The next morning, Ray woke up with a bad hangover. Marcella had left him a note saying that she had gone out shopping. Ray searched the medicine cabinet for aspirin and, finding none, got dressed and drove to a convenience store. He purchased a newspaper, as well as aspirin, and drove back to his villa. He sat on the couch and took the aspirin with a glass of warm beer. He sparked a joint. Thirty minutes later he felt much better, the hangover was still there, but not as intense.

He opened the newspaper and started reading. There was a story out of Ormond Beach, Florida, about a missing Maryland couple found dead in a survival raft which had washed up on the beach. The badly decomposed remains had to be identified through dental records. Relatives had reported the couple missing ten days ago. The cause of death was undetermined pending an autopsy report. A hot prickly adrenaline flash washed over Ray as he folded the paper and set it down on the coffee table. Tomorrow, he would take the article over the state line to Max and Gina's house. Would the names listed in the paper match the IDs Gina still had in her possession? He desperately hoped not, but what were the odds?

Ray related all of the details about his trip to Baltimore at Max and Gina's house the next day. They were both fascinated and horrified by what they heard. Ray described the deal he had set up with Otis Williams. Max offered to take over the task of purchasing the old car and truck engines that would be needed to smuggle the product up Interstate 95N. He would use his basement workshop to partially disassemble the engines, load them with product, then reassemble the engines and transport them to a freight terminal in Savannah.

It was the very least Max thought he could do in this endeavor. Ray had done all the legwork. Prepping the old engines for transport would keep Max busy. Max, like Wolf before him, was meticulous about his work. He could definitely be trusted with this all-important part of the process. Gina even offered her assistance as well. It would be up to Max to find an engine suitable for their first order with Otis Williams, sixty kilos for six hundred thousand. This deal would push their earnings so far into the 1.3 million range. Ray would fly to Baltimore/Washington International Airport. From there, one of Otis Williams's hired hands would pick him up and take him to Felicia's. Ray would personally receive the cash, pack it into a shipping crate, and have it sent back to the same freight terminal in Savannah where Max could pick it up. Ray would stay overnight, then fly back to Savannah the next day.

Satisfied that they had a foolproof plan, the three friends decided to celebrate with drugs and alcohol. About halfway into the party, Ray remembered the second reason he had come all the way out here. He went to his car and retrieved the newspaper. Gina read the article and gasped. The recovered bodies were in fact the previous sailors aboard the *Winsor2*, John Allen Webster and his wife Becky Simpson Webster, of Ocean City, Maryland. The couple had drifted in the ocean, in their life raft, for probably hundreds of miles before winding up on Ormond Beach, Florida. But whatever happened to the older couple from New York, Juan Pablo Hernandez and his wife, Esmeralda Lopez Hernandez? Were they still alive, and if so, where? Did they somehow know the location of the stricken vessel once it foundered on the Joyner Banks? Max assured them that with modern GPS technology, it was not outside the realm of possibility. That information served to make everyone a little uneasy. But there was absolutely nothing they could do about it right now, and so the partying continued. Ray called Marcella and told her he was too wasted to drive back to the island tonight. He would be home tomorrow morning some time. He wished her good night, just before he passed out on the sofa.

Three days later, Max had the truck engine prepped and crated up ready to be taken to the freight terminal in Savannah, and from there up the interstate to Baltimore. Max had removed the camper shell from his truck and enlisted the help of his neighbor who owned a tree service company with a crane truck. Max explained to the nosey neighbor that he was rebuilding old engines and sending them up north. Upon seeing the pile of discarded engine parts in Max's backyard, the neighbor lessened his suspicions and used his company crane to hoist the crate into the back of Max's truck.

The truck's rear suspension sank low under the heavy load that had just been placed upon it. Max decided that his next project would involve modifying it to handle more weight. Max paid his neighbor two hundred dollars for his assistance. The neighbor gladly pocketed the cash and wished them luck in their new business venture. Gina held up her middle finger as the crane truck slowly pulled out of the driveway and turned onto the main road. She did not like that nosey motherfucker one bit. He always asked a zillion questions while gawking at her tits whenever he was around.

A few hours later, Max called Ray and told him that the "dog was missing from the kennel," which was their prearranged code for the first load was on its way. Ray made the airline reservations then took Marcella out to dinner to their favorite island restaurant. They both planned on getting wasted so they called a cab. In the restaurant bar, two men stood out from the other patrons who were all mostly locals. Aside from staring at Marcella almost the entire time, they acted and dressed weird, as in "wearing sunglasses indoors at night" weird.

All during dinner, the two creepy-looking individuals kept looking over at Ray and Marcella as they ate, drank, and pretended to not notice the two strangers. Ray had an idea and excused himself from the table. Sandy, the bartender, was an old friend. Ray asked her about the two strange dudes seated all the way at the other end of the bar. Sandy told him there wasn't much to tell, really. They both had thick New York accents and they both were in here every single night this week about this time. Ray thanked her for the information and rejoined Marcella at their table. Marcella was tipsy from all the booze, but then again, so was Ray.

Ray paid the dinner bill and politely asked their waitress if she would be so kind as to call them a cab. She said it wouldn't be a problem. By now Ray could not help but notice that the two strangers were gone. Ten minutes later, the waitress told Ray that their taxi was waiting outside the front door. Ray helped Marcella into the cab and looked around. There was no sign of the two men anywhere. Ray told the driver to please take them to the Coligny Circle Beach Access, a short walk from their oceanfront villa.

After paying the driver, they both stepped out into the hot summer night. A slight breeze blew in from the ocean. It was a beautiful night. Ray suggested they take a stroll on the beach. Marcella thought it was a fine idea. They walked the thirty yards or so to the beach. Marcella removed her high heels before stepping out onto the sand. Ray looked over his shoulder one last time. There was a car in the traffic circle, which began to slow down and pull into an area where vehicles could drop off their passengers.

Grabbing Marcella's hand, they began walking while Ray explained to her they were being followed. The beach was dark, and Ray figured it might be easy to lose the men tailing them. They could just blend in with other folks out walking on the beach on this perfect summer night. It was so dark that unless the men were relatively close, they would have a hard time distinguishing between their intended targets from the other beach walkers. But Ray had a better idea. If they did lose the men following them, then what? There would still be a problem. The men would still be out there somewhere, still looking for them. He knew he was going to have to confront this problem head-on, and end it right here, right now.

Still holding on to Marcella's hand, he pulled her in the direction of a beached catamaran, up near the dune line, about fifty yards away. They now crouched behind the sailboat and waited. Sure enough, one of the heavy-set would-be assassins appeared at the beach access. The man pulled a black revolver out of a waistband holster and looked around carefully. They waited.

Soon the other man appeared and drew his weapon as well. The two men exchanged words and split up. The first headed north along the beach, while the second headed south, directly toward the sailboat and Ray and Marcella. Ray laid the barrel of the .44 down against the deck of the sailboat and took careful aim. Marcella cupped her hands over her ears. The fat man closed the distance with his weapon held at arm's length. Holding his breath, Ray slowly squeezed the trigger, and *ka-boom!* The discharged weapon lit up the entire beach for a split second. The fat man flew backward landing on his back, arms outstretched. People on the beach began screaming and running in all directions. Marcella tried to stand up, but Ray pulled her back down. Soon the other man appeared and began firing in the direction of the sailboat. Fiberglass splinters flew everywhere as the bullets penetrated the hull.

The man was now dry firing, he was out of ammo. Taking careful aim, Ray pulled the trigger, and *ka-boom!* Ray's ears were ringing as he told Marcella to stay put. Both men were still moving. Ray stood over the two men who were now gasping for air. They had both been wearing bulletproof vests. Ray kicked their weapons away from their hands as the two men writhed in pain. Ray holstered the heavy gun and pulled a small semiauto from his ankle holster.

"This is the end of the road for you, fat man!" Ray said as he squeezed off a round into the man's forehead. Ray now stood over the other man who tried to grab him by his pants leg. "Same goes for you … asshole!"

Satisfied that both men were dead, Ray ran over to the sailboat and grabbed Marcella. They ran south on the beach before turning onto a wooden walkway that took them over the sand dunes. Soon they were standing at the keypad that would open the pedestrian gate to their villa complex. Ray punched the code and a second later they were inside as the spring-loaded security gate closed behind them. They now walked to their villa where Ray fumbled with the keys. Once inside, Ray headed for the liquor cabinet and poured a water glass full of whiskey. Ambulance and police sirens could be heard right outside.

Soon, there were red and blue flashing lights on the beach. Ray and Marcella stepped outside onto the balcony and looked to the north, watching the spectacle Ray had just caused. In less than a month after finding the *Winsor2*, Ray had killed four men. He thought about it now, as he watched the commotion down on the beach. Yes, four men were dead because of him, but they were all fucking assholes who had it coming. Nervous energy still ran through his body, but he felt charged. Marcella began rubbing his stiff shoulders as she suggested that they go inside, they had seen enough. Ray sat on the couch as Marcella lay on her stomach beside him, unzipping his fly and taking him into her mouth. He tilted his head back and closed his eyes, trying to make this moment last forever. Thoughts raced through his mind, he could not concentrate. But Marcella made him!

It was Saturday and they drove across the state line out to Max's house, this time in Marcella's Cadillac. Max and Gina had invited them to a cookout. Their neighbor Amy would be there as well as a few other friends. Ray was looking forward to steaks on the grill and cold beers. He reclined in the soft leather passenger seat as Marcella drove humming to herself. The tranquility of the moment made him fall asleep. Marcella pinched his thigh, waking him as soon as she pulled her car into Max and Gina's driveway. There were about twenty people or so at the party which appeared to be in high gear. There was loud music coming from a sound system set up on the rear patio, and barefoot women danced on the soft grass in the backyard. Men threw horse shoes and shouted drunkenly at their opponents. Max's dorky tree surgeon neighbor stood with a beer and a cigarette, talking to Max's neighbor Amy, staring directly at her large breasts as he spoke. Ray immediately decided he didn't like this dude.

Max stood in front of the grill flipping steaks, while Gina went around making sure everyone was having a swell time. Ray and Marcella sat on lawn chairs and drank beer. Marcella turned to him and smiled. After a few beers, she was dancing with the other women to the loud dance music. He was glad to see her enjoying herself at the party. They ate, they drank, they partied as the sun began to set. Ray sat on a picnic bench across from Max. The two men talked business. Ray explained that he had guns that needed rifling alterations. Max told him to grab them and meet him in the workshop.

In the workshop, Ray saw that Max had procured another old engine in preparation for the next order. He was on the ball! Max now held the guns Ray had brought with him, explaining that the small .25 semiauto wasn't worth saving, Max would destroy it by melting it with an acetylene torch. The .44, on the other hand, the one that used to belong to Max's father, now that was a different story. Max pinched the barrel in a vice between two blocks of wood and proceeded to chuck up a knurling tool in his drill motor.

Just as Max was about to run the tool into the barrel, the door to the workshop opened and in came Rob, Max's dorky lumberjack neighbor. Ray eyed the man with disdain as Max set the drill motor back on the workbench. Rob asked what they were doing. Max, a little edgy now from the rude interruption, told him they were cleaning up an old gun. Rob went on to profess that he knew a great deal about guns, but it soon became obvious that neither Ray nor Max cared anything about that, they were busy at the moment. Rob took the hint and left the workshop.

The two men talked business now once they were alone. Ray explained that he was flying to Baltimore at the end of the week to pick up the cash from their last deal. Max told Ray that he would be picking up the lumber to build another shipping crate on Monday. As soon as Ray knew the quantity of the shipment, Max needed to know. The sooner they emptied the contents of the storage closet, the sooner they could all relax. As Ray left the workshop, he noticed Rob seated at a picnic table talking to Marcella. Rob was doing all the talking and he reached across the table and touched Marcella on the forearm. Ray grabbed Rob by the shirt and pulled him backward off the picnic table to the ground.

Rob quickly got back on his feet and defiantly looked at Ray.

"What the fuck are you doing, fool?" Ray yelled in Rob's face.

Rob was caught completely off guard and he stammered, "I didn't know you two were together!" he said unconvincingly.

"Bullshit … you just watched us get out of the car when we arrived … moron!"

Rob looked over at his friend Max. Max just shook his head at Rob as if he were saying, "Don't do it!"

"Look … I'm sorry … all right," Rob said nervously, extending his hand.

Ray spat on the ground and got right in Rob's face. "You got one thing right … you are sorry!"

It was Gina now who stepped in to defuse the situation. "Both y'all need to leave, now!"

Ray grabbed Marcella and headed to their car. Rob walked over to his pickup, got in the driver's seat, and started the engine. As the pickup backed out of the driveway, Ray sat and waited. His blood was boiling, he was so angry at this moronic idiot. Gina walked over to the Cadillac. She told Ray and Marcella they could stay, she just wanted Rob to leave. All day he'd been bothering her and her friends. He was single, she explained, for a reason. Ray's hardened heart softened just a little.

Gina invited Ray and Marcella in the house for the after-party party. All the guests were leaving anyway. Max went around making sure all the drivers were okay to drive as they got into their cars and trucks. The four friends now sat in the living room. Ray apologized for the scene he had caused. He could have handled it differently. Everyone agreed. Gina did not want to invite Rob anyway, but Max insisted they should because he was going to need Rob's help in the future. Max assured Ray he would be able to smooth over the situation with Rob.

Back on Hilton Head, investigators were still trying to piece together the recent murders that had occurred there. Seven homicides and two separate crime scenes. Authorities were positive the two were related. Somewhere out there, someone was killing lowlife crime bosses and thugs. The sheriff's department, the state police, and the FBI were all convinced that the people responsible for the murders were extremely dangerous, much more so than most of the violent crime cases most of them had handled so far in their careers. These killers were motivated, brazen, and well-armed. These murderers were taking out other murderers, extremely dangerous people themselves. All of the deceased had long rap sheets and very bad reputations.

There were some who believed that whoever was responsible was doing society a favor, taking out the garbage so to speak. But they were just snakes preying on other snakes. And so it came to be that Operation King Snake was hatched. There were no known suspects thus far, but there were eyewitnesses and there were clues. There was information yet to be disclosed to the public. It was only a matter of time before these dangerous professionals made the mistake that would crack the case wide open.

Sitting on the couch in his living room, Ray read about the crimes he had committed in the newspaper. If the authorities had any leads, they were not divulging it to the media. That's pretty smart on their part, he thought. Seven homicides in a matter of weeks was unheard of in the otherwise sleepy beach town. Right now, he was concerned about the investigation, but not sweating it.

Inside, he was dreading the flight to Baltimore. He hated flying and he hated that town. He wished he could just pay someone to do this for him, but there was no one he could think of that could be trusted to do his job. Marcella, Gina, and Max had their own responsibilities. This was his elephant and his circus. Six hundred thousand was a lot of dough. This absolutely had to be done correctly.

Marcella gave him a kiss before he got out of the car as she dropped him off at the Savannah International Airport. Once inside the terminal, he was surprised to see a huge display of all the weapons that had been confiscated from people trying to bring them onto passenger aircraft. There were firearms of all types as well as other weapons mounted in a display case on the wall. Ray could not get over the number of weapons as well as the number of stupid people that thought they could somehow bring these things on a plane. Ray felt almost naked without a weapon. But he would be spending less than twenty-four hours in the city, and he was not anticipating any problems. Otis had promised him everything would be cool.

At 6:00 p.m., Ray stepped off the plane and into the airport terminal. There was a beautiful, smartly dressed black woman holding a white cardboard sign that read Ray Bangor. He approached her and introduced himself. She introduced herself as Sharice. She asked Ray if he knew who she worked for.

That would be Mr. Otis Williams. That was all she needed to know, she asked Ray to accompany her. Otis had taken the trouble to send a limousine. Ray and Sharice sat in the backseat of the limo as it cruised on the highway headed toward Baltimore. She asked Ray if he'd had dinner yet. He had not. Sharice hit the call button and told the driver to take them to a restaurant downtown. Ray told her she didn't have to bother herself. Sharice said it was no bother at all, she was hungry also. Besides, Mr. Williams owned the restaurant. He also owned the limo. Sharice offered Ray a drink from the limo minibar. He had a whiskey, neat. Sharice handed the drink to Ray and made a drink for herself.

They had a nice drive ahead of them, so Sharice asked Ray about Hilton Head Island, she had never been there, but she heard it was nice. Ray told her that it wasn't the real world, yes, it was nice. Over a delicious meal and a fine bottle of wine, Sharice told Ray that it was her job to make sure he was comfortable while he was here. She was there to take care of everything, and she did stress "everything" as she put her hand on Ray's leg. Slightly uncomfortable now, Ray told Sharice he had a steady girlfriend that he was in love with. Sharice just smiled and said he was a long way from home. Taking the hint, Ray began avoiding eye contact with her. This woman was fine. She had a great figure. Ray imagined what it would be like to go to bed with her. Somehow, he just knew it would be out of this world. He thought about Marcella, over six hundred miles away. No, he thought. He could not do that to Marcella, no matter how fine this other woman was.

The building where Felicia's was located had its own indoor garage. The limo driver pushed a remote switch and the door began to roll up. Once inside, Ray was astonished. Not only were there other high-end automobiles, there was a mechanics bay. Otis had a self-contained operation going on here. Ray was impressed. Sharice and Ray exited the limo and headed toward a freight elevator that took them to the second floor. Ray felt a little uncomfortable standing in the office where the murder had taken place. Otis was on the phone with a family member, he was laughing. Sharice offered to make Ray another drink. He accepted. They sat together on a couch in the office until Otis was done with his phone call. Ray picked up a magazine and began flipping through it. Sharice was sitting close to him, maybe a little too close. Ray kept thinking about Marcella back home.

Finally, Otis said goodbye and hung up the phone. He greeted Ray like an old friend. He wanted to know if Sharice was making his stay comfortable so far. Ray assured him that she was. Ray got right to the point asking Otis about the sixty-kilo shipment and the six hundred thousand that was due. Otis assured him it was all taken care of. All the money was already packed inside the same crate with the 3406 engine Wolf had sent him originally. Tomorrow, his people would load the crate onto a truck and take it to the freight terminal on the other side of town. From there Sharice would escort him back to the airport.

This posed a huge problem. The crate was already sealed and ready to go. There was no way of knowing exactly what was inside it. Asking Otis to open the crate would be the same as Ray saying that he didn't trust the man. It would be an insult. Ray decided that the very last thing he needed to do right now was to call Otis out on this one. That would be a huge mistake. It now occurred to Ray that Otis had been in the drug business a long time. The man obviously knew exactly what he was doing. There was no way Otis would jeopardize his relationship with a good supplier. Otis would not purposely destroy a business arrangement that was making him a lot of money. It made Ray wonder what had happened to the last coke supplier Otis had used. In this business, Ray knew, that could have been anything.

The last time Ray had spoken with Otis about this deal, Otis told him not to worry about booking a hotel room. Above the office, where they were right now, were luxury apartments, on the third and fourth floors. Otis had promised to set him up in one for the night. So far, all the accommodations Otis had made were first class. Otis had gone above and beyond what Ray had been expecting on this trip.

He was actually enjoying it so far. Otis suggested that Ray meet him in the private dining room on the first floor for breakfast tomorrow morning at nine. Otis told Sharice to take Ray upstairs to his room and make sure he was well taken care of. Ray was nervous about the implications of that. The two men shook hands. Ray followed Sharice to the elevator. On the fourth floor, she led him down a dimly lit corridor to an apartment all the way at the other end.

Sharice unlocked the door, and Ray thought for a second he was dreaming. It was a large and well-furnished corner apartment, but what really had his attention now was the magnificent view of the downtown skyline. The tall buildings were actually quite beautiful at night. Ray surveyed his new surroundings. There was a nice-sized living room with leather sofas and chairs. On the coffee table, there was a small glass bowl full of high-grade marijuana. Damn, Otis really had thought of everything. There was a kitchen stocked with food, a case of beer in the refrigerator along with a couple bottles of champagne. The kitchen led out into a nice dining room with placements for six. This apartment was actually more luxurious than his villa back on Hilton Head Island. Ray asked if all the other apartments were this nice. Sharice told him this one was reserved for special guests only. She now stood in front of Ray, next to a huge window that afforded a nice view of the neighborhoods on the west side of the building.

"Is there anything else that I can do for you, Mr. Bangor?" Sharice asked, batting her long eyelashes at him.

"Actually, there is. Would you stay and party with me?"

"It would be my pleasure."

Ray opened a bottle of champagne and poured glasses for each of them. They sat on the sofa and watched some ridiculous romantic comedy on cable that was actually quite funny. Ray rolled joints for each of them, and they smoked and laughed out loud at the silly movie. Next Sharice did something that took Ray by surprise, if only because he had never seen it done before. Sharice lit a crack pipe with a butane torch. She reloaded it and passed it to Ray who held it in his hand, while nervously telling Sharice he had never smoked crack before.

It's good crack, she informed him, cooked up from the first shipment of coke they received from Wolf Zeigler. Ray didn't quite know what to expect as he took that first hit. He exhaled and, now for the first time, understood why crack was so addictive. Sharice kicked off her shoes and sat very close to Ray now. Ray could feel his heart beating through his chest. He awkwardly excused himself to use the bathroom.

On the way back to the living room, he stopped in the kitchen and grabbed a couple bottles of beer, which upon closer inspection, turned out to be malt liquor. He offered one to Sharice who respectfully declined, preferring the combination of champagne, weed, and crack cocaine. Ray was high, really high. He sat back down on the sofa and Sharice edged closer to him. She began rubbing his throbbing erection through his pants. They kissed. Sharice pressed her body against him now, pushing him backward down onto the couch. She kissed her way down his chest and stomach, unbuttoning his shirt as she did so. A few seconds later, he was in her mouth. This was the point of no return. He thought about Marcella back home, but was now more focused on Sharice's oral technique, which was better than he ever thought humanly possible. So good was she, he almost lost it. She stopped briefly, letting the sensitivity subside, only to resume again.

How could she be so good at this? How could any woman be so good at this? But she kept at it and kept at it until he felt like his heart was going to explode. She stopped. She stood. She began taking off all her clothes. Ray did likewise. He knelt in front of her now and began to explore her with his mouth and tongue, while Sharice stroked his head and pushed her hips against his face. When she could no longer stand the sensation, she grabbed Ray's head in her hands and pulled him to a standing position. She pushed him down onto the sofa and mounted him. She ground her pelvis against him. Pressing her hands against his chest, she arched her back and ground into him harder. How could this be happening? How could this be happening to him? He somehow felt unworthy of this woman who knew exactly how to make a man feel like a man. She looked down into his eyes, grabbed his shoulders, and thrust the whole weight of her body against him. Sweat was now making her hair stick to her face, as she continued to hold him down, making him her bitch. Just when he thought he could stand it no longer, she stopped.

Extricating herself from him, she turned around and mounted him reverse cowgirl style. Ray lay rigid and still as she worked it, and worked it. She grabbed his thighs tightly in her hands and squeezed as she pounded her body against his. Ray could stand it no longer and pulled his pelvis down into the couch cushion, the sensation was just too overwhelming. She pushed herself even harder now onto him, forcing them both to climax simultaneously.

Breathing heavily, Ray thought about what had just happened. It occurred to him that he did not just fuck this woman. She had just fucked him. And what a fucking he had received. Sharice climbed off of him and stood, using her thumbs to pull the hair back away from her face. She fished a cigarette out of her purse and lit it with the butane torch. She took a deep drag and exhaled. She sat on the couch next to Ray. "You're pretty good, honey," she said, smiling.

"I was thinking the same thing about you!" Ray exclaimed.

Over breakfast, Otis explained that his man Leroy was going to load the crate with the 3406 and the cash hidden inside onto a truck. Later, Ray and Sharice would follow the truck through town to the shipping terminal. Ray would make sure that all the paperwork was in order and the crate would be on its way to Savannah. He would have the rest of the day to kill after that. Otis said that in the future, his people would handle everything on this end. Ray would not have to come here unless he really wanted to. Otis said this while smiling at Sharice. So it was Otis who had prescribed the fucking for Ray all along. Yes, this man knew exactly what he was doing.

A little after 12:00 p.m., the truck and limo parted ways at the shipping terminal in South Baltimore. Sharice suggested they have lunch. She ordered the limo driver to take them to a diner in the area. Over lunch they talked of the possibility of Ray coming back to Baltimore, or she could come visit him some time on Hilton Head Island. Ray said that both scenarios were possible. They still had plenty of time to kill before Ray's flight back to Savannah. Sharice asked him what he would like to do during that time. Ray told her he wanted to do the same thing they did last night.

Sharice agreed and suggested that they go to her midtown apartment. She told Ray she normally does not bring work home with her, but he was a special client, she liked him. Her apartment was nice, a little small, but nicely furnished and impeccably clean and organized. She began taking off all her clothes right there in her living room. She looked at Ray and asked what he was waiting for. Ray did not have to be asked twice.

On the limo ride out to the airport, Ray had several cocktails. He was dreading the flight home and was now feeling extremely guilty about his sexual encounters with Sharice. As they pulled up to the departures terminal, Ray now said goodbye to Sharice. She kissed him on the cheek. He got out of the limo with his single suitcase and headed into the terminal. The guilt began to wash over him in waves. He suddenly realized he smelled of perfume. He was as good as busted.

The woman at the airline counter looked at Ray strangely as she handed him the boarding pass. "Sir, you have lipstick on your cheek," she said to him.

Embarrassed, Ray headed to the men's room and found that the woman at the counter was not kidding. Checking his overall appearance, he left the men's room and waited for his plane. It was guilt now that totally overwhelmed him. He had a few more drinks on the flight and still the guilt racked his brain. By the time they landed in Savannah, he was pretty lit. He stood outside the terminal building and looked for Marcella's white Cadillac which was nowhere to be seen. He waited. Guilt consumed him. He wasn't sure if Marcella would be able to tell what had happened by looking at him or talking to him on the ride back to the island, let alone the fact that he was carrying the scent of this other woman home with him.

After a forty-minute wait, Ray was a little alarmed. This was not like Marcella. He got into a taxi and told the driver to take him to the south end of Hilton Head Island. Standing in front of the pedestrian security gate, he entered the pass code and was surprised to see Marcella's Cadillac parked right out front, right next to Max's truck. This was extremely odd. He opened the front door to his villa and was greeted by the sight of Marcella bent over the couch, and Max behind her letting her have it.

It now occurred to Ray that Marcella had simply gotten his travel plans mixed up, thinking he would be arriving tomorrow. Max and Marcella turned to face Ray. Ray could not believe what he was seeing. All the guilt that he had felt, and now he came home to find this. Ray stood with his suitcase in hand and looked awkwardly now at Max and Marcella. He felt as though he'd been mule-kicked.

"Hey, man, I let you fuck my girlfriend!" Max said to Ray.

Marcella, still bent over the couch, opened her mouth in shock forming an O with her lips in reaction to Max's comment.

"That was before I even met you, Marcella!" Ray exclaimed.

Marcella's face still registered shock, as Ray turned to leave through the front door. He was not about to sit there and watch his best friend fuck his girlfriend. Suitcase in hand, he walked and walked for over a mile to a pub that he frequented sometimes. He ordered beer and whiskey. He could not shake the image of what he had just seen out of his mind. He was numb. Sitting there at the bar by himself, he realized something that had never occurred to him.

It was the drugs. All the drugs they were doing were affecting everyone's judgment, to the point where people were doing things they never would have done otherwise, himself included. The violence, the opportunistic sex. All these things were a direct result of the drugs and the alcohol, Ray was certain. But he could not just walk away from these people. He would have to man up. He decided to treat this situation like it never happened. It would be hard, but he had to do this, he had to see this thing through to the end. Then he could make a choice one way or the other.

"Hey, asshole, remember me?" came the voice.

Ray realized that the voice was addressing him. He spun around on his barstool to face a man with whom he'd had a problem with a couple of months ago. The other man had bumped into Ray, causing Ray to spill his drink on the man's shirt. Words were exchanged. They were about to go at it when a large dude got between them and told them to knock off the shit. Now he was looking at the same man who just wouldn't let it drop.

"Well, if it isn't the clumsy fool who bumps into people trying to start fights!" Ray said, now drunk off his ass.

Lights out!

When Ray regained consciousness, he realized he was in the hospital in the ER. He'd felt like he'd been hit in the head with a sledgehammer. A doctor stood over him, shining a flashlight in his eyes. Diagnosis, intoxicated, and highly beaten up. Ray told the doctor he could have told him that, and he didn't even attend medical school. The doctor, having lost his sense of humor, left the exam room.

The next person to walk into the room was a young sheriff's deputy, there to take a report of what happened from Ray. Ray told the deputy he didn't know the guy, it was just someone he'd had a problem with a couple months before. The deputy told him he was lucky to be alive. He had been left outside of the bar for dead. The deputy handed Ray a business card and told him to call this number when he was ready to change his story.

A pretty nurse asked him if there was anyone he could call. He reluctantly gave the nurse a phone number. An hour later Marcella was helping him to her car. On the way home, Marcella apologized repeatedly for fucking his best friend. Ray thanked her for picking him up from the hospital and told her not to worry about that other thing, he would get over it. He didn't believe it himself, he just hoped that right now Marcella would. Marcella explained that she felt so bad about all of this, Ray didn't have to go around letting people beat him up. Riding in Marcella's car on the way home from the hospital,

Ray knew he'd hit rock bottom. All the stupid things he had done in life were now coming back around on him. The only positive thing that he could think of right now was that things couldn't get any worse. Then it occurred to him that, hell yeah, things could be much worse. He could be busted and on his way to the Big House. It was right then that he thought he needed to just stop thinking, but he just couldn't do that right now.

Marcella bent over him now as he lay on his bed. She asked if there was anything she could do for him right now. The only thing Ray could think of was to please stop fucking Max, but he let that one go. Instead he told her he was fine. It wasn't like he'd never been beaten up before. He was angry at himself. It was no one other than he who put himself in the fucked-up situation he was in right now. If it were only possible to turn back time, he would have pretended he never saw the *Winsor2* aground on the Joyner Banks.

A week passed and Ray finally received the call from Max. He had possession of the crate that was sent from Baltimore. He told Ray to come on out and bring Marcella, Gina would make dinner. Max said there was something that Ray just had to see for himself. No, there wasn't a problem, well yeah, there was, kind of. They drove to Max and Gina's without saying a word the entire trip. When they arrived, he found Max in the backyard with the crate. The top of the crate had already been removed.

Other than the engine which stood upright on a homemade stand made of angle iron, there were plastic trash bags. The entire crate had been stuffed full of trash bags which had been stuffed full of stacks of money. Max grabbed one of the bags and dumped the contents on the ground. There were stacks of hundreds, but there was also stacks of fifties, twenties, and tens. There were even stacks of fives and ones. Ever wonder what six hundred thousand looks like in small bills, well, this is what it looks like.

Ray did the math. Otis had obviously used cash from the proceeds of his nightclub. Most of the bills were worn. Currency passed around in a large city, didn't have a long life expectancy. Ray picked up one of the stacks and thumbed through it. Hey, it's still money! They pried the crate apart with a crowbar, and the trash bags fell out under their own weight. They began to pick them up and carry them into Max's basement and put them in a pile. Ray just hoped it was all there. Of course, they would never know until it was all counted, and who knows how long that was going to take?

Max handed Ray a piece of paper with a set of instructions. There was more cash inside the engine. Ray noticed that the engine was now missing the crankshaft. Apparently, Otis's people had removed it to make more room. Now the engine was nothing more than a cylinder block, a cylinder head, and an oil pan. Ray took this opportunity to explain to Max they wouldn't need any more truck engines, they would keep sending the ones they already had, back and forth. Anything that saves time and work was greatly appreciated.

Over dinner, they talked of how drug dealing, on a scale such as this, was a lot of work. It was just like a job, Ray told them, they all had to work it. Ray still wasn't sure if Gina knew about Max and Marcella. If so, she didn't act like it. That, or she just didn't care, they had a pretty open relationship.

All Ray knew at this point was that if Gina ever offered herself to him again, he would take full advantage.

It took Gina twelve hours to count all the money the next day. It was short about two thousand. Ray wasn't worried about it, but everyone else was. He told them he would call Otis and let him know. What was two thousand next to six hundred thousand? It was just the principle, and it was sloppy work. Ray asked Gina on the phone if she was absolutely certain about her count? She said that she was, and Ray believed her. Gina was good like that.

The next day, Ray decided to take a day off. He went to the beach. He swam in the warm ocean. He took an incredibly long walk. He never imagined who he might meet that day, and in retrospect, he wished he'd never taken that walk. He had walked so far that he was now on a public beach about mid-island. A young woman with tattoos on her arms, legs, hands, and feet, approached him and called out to him by name. It was Janie from the Ingrate Order MC. She was on Hilton Head for the day with her sister. What were the odds? Ray asked her how she was able to recognize him, he was wearing a wide-brim straw hat and sunglasses. Janie said she recognized a scar on his leg. She was front and center the night the Ingrate Order MC stripped his clothes off thinking he was a narc.

Janie wanted to talk, but this was neither the place nor the time. Ray offered to buy Janie and her sister lunch. Looking at Janie now in a bikini, Ray wished he had never passed up on that blowjob. She looked pretty good. Janie and her sister, almost a carbon copy of Janie herself, packed up their gear and walked to the beach parking lot, a good distance away. Riding in the car, Ray asked Janie what had happened to the Ingrate Order MC. After Wolf died in the accident, the authorities raided the compound and confiscated illegal weapons and drugs. There were also stolen bikes, as well as a host of other stolen items. Most of the members were still in jail and looking at lengthy prison terms. Janie was freed for lack of evidence. She told the cops that she was just a bartender at the clubhouse. Of course, they didn't believe her, but she could not be directly tied to the weapons or the stolen items or the narcotics. Just about all of the women of the Ingrate Order MC had been released in similar fashion.

Janie and her sister put on street clothes over the top of their bikinis, and Ray led them inside a restaurant that he'd never been to, he'd heard they had a pretty good lunch menu. The women ordered food and cold beers, as did Ray. Janie told Ray that they wished they could stay, but she and her sister were low on funds. Ray said he could help them with that, and even offered to put them up in a hotel for a couple of days. Janie's sister Beth asked Janie why she never tried to marry this Ray dude.

They stopped to pick up beer and a few other necessities, and Ray checked them into a nice hotel. Beth was impressed. Sitting in the hotel room, they popped open beers. Beth had hers to go, saying she was going to the pool. She really wanted to give Janie a chance to be alone with Ray. Once they were alone, Janie explained to Ray that she had wanted to contact him as soon as she got out, but had not only lost his number, but every single contact number that she had in the raid. She asked Ray if he was ever able to get in touch with Otis Williams. Ray said that he had and even went to Baltimore himself to meet the man. They did one deal and were shorted on the cash. So far, he was telling her the truth.

Otis, he told her, was difficult to work with, and that Ray was actually afraid of this guy, he would kill a person without even thinking about it. Baltimore was a dirty, nasty city anyway. Ray decided he could not continue to do business with this man. Ray asked Janie if she knew anyone other than Otis who was in the market. Janie said she personally did not. They were all associates of Wolf's and she had no way of getting in contact with them since the raid.

Although Ray felt like he didn't owe Janie anything, he still felt bad for her situation, no money, no job, and no prospects. Janie's sister was probably in the same situation, he figured. Sitting across the small hotel room table, Ray looked at Janie. Underneath all her tattoos was a woman who was just as vulnerable as anyone else. She had fallen on hard times, or more appropriately, hard times had fallen on her. Ray decided he was going to try to help her out. He told Janie that he would front her one kilo. She could pay him back the ten grand whenever she was in a position to. Stomped with cutting agents, she could make over two million at street level. Invested properly, that money could go a long, long way. She and her sister would never have to worry about money again. They could just live their lives however they chose.

Realizing the implications of what Ray had just said, Janie grabbed Ray in a bear hug and laid a big sloppy wet kiss on his face. Nobody in her whole life had ever afforded her such an opportunity, and she was overcome with emotion. There were tears in her eyes. She just couldn't believe what had just happened. Ray called a taxi from Janie's room and told her he'd be by tomorrow early, say, 8:00 a.m. As he left the room, Janie's sister Beth passed him in the hallway. He told her it was nice meeting her and Beth said likewise, smiling.

By the time Ray got to the elevator, he could hear the women screaming with excitement in their room down the hall, Janie must have told Beth the news. Ray left the hotel thinking of that day, fishing in the Savannah River Shipping Channel with Max and Gina. That was the day that changed his life. He would never forget it. What if he had just said no to Max's offer? He'd still be a working-class man, but with a lot fewer headaches and a lot less worries.

At 7:00 a.m., Ray woke. He showered, got dressed, grabbed a package from his closet, and was on his way out the door all without waking Marcella. He stopped for coffee and a newspaper, which informed him there were no new leads in the murder cases and anyone with any information was urged to contact police. They could remain anonymous and receive a reward. Ray wondered if they did have anything at all on him and his friends.

At precisely 8:00 a.m., Ray was knocking on the door of Janie and Beth's hotel room. Ray heard one of the woman say just a minute. He heard locks open. A couple of seconds later, the same female voice said, "Come on in." Ray did just that and was greeted with the sight of both women completely naked on the bed on all fours, side by side. Ray acted as though they weren't there, but inside his heart was pounding as he casually strode across the room and put the kilo on the small table.

Ray looked at the two women on the bed. They were both ready for whatever Ray had in mind. Ray was more than ready for this, and was actually hoping for it all along. He had played his hand correctly and it was about to pay off big-time. If he was still a motor mechanic, he'd be working right now. He climbed onto the bed. Let's start with Janie, he decided. He would have a lot of decisions to make in the next couple of hours, and he was looking forward to it greatly!

The problem for Ray now was that sex just made him even more horny. Sex, he knew, was the last good thing on earth. Everything else can and will turn to shit eventually, but sex will always be good. He could not ever remember having a bad sexual experience, then telling himself, I'll never do that shit again. He knew that Janie and her sister Beth were sex addicts just like himself. Damn if he wasn't right.

Stepping out into the midday heat, Ray felt good. He felt relaxed, a little tired maybe, but he felt a sense of accomplishment. He was convinced that he had just bought off Janie. Their previous deal was now null and void. Janie had no way of knowing that Ray had entered into a business agreement with Otis Williams, and she had no way of contacting him either. It didn't even matter if Janie ever paid Ray back the ten grand she owed him. By his figuring, he had just saved hundreds of thousands of dollars.

In a beachside bar, Ray relaxed with a cold beer while watching bikini-clad women play volleyball. The outdoor bar was crowded with tourists, and by all appearances, he blended right in with them.

An attractive woman in her late thirties in a one-piece stood at the bar, and Ray admired her figure from behind. She paid for her drink and headed off to a beachside table. She looked familiar, but Ray could not remember where he knew her from. This bothered Ray. He should know who this attractive woman was, with her wavy black hair and full pouty lips. She had a full hourglass figure, and she looked really good in the one-piece, but who was she? Ray pretended to read a newspaper, all the while staring at her face, searching his memory. Her snooty, slightly upturned nose was her most prominent facial feature.

A hot prickly adrenaline flash came over him as he realized he was staring at none other than Esmeralda Lopez Hernandez. He had seen her picture at Max and Gina's house on a New York driver's license, the same one they took off the *Winsor2*. What in the hell was she doing here on Hilton Head Island? Ray began formulating a plan. All afternoon he watched her, laughing and talking with her friends. At about 3:30 p.m., she told her friends she was retiring to her room for a nap before dinner.

Ray followed her inside the hotel and even got on the elevator with her. He walked right past her as she let herself into room 224. Rushing to the hotel lobby, he called Max on a payphone explaining that he needed his help. An hour and a half later, Max's truck with the camper shell reinstalled pulled into the hotel parking lot. The two men now sat in the hotel lounge sipping cocktails as Ray went over the plan he had devised. It wasn't going to be easy, but they had to do this.

After an hour, Ray saw Esmeralda and her husband Juan Pablo Hernandez get off the elevator and walk toward the main entrance out into the parking lot. Max and Ray followed them outside. Max went straight to his truck and started the engine. Ray continued to follow the couple and watched them get into a silver Acura. Ray rushed to the parking lot entrance where Max was waiting for him.

They followed the silver car to a restaurant popular with tourists. They watched the couple go inside. They waited.

The sun had already gone down, and the sky was beginning to darken when the couple finally came back outside two hours later. As the couple got into their car, Max pulled in behind them, blocking them in their parking space. Juan Pablo Hernandez, now clearly pissed off, exited his vehicle holding a small revolver which he pointed at the truck. Ray snuck up behind Juan Pablo and clobbered him on the back of the head with a heavy-duty flashlight. Juan fell to the ground unconscious.

Esmeralda exited the passenger side and produced her own gun, shooting Ray in the upper arm. Max snuck up behind her and grabbed the arm with the gun and twisted it up behind her back until she dropped it. Grabbing her other arm, he held both wrists behind her back, placing a wire tie around them and pulling it tight. She began screaming just as Ray tied a ball gag around her mouth. Ray held her legs together while Max placed another wire tie around her ankles. The two men lifted her and threw her into the back of Max's truck. They next performed the same procedure on the unconscious Juan Pablo.

Ray got into the truck bed with the hostages as Max closed the tail gate and rear windshield. Max got into the driver's seat, and they were off. Hopefully no one had seen them. Ray grabbed Esmeralda's blouse and tore it, using the ripped portion to apply direct pressure to the gunshot wound. Esmeralda began writhing and kicking until Ray held a gun up underneath her chin. Off into the night they drove to Max's house. Max yelled for Gina as soon as he stepped out of the truck.

Gina gasped when she saw that Ray had been shot. She ran back to the house to get the first-aid kit.

Cleaning the wound with hydrogen peroxide, Gina told Ray he was going to need stitches. Ray told her that there was no way he was going to the hospital with a gunshot wound. Max looked at it. It was just a graze, but it was deep and bleeding a lot. They would have to cauterize the wound. Max fired the gas grill and disappeared inside the house to retrieve a fireplace poker. When the poker was glowing red, Gina stood behind Ray and placed a washcloth in his mouth for him to bite down on. Gina held Ray by the shoulders as Max applied the red-hot iron to the wound. It was the most excruciating pain Ray had ever felt in his whole life.

Gina bandaged the wound. Max handed Ray a bottle of whiskey and some pain pills. That would have been a lot better fifteen minutes ago, thought Ray, but he knew he had lost a lot of blood, there was no time to waste. The two men now turned their attention to the hostages. They pulled out Esmeralda feet first and sat her in a lawn chair. They held her still, while Gina tied her to the chair with rope. Next, they did the same for Juan Pablo, still unconscious. Max shot Juan Pablo in the face with a garden hose. He regained consciousness, cursing and swearing in Spanish. Ray told Gina to call Marcella.

Ray turned to Max. "These two are going to tell us everything we need to know!"

Max drew his gun and held it in the face of Juan Pablo.

"No hablamos Ingles!" Esmeralda yelled at them.

"Bullshit!" said Ray. "I've been watching you all afternoon sitting and talking with your friends at the beach bar!"

"Puto!" Esmeralda yelled at Ray.

Gina came forward and showed the prisoners their own IDs. Juan and Esmeralda turned to look at each other, then turned to face their captors. The couple began cursing defiantly. Max squeezed off a round that hit the ground right in front of Juan Pablo. They both simmered down. Ray leaned forward and asked Juan to his face what they were doing on Hilton Head Island. Juan defiantly spit in Ray's face. Ray grabbed Juan by the neck and started choking him. Max pulled him off, saying this isn't going anywhere. They would just sit back and wait for Marcella to arrive.

Max and Ray pulled up lawn chairs and now sat in front of the prisoners, while Max held them at gunpoint. Gina handed each a cold beer. Ray and Max popped open the beers and guzzled, but never took their eyes off the two prisoners. On the off chance that Juan Pablo did speak English, Ray and Max played mind games with the captives. Max asked his friend which one should they kill first.

Ray responded by saying that it didn't much matter, they were going to kill them now or kill them later.

After ninety minutes, Marcella's Cadillac pulled into the driveway. Gina met her at the car and explained that Ray had been shot, but he was okay. Which one did the shooting? Marcella wanted to know. Gina pointed to the woman. Marcella bitch-slapped Esmeralda in the face. She then began beating on the restrained woman with her fists. Ray grabbed her around the waist and told her he needed her to do some translation.

"Ask them what are they doing on Hilton Head Island?" Ray told Marcella, who repeated the same question in Spanish. Cold, blank stares were all they got from Juan Pablo and his wife. "Tell them that if they don't start talking, they are going to die!" Marcella repeated the question and Juan Pablo answered angrily. Ray asked her, "What did he just say?"

"He said that we are all going to die, his people will track us down and kill us."

Max told Juan Pablo not to be so sure of that, right before shooting him in the foot. Juan Pablo winced in pain. Esmeralda was now visibly affected, realizing that their predicament was very serious now. Juan Pablo started screaming at his captors. He went on and on in Spanish for about a minute. Ray asked Marcella what he was saying now. Marcella told Gina, Max, and Ray that Juan Pablo said he was a very powerful and dangerous man, and that they were all going to pay dearly for this.

"We will see about that," Max told him as he fired a round into Juan's upper body causing a sucking chest wound. Juan began choking on his own blood. Esmeralda began vomiting down the front of her blouse. Max raised the weapon slightly and shot Juan Pablo in the forehead. Ray got up from his lawn chair, grabbed the garden hose, and began spraying the spattered blood and vomit off Esmeralda's blouse. Ray now waved the garden hose nozzle directly in the face of Esmeralda Hernandez. Ray turned his head toward Marcella and asked her, "Tell this woman that she'd better start talking, or this thing is going straight up her ass!"

"All right!" Esmeralda screamed in English.

Ray pulled his chair forward and sat face-to-face with Esmeralda. "So … Mizz Hernandez … is there anything you would like to say at this time?"

Esmeralda began to speak in fluent English. In between tears and gasps, she explained that she and her husband, along with the American couple, John and Becky Webster, worked for an organized drug ring in New York State. They all met in Miami Beach, Florida, for the purpose of stealing an oceangoing yacht from a marina on the bayside. John Webster was an expert sailor, and he plotted a course that took them to Santa Marta, Colombia, in South America. In Santa Marta, they loaded the *Winsor2* with six hundred kilos of cocaine.

It was hurricane season, and John Webster plotted a course that would take them around a storm that was poised to hit South Florida. But ten miles offshore, in the middle of the night, a huge wave capsized the *Winsor2*. They abandoned the vessel believing that it would eventually sink. But John Webster activated a homing beacon in the event that it didn't. They drifted in the survival raft for days, surviving off provisions they took off the stricken *Winsor2*. When they landed on Ormond Beach, her husband shot the American couple. Her husband blamed John Webster for the loss of the *Winsor2* and its cargo.

Ray asked her about Diego Ortiz. Esmeralda told him that Diego was part of the same drug ring in New York State. It was Diego that sent a driver down to pick them up in Ormond Beach. As Diego Ortiz motored his yacht *PRINCESS* down the East Coast, sophisticated electronic equipment picked up the signal that placed the stricken *Winsor2* off the coast of Hilton Head Island. Ortiz homed in on the signal, but it vanished before he got there. Ortiz cruised toward the *Winsor2*'s last known position, but when he got there, he found the sailing vessel missing.

Ray thanked Esmeralda for the information she had just provided them. He apologized for Max killing her husband. Esmeralda then did something no one was expecting. She said she hated Juan Pablo, he had a violent temper and beat her often. She was afraid to leave him for fear that he would track her down and kill her. She then turned and spat on the corpse that was her deceased husband. Gina, Max, Marcella, and Ray all looked at each other now. Esmeralda continued, she didn't like Ortiz or his people either. They were all lecherous pigs. Some of them would grab and fondle her in front of her husband and he would just laugh it off, leaving her feeling degraded and humiliated. She once tried to complain about it and Juan just slapped her. She told them that no one had ever stood up to her husband. Even some of the higher-ups were careful what they said to him for fear of setting him off.

She went on to apologize to Ray for shooting him. She feared for her life, it was a gut reaction. Ray told her no worries, he understood where she was coming from; he would have done the very same thing. Ray looked into Esmeralda's eyes. Somehow, he knew she was sincere and not just trying to save her own ass. He didn't quite know how he knew it, he just did. Ray asked Gina, Max, and Marcella to speak with him privately. They went into the basement, leaving the door open just to make sure Esmeralda didn't try to escape. The question on everyone's mind now was, what were they going to do with her? Everyone agreed that she seemed sincere. If she was, it would be wrong for them to kill her. But they couldn't just let her go either. Who knows what she might do then? Ray came up with a solution. Keep her around, and just keep an eye on her.

Keep her around where? Ray suggested that they let her stay at Max and Gina's. Esmeralda had no idea where she was right now, and Max and Gina lived out in the middle of nowhere. No one but Ray thought it was a good idea, but Ray persisted. Keep her locked up for now and see how she behaves.

If she was not on the level, it would become apparent after a while. Right now, she knew that her life was on the line. She would, of course, be on her best behavior. But given enough time, her real personality and motives would come through.

She's a human being who just got caught up with the wrong people. It happens. So far, everyone that they had killed had it coming. All of the deceased were the shit of the world. They just tried to screw and fuck with the wrong people. If they were to just kill this woman, they would never find out if she was sincere or not. Why take that chance? It was bad Karma! Ray looked around the room at his friends. The consensus was that if he was wrong about this, it would be catastrophic for them. But they all unanimously decided to give her a second chance anyway.

The four friends now gathered around Esmeralda. They untied her. They cut the wire ties binding her wrists and ankles. Ray motioned for her to have a seat at the picnic table. They all sat down with her.

It was Ray who explained the situation to her. They would spare her life. But there was something that she needed to know. The people seated at this table with her right now were the same people who killed Diego Ortiz and his four bodyguards. It was Ray who killed the two assassins that came after him and Marcella. All of these people had one thing in common. They all thought they were bad-asses, and they were all dead. He paused to let that sink in.

Max asked Gina and Marcella if they would be so kind as to fix everyone a drink, they could all use it. Alone now with Ray and Max, Esmeralda thanked them both for not killing her. All of her adult life, she had lived in fear. Now, for the first time, she felt strangely at peace with the world. She felt as though she had been given a second chance at life. This was a turning point for her. Esmeralda promised the men they would not regret their decision. Max and Ray believed her.

The next morning, Gina walked into the kitchen to find Esmeralda not only awake, but standing at the kitchen sink washing dishes and glasses. Max had chained Esmeralda's ankle to the sofa bed frame, but the chain was long enough for her to use the bathroom in the middle of the night. Gina thanked her and told her she didn't have to do that. Esmeralda simply said she did it because she wanted to. Max would be busy all day, reassembling the 3406 engine with another sixty kilo order and prepping it for transport to Baltimore. It would take him most of the day. He asked Gina if she felt okay being alone in the house with Esmeralda. Gina said it would be fine, all the guns were locked up except for the pistol she now carried on her hip. Max asked her how Esmeralda was doing. Gina said she was doing okay, she folded all the laundry and vacuumed the living room, now she was sitting on the couch watching soap operas. Gina told him to relax, everything would be just fine.

Such was not the case back on Hilton Head Island. Ray pulled out of his villa complex and noticed a dark blue Ford parked across the street with two men sitting inside. They looked like undercover cops. Ray went to the convenience store to buy a paper, then stopped by a local coffee shop. He went to an auto parts store to buy wiper blades, and a hardware store to buy lightbulbs. As he was leaving the hardware store, he saw the same car with the same two men all the way in the back of the parking lot. He was being tailed. This changed everything.

He drove back to his villa complex. He took a shot of whiskey, then another. His mind was racing. What mistake did he make that tipped them off? Then it occurred to him, it didn't matter, they were onto him, and that's all that mattered right now. What should he do? All his planning never included this. He decided he needed to get out of town, let things simmer down for a while. When Marcella came home, he would suggest that they go to Charleston for the weekend.

Looking out through the bedroom window, he could see the parking lot across the street. There was no sign of the dark blue Ford. Maybe he was just imagining everything. Maybe all the drug usage was making him paranoid. At any rate, he needed to just calm the fuck down. He poured another drink. All afternoon he sat on the sofa, channel surfing and drinking whiskey. He fell asleep.

When he woke up, it was early evening. Marcella was still not home. Groggy from all the whiskey, he suddenly remembered the predicament he was in. He grabbed a pair of binoculars and went to the bedroom. There it was, in the same parking spot no less! Looking through the high-power binoculars, he could see that one of the men was flipping through a magazine, while the other stared straight ahead, appearing to stare right at the window that Ray was looking out of right now.

Completely motionless now, Ray focused on the man behind the wheel, still flipping through the magazine. It was a girlie magazine, for fuck's sake! How unprofessional! Meanwhile the man in the passenger seat took a sip from a silver can. It was a beer. It was a light beer, but it was still a beer. The man in the driver's seat passed the magazine to his partner and lit a cigarette. He pulled on it deeply, then passed it to his partner. They were smoking a joint. It now occurred to Ray, these guys weren't cops, they were just goons pretending to be cops.

What should he do? His first reaction was to climb down the balcony on the ocean side, walk around the complex, sneak up behind them, and blow their brains out. It would be messy, and it would attract attention, but it was doable. Then he thought of a better idea. He would just call the cops on them.

He picked up the phone and dialed 911. The dispatcher picked up on the first ring and asked him what type of emergency he was calling in? He told her that he was a concerned citizen, reporting a suspicious vehicle. The dispatcher asked him what was suspicious about the vehicle. It was parked with two men sitting inside it, drinking beer, and smoking marijuana. They'd been there for a while.

Apparently, not much else was going on right now because within thirty seconds, three sheriff's deputy patrol cars screeched into the parking lot blocking the dark blue Ford in place. They surrounded the car and asked the men to step out. The men were led to the back of the dark blue Ford and told to place their hands on the trunk. The third deputy searched the Ford and began removing items, placing them on the hood as he did so. Open cans of beer, a bag of weed, a girlie magazine, and wait, what's this? It was a gun. Ray was pretty sure they were not concealed weapons permit holders.

The deputies placed handcuffs on both men, while a third deputy stood by with his weapon drawn. Even more concealed weapons were found and soon both suspects were placed in the backseats of separate patrol cars. Ten minutes later, a rollback was impounding the dark blue Ford. With all the commotion going on outside, Ray had failed to notice that Marcella was now home. She came into the bedroom and asked Ray what was going on with all the police across the street. Ray simply told her it was suspicious activity of some type with two in custody.

Someone must have called the police to complain, he told Marcella now. In the back of his mind, he was thinking what a chicken-shit, cowardly thing to do. Anyway, that didn't matter now. He could relax. Yeah, he'd sent these two morons up the river, and they probably wouldn't be getting out any time soon. But there would be more right behind them. Ray would have to move out of this villa quickly. He would just call Lester Price and tell him they didn't like the neighborhood, too many tourists. They needed something a little more secluded.

Lester set them up in a long-term rental house in a quiet neighborhood on the north end of the island. It was four hundred a month more than what he was paying now, but worth it. It had three bedrooms, three bathrooms, and a front and back yard. It was a lot more room than they needed, but it was a great location. As for security, Ray would have to handle that himself. The best part of all was the fact that once again, no one but Lester Price knew where they were living.

They would have to get new cars. They went back to the same dealership and dealt with the same sales manager. Once again, Marcella put on a performance worthy of an Oscar. They drove out of the dealership with two identical, lightly used full-sized Chryslers. The two cars were even the same color. That would keep everyone guessing, Ray thought now as they drove back to their new residence. Pleased now with the new house and new vehicles, Ray felt as though he could relax again. Once inside the house, he threw Marcella on the bed and pulled her pants off.

The last sixty kilo order for Otis Williams had been sent and the money had been received. This pushed their total earnings so far into the 1.7 million range. Otis even made good on the two thousand that was shorted the last time. Again, it was a lot of small bills, but they weren't complaining. It was money, and that's all that mattered to them. Ray and Marcella would take a much-needed vacation, he decided. Business was good, and they needed to unwind anyway.

For the next couple of weeks, Ray and Marcella drove all over the state of Florida, staying in fine hotels, dining in fine restaurants, and dancing in popular nightclubs. They were living the high life. Jacksonville Beach, Vero Beach, West Palm Beach, Miami, Naples, Clearwater, all the places Ray had wanted to visit in the past became the vacation of a lifetime for them. Ray was so happy that Marcella was enjoying herself, he was too for that matter. Ray especially enjoyed the fact that he didn't have to look over his shoulder constantly. They were living the dream. So much hard work had gone into this to make this all happen, and now they were reaping the rewards of their labor.

About halfway through the vacation, Ray called Max and Gina to make sure everything was fine with them. Gina told Ray that Esmeralda had settled in nicely and was helping them any way that she could. She was free to come and go as she pleased, and Max had even bought her a car. She even had begun dating Max's goofy lumberjack neighbor, Rob. Ray was glad for them, he really was.

After two solid weeks of traveling, partying, going to the beach, and lots of hotel room sex, Ray and Marcella drove back to South Carolina. Back on Hilton Head Island, they settled back into their old routines. They had both changed their appearances dramatically over their vacation. Marcella changed both her hairstyle and hair color and she dressed more conservatively now. Ray had grown a beard and began letting his hair grow. He also stopped wearing outfits that made him look like he just stepped off the set of Miami Vice, opting for a more laidback appearance.

Max and Gina hardly recognized the couple when they pulled into their driveway in one of the Chryslers after they returned from Florida. Marcella, Gina, and Esmeralda all sat in the backyard enjoying the late summer afternoon. They sipped on cocktails while Marcella related every single detail about their trip to Florida. Only thirty feet away was the steel drum Max used to incinerate the body of the late Juan Pablo Hernandez after dismembering it. He had burned it for days, he told Ray.

The two men drank beer, smoked dope, and talked about Ray's last run-in with the New York–based criminal enterprise that had made two unsuccessful assassination attempts so far. That would be three, including the aborted drug deal with Diego Ortiz. Ray was convinced that Ortiz and his men would have captured them and tortured them into revealing the location of the coke they had taken off the *Winsor2*. What Ortiz didn't count on was how motivated and ruthless Max, Gina, and Ray had become once they entered the drug business. Eight individuals connected to the New York criminal enterprise were now dead because of Gina, Max, and Ray. The assassination attempts would continue, Ray knew, as long as the leader of the criminal organization were still alive. But suppose something were to happen to him, what would be the end result of that?

Not knowing where to begin, the two men decided they had to find out for themselves who this person was. They themselves had no idea, but both men were now looking at someone who might.

She was sitting in the sun right now, talking to Marcella and Gina. After dinner, the five adults sat around the dining room table to discuss the matter. Orlando Rodrigues, Esmeralda explained, was the top dog in the criminal organization that engaged in heroin and cocaine trafficking, human trafficking, prostitution, and pornography.

Rodrigues, she explained, was a criminal mastermind who never worked a real job in his life. Now, aged sixty-five, he still ruled over the criminal empire he himself had created from scratch as a young man. He was a heartless and unrelenting businessman, who thought nothing of killing innocent people, if they were merely in the way, or at the wrong place at the wrong time. The major weakness in his organization were his own people. Rodrigues never hired people he perceived as more cunning and more intelligent than himself.

Esmeralda said that if someone were to take out Rodrigues, his whole organization would collapse from within. None she felt were capable of stepping into his shoes. They were predominantly uneducated, unsophisticated individuals with no regard for others. Her dead husband was a typical example of the type of individuals he employed. With Rodrigues out of the picture, the remaining people would fight over the scraps of his empire and would ultimately wind up killing each other. The whole organization, she felt, would implode in a matter of weeks.

How difficult would it be to take out Rodrigues was Ray's question to Esmeralda. She sat puffing on her cigarette as she pondered the question. Her answer, next to impossible! Rodrigues had survived numerous assassination attempts throughout his criminal career, and these attempts were all perpetrated by experienced underworld hit-men. As a matter of fact, every individual who had ever attempted to kill Rodrigues was killed in the process of trying to do so. It would take meticulous planning and flawless execution, no pun intended.

Esmeralda snubbed out her cigarette and looked around the table. The only chance they stood of killing Rodrigues would be to employ the services of a criminal mastermind more heartless, more sophisticated, and more cunning than Rodrigues himself. If they were able to do this, they would essentially be cutting the head off a snake.

On the entire planet, Ray Bangor knew of only one person who might know someone capable of pulling something like this off, and his name was Otis Williams. Everyone seated at the table, with the exception of Esmeralda, rolled their eyes and shifted in their seats. They all knew of Otis Williams, and they all knew Otis would never engage in something like this out of the goodness of his heart. How much was this going to cost? They all had no earthly idea.

Ray contacted Otis and booked a round-trip flight for two to Charm City, USA. He would be taking Esmeralda with him. Only she could provide answers to the questions regarding logistics and specific information necessary to put the plan in motion. Marcella was not pleased, but agreed to take them to the airport. She didn't trust Ray being alone with Esmeralda, but these days, trust was a pretty hard thing to come by. Ray assured Marcella she would have nothing to worry about, this was business. She needed to decide right now if they wanted to live or wanted to die. This trip was going to determine whatever might happen in the future. Marcella would just have to trust his judgment.

Ray hated flying so much so that he had booked first-class seating, figuring maybe he wouldn't hate it as much. Having never flown first-class, Ray was impressed with the accommodations. He could get used to this. During the flight, Esmeralda put her hand on Ray's hand and told him she enjoyed being in the company of a man without the fear of being slapped upside the head if she said or did something wrong. She also confided that she was afraid of flying, while she squeezed his hand even harder. Ray told her not to worry. These were senior pilots, with years of experience, he had said hello to them as they boarded.

As soon as they touched down on the runway, the pilots aborted the landing and pushed the throttles all the way forward as they pointed the nose of the large passenger aircraft skyward at a steep angle, causing butterflies in the stomachs of all aboard. When they reached a prescribed altitude, they circled the airport below. The pilot came over the intercom and explained to the frightened passengers that a large piece of construction plastic had blown across the runway and narrowly missed being ingested by the plane's engines.

When they finally did land and disembarked, they walked right by the pilots standing outside the door to the cockpit. Ray nodded at the pilots and turned to Esmeralda, telling her that he knew these guys were seasoned pros just by looking at them. The pilots beamed when they heard the compliment. Esmeralda put her head on Ray's shoulder, thanking him for making her feel so at ease. He told her she was welcome, knowing full well he had his foot inside the door to winning her trust.

Sharice was waiting for them at the arrivals terminal. They exchanged greetings and Ray introduced his associate Esmeralda Lopez. He had used Esmeralda's maiden name by accident, but she didn't seem to mind as she slipped her arm around his and allowed him to lead her to the baggage claim and from there out to the waiting limo. Esmeralda had never been in a limo before and was very impressed. They had cocktails on the long drive from the airport to North Baltimore.

Arriving at their destination, Sharice escorted them to a room, this time on the third floor. It was every bit as nice as the one he had stayed in on his previous trip, except that it did not have the impressive view owing to the fact that there was a three-story building directly across the street blocking the view of the downtown skyline. Sharice informed them that Otis would join them for dinner in his private dining room on the first floor at 7:00 p.m.

They had about four hours to kill until then. Ray went to the fridge and grabbed a bottle of champagne. They sat on the couch and discussed their upcoming dinner meeting with Otis. Ray told

Esmeralda that Otis was a straight shooter and was well spoken. All conversation needed to be direct and to the point.

A little buzzed from the cocktails and champagne, Ray told Esmeralda he was going to lie down and take a nap before dinner. He awoke to find her on the bed, sleeping peacefully next to him. He woke her and informed her they only had about thirty minutes to get ready. Esmeralda stripped down to her bra and panties and dressed in a conservative business suit, making her look like a business executive. Ray admired her curvy figure from across the room as he put on a tie and sport coat. He was greatly looking forward to being alone with her later on, but right now, they had important business to attend to.

Ray introduced Esmeralda to Otis, explaining that she was a trusted associate, here to assist with a matter of the utmost importance to their organization down south. Otis was impressed with her demeanor and invited them to take seats at the table with him. Otis suggested that they enjoy dinner first, before moving on to the business at hand. The meal was a banquet fit for royalty, lobster tails and huge porterhouse steaks grilled to order. Esmeralda was very impressed with the people Otis employed. She was totally unaccustomed to well-mannered servants who made sure their dining experience was first class.

After the fine meal, Otis lit a huge cigar, sat back in his chair, and asked Ray what had brought them to Charm City. Esmeralda lit a cigarette as Ray outlined the problems he was having with multiple assassination attempts ordered by one Orlando Rodrigues based in New York City. They needed Rodrigues taken out and needed to know what it would cost to do so. Otis didn't know Rodrigues or his organization and began to ask a series of questions that only Esmeralda was capable of answering. She gave precise and succinct answers as to the structure of the organization in question and how well Rodrigues was protected by his people.

New York City was alien territory to Otis and his organization. Given the number of unsuccessful assassination attempts on Rodrigues, it would take the skills of a highly experienced professional who knew the city well. Otis knew exactly who was capable of pulling this off, but unfortunately, the individual did not work for him directly. The individual was an independent contractor with whom Otis had used with great success in the past. Otis asked Ray and Esmeralda how long they were planning to be in town. Ray told him there was no time limit, they could stay as long as necessary. Otis told them that he would attempt to contact this individual and that they could meet again for dinner tomorrow night to discuss the matter further. In the meantime, Esmeralda and Ray were free to stay and enjoy themselves while they were here. He gave Ray a business card with Sharice's pager number. Anything they needed while they were here, they could contact Sharice, and she would see to it.

Ray switched gears and now asked Otis how his business was doing with the product Ray's organization was supplying. Otis was all too happy to explain that the product offered by Ray was being used to produce the purest crack cocaine on the market. Otis went on to say that the quality of the crack produced was not only undermining his competitors, but his organization was now branching out into neighboring cities such as Pittsburg, Philadelphia, and even south into Richmond, Virginia. His organization was able to expand greatly thanks to the quantities of Ray's high-quality product.

Otis now excused himself, shaking hands with the couple and urging them to enjoy themselves as much as possible while they were here. Esmeralda really wanted to go out, but Ray told her that Baltimore was dangerous, especially at night. Out on the city streets they would be immediately pegged as tourists and would be no doubt be harassed by street criminals, who preyed on people unfamiliar with the city and its culture. Esmeralda seemed disappointed, but accepted Ray's explanation. She had no reason to doubt his judgment so far. Ray suggested that they retire to the room and relax. They could always go down to the after-hours nightclub when it opens at 2:00 a.m.

Ray examined the contents of the refrigerator. They needed groceries: beer, wine, orange juice, eggs, bacon, bread, ham and cheese. He called the pager number Otis had given him. Sharice called him back and told him that someone would bring the grocery items he requested to their room within a couple of hours. He thanked her, all the while grateful he would not have to go outside at night and obtain these items himself. Ray opened another bottle of champagne and sat on the couch and turned on the television. He rolled several fatties and chopped up a couple grams of coke. Esmeralda sat down and joined the party. It wasn't long before they were both really, really high. They watched a movie on cable, with Esmeralda sitting close beside him, her head on his shoulder.

The doorbell rang. Ray looked through the peephole, but didn't recognize who it was. He opened the door anyway, and in walked two black males with the groceries Ray had ordered. Ray thanked and tipped the young men as he grabbed a couple cold beers out of the case they had just brought. He made grilled cheese sandwiches and brought them into the living room, setting the tray down in front of Esmeralda. Grilled cheese and beer was a delicacy, especially while stoned, he told her.

Esmeralda just stared at Ray now, who sat bug-eyed watching the television. She decided he needed a blowjob right about now. Ray was cool with that. He sat back, relaxed, and continued to watch a science-fiction horror movie while Esmeralda did her thing. It just doesn't get any better than this, Ray thought as alien creatures seemed to pop out of the television screen while Esmeralda serviced him with genuine desire to please. He thought of Marcella back home. Who in the hell knew what she was doing right now?

Ray looked at his watch. Oh shit, he thought, it was almost 2:00 am. Ray asked Esmeralda if she would like to go down to Felicia's for a night of dancing. Esmeralda was thrilled by the prospect and asked what she should wear. Ray told her to dress as slutty as possible and she would fit in nicely. She wore a tight-fitting, very short, red satin dress, and she looked great. Ray wore a leisure suit. The couple took the elevator down to the first floor where people, who had been standing in line all night to gain admittance, were filling the club to capacity. Esmeralda grabbed Ray's arm and whispered in his ear that they were the only white people in the club. Ray told her not to worry, they would be just fine.

A pretty cocktail waitress took their drink orders. After a couple of mixed drinks, Esmeralda grabbed Ray and pulled him onto the dance floor, where she began to shake her booty to the pulsating, funky electronic dance music. Ray was a pretty good dancer himself, and the two dance partners were so good together that the other dance patrons made room for them in the middle of the dance floor. It was incredibly good fun. Felicia's was actually hipper than any nightclub Ray had been to down in Florida.

All hot and sweaty, and out of breath, they retired to their room for the night. They were both lit up pretty good. Esmeralda told Ray that she needed to take a shower. Ray said to her that hell no, she didn't. He picked her up and threw her on the bed. He pulled off her high heels and stripped out of his clothes. He climbed on the bed, kissing his way up her body, to her waiting, pouty lips. He pulled off her panties and buried his face between her thighs. Esmeralda writhed in pleasure as Ray returned the favor previously given to him earlier in the evening. He climbed on top of her and pressed himself against her warm, soft body. It was Ray's intention to restore Esmeralda's lost desire for intimate relations with men, and he was succeeding. He stared deeply into her dark brown eyes. He could not control himself any longer and he let lose, collapsing on top of her.

Their sexual escapades continued into the early morning hours, when the sun started peaking in through the windows of their room. They slept the entire day. They made lunch. They resumed sleeping. They woke a little after 6:00 p.m., realizing they had less than one hour to get ready for dinner. They took a shower together to save time, and it was more fun that way, of course. They met Otis for dinner right at 7:00 p.m. He told them he had met with the contractor earlier in the day. His price, one hundred thousand plus travel expenses, firm. Ray didn't like the sound of that at all. His partners back home would never go for it. They would just insist that Ray move to another state if he had to. But Ray didn't want to move, he just wanted these goons to stop coming after him and Marcella. He would do the hit himself if it came down to it, but he realized he was now in the big leagues of contract killing. His chances for success were exponentially low.

Otis went on to say that in the event Ray did decide to go through with the hit, the contractor would have to take Esmeralda with him to make a positive identification while doing preliminary surveillance. Oh hell no, thought Ray. A complete stranger alone with his latest sexual conquest, out of the question. Besides, it would be too dangerous for her. She could be easily recognized by Rodrigues and his people. Ray calmly tried to explain to Otis, this option was just not viable.

An unstudied expert in human psychology, Otis tried a different tact. He knew that Ray, like himself, was a businessman. In almost all business transactions, there had to be some room for negotiation. Ray had indeed proven himself to Otis. If something were to happen to Ray, this whole arrangement could fall apart. Otis did not relish the idea of having to deal with Ray's associates. It wasn't just the fact that Otis had never met them, they had yet to prove themselves worthy of his trust. The impression he had of Ray's associates, from Ray's own description, was that they were cheapskates, and a lot less sophisticated than Ray.

And so, after careful consideration, Otis proposed that he himself would finance the hit, on the condition that Ray held firm to their original agreement and kept those shipments coming. Otis knew that Ray was a greenhorn in the drug business, having been involved for what, six weeks maybe? One hundred thousand was a lot of money to this young man and his friends. It was nothing for Otis Williams. Otis calculated that this course of action would continue to make him millions of dollars. If something were to happen to Ray, he would have to find another high-volume supplier, and they were extremely hard to come by. This assassination was just an unforeseen cost of doing business.

Ray insisted that he go along with Esmeralda and the contractor. Otis agreed. Ray and Esmeralda were going to the Big Apple. Sharice would make all the travel arrangements. Ray and Esmeralda would lend logistical support and assist the contractor in whatever capacity was needed. Otis and Ray shook hands on the deal. Both men were pleased. Otis grabbed Ray by the lapel of his sport coat, pulling him close and advising him right to his ear to stay clean and sober for the next twenty-four hours pending further instructions. Otis, knowing that Ray was a party animal, asked him if this was going to be a problem. Ray looked at Esmeralda in her stunning satin silver evening dress. No, it would not be a problem at all, he reassured Otis.

They did not have to wait long. The next morning, Sharice called Ray and told him to be ready by 9:00 a.m. They would be taking the train from Penn Station in Baltimore to Grand Central Station in New York City. Departure time was 10:00 a.m. sharp. Penn Station was only a few city blocks away, leaving plenty of time for them to get there and board the train. Ray and Esmeralda packed and left their room, only to see Sharice leaving another room on the same floor with an as yet unidentified short white bespectacled male. They all met in the garage on the first floor. Sharice introduced Ray and Esmeralda to Jimmy, a very small unassuming man in his thirties. This was the cold-blooded contract killer Otis had hired? No way! Ray shook his hand and introduced him to Esmeralda who also shook his hand. They had time to kill before departure, so Sharice took the opportunity to get coffee for everyone. Jimmy excused himself to use the restroom. Esmeralda leaned in close and asked Ray if Jimmy's hand didn't feel weird. He told her it did not.

When Sharice returned with the coffee, Ray could not help but noticed that Jimmy's palms were abnormally smooth and devoid of surface features as he reached for the coffee in the drink carrier. It became obvious to Ray that Jimmy, at some time long ago, had burned off his finger and palm prints with acid. Jimmy was the real deal. It all began to make sense to Ray now. This ordinary-looking man looked nothing like a murderer. No one would suspect that this short, bald, and even frail-looking man was a professional contract killer, with a fearsome reputation no less.

They sat across from each other on the train to New York. Esmeralda tried to engage Jimmy in simple conversation, but it soon became apparent that Jimmy was not much of a conversationalist. The man was simply devoid of personality. He was just a stone-cold professional killer without any remorse. That's what made him so good at what he did, Ray figured. Jimmy was just fine with killing complete strangers in furtherance of financial gain.

When they arrived at Grand Central Station, it all hit home for Ray. Having never been to NYC, it was culture shock on a new level for him. Jimmy had been to the city many times before, and he was the one who now hailed a taxi that would take them to their hotel. Ray could not get over the sheer size of NYC. It was Baltimore multiplied by one hundred. The buildings alone defied imagination. Ray marveled at the engineering genius that was required to design and build them.

In the lobby of their hotel, Jimmy instructed Ray and Esmeralda to meet him at the hotel coffee shop at seven the next morning. Esmeralda said she was hungry and suggested to Ray that they have dinner in the hotel restaurant after they settled in and unpacked. Over dinner, she told Ray that Jimmy was perhaps the strangest man she had ever met. Ray thought he was weird also, but was not the least bit concerned about Jimmy or his personality, or lack thereof. Jimmy was there to do a job, and that was all they needed to concern themselves with right now.

In the privacy of their room, Esmeralda gave Ray a massage. She worked her hands and fingers into the muscles of his shoulders and back. Ray, already extremely high at this point, wondered to himself where has this woman been all his life. Juan Pablo Hernandez was an idiot for not appreciating this woman. It further reinforced Ray's complete and total disdain for the man who was now nothing more than a pile of ashes in a backyard down in Georgia. The only regret Ray had was that fact that he did not kill the man himself.

Jimmy was waiting for them in the coffee shop the next morning. He hardly recognized Esmeralda who had changed her hairstyle. She looked like a completely different woman now with her long, wavy red hair. The three sat in the hotel coffee shop and devised a plan. They would take a taxi to the office building in lower Manhattan, where Rodrigues had offices on the tenth floor. Ray would attempt to schedule a meeting with Rodrigues.

Standing in front of the building directory, Ray found what he was looking for, Rodrigues and Associates Consulting Inc. Ray was immediately met by armed security as he tried to gain access to the tenth-floor office complex. They gave him a thorough screening with metal-detecting wands, before allowing him to approach the reception area. A pretty receptionist informed Ray that Mr. Rodrigues was unable to accept any new appointments at this time, his schedule was booked into next week. Ray insisted that he had an urgent matter that he needed to discuss with Mr. Rodrigues.

The receptionist handed Ray a business card and told him to call in a week, and maybe they would be able to set something up then. Ray felt as though he'd been given the bum's rush, but he was expecting that. He rejoined Jimmy and Esmeralda in the lobby on the first floor. Esmeralda said she would go and attempt to set an appointment with Rodrigues. Ray thought it was too dangerous. What if someone recognized her?

Esmeralda explained that she had personally not seen Rodrigues in over a year, he probably would not remember her. Not only that, her new appearance would throw him off. Ray was still opposed, but Jimmy thought it was worth a try. He said that when he saw Esmeralda first thing this morning, he had no idea who she was. Her heavy makeup and radically different hairstyle had made her unrecognizable to him. Looking at Esmeralda now, Ray had to admit, she did look like a completely different person. It just might work. Ray wished her luck. She was taking one hell of a chance, and he wasn't comfortable with it at all. Jimmy and Ray sat in the lobby as Esmeralda disappeared inside an elevator. They expected her to return rather quickly just as Ray had. Instead they waited for thirty minutes before she got off the elevator and rejoined them.

She explained to them that not only had she made an appointment with Rodrigues, they were meeting for lunch at a restaurant a block and a half away. Against all odds, she had pulled it off. They took a taxi back to their hotel, where in the privacy of Jimmy's room, they discussed how to proceed further. Upon leaving the front door of the restaurant with Rodrigues, Esmeralda would break free, allowing Jimmy the chance to open up on Rodrigues and his associates with a sub-machine gun. It was a bold plan, in broad daylight, in front of hundreds of witnesses.

Jimmy explained to them that under circumstances such as these, people would just run for cover as soon as they heard shots fired. It would be total chaos. This would allow them to escape by blending in with the fleeing pedestrians. They would discard their weapons and disguises and blend in with the thousands of other pedestrians on the crowded sidewalks of Manhattan. Jimmy opened a small suitcase. It contained wigs, fake beards and mustaches, along with sunglasses and hats.

He next opened another suitcase. It contained a full-auto Israeli Uzi, extra magazines, and assorted handguns. Jimmy handed Ray a 9mm semiauto pistol, with instructions to kill anyone who attempted to escape the ambush. Ray ejected the gun's magazine and, satisfied that it was fully loaded, reinserted it and tucked the weapon into his waistband. He next picked a disguise out of the other suitcase, a long black beard and a short-brimmed fedora. Jimmy picked out a blond wig and matching beard.

After the killing, they would all meet back at the hotel and prepare to leave for Baltimore. Ray donned the fake beard and hat and looked at himself in the mirror. He didn't even recognize himself. This is going to work, he thought. Jimmy instructed Ray to take up position in the restaurant bar. Jimmy was a real professional who was completely prepared. If there was a Hall of Fame for contract killers, Ray would be the first to nominate Jimmy as an inductee.

Esmeralda and Ray went back to their room, they had a couple of hours until it was time. Ray asked how was it that Esmeralda was able to secure a lunch meeting with Rodrigues. She told him that she had introduced herself to the receptionist as Monica Lopez, sister of Esmeralda Lopez Hernandez. She had not heard from her sister in months and wondered if Orlando Rodrigues might know where she was. That was pure genius on her part, thought Ray. He asked her if she was nervous. Her answer was, hell yes, she was nervous.

They all took separate taxis to the restaurant in the hopes that no one would identify them as being together. Esmeralda went inside, while Ray and Jimmy took their respective positions. Jimmy stood at a city bus stop while Ray entered the restaurant and sat at the bar. He ordered a martini, in the hope that it would calm his nerves somewhat. He could not see Esmeralda or Rodrigues from his vantage point seated at the bar. He didn't even know what this Rodrigues character looked like anyway.

After one hour and twenty minutes, Ray saw Esmeralda, arm in arm with the man that had to be Rodrigues. Accompanying them were three large bruisers, who Ray figured were bodyguards. This is it, thought Ray as he got up from his barstool and followed the entourage outside. As soon as they were outside, Esmeralda pulled her arm away from Rodrigues and fled. Jimmy grabbed the Uzi, still concealed in the duffle bag, and began to spray the men with bullets.

Four men now lay on the ground bleeding as people began screaming and running away from the sound of gunfire. Jimmy approached the restaurant entrance and emptied the weapon's magazine into the fallen bodies, insuring no chance of survival. Ray looked for Esmeralda in the chaos that now surrounded him. He saw her several yards away, face down on the sidewalk. A ricocheted bullet had struck her in the back of the head, killing her.

Without thinking, Ray pulled the 9mm from his waistband, chambered a round, and shot Jimmy in the face, at close range. Ray, now overcome with grief and terror, threw down his disguise on the sidewalk and joined the fleeing crowd, still holding on to the weapon now tucked under his sport coat. As he got further from the crime scene, he slowed down to a walk, turning west onto a side street. He continued walking several blocks before hailing a taxi. He asked the driver to take him to Grand Central Station.

He purchased a train ticket back to Baltimore, but was informed the next train would not be departing for three more hours. He found a bar and began drinking heavily. He could not believe what had happened. Seeing Esmeralda dead on the sidewalk had affected him so badly, he was sure he would never be able to shake that horrible image from his mind. He was overcome with sorrow and grief and had to suppress the urge to cry. It was getting late, he had a train to catch.

Sleeping almost the entire way from Grand Central to Penn Station, he awoke only to realize the precarious situation he was now in. Calling Sharice on her pager, she called him back at the phone booth in Penn Station. He explained to her that there was a huge problem in New York City. Jimmy and Esmeralda were not coming home, ever. Sharice told Ray this was in fact a huge problem. Otis and Jimmy were, well, let's just say more than friends. Ray was completely shocked by the disclosure.

He told Sharice that he could not, right at this moment, face Otis and explain the dreadful news. Sharice was also in a state of shock and pressed Ray for more details. Ray said he just couldn't bring himself to talk about it right now. Explaining that he would contact Otis in a couple days, he hung up the phone. Outside the train station, he hailed a taxi and told the driver to take him out to Baltimore/Washington International Airport.

While waiting for his connecting flight in Charlotte, North Carolina, he saw the story on national television. Unable to watch it, he turned away, until the news anchor reported that the authorities were looking for this man in connection to the crime. There on the television screen above him was a police sketch of a man who looked just like him. Looking around him nervously, he was temporarily relieved that no one else around him was paying any attention to the news story out of New York City.

Back at his residence on Hilton Head Island, he found Marcella asleep in their room. Grabbing a liquor bottle, he sat on the couch and replayed the events over and over in his mind. How could things have gotten so incredibly fucked up? He felt so bad for Esmeralda. He even felt bad for Jimmy. Esmeralda's death was just an unfortunate accident. Now the authorities were looking for him. How long would it be before someone recognized him from the police sketch? He would have to change his appearance again, but he was fast running out of options on that one. Every single bad thing that had happened so far was his own fault. Since finding the *Winsor2*, he had killed five men. It was only a matter of time until all the things he had done would catch up with him.

Marcella found Ray passed out on the couch. He looked incredibly bad, like he had aged twenty years in the past three days. She woke him gently, only to see him run to the bathroom and vomit profusely. She desperately wanted to know what had happened, but there was also a part of her that didn't. Whatever it was, it must have been bad, very bad. She decided it would be best to just let Ray explain what had happened when he was ready.

They drove out to Max and Gina's the next day. There, seated around the dining room table, Ray laid out the horrific story of how the assassination of Orlando Rodrigues had gone terribly wrong. Gina started crying when she heard of Esmeralda's death. Max wanted to know how the death of Jimmy was going to affect the business relationship with Otis Williams. Ray didn't have an answer for that. Until someone came forward and reported otherwise, everyone—including Marcella, Max, and Gina—believed that Jimmy's death was caused by one of bodyguards hired by Rodrigues. Ray was not about to tell anyone the truth about what really happened to Jimmy. He could not even handle the truth himself.

Then came the day when Ray called Otis Williams. It was obvious that Otis had taken Jimmy's death very hard. Otis wanted to know exactly what had happened that day, but Ray explained that everything occurred so fast, he did not know exactly what had happened. Otis wasn't buying any of it. Ray was there, how could he not know? There could only be one reason for the lame explanation-Ray Bangor was lying.

For the next week, Ray became reclusive, leaving the house only when he ran out of booze. He did not answer the phone, he did not return messages. Then came the day he woke, only to find Marcella had moved out. Every single one of her belongings were gone, as was her car. Standing in the doorway of the room they once shared, he stared at the empty closet that had previously held all of her clothes. This was the end of the road for Ray Bangor. He was circling the drain and he knew it. Picking up a revolver from the coffee table, he opened the cylinder to find that it was fully loaded. He placed the barrel against his right temple. For several minutes, he sat with the loaded weapon pointed at his head. There was no reason for him to go on. He had nothing to live for. He had fucked up his own life and the lives of others around him. He had purposefully caused the deaths of five men. Squeezing the trigger ever so lightly, he stopped, right as the sweet spot was about to snap the hammer down on the live round in the cylinder. He set the gun back down on the table and began crying. He did not have the balls to end his own life, and he wept uncontrollably.

He woke to the sound of a raging, roaring surf. Huge waves crashed upon a rocky beach littered with boulders of all sizes. A wave of nausea swept over him producing dry heaves. Gasping for breath now, he stood and looked around. There were huge mountains in the distance. There were species of plants and trees he had never seen before. If this was hell, it was quite beautiful in a natural rugged sort of way.

Reaching into his pockets, he found they were empty. The spray from the violent surf soaked him through to the skin. He wore the same clothes he was wearing the day he found Marcella had left him. It now seemed like such a long time ago. His body ached all over and his head felt as though someone were driving a railroad spike into the base of his skull. There were ligature marks on his wrists and ankles. Trembling now from the whipping wind coming in from the sea, he urinated in his already-soaking wet pants.

Looking up and down the coastline, he found that it was rugged and desolate in both directions. He began walking along the surf line, hoping it would dry his clothing and begin to generate body heat. Coming to a stretch of beach that opened up and seemed to go on for miles, he saw something far off in the distance. As it got closer, he realized it was a horse in full gallop, running directly toward him. As it ran right past him, he noticed something horrible. There was a naked man tied underneath the horse with his face directly underneath the hindquarters. The man appeared to be either unconscious or dead.

Ray continued to watch the horse as it disappeared down the coastline. He had just witnessed an act of cruelty, unmatched by anything he had ever seen before. Not wanting to believe what he had just seen, he continued walking, replaying the image of the man under the horse over and over in his mind. In another mile of so, he came upon an old wrecked freighter, its hull severely damaged by the rocky coastline. The wreck was so old that not a single chip of paint remained on it. The entire wreck was covered with rust. It had probably been here, disintegrating for a hundred years or more.

Huge waves crashed over the wreck, and seawater poured out of cracks in the hull so large, a truck could have easily driven through them. Sitting on a rock, he could not take his eyes off of what was once a proud oceangoing freighter. Now, it was just a mere rusty skeleton of a ship, abandoned and long forgotten. Whatever cargo it held when it ran aground had long since been destroyed and consumed by the violent sea

Despondent, he continued walking on the deserted beach, only to see something in the distance that made him wretch with the dry heaves again. He was now standing in front of a series of post driven deep into the sand. Attached to each one was a naked man or woman, secured to the post by ropes tied tightly around the torso and neck. Their arms and legs had been sawed off at the body. The facial expressions on the deceased grimaced with the agonizing pain each must have felt in their final moments.

Was this hell, or hell on earth? Ray had yet to decide. Whatever it was, it was now obvious to Ray that he had been placed here by persons unknown. He had been placed here to die, painfully, slowly. In the back of his mind, he somehow always knew that his past would catch up with him, all starting with the discovery of the cocaine aboard the stricken *Winsor2*. But nothing in this world could have prepared him for this day and the gruesome things he had seen thus far. And the day was far from over.

Drenched in sweat, he awoke from the nightmare. His heart was pounding and his breathing shallow. Sickness caused by alcohol consumption made him dizzy and queasy. It was dark outside, and the house was deathly quiet. He looked at his watch, it was almost 5:00 a.m. He reached for the gun on the coffee table, pointed it to his temple, and fired a bullet into his brain. Unbeknownst to him, the authorities were just outside his house, preparing to execute a search warrant.

Gina gasped when she read the newspaper article about the police raid and subsequent suicide of Raymond Bangor. According to the paper, two full-auto AK-47s were found inside the house along with two kilograms of high-grade cocaine. Raymond Bangor was a murder suspect, wanted in New York State for questioning in the deaths of Orlando Rodrigues and five other, as yet unnamed individuals. She ran out of the house and found Max working in the backyard. She handed him the newspaper.

Annoyed by the interruption, Max took the paper and read the article in its entirety. Max was pissed. His former friend was responsible for all the problems all of them had experienced over the last two months. Max wondered aloud if the authorities could somehow connect Ray Bangor to himself and Gina. In the meantime, they were still sitting on almost nine hundred pounds of coke and nearly two million cash.

Max grabbed Gina by the shoulders and spoke directly to her face. Ray Bangor was a fucking asshole. Ever since they took the coke off the *Winsor2*, Ray lived his life like a fucking asshole, and he died like one. Gina became upset and asked Max what they were going to do now. Max told her he would have to think about that carefully. He couldn't just decide the course of their lives in the next five minutes. Right now he had to struggle with the possibility that the authorities were already onto them.

But Max had known Ray well enough to know that Ray almost never wrote anything down. The authorities would be hard pressed to link Gina and himself without any physical evidence. Also, Ray was tightlipped about his business dealings. For example, Max didn't even remember the last name of Ray's customer in Baltimore. Max didn't know the man and didn't want to know him. As far as Max was concerned, that man did not even exist in his world.

The first priority, Max decided, was to get that fucking coke off his property. The next would be to stash the money somewhere where it could never be found. Max spent the rest of the day formulating a plan. Tomorrow, he would take Gina to Savannah for the purpose of purchasing a new vehicle.

They would load the coke into Max's old truck and park it at Rob's place. For his trouble, Max would pay Rob two hundred dollars a month just to park the old truck in an old garage on Rob's property. Max was sure Rob would go for it. Hey, it was an extra two hundred a month. Next, he would load the cash into five-gallon buckets and bury it. But not on his property of course.

Max owned about one acre in the Georgia countryside. Directly behind his property were hundreds of acres of undeveloped land that belonged to a wealthy family. The property had been handed down over generations since before the Civil War. Max knew they were not planning to develop or sell it any time soon. It would be there on that adjacent property where Max would bury the loot, unbeknownst to his neighbors of course. Whenever they needed it, it would be there for them less than one hundred yards away.

Early the next morning, Max and Gina set the plan into motion. Max purchased a fully loaded, brand-new four-wheel-drive Ford truck. Gina followed him back to their house where they spent the rest of the morning loading the coke into the bed of Max's old truck and covering it with a heavy canvas tarp. Max had already nailed down his agreement with Rob the previous night, and they parked the old truck in a garage that held several other vehicles Rob was planning to restore someday.

Max and Gina spent the rest of the day loading the cash into dozens of five-gallon buckets and began the process of burying them. It would take them into the night to complete the process as they worked under the light of a gas lantern. Max carefully mapped out the locations of the buried buckets and hid the map in a fire-resistant safe in his house. Anyone who did find the map would not be able to understand what it was exactly. Only Max and Gina knew the key to reading and understanding it.

Satisfied now that their assets were protected, Max proposed that they take a well-deserved vacation. He asked Gina if she would ask her friend Amy to accompany them to Charleston for a week of deep-sea fishing aboard *The REEL OPPORTUNITY.* Gina thought it was a great idea. The next morning, they drove to the marina in Charleston, and by noon, they were loading provisions onto the sport fisher. They spent the night aboard the boat, and by six the next morning, they were headed down the Ashly River, toward the Atlantic Ocean, and out to the Gulf Stream.

Once they were well offshore, Amy began to complain of seasickness. Amy was not a pot smoker, so Gina offered her some motion-sickness medicine. She began feeling a little better, but Max and Gina were feeling no pain. They smoked weed, snorted rails, and drank countless twelve ounce beers. Max showed Amy how to pilot the large sport fisher, knowing that they would need her help if they hooked into something big.

Out in the Gulf Stream, they were the only vessel in sight. They set some hooks and began trolling. Within minutes, one of the large bait caster reels began to pay out rapidly. Gina grabbed it and set the hook. Max reeled in the other lines as Gina let the fish on the end her line run like it had just stolen something. Max climbed up on the bridge and gave Amy careful instructions: stay in the dark blue waters of the Gulf Stream and continue motoring at low idle. Max joined Gina down on the deck and strapped her into the fighting chair.

After what seemed like forever, the reel began to slow down. Gina began to reel in the line slowly. Off the starboard stern, a large marlin broke the surface and danced on its tail before falling back down into the sea. Max yelled to Amy to keep an eye on the fish when it broke the surface and keep the bow pointed away from it. Max stood by and encouraged his girlfriend. He offered her cold beers and hits off a joint which she gladly accepted.

Amy did an excellent job piloting the boat as Gina began to reel in her prize. All afternoon she fought the marlin in the hot sun. After almost three hours, the large fish was alongside *The REEL OPPORTUNITY.* Max grabbed the camera and took pictures of Gina holding the rod with the marlin on the other end.

It was a magnificent specimen. Max hollered to Amy up on the bridge to place the steering system in auto pilot and join them down below.

They had no way of measuring the fish or estimating its weight, all they knew was that it was big and it weighed a lot. Gina wanted her picture taken with the fish and she handed the rod to Max while she dove in the ocean and swam alongside it to give a sense of scale as Amy snapped pictures. Max helped Gina back on board and told her that was the bravest thing he'd ever seen. How did she know that an opportunistic, hungry shark wasn't about to show up and take a bite out of her or her fish? Gina was not the least bit bothered by that, she was so proud of the beautiful fish she had just landed.

Gina now held the rod steady as she could while Max put on a set of gloves and grabbed the marlin by the bill, as he used a pair of heavy lineman's plies to cut the barb off the hook. He gently backed the hook out and the fish was free. It lay still in the water for a moment, recovering from its ordeal, then bolted for the ocean depths. The three friends all gave each other high-fives, and even Amy drank a beer to celebrate the magnificent catch.

It had been a long day indeed. They headed back toward the marina with Amy piloting the whole way until they reached the mouth of the Ashley River. She told Max and Gina she had never had so much fun on a boat before. Max welcomed the news, he was planning to take the boat out each day this week, weather permitting. Gina suggested to Max that they get hotel rooms, which would allow everyone a little more privacy. Max said that would be fine.

And so all week they fished the Gulf Stream catching wahoo, sailfish, tuna, and mahi-mahi. It was good fun for all. Amy really enjoyed piloting *The REEL OPPORTUNITY.* Gina loved fishing almost as much as she loved sex. Max enjoyed watching both women enjoy themselves. They ate in fine restaurants and explored the city of Charleston at night.

One night after dinner, they were walking the busy city sidewalks and came upon a group of punk rockers. They wore black leather jackets, had pink and purple Mohawks, and wore safety pins as earrings. When they saw Amy, Gina, and Max approaching, they all stepped aside to make room for the three adults to pass. Max commented that one of the reasons he loved Charleston so much was that even the hoodlums were polite. By the end of the week, Max was not looking forward to returning to their ho-hum lifestyle in Georgia.

To make matters worse, Gina's oldest brother Martin was coming to visit them from Los Angeles, California. Martin was a successful recording engineer and he never passed up the opportunity to brag to anyone who would listen about what it was that he did for a living. And he made a damn good living at it. He got to meet famous performers, and he even counted some of them as friends. To Max he was just an arrogant, condescending braggart. The two men were bitter enemies, but Martin tolerated Max because, after all, Max was his little sister's boyfriend. Max, in turn, tolerated Martin because Gina thought the world of him.

They picked up Martin and his new girlfriend Vicky at the Savannah International Airport. Martin did most of the talking on the ride out to Max and Gina's house. Vicky, as it turns out, was a real looker. She was a knockout. She had attended college to become an actress and was just getting started in the business. With her vibrant personality and stunning good looks, it wouldn't be long before she found someone a lot better than Martin, Max figured.

Max grilled steaks and drank beer, while Martin went on and on about how great California was. Martin even suggested that Max consider moving out there with Gina. She would be a lot happier there, he explained. Max could feel his brain tighten up with every word that came out of Martin's mouth. Max told him that that horses from hell could not drag him to California to live or even visit. Max was greatly looking forward to Monday when he would be driving Gina's brother and his girlfriend back to the airport. In the meantime, Max would have to suck it up and deal with this sorry asshole all weekend.

After dinner, Martin asked his sister if she had anything for the head. Gina replied that, yes, indeed she did and provided her brother with a personal stash of weed and coke. Great, thought Max, now he's never going to shut up. But after snorting a couple of rails, Martin turned serious and asked his sister where she had gotten this coke. He said it was the best he'd ever had, much better than anything he could get his hands on in LA. He asked her if she could get more of this, and Gina responded by saying, maybe.

They sat at the dining room table and snorted rails well into the early morning hours. Martin told his sister that this cocaine was so good, he wondered if she could send some to him in LA. Gina said she wasn't sure about that, she would have to check and see. Max had already retired for the night, but Martin, Gina, and Vicky continued their party, speaking in hushed voices so as not to disturb Max. The brother and sister, having not seen each other in a couple of years, had a lot of catching up to do.

Vicky just sat back and enjoyed the weed and the wine, coke just wasn't her thing.

Max was up at the crack of dawn as was Vicky. He made breakfast for her as Gina and Martin continued sleeping well into the afternoon. When they did finally wake up, Martin announced that he wanted to spend the rest of the day in downtown Savannah. Max was all too happy to drop the couple off on River Street. Martin told Max and Gina not to worry, they would take a cab back to their house later that night. That was just fine with Max.

On the way home, Gina took the opportunity to tell Max that her brother was so impressed with the quality of the coke, he told her he could get rid of as much as she could come by. He said that coke of this quality would go over huge in LA. He said he knew a lot of folks who would love to get their hands on this, and the truth was, he probably did with all the people he knew in the entertainment industry. Max was all against it. He didn't like nor did he trust Gina's brother.

But Gina pressed her case even further. This was the key to getting rid of the eight hundred eighty pounds they still had. Even if Martin were to screw up big-time and get nabbed by the police, he would never roll over on his little sister. By the time they reached the house, Gina had Max convinced that Martin was the path forward to getting rid of the stuff once and for all. Max said he would front Martin one kilo for now and just sit back and see how that panned out. Down in his basement, Max retrieved a kilo he had hidden in the rafters and brought it upstairs. Gina couldn't wait to tell her brother.

But Martin and Vicky never came home that night. Instead they arrived the next morning saying that he had gotten a room downtown so that they could spend some quality time alone together without disturbing Max and Gina. Later in the day, while Max was grilling the mahi-mahi they had caught in the Gulf Stream, he told Martin that he would, in fact, front him one kilo of pure coke for ten grand. For the first time since his arrival in Georgia, Martin was actually silent for all of thirty seconds. He thanked Max profusely and said that he would not let him down. Max sure hoped not.

Max asked him where he would like it sent to, and Martin responded that he would just pack it in his checked baggage. Whatever, thought Max, as he handed Martin the package. Max grabbed Martin's arm and whispered to his ear, if anything happens, Martin did not know where he got this from. Martin told Max everything would be cool, he did this very sort of thing all the time, and he'd never had a problem. It wasn't like he was flying to a foreign country. Besides, he would never do anything to jeopardize his little sister Gina.

They all rode in Max's new truck to the Savannah airport where Max was all too happy to help Martin and Vicky with their luggage. As they said their goodbyes, Martin looked Max in the eye, shook his hand firmly, and told him, "Thanks, bro, you won't regret this." On the way back home, Max wondered aloud if he had done the right thing. After all, Martin had a big mouth. Gina told him to relax. Martin wasn't an irresponsible teenager, he was a full-grown man with a lot to lose if things went wrong. The last thing in the world Martin wanted was to get into any trouble that would land him in prison.

Max trusted Gina's judgment. She always seemed to be right about everything. She was a keen observer of human behavior and a good judge of character, she did after all choose him as a boyfriend. That morning, driving home from the airport, Max decided he wanted to marry Gina. Tomorrow he would buy a ring and propose to her. They had been together for three years, it only made good sense.

The very next day after dinner, Max proposed to his longtime girlfriend. He presented her with the ring he had bought earlier in the day and she slipped it on her finger. She began to cry, she was so happy. Yes, of course, she would marry him. Holding it up to the overhead light over the table, she marveled at the sparkling facets. She was so happy right now, she couldn't wait to call her parents and give them the good news. Max was so happy that Gina was happy. He'd been wanting to do this for a long time and now seemed just like the right moment. He looked forward to the future with Gina as his wife. Hopefully, she would want a family, and it might even serve to settle down her wild streak. Even if it didn't, he still loved her anyway. She was his soul mate. They had been through so much together, dealing illegal narcotics, committing murders, and the unfortunate suicide of Max's former friend and business partner, Ray. Max just wished the future would hold good luck and good fortune for them.

An overnight delivery truck pulled into the driveway as Max was burning debris in the backyard. He hadn't ordered anything and wondered if Gina might have. Signing for the package, he took it into his basement workshop and opened it. It was from Gina's brother Martin. It contained one hundred and fifty crisp new one-hundred-dollar bills. There was a note from Martin thanking Max for the package he had taken back to LA. It went on to say that Max didn't know what he had, hence Martin had included the extra five thousand. It also said to contact him at his home when Max had the chance. Martin said he would take all that Max could get.

This was a pleasant surprise indeed. Max figured he had misjudged Gina's brother all along. Now there was a way for Max and Gina to unload the remaining coke and be done with this shit forever.

Max got into his truck and drove the quarter mile or so to Rob's house. He pulled into the driveway and drove on back to the garage where he had parked his old truck. He was shocked to see that it was missing. He found Rob and a couple of Rob's employees working on the crane Rob used for his tree service company.

Max asked Rob where his old truck was. Rob explained that he thought Max had taken it. Max could not believe what he was hearing. He felt his blood begin to boil in his veins. It now occurred to him that the old truck had been stolen. He asked Rob when was the last time he saw the truck still parked in the garage. Rob told Max there had been a tornado outbreak in a neighboring county, Rob and his crew were there for a week during the recovery effort. When they returned, he noticed the truck missing and just figured Max had taken it.

That would have been the previous week when Max and Gina and Amy were sport fishing. He now asked Rob if he knew of anyone who may have stolen it. Rob though for a moment and explained that there was a disgruntled employee that he had fired recently for missing too many work days. Max wanted the man's name. Rob went inside the house and returned with the former employee's file, handing it to Max. It contained the former employee's original application as well as a copy of his Georgia driver's license. Max now asked Rob if he could borrow the file to make a copy. Rob told him sure. Max thanked Rob for his help and left in a hurry. Rob didn't quite understand why Max was so edgy and upset. It was just an old truck, probably not worth a whole lot. Why didn't Max just call the police and let them deal with it? There was obviously something else, Rob thought, but it wasn't his concern. Rob and his employees resumed replacing the lift cable on Rob's crane which was damaged during the tornado recovery effort.

Max examined the copy of the driver's license. The man he was looking for was named Dale Mitchell Tomkins Jr., aged thirty-one. Looking at a state map, he located the area he was looking for, about a thirty-minute drive from where he was right now. Max's truck spit gravel as it pulled out of the driveway onto the main road. He was so pissed off he couldn't think straight. Taking deep breaths, he regained his composure and found the address he was looking for.

It was a trailer park out in the sticks. Max put his .40 caliber semiauto in his waistband holster and knocked on the trailer door. A very pregnant and very young woman answered the door. She could not have been any older than seventeen or eighteen, maybe. Max produced the copy of the driver's license and showed it to the girl. Max told her he was looking for Dale Tomkins in an attempt to recover some stolen property. She asked Max he if he was the police to which Max replied no, he was the owner of the stolen property.

The young woman invited Max inside her trailer. She invited Max to take a seat and went on to explain to him that Dale was her common-law husband and the father of her unborn child. He had disappeared about a week ago, and she had not heard from him since. Son of a bitch, thought Max. He asked the girl where Dale might be at this moment. She said she had no idea. Max tried to relax as he attempted to gather as much information as possible.

The girl told him Dale was an ex-con, who had been released from prison about a year ago. His parents in Chicago, Illinois, bought him a bus ticket south so that he could stay with his aunt and uncle and start a new life. Dale was a former gang member, the girl explained, and his parents figured that the move south to Georgia would help him straighten out his life. He took a job with Rob's Tree Service and rented this trailer. They were already a month behind in the rent and facing eviction.

Max looked at the girl who was wearing a ragged T-shirt and dirty flip-flops. He felt empathy for her. Reaching in his pocket, he pulled out the huge wad of money he had just received from Martin and placed it on the table in front of her.

He told the girl that Dale was probably never coming back. The money was hers to keep, she did not have to pay it back. The girl was overcome with emotion and, with tears in her eyes, gave Max a big hug thanking him for his generous gift. Max asked her if there was anything else she could tell him about Dale. She was all too happy to comply with his request. She handed Max an unopened piece of mail Dale had received from his parents just this past week, there was a return address on it.

Max thanked the girl and gave her a phone number to call if she had any other information that might be helpful. The girl gave Max another hug and wished him luck in recovering his stolen property. Bursting with rage, Max drove back to his house to give Gina the news. He did not relish the idea of going to Chicago. There were so many stories in the national news about the gang problems in Chicago and the associated gang violence that went with it.

Gina literally went ballistic when told that the old truck was stolen along with the eight hundred seventy-eight pounds of coke. Max explained to her that the man who stole the truck probably did so not knowing what was hidden in the truck bed under the tarp. He produced the letter with the return address. They had a starting point anyway. They began to pack in preparation for their trip to Chicago. Among the items Max planned to bring, one of the five-gallon buckets that contained one hundred thousand dollars and an assortment of weapons, including two full-auto AK-47s they had taken off the *Winsor2*.

They would inform their neighbor Amy of their travel plans and leave at dawn the next morning. Max sat at the dining room table and carefully planned their route from their house all the way to Lincoln Park, Illinois, in the hope that Dale's parents could be of some help in locating him. It was a huge gamble they were taking. They were not even sure if that's where Dale Tomkins was headed.

But Max figured, once a fuck-up, always a fuck-up. Once Tomkins figured out what was under the tarp, his only logical choice would be to return to Chicago where he knew the territory and people who could help him get rid of it.

And so at the crack of dawn the next morning, they left. They took I-16 to Atlanta where they stopped to have lunch and refuel. Taking the beltway around Atlanta, they continued on I-75 to Chattanooga, Tennessee, and from there to I-24 to Nashville where they got a hotel room. Max and Gina were unprepared for Nashville. They never realized what a tough town it was. Trying to unwind in their room, they heard gunshots right outside the hotel. They smoked weed and drank beer, never leaving the comparative safety of their room.

Of course, Gina wanted sex just like she always did, especially in strange places, but Max couldn't concentrate. His mind was overrun with thoughts of what the immediate future held for them. Inwardly, he cursed himself for parking the load on Rob's property, but how was he to know that someone would steal his old truck? What if this Tomkins character broke down or got himself picked up by the police? There were just too many things that could go wrong. Max always kept the truck in good running order. But what if this idiot got into an accident? Max had to force himself to stop thinking, so he just tried to clear his mind and let Gina do her thing.

But there was only one problem, he couldn't clear his mind. He had already decided that he was going to kill this Dale Tomkins if they ever found him. Even if they did recover the stolen coke, Dale was a dead man. Max remembered his father telling him once that we, as individuals, have absolutely no control over what others do.

How right he was about that. Max hoped that once they reached Chicago, he would not make the mistake that would lead to their deaths.

After a huge breakfast the next morning, they drove on to I-65 which took them to Louisville, Kentucky. They continued on through the day to Indianapolis, Indiana, and from there to Greater Chicago where they stopped for dinner. They continued north to Lincoln Park, passing through some very rough neighborhoods. It was early evening when they pulled up in front of the house which matched the street address on the envelope. It was actually a very nice neighborhood. Max wondered what happened to Dale Tomkins that made him take the wrong path in life. It was probably the very same thing that happened to Max's life; drugs.

They were met at the front door by a very nice Dale Tomkins Sr. who invited them inside. There, sitting in the living room with Dale's mom, Linda, and her husband, Max explained that they had traveled a great distance from Georgia looking for their son, Dale Tomkins Jr. Dale's mother wanted to know if her son was in any kind of trouble. Thinking quickly, Max told her yes and no. Dale had borrowed a truck from Max and had not returned it. Dale's common-law wife in Georgia told him he might find Dale here in Chicago. All they wanted was for Dale to return the truck, and they would be on their way.

Dale's father became edgy. Obviously, his son was not something he wished to talk about. Linda now led the conversation by explaining that Dale was an only child and had received a very good private school education right up through high school. He began experimenting with drugs and everything went downhill for him from there. During his senior year, he was arrested for grand theft auto and served time in prison, where he met up with the wrong element. Upon his release from prison, he joined a gang and got into even more trouble with the law.

Gang life had affected him in ways they could never accept. In and out of prison through his young adult life, he became hard and uncaring, eventually becoming a heroin addict. Most of his fellow gang members were eventually killed or incarcerated, and the remaining members were displaced by the tearing down of the projects they inhabited. Broke and suffering from heroin withdrawal, Dale showed up on his parents' doorstep one day. They took him in and helped him kick his heroin addiction. When he regained his health and his senses, his mom suggested that he move down south to live with her brother and his wife, far away from the bad influences that could one day pull him back into gang life. He found a job and got his own place. It was in the very same trailer park that he lived where he met his common-law wife, Peggy, who was expecting a baby in a couple of months.

Finally, Dale Tomkins Sr. spoke up. If they wanted to find Dale, he could probably be found on the West Side, in a basement apartment where his former girlfriend lived. The two had been sweethearts since they were teenagers, and together they got involved in drugs. Dale's father rose from his chair and removed a picture form the mantle, handing it to Max and Gina. It was a very young Dale with his girlfriend Laura at their high school prom. They made a handsome couple.

What were the chances that Laura still lived in the same apartment? Max wanted to know. Pretty good, said Dale's father, her parents owned the building. Dale's mom became concerned, wanting to know if they were going to hurt their son. Thinking fast, Max told her no, all he wanted was his old truck, it had sentimental value. It belonged to his deceased brother who died in a drowning accident.

It was all a lie. Max didn't even have a brother, but the explanation seemed to placate Dale's parents. Dale's mom wrote down a street address and handed it to Max. It's not a real good neighborhood, she warned them. Max and Gina both graciously thanked Dale's parents, and they left the house. They discussed tactics on their way to the West Side apartment. This isn't going to work, Max told Gina as they passed by the building. Max's truck and their physical appearance would make them stand out, calling unwanted attention to themselves.

Max suggested they head out into the suburbs and find a hotel. They had been driving all day and they were exhausted. On the way, they passed a used car lot, giving Max an idea. He picked out an old beat-up Chevy and paid five hundred cash for it. When asked for his proof of insurance, he gave the salesman his insurance card from Georgia, saying that he would have the coverage transferred. They next stopped at a novelty store where they picked out a book of fake tattoos, bandanas, sunglasses, and a headbanger's wig.

At the hotel, they used the entire book of tattoos on each other's arms and necks. Max put on a flannel shirt and tied a black bandana around the long stringy black-haired wig to keep the hair out of his eyes. Gina wore tight-fitting jeans and a black tube top. She also tied a bandana around her head. They stood in front of the mirror admiring their disguises. They would look like any other street urchin couple that could be found in the rough-cut West Side neighborhood. Gina suggested that they make love wearing their disguises. Max thought it was a great idea.

Early the next morning, they headed straight for the West Side in the old Chevy. They circled the block a couple of times until a parking space became available. Finding the front door to the building locked, Max pick-gunned the locks, and soon they were standing in front of apartment F, all the way in the back of the building, furthest from the street. There were four locks on the apartment door. Max carefully pick-gunned all four locks as quietly as he could.

He grabbed the door handle and twisted it, pushing the front door open. It was completely dark inside. Max used a penlight to survey the room. On a table, there was one of the kilos, sliced open.

Bingo! On the couch was a half-naked woman in deep sleep. Max checked the rest of the apartment, it was empty. Max returned to the living room and turned on the overhead light just as Gina grabbed the sleeping woman by the hair and woke her up with a gun pointed right at her face.

"You must be Laura!" Gina said to the stunned woman, now half awake.

Gina sat on the woman while holding the gun in her face. Max put handcuffs around her wrist and ankles. Gina tied a ball gag around her head. Next, Gina placed an electric shock dog collar around the woman's neck. Fully awake now, the woman sat upright on the couch, clearly frightened out of her skull. It was Laura alright, but she looked nothing like the beautiful girl in the high school prom photo.

"Where's Dale?" Gina asked.

Laura mumbled something unintelligible, but the she couldn't speak with the ball gag.

"Wrong answer!" Gina pressed the switch on the dog collar remote, causing the woman to moan in pain.

"Now … let's try this again." Gina pulled the ball gag out of Laura's mouth. "Where is Dale?"

"He's out with his homies … they're all jacked up on coke!" Laura exclaimed.

"When's he coming back here?" Gina said as she held the gun up against the frightened woman's skull.

"I don't know … he has to come home and eat and sleep sometime, I guess?"

"Then we'll just have to wait for him." Max said as he pulled the wig off his head. It was getting too hot.

Gina placed the ball gag back in Laura's mouth, Max used the opportunity to search every square inch of the apartment. The only coke he found was the sliced open kilo. Max was getting more and more pissed off by the minute. This Dale Tomkins had caused him enough trouble already. He began taking his frustrations out on Dale's girlfriend. Pulling the gag from her mouth, he asked her where was the coke, where was his stolen truck? Laura said she didn't know exactly. Gina zapped her again.

Laura told them that Dale just appeared one day out of nowhere. He said he had ripped off some kingpin coke dealer and that they were going to be rich. When Dale found out that Laura had taken up with another man, Dale ambushed him in an alley and killed him. To the police, it was just another victim of gang violence that would go unsolved. Her live-in boyfriend was a deadbeat anyway. Dale promised her that he would make them rich. She believed him. She said she would do anything to be able to move out of the city, and Dale told her that after he sold enough coke, they could move anywhere they wanted to.

Max pulled up a chair and sat face-to-face with Laura. He told her that he was the kingpin dealer Dale had ripped off. Dale was so stupid, he probably stole the truck without knowing what was in it.

He'd been fired from his job and was just trying to get even with his former boss by stealing the only vehicle on his property that was in running condition. Once Dale discovered the coke, he ditched his pregnant common-law wife. Dale Tomkins was just an opportunistic piece of shit.

Laura admitted that she knew that already about Dale. Ever since he was released from prison the first time, he was never the same after that. He would always come back to her and she would always take him back, thinking that someday he would get his act together, but of course he never did. When he showed up with a truckload of dope, she figured this was her ticket out of this horrible city that she hated so much. Just like the abandoned pregnant common-law wife down in Georgia, Laura was just another victim of this opportunistic moron. Max felt compassion for her. He offered her a deal. If she cooperated with them, they would take her back to Georgia where she could start a new life. He would give her money to live on till she got on her feet. If she chose not to cooperate, well that would be something else entirely.

Of course, she would cooperate. She would do anything they wanted her to. Max looked into her eyes. He believed her. Gina was not necessarily happy about it, but she did feel bad for this woman. They removed the handcuffs and electric dog collar. They told her that when Dale did come home, Laura was to offer him sex and lead him to the back bedroom. Halfway there, Max and Gina would jump out of the bathroom and subdue him. So they waited.

A little before noon, someone was fumbling with the locks to the front door. The trap was set. Dale entered the apartment. Laura told him that she had missed him and grabbed him by the shirt and led him to the back bedroom. Just as Dale passed the bathroom door, Max struck him on the back of the head with the butt of his gun. On the floor of the hallway, Dale lay there semiconscious. Gina placed a stun gun on Dale's neck and stunned him into submission. Max cuffed him up, while Gina placed the electric dog collar around his neck. Max dragged him to the back bedroom.

"Do you know why I'm here?" Max asked Dale, who didn't answer.

Gina zapped him for about ten seconds while he winced in pain.

"Normally, I would shoot a cretin like you on sight, but I'm going to make an exception for you, Dale Mitchel Tomkins Jr. I want my truck, I want the coke that you stole, where is it?" Max asked Dale directly to his face.

"Am I going to have to use this again?" Gina said, holding the remote to the electric dog collar.

"Please no!" Dale begged. "The truck is in a garage in Lincoln Park! A buddy of mine lives there."

"Okay then," Max said to him. "You're going to take us there, or my fiancée here is going to do terrible things to you. Do you understand what I just said?"

Dale looked up at Laura. "Are you in on this?" he yelled at her.

Gina zapped him again for ten seconds.

"All right!" Dale gasped.

"Now, I'm going to remove these cuffs … and you will take us there! If you try anything, and I mean anything, Gina is going to shoot you in the nuts … you won't be the first man she's ever shot!"

"Um … by the way … your fake tattoos are disintegrating," Laura said to Max.

Max put on his headbanger's wig. "Girl, that is the very least of my concerns right now," Max told her.

Gina pulled a small revolver out of her purse and handed it to Laura who pointed at Dale. Once outside the building, the two women stood on either side of Dale, with their arms around his neck, and their guns pointed at his abdomen. To any passerby, Dale looked just like some lucky bastard with two dates. Gina got in the driver's side backseat of the Chevy. Max opened the door and pushed Dale inside the rear passenger-side seat. Laura sat up front with Max who began driving to Lincoln Park.

As it turned out, the address Dale gave was right down the street from his parents' house. Must be some childhood friend who still lived with his parents, thought Max. What a loser! Gina still had her gun on Dale and asked if anyone was home. Dale explained that all the vehicles normally parked in the driveway were gone. He said that his buddy lived there with his wife and had inherited the house from his parents who passed away years before.

Gina and Laura both held guns on Dale as Max went to the garage and attempted to open the rollup door. It wouldn't budge. Max went around the garage to a side door, it was also locked. Max used his gun to break a window in the side door. He reached inside and unlocked the deadbolt. He walked to the front of the garage and hit the electric garage door opener. Pulling open the camper shell window, he stuck his arm inside and lifted the canvas tarp. The coke was still there, well most of it was anyway. Walking around the truck, he saw that the passenger-side headlamp was smashed as was the entire passenger side.

Max was planning to drive it back to Georgia, and now he couldn't. It wasn't road-worthy. He walked back to the Chevy, opened the passenger-side door, and grabbed Dale by the dog collar.

Gina pressed the barrel of her gun directly at the base of Dale's skull. Max asked Dale where they could find a place to transfer the load. Nervously, Dale thought for a moment. He said there was an industrial park a few miles away from where they were right now. There they could find an abandoned warehouse to do the transfer. Max warned him that he better not be jerking him around. Max let go of the collar and Gina zapped Dale yet again.

Max handed the keys of the Chevy to Laura and told her to follow closely. Max pulled Dale out of the backseat while Gina followed them, sticking her gun in Dale's ribcage. Max threw Dale into the backseat of the old truck and Gina got in there with him. Max got in the driver's seat and found the ignition cylinder had been pulled out of the steering column with a slide hammer. Max found the wiring harness hanging out from under the steering column. He angrily asked Dale which wires would start the engine. Dale reached over the seat and pointed, instructing Max as to which two wires to connect and which two to touch together to engage the starter motor.

Gina zapped Dale again. Max drove the truck back to the hotel while Laura followed in the Chevy. On the way, they stopped by the dealership where Max bought the car. He handed the keys to the same salesman and told him he didn't want the car anymore. The salesman asked Max what about the money. Max told him to keep it, the title was in the glove box. Laura got in the front seat of the old truck with Max who now drove straight to the hotel they stayed in last night.

Now it was Max who held the gun on Dale, while Gina went inside to retrieve their belongings. She did so quickly and loaded the items into Max's brand-new truck and started the engine. She followed the old truck closely as Laura held her gun on Dale as he nervously spat out directions to the industrial park. Once they reached the industrial park, there were dozens and dozens of abandoned buildings covered with gang graffiti. Max didn't like this at all.

Finding a building with a large open rollup door, Max pulled inside. Gina backed the new truck right up to the rear of the old one. Max pulled one of the full-auto AKs out of the back of the new truck and chambered a round. He flipped off the safety and pointed it directly at Dale's head. Max told him to get moving quickly. Dale reached into the bed of the old truck and began tossing kilos into the new one. Max poked Dale with the barrel and told him to move faster. Gina zapped him again for good measure. Laura looked around nervously.

Nearly halfway through the transfer, there were the sounds of screeching tires and loud music. Two tricked-out low-riders pulled inside the building and began circling the two parked trucks, burning rubber as they did so. Gina pulled out the other AK and chambered a round, while Laura held her gun on Dale. This was exactly what Max had been afraid of all along. The two low-riders stopped on either side of the parked vehicles and began manipulating the hydraulics. After a minute, they both used the hydraulics to lower the vehicles to within centimeters off the ground. The doors opened and five armed men stepped out of each car.

Max and Gina leveled their weapons at the gangsters as they attempted to surround the two parked trucks. Max squeezed off a three-round burst into the ceiling with the AK, stopping the men in their tracks. It was now a standoff. Max and Gina had the advantage of superior firepower, they could have easily mowed down the intruders. But it occurred to Max that they were the intruders, this was gangster turf, and who was to say there weren't more gangbangers on the way behind these guys?

A scary-looking dude with an eyepatch stepped closer to Max who held the AK right at the man's chest. These damn gangbangers have some balls, thought Max. In a spit second, everyone in the building could be dead in a crossfire. It was deathly quiet, other than the sound of dripping water. Smoke from the burning tires still hung in the air. A wet spot appeared on the front of Laura's jeans, she was shaking, still holding the gun on Dale.

"What's up, homie?" the one-eyed man asked. He was obviously addressing Dale who stood there nervously with a kilo in each hand.

"Oh … nothing, Cyclops, just helping out some friends," Dale said.

It was a ghost from Dale's past, a rival gang member with a grudge.

"We all thought you were dead, homie."

"Naw … I just moved away for a while."

"Well … you should have stayed gone!" the man called Cyclops said and then spat on the ground.

"What do you guys want?" yelled Max at the one-eyed man.

"We just want what you guys are having!"

Max fired his AK from the shoulder sweeping back and forth, while Gina on the other side did the same. Some of the gangsters had managed to squeeze off a few rounds, but now they all lay about on the floor of the warehouse. Some of them were still moving. Max approached the survivors and dispatched each one with a shot to the head from his .40 caliber. Laura stood over one of the fallen men still moving and fired five shots into his head emptying her weapon. Max and Gina each loaded fresh magazines into their AKs. Dale lay on the ground directly between the two trucks with half his head blown off.

Other than ringing eardrums, Laura, Gina, and Max were unscathed. Laura began kicking Dale's lifeless body until Max pulled her back. Right now, they needed to finish the transfer and get the fuck up out of here. Max pulled Dale's body out from between the two trucks, and the three survivors worked quickly. Max told Gina to get behind the wheel and pull out of the building onto the street. He chambered a round and emptied the weapon before one of the bullets found its mark and struck the fuel tank of his old truck, causing it to explode. It did so with such force that it flipped the old truck upside down.

Max now climbed in the driver's seat and the three survivors sped off. Laura, who knew the area somewhat, shouted directions, and after a few wrong turns, they were on the interstate headed south. The three said not a word until they stopped for fuel. Max recommended that they keep on driving to Louisville, Kentucky, before they stopped to get a room for the night. The more distance they put between themselves and the crime scene, the better off they would be.

They got a room for the night and Max even offered to get Laura her own room but she declined, saying she didn't want to be alone after what had happened. Max told the girls not to leave the room, he was going out for food and drinks. Gina and Laura started to worry after forty-five minutes of Max being gone. What would they do if something happened to him? But their fears soon evaporated when Max came through the door with bags of take-out, six packs of beer, and bottles of wine and liquor.

They were all so wired by the day's events that they had all forgotten how hungry and thirsty they were. They devoured the food and started in on the beer, wine and liquor. It wasn't long before all three were crazy drunk and stoned. Max put on a show for the girls by tying one of Gina's black bras around his head, imitating an eyepatch, and doing his best impression of the gangster called Cyclops. The two girls rolled on the bed, doubled up with laughter.

They finally passed out for the night and upon wakening realized they had slept past checkout time. No problem, Max went to the hotel office and paid for another night. He went out for more food and alcohol, and they repeated the process all over again. After all they had been through, Max felt as though they could use the opportunity to unwind and get over the experience they had been through in Chicago.

Gina, ever the wild one, pulled Laura into the bathroom. Ten minutes later, both women came out and startled Max. They were both completely naked and covered head to toe in baby oil. Gina teased Max by saying there was no way they were going to have sex with him, unless he made them. Max stripped down and wrestled with the two oily, slippery women, but was never able to pin either one. Instead, they wound up pinning him. Max was just fine with that. Just like their deceased friend Ray Bangor, Max and Gina were insatiable sex addicts.

But the next morning, Max was all business trying to get the girls to hurry so they could be on the road. They did manage to get an early start, and by early that evening, they were at Max and Gina's house. Max grilled up some steaks and seafood and they had a banquet. They offered Laura the guest room formerly occupied by Esmeralda. Laura said the room gave her the creeps and opted to sleep on the sofa bed in the living room. Gina asked her why the room made her feel uncomfortable.

Laura told her she didn't know why, it just did.

Max called his answering service. There was a message from the Illinois State Police informing him that a vehicle registered to him was found at a crime scene in a deserted warehouse in Chicago. He was urged to contact them and give the case number they had assigned. Max called and spoke with an investigator. He told the officer that they had just returned from vacation and found the truck had been stolen. The investigator told Max the vehicle was a total loss and was being processed for evidence. Max informed the investigator that it was an older vehicle and that he only had the minimal liability insurance required. The investigator thanked Max for the information he had provided.

The following day, Max made it his number one priority to find a safe location to stash the coke. He checked the newspaper and found a house for rent only fifteen minutes from his house. If this worked out, it would be perfect. He contacted the owner and said he was interested in renting the property for at least a year, possibly longer. Later, he met the owner and checked out the small house. It would be the perfect place for Laura to live and a perfect place to stash the coke.

Max invited Laura to take a ride with him. He took her to a used car dealership and let her pick out a car. She chose a late model foreign sports car in great condition. She was so happy that Max was doing this for her. Next, she followed Max to the rental house. He told her this was her new home. Again, she could not get over her good fortune and gave Max a big hug. He handed her five thousand dollars and told her to start looking for a job, he would take care of the rent for at least a year.

Laura told him that finding a job might be a challenge for her, she had never had one, and she didn't have any job skills. Max told her not to worry about that, just enjoy her new lifestyle. That night, Max and Gina returned to the rental house and, together along with Laura's help, stashed the coke inside the basement of the house. They counted three hundred ninety-five kilos remaining. Only four could not be accounted for. Max pulled Laura aside and told her that her new job was to guard the coke, he would pay her two hundred dollars a week.

Gina was not at all pleased with the new arrangement, but Max explained that they had just solved two problems at once. It was just the cost of doing business, he explained. He next contacted Gina's brother in LA and told him to send a next-day letter outlining what he thought he would need in the near future, as well as a shipping address. The next day, Max received a letter informing him that Martin wanted ten kilos sent to the address printed in the upper right corner of the letter. Max showed the letter to Gina, and she told him that was Martin's home address.

Max sure hoped that Martin knew what he was doing. Within a few days, Max received an overnight package that contained one hundred fifty thousand dollars, all in hundreds. Apparently, Martin did know what he was doing. Max gave Gina the good news, and they decided to celebrate with dinner in downtown Savannah. They were exuberant. Everything was going well. Their assets were hidden, and their new customer on the West Coast was paying one and a half times the asking price. Max and Gina could not believe their success so far.

Then it came by way of a letter. Max opened the envelope and felt a lump in his throat. His stomach felt as though it had been twisted into a knot. It was that which he feared most of all. He examined the plain white envelope and saw that it was postmarked in Savannah. Just when he felt everything was going along fine, this single piece of paper with one single sentence written on it turned his world upside down. He handed it to Gina for her to see for herself.

"I KNOW YOUR SECRET!" was all it said.

They sat at the kitchen table. A thousand thoughts raced through Max's mind as he contemplated who the sender might be. Who out there in the world knew his last name, his home address, and his secret? A list of possible suspects began to emerge. It could be almost anyone he had been in contact with over the last three months. He began to narrow down the possibilities.

"It's Marcella De Silva!" Gina said.

How could Gina be so certain? Gina began to explain that Marcella knew exactly where they lived and what they were doing. She had disappeared off the radar just prior to Ray's suicide. Gina was convinced that Marcella was going to try and shake them down for money, probably a lot of money. They had to find her before she could do any real damage. Gina thought that Marcella would be reluctant to report their illegal activities to the authorities. If she did, she wouldn't stand to gain anything. This was a game to her, and it was only just beginning.

The more Max thought about it, the more convinced he was that Gina was right. Ray had confided to him that Marcella initially threatened to call the authorities after she found the coke in Ray's villa. Ray had somehow managed to buy her off. But then there were the problems with her underworld associates, all of whom were dead right now as far as Max knew. He came to the conclusion that it only could be Marcella who sent the letter. But how would they go about finding her?

They drove to Hilton Head Island. They found a private investigator there who would take their case. His fee was exorbitant, but he told them he was extremely good at what he did and never had a dissatisfied client. Max and Gina were willing to bet that he said that very same thing to all his prospective clients. The investigator wanted twenty-five hundred up front, saying he would make this case a priority. He'd be in touch.

This was going to be a lot harder than they thought. Who knew where Marcella was right now? She might not even be living in Hilton Head Island anymore. But the letter was postmarked in Savannah, so they figured she had to be in the area somewhere. If this private investigator was half as good as he said he was, he should be able to find her no problem. They would just have to sit back and wait.

Max and Gina knew something was not right as soon as they pulled in the driveway. Both Max's dogs were dead in the front yard of gunshot wounds to the head. The basement door had been kicked in, and the locked storage closet that formerly held the coke had also been kicked in. It had contained two of the assault rifles taken off the *Winsor2.* They were both missing, as was a crate which contained extra magazines, also taken off the *Winsor2.*

Max's collection of handguns were still locked inside a safe, but every other firearm that wasn't secured was missing. The house had been ransacked. Max and Gina both knew what the intruders were looking for, but they weren't going to find it here. They both felt violated and vulnerable. What bothered them most was the fact that whoever was responsible knew that they wouldn't be home at the time, or would they have? Either scenario was frightening.

Against his creed, he reluctantly called the sheriff's office to report the crime. He handed one of the young deputies a list of all the weapons that he knew were stolen, minus the AKs. The deputy asked him, was it not he who had his truck stolen recently. Max admitted that he was. The deputy asked him if he had any idea of who might have broken into his house, and if it was in any way related to the stolen vehicle. Max told the deputy he did not think the crimes were related, and as to who was responsible for the break-in, Max lied and said he didn't have any idea. Max wanted to find who it was before the police did.

They took fingerprints from Max and Gina and dusted the crime scene for prints that might identify the culprits. They took pictures and snooped around everywhere on the property. They even took both of Max's dead dogs in the hopes of recovering ballistic evidence. When the police did finally leave, Max and Gina felt even more violated than they did before. One thing did stand out in Max's mind though. There was no way Marcella herself had participated in this crime. She probably had someone else do it for her.

With no dogs to guard the property at night, Max devised a primitive but effective way of detecting anyone who might attempt to enter the property at night. He strung a monofilament fishing line across the front of his property and attached it to empty metal garbage cans. Tomorrow, he would look into more sophisticated home security measures. That night both he and Gina slept with guns under their pillows. But they didn't really sleep well at all. About 1:00 a.m., they were awakened by the sound of clanking metal. Max grabbed his gun and flashlight and went outside to confront the intruders. There was no vehicle, and no one in sight. He scanned the entire property with the powerful flashlight beam and saw iridescent eyeballs staring back at him from the backyard. It was a deer. They were definitely going to need a better security system. He found Gina waiting for him in the house with her own gun at the ready. False alarm, he told her.

The next day, Max hired a security systems specialist to evaluate and design a security system that would minimize false alarms and suit their needs more appropriately. It would include infrared cameras and an alarm system for the house with remote monitoring. Max also had the specialist do the same for the rental house. When he asked the specialist how much all this was going to cost, he told Max he'd better break out the gold card. A lot of money had been spent so far protecting the coke, but Max knew that their early retirement scheme was not going to protect itself.

A call from the private investigator gave them very bad news indeed. The woman they were searching for did not exist. How could this be? Max wanted to know. The investigator told him that Marcella De Silva was an alias. It was a false identity created using the name of a woman who had been killed in a car accident over ten years ago. The person they were looking for probably had a criminal record they were trying to hide. The investigator asked them if they had a picture of the woman. They did not. The investigator said he would continue to work the case, but it would require more money. Max told him no thanks, he had already spent enough on the useless information the investigator had provided so far.

Gina berated Max when she was told of the investigator's findings. She told Max that guy reminded her of a beady-eyed snake. She didn't say anything initially because she wanted to believe this guy was going to help them. But her primary instincts had been correct all along. She cursed herself for not speaking up earlier. She knew that Max was trying his best to figure this all out, he just needed to try a little harder. Fed up with Gina's chastising, Max got into his truck and decided to take a ride to clear his mind. He decided he would check on Laura, see how she was doing. About halfway to her house, he stopped at a gas station. As he pulled in, there were six full patch members of the Ingrate Order MC fueling their bikes. What in the hell were these guys doing? What were they doing out of jail, and why were they out here on the very same road that he lived on? Max had been to their compound in South Carolina, and here they were out here in Georgia, probably on some other club's turf. Not only that, they were heading north on the same road that would take them right by his house.

His first instinct was to follow them out of the gas station, but he was dangerously low on fuel. The bikers pulled out onto the main road, just as Max pulled up to the fuel pump. Impatiently, he waited for the old pump to finish clicking off the dollars and cents. It seemed to take forever. He paid for the fuel and tore out of the gas station heading north. He pulled into his driveway and ran into the house, only to find Gina cleaning the house with the stereo turned up.

He asked Gina if she had heard any bikes rumble past their house. How could she, she was listening to her favorite music. Max advised her to use more caution, he'd just seen six members of the Ingrate Order MC headed their way. Gina told him not to worry so much, patting the nine millimeter she wore on her hip. From now on, she was to keep the house locked and the alarm engaged at all times. Max told her to get ready, they needed to take a ride. She asked where to. He told her just do it, it was important.

Riding in the passenger seat with her feet propped up on the dash, Gina asked Max once again where they were headed. They were going to Laura's house to see if she was all right, then they were going to Charleston. At Laura's house, they found her alone, sitting on the couch, drinking beer, smoking weed, and snorting coke, all while watching her favorite soap operas. At least she was good at multitasking. Max knew that Laura already had a gun, but he gave her another semiauto with a fourteen-shot magazine and told her to be vigilant. She promised him that she would, though she didn't quite know what the word "vigilant" meant.

Gina wanted to know why they were going all the way to Charleston. Max told her that of the seven full-auto AK-47s they took off the *Winsor2*, there were still three remaining, hidden aboard *The REEL OPPORTUNITY.* He reminded her that in addition to the two stolen from their basement, two had been confiscated by the authorities after Ray's suicide. They would need superior firepower if things went south. Even a bulletproof vest wouldn't stand up to an AK-47.

When they finally reached Charleston, Gina said she was hungry. Max told her they would eat later, right now they needed to get those weapons off his boat. At the marina, they found *The REEL OPPORTUNITY* just as they had left her. Max went aboard and retrieved two of the full-auto weapons, as well as extra magazines and ammo. Max wrapped up the heavy assault rifles in a blanket and carried them back to his truck. Now they could eat dinner.

Back on the road, Max decided to take a detour and drive past the old Ingrate Order MC compound. Just as he suspected, they were back in business. The place was lit up like a baseball field. A tractor trailer was pulling out of the complex just as they were driving past. Satisfied now that his original suspicions were confirmed, they headed back to Georgia. On the long drive home, Max and Gina discussed their next course of action.

They needed a way to infiltrate the Ingrate Order MC. Max could not do it himself. He called an old buddy he used to work with named Buster who had moved out of the area in search of better employment opportunities. Buster was an expert welder and had taken a job in Jacksonville. He had just been fired for getting into an altercation with another employee and was in the process of looking for another job. Knowing that Buster loved motorcycles, Max asked him if he still rode a hog. Buster replied that of course he did.

Max explained that he had an opening available. It was part time, but it paid well. How about ten thousand dollars a month? Buster didn't need any more convincing than that. Max instructed him to bring his bike and/or bikes to Max's house in Georgia. Buster said he would load up and be at Max's house tomorrow sometime. Max couldn't wait to see his old friend. He would be perfect for what Max had in mind. Buster was rough-cut, and he could hold his own in a fight. That was precisely the kind of individual they were looking for.

After hanging up with Buster, Max called Laura. Would she mind sharing her house with a friend of his for a while? Laura's first question was, "What does this guy look like, is he handsome?" Max told her he couldn't look at another man and decide whether or not he was handsome, she would have to do that herself. Now, would she be willing to do this favor for him? Laura said she would have to meet this guy first, then decide. Whatever, thought Max. If Laura didn't feel comfortable with Buster around, he had a backup plan. But Gina wouldn't like it. She didn't like Buster at all.

Buster showed up the next day in his truck, which looked like a life-sized Tonka Toy. On a trailer, he had two beautiful custom bikes. It had taken him a couple of years to build them himself from the ground up. They were his prized possessions, other than his monster truck. Gina wouldn't even come outside to say hello, so Max and Buster sat at the picnic table. Over cold beers, Max laid out his proposition.

Leaving out sensitive details, Max explained to Buster that he was having some issues with a motorcycle club over in South Carolina. The club had been busted a while back, but now they seemed to be in the process of reforming. They were suspected of stealing firearms from Max's house, including two Chinese-made full-auto AK-47s. He needed Buster to infiltrate the club as a prospect, find out what they were up to, and report his findings back to Max. For his services, Max would pay him two thousand five hundred a week.

Max placed twenty-five one-hundred-dollar bills on the picnic table. Buster looked at the money and looked back up at Max. He asked if Max was still with Gina. Max told Buster that he was. Buster said he would need a place to stay. Max told him he had a place lined up for him, but he would have to share it with a female roommate, but only if she agreed. Buster asked what does this female look like. Max replied that he would fuck her, leaving out the part about having already done so.

Laura answered her door, and Max barely recognized her. She had fixed up her hair, applied just the right amount of makeup, and wore a conservative but tight-fitting outfit. She looked absolutely nothing like the woman they had brought back from Chicago. Laura was pale as a ghost when Max first saw her, now she was tanned from the Georgia sun, and she looked hot as hell. She brushed her hair back from her eyes with her hand.

"You must be Buster," she said.

"And you must be Laura," answered Buster.

Max was certain this was going to work out just fine. He excused himself and made the short drive back to his house. Gina was waiting and demanded to know how long Buster was going to be around. Max asked her why she hated Buster so much. Gina said that nobody had to tell her she didn't like chicken livers, she just didn't like them. The same was the case with Buster. Max told her that was a really fucked-up reason to not like somebody. Did Buster ever do anything to her? She said no, of course not. She just didn't like the dude.

The next morning, Max showed up at Laura's house. It was early, and she answered the door wearing nothing but a bra and panties. It was nothing Max hadn't seen before, of course, recalling their hotel stay in Louisville. Max told her to please tell Buster to get ready and meet him outside. Well, it didn't take those two very long to get acquainted, Max thought, as Buster left the house wearing his riding leathers and black leather vest. They had a long ride, and Max was looking forward to it.

Buster lent Max one of his prized custom bikes and asked Max if he remembered how to ride one. Max said it had been quite a while, but he would be fine. Buster told him that if he laid it down, he would kill him. Buster said he was only kidding, but just in case Max did lay it down, don't. They kick-started the bikes and pulled out of Laura's driveway onto the main road. Max was impressed with Buster's creation and how it handled. It looked and sounded good also. About halfway to their destination, they stopped at a roadside country diner for a bite.

The two men sat across from one another in a booth, well away from the other patrons. They didn't want anyone hearing what Max was about to say. A pretty country girl took their orders and Max got right to the point. Once Buster was inside the compound, he was to introduce himself and ask if he could talk to Wolf Zeigler. When told that Wolf was no longer alive, he was to bow his head in respect and say that Wolf had once asked him if he was interested in prospecting for the Ingrate Order.

About how long ago would that be? Buster wanted to know. "Just tell them three or four months ago, but you had to respectfully decline saying you had a job offer in Florida. The job just didn't work out."

Max went on to say that once Buster was inside, it was totally up to him to walk the walk and talk the talk. Buster assured Max that he had this wrapped up. Also, he thanked Max for introducing him to Laura. She was really cool. Max told him he was welcome.

As they approached the compound, they got behind a tractor trailer that Max was sure belonged to Zeigler Trucking. Buster followed the tractor trailer into the compound and Max continued straight past the entrance, heading back to Georgia. Buster was now on his own, but Max had complete and total faith in his friend. Buster seemed to relish the idea of joining the Ingrate Order, he'd heard they were a bunch of bad-assess that didn't take any shit.

Riding back to Georgia, Max could see the appeal of the biker lifestyle. He personally wasn't cut out for it, but he could see why others were. Pulling into his own driveway, he was met by an angry Gina, armed with one of the AK-47s, thinking he was somebody else up to no good. She lowered the weapon upon realizing it was her man. She taunted him by saying, "So you think you're some kind of bad-ass biker dude now, huh?" Max felt empowered after the long ride and told her yes, yes, he was some kind of bad-ass biker. He grabbed the assault rifle from her and leaned it against a tree. He grabbed her by the arms, spun her around, pulled down her shorts, and bent her over the picnic table.

"Who's your biker daddy now, bitch?"

It was all in good fun, right up until Max's neighbor Rob pulled into the driveway.

"He's not hurting you … is he?" Rob asked Gina, genuinely concerned.

"Not really," Gina replied, pulling up her shorts, going in the house.

Max told Rob that he just ruined a very romantic moment, he really should have called first so Max would have known not to answer. Clearly embarrassed, Rob apologized. He said that he just stopped by on his way home, wanting to know if Max knew anyone looking for a job. Max shook his head no. Rob asked Max if he ever found his old truck. Max told him that the Illinois State Police called and informed him that the truck was completely destroyed. It was found at a crime scene, and Rob's former disgruntled employee, Dale Mitchell Tomkins, had been driving it. Rob apologized again saying that he always knew Tomkins was a bad egg. Max excused himself saying that he had to finish pounding his girlfriend. Rob apologized again.

On the kitchen table, Max found today's mail. Flipping through it, he found another envelope with no return address. The suspense was killing him. He couldn't wait to see what his pen pal tormenter had to say this time. Gina stood by and watched him fumble with the envelope as he tried to open it with his thumb. She teased him by saying that the sender had neglected to send opening instructions, how rude. "FIRST PAYMENT DO ON NOVEMBER FIRST FURTHER INSTRUCTIONS TO FOLLOW," the letter read.

That was a week from tomorrow. He handed the letter to Gina, who read it and giggled. "Now you're really going to get it!" he teased, grabbing her by the hair and bending her over the kitchen table.

Two days later, Buster showed up at Max's house as planned. Max couldn't wait to hear his report. Even Gina stuck around, just to hear what Buster had to say. The first thing he did was to show Max and Gina the patch on his vest which read PROSPECT. Oh, he was proud of it, all right. Gina giggled and told Buster that it was spelled wrong. He actually took off the vest to see for himself as Gina laughed hysterically.

Buster was not amused, but he went on with his story. He said that after he introduced himself, a full patch member invited him into the clubhouse for a beer. As soon as he stepped inside, some dude stuck a gun in his face while two biker chicks stripped his clothes off checking to see if he was wearing a wire. Max told Buster he forgot to mention that might happen. Buster looked at Max, but continued with his story. They gave his clothes back and invited him to have a seat at the bar.

Taking a seat, Buster said the bartender was shooting up between her toes. That must be Janie, Max thought, not wanting to mess up her tattoos with track marks. After a few beers and several shots of whiskey, one of the full patch members asked him if he could "bounce." Not sure what the dude was asking him to do, the patch member pointed to some dude, sitting on a barstool, passed out face-down on the bar. Buster said he grabbed the dude who immediately regained consciousness, and they started going at it. After beating the guy senseless, Buster described how he dragged the dude out of the clubhouse and left the guy facedown in the dust.

When he came back inside, the same full patch member said, "Not that guy … that guy over there!"

Buster said he was now looking at some guy that must have weighed three hundred pounds. When he started walking toward the guy, the original patch member stopped him, and everyone in the whole clubhouse started laughing and pounding their beers on the bar and tables. Then, the same guy handed him a mop and a bucket and told him to clean up all the spilled beer. He wasn't kidding about that. Buster said it took him an hour to clean the place up.

After finishing his janitorial duties, they invited him back to the bar and they all got shit-faced drunk. Buster said that he woke up on the floor of the clubhouse the next morning and found that someone, probably one of the biker chicks, was kind enough to cover him with a dirty tablecloth while he slept.

The same patch member who started all the shit in the first place introduced himself as Dick and invited Buster to sit down and join him for a bowl of crunchy oat cereal and milk. Buster wasn't hungry, but he ate it anyway.

Buster said they spent the rest of the day riding through the South Carolina countryside. Max asked Buster how many full patch members were there on the riding event? Buster said only about fifteen. Max asked if there was anyone named Ace or Buzz. Buster said that no, he didn't meet anyone by those names, and he had met them all. Max asked him what they did after the ride. Buster said they went back to the clubhouse and got drunk and stoned all over again. Buster added that there was plenty of coke going around.

The next day, Buster told Dick that he needed to go see his woman, she was probably worried about him. Dick told him to come on back after he got some. Buster said he got on his bike and went straight to Laura's house, then he came here. Buster said it was all good fun with these guys. He couldn't believe Max was paying him to do this. Gina giggled, said that Buster was an idiot, and left the room. Buster asked Max why Gina disliked him so much. Max told him he was still trying to figure that out himself. Buster returned to Laura's house for the night, planning to go back to the Ingrate Order compound the following day.

Early the next morning, Max found a bright yellow thirty-gallon steel drum in the middle of his driveway out by the road. He approached it with extreme caution and found that the lid had been removed and was lying beside it. He went back in the house and retrieved a handheld mirror. Holding the mirror at arm's length, he tilted it so that he could see down into the barrel. It appeared to be empty, except for a plain white envelope. Kicking the drum on its side, he reached in and removed the envelope carefully. Inside was a letter.

"LOAD THIS WITH ONE MILLION SEAL IT UP WATER TIGHT DROP IT AT BASE OF R7 TOWER ON SOUTH LEG YOU HAVE TWENTY-FOUR HOURS."

Whoever wrote this knew that Max knew that the R7 Navy Tower was about ten miles off the coast of Hilton Head Island. It was an unmanned platform that stood in about eighty feet of water. It was a popular fishing spot. Max didn't really know its true purpose, but he had heard that it might be used for climate and weather observation. He'd also heard that it might be used for petroleum extraction. Max picked up the empty barrel and brought it into his backyard. He had a big surprise for the would-be extortionist.

He loaded the drum with neatly stacked common bricks to within about one inch of the rim. On top of the bricks, he placed a specially modified rat trap. Using a flint and steel fire starter's kit he had since he was a Boy Scout, he wired the flint to the base of the trap and the steel to the killing spring. He next filled the drum about three quarters full of gasoline mixed with detergent. Very carefully, he cocked the killing spring, holding it backward with his fingers as he placed the steel lid on top and went around the perimeter with a rubber hammer, tapping the protruding tabs on the lid, thus sealing the drum water tight. At least he hoped it was water tight, or it would mess up a perfectly good petroleum bomb.

There was no time for him to go to Charleston and motor his sport fisher down the coast. He would have to use *The REEL BITCH* to deliver the bomb. He just hoped the seas were calm. *The REEL BITCH* was not designed for the open ocean. He asked Gina to help him load the drum into the stern of *The REEL BITCH*. When Gina asked what he was planning to do, he explained that he was delivering a gasoline bomb to the would-be extortionist. Gina was a sport and said she wanted to go with him. He told her absolutely no, it was too dangerous. She said she was coming anyway.

They drove to Hilton Head Island and launched *The REEL BITCH* at a public boat ramp, just as it began to rain. As long as there wasn't any lightning, they would be just fine. It wound up taking them two hours to reach the R7 Tower from the landing. When they did reach the R7 Tower, the rain had slacked off, and there were no other vessels in sight. Max picked a spot between two of the three legs and tilted the barrel over the stern into the sea. The would-be extortionist wanted the barrel on the south side of the tower to make it easier for a diver to find, Max figured.

When they got back home, Max told Gina to pack up all her necessities; they were spending the night at Laura's house. When the truck couldn't hold any more, they tossed the remaining items into *The REEL BITCH*. At Laura's house, they had a party. By midnight they were all asleep. They were awakened by the ringing telephone at 7:00 a.m. It was Amy, Max and Gina's neighbor. She was all panicky and out of breath. She said it sounded like a war zone across the street from her house and now there were a zillion cops out in front of Max and Gina's house. Gina, Laura, and Max piled into the truck and headed that way.

Amy wasn't kidding about the number of cops. It seemed like every cop in Georgia was there. Max and Gina's house looked like Swiss cheese. There were hundreds and hundreds of bullet holes in the front of the house facing the main road. Amy was still in her nightgown standing at the end of her driveway. She was telling the cops she heard automatic weapons fire that seemed to go on and on. Max was willing to bet that stolen AK-47s had been used. Just as they were getting out of the truck, Max was approached by a young sheriff's deputy.

"You're the guy who had his truck stolen a couple weeks ago!" said the rookie deputy.

"Yep … that would be me," Max said

"And you're the same guy who had his house broken into and ransacked?"

"Yep!"

"And now you're the same guy who just happened to not be home while his house was all shot up?" the deputy asked Max sarcastically.

"I guess there's someone out there that doesn't like me," Max said sincerely.

"You mind telling me where you just happened to be last night?"

Max directed the deputy's attention to Gina and Laura, both girls didn't even bother getting dressed, both were wearing long T-shirts and were naked from the waist down.

"Uh … I was at a sex party last night," Max said, pointing at the girls.

Gina was bent over petting one of Amy's dogs, flashing a little camel toe at the young deputy.

"And you don't have any idea who did this?" the deputy said, pointing to Max's destroyed house.

"Yeah … I think I do … I think it might be a jealous ex-boyfriend."

"Really?"

"Yup!"

The cops separated the two girls and began interrogating them individually.

"And how many boyfriends have you had, young lady?" asked one deputy.

"I dunno … maybe seventy-two," Gina said.

"How many boyfriends have you had, miss?" another deputy asked Laura.

"I'm guessing right around fifty," said Laura.

"How many women have you had relationships with?" a veteran sheriff's deputy asked Max.

"That would be one hundred and three … I mean one hundred and four counting the one over there in the light blue T-shirt," Max said, pointing at Laura.

A Georgia State Police sergeant could be heard discussing the case with the sheriff's department.

Maybe they were dealing with sex-crazed young adults who happened to piss off the wrong guy. But every law enforcement officer present knew there was much more to this than these folks were letting on. All three were taken in for questioning and interrogated in separate rooms. The only one out of the three who seemed to have her story confused was Laura. But at least she was smart enough to give the cops her sister's name and birthdate. Laura and her sister were a year apart and could have been mistaken for twins. Her sister had a squeaky clean record and lived in Wyoming. In the end, they were all released from questioning.

The next day the newspaper ran the following story under the following headline:

COAST GUARD FINDS BURNING VESSEL OFF HILTON HEAD; INVESTIGATION UNDER WAY

Hilton Head Island: A Coast Guard helicopter patrolling the coast off Hilton Head reported a vessel fully engulfed in flames early Saturday morning. The vessel was approximately one mile south east of the Navy Tower R7 when spotted. Authorities are investigating the cause of the fire which nearly burned the vessel to the water line. A search for survivors is under way …

Max showed the article to Gina who gasped when she read it. Other than Max, she was the only other person on the entire planet who knew what had happened. On this early Sunday morning, Max now sat at Laura's kitchen table on the phone with Rob of Rob's Tree Service. Max was asking Rob about leasing a portion of his seven-acre property to accommodate a single wide. Rob must have been okay with that, as Max went on about getting the permits.

Buster showed up at Laura's house around 10:30 a.m. and told Max he had just come from Max's house and could not believe what he had seen. Max immediately began to press Buster for information regarding the Ingrate Order MC. Buster told Max that Friday night the club president, Dick, had assigned him and a full patch member named Napoleon to stand guard duty at the compound when about fifteen full patch members left the compound in automobiles dressed in civilian clothes.

Knowing better than to ask questions, Buster stood at attention as club president, Dick, handed him a semiauto combat shotgun and instructed him along with his sergeant at arms Napoleon to guard the compound and the women. They were instructed to block the compound gate with a tractor trailer. When the passenger vehicles returned about noon on Saturday, there were only twelve full patch members. They all headed for the clubhouse and started drinking. There was a lot of shouting and swearing, and there was even a fist-fight between two of the hardcore members which had to be broken up, or they would have probably killed each other.

When it got dark, this crazy woman with a killer body came into the clubhouse wearing a gun belt with twin holsters. She pulled twin .44 magnums with six-inch barrels and began shouting and cursing while firing the guns into the clubhouse ceiling, waking up every passed-out drunk in the process. Everyone got on their feet and ran out of the clubhouse fearing for their lives as the crazy woman reloaded both weapons with speed loaders and went outside after them. Buster said he looked outside a window and saw dudes scrambling to get on their bikes and take off as she started firing again, this time right over their heads. Max asked Buster if this woman had long, straight black hair, a thick Spanish accent, big tits and a perfect heart shaped ass. Buster shook his head no, saying she had short blond hair. But she did have an accent and a killer body. Max had one more question for Buster. Did she have a dragon tattoo on her arm? Buster said yes, she did. Max looked at Gina. That's her! Gina rolled her eyes and said it sounds like Marcella might have developed a psychotic disorder since the last time they saw her.

Buster was instructed to get back out there, gather as much intelligence as possible, and report back to Laura's house in a couple of days. Max asked if Buster felt that his own personal safety was in jeopardy? Buster said no, he didn't think so. Everyone had been real cool with him. But everyone seemed to be at odds with each other since Saturday. Max told Buster that if he had the least bit suspicion that he was in danger, he needed to get the hell out of there as quickly as possible.

Buster climbed on his bike and sped out onto the main road. Max wondered what the next course of action should be. Now he knew for sure that Marcella was using the Ingrate Order in furtherance of financial gain. How was she able to do this? he wondered to himself. The more he thought about it, the more convinced he was that he knew the answer. Of course, he wasn't one hundred percent sure he was right about this, he was just guessing.

When Ray first met Marcella, she must have found out that he was dealing coke, so she probably tried to shake him down for money. Not being liquid, Ray probably offered her coke in exchange for her keeping her mouth shut. Marcella was a very social person and knowing a lot of people, probably did some street-level sales at nightclubs on Hilton Head Island and Savannah. Somehow, some of the coke wound up in the hands of Diego Ortiz who analyzed it and determined it to be the same coke that was destined for New York City aboard the *Winsor2*.

When Ortiz set up the one-hundred-kilo deal, he was probing Ray. Ortiz was trying to recover a portion of the coke and probably would have tortured them all into revealing the whereabouts of the remaining five hundred kilos. Only Ortiz severely underestimated Ray's hair trigger temper once Ray figured out Ortiz was going to short them a half million. After failed assassination attempts on Ray and Marcella, Ray figured out a way to assassinate the man calling the shots in New York City, Orlando Rodrigues.

At any rate, Marcella pocketed a lot of money from the wholesale deals as well as the street-level deals. Marcella had been to the Ingrate Order MC and probably met most of the players. When the Ingrate Order MC was busted, Marcella was able to use this money to bail out some of the members charged with lesser offenses. With false identity and phony real estate titles, the authorities would have no way of tracking her when these guys failed to show up for trial.

Marcella was now using the Ingrate Order to terrorize and extort himself and Gina. There was no doubt in Max's mind now that Marcella wanted all the coke and all the money. What she had not counted on was Gina's and Max's viciousness when it came to protecting their ill-gotten gains. Max was planning on killing Marcella, or whoever the fuck she was, and killing any member of the Ingrate Order MC who tried to cause problems. They had just killed three at one time with the petrol bomb at the R7 Tower.

Now Marcella and the Ingrate Order MC were at a distinct disadvantage. Not only did they have a well-placed spy in their midst, they had no way of finding him or Gina or Laura, for that matter. Max decided that it was time to fuck with Marcella and the Ingrate

Order MC big-time. When it was all said and done, Max hoped that Marcella and her boys deeply regretted not only fucking with him and his bride-to-be, but ever being born as well.

But there were other matters at stake. Max purchased a single-wide trailer and had it placed all the way in the back corner of Rob's property. All they were waiting for now were the well drillers and the septic tank installation. Rob could not have been more pleased. He was happy there was another dwelling on the property that would serve to deter thieves and trespassers. Also, he knew that once Max and Gina moved out, he could rent the place to another family. On top of all that, Max was paying to lease the land on a monthly basis, with one year's rent paid in advance. Rob had strong suspicions about Max and Gina and their finances, but he was not about to kill the golden goose.

Max even paid a specialty contractor to design and build an oversized subterranean tornado shelter complete with running water, electricity, and an impenetrable steel door. The structure even had an escape tunnel which ran into the woods. The contractor was a little suspicious of the fact that this emergency shelter cost more than the trailer. Max told the contractor that he was a "prepper" planning for the worst.

Then came the all-important task of digging up the two-dozen, five-gallon buckets loaded with cash and transporting them to the shelter. It was tiresome, backbreaking work, but Gina was there to help every step of the way. After registering his new address with the post office under an alias, they were ready to move in. Also, they were ready to resume cocaine shipments to Gina's brother on the West Coast. To any visitor to Rob's property, the single wide looked like it belonged to a moderately low-income family. And that's precisely the impression Max wanted people to have.

They had a party to celebrate their new residence, the very same day Max had a contractor demolish his old shot-up house. He had just sold the land for cash and spared no expense at the outdoor party, which included a live band. In attendance were Rob, Laura, Amy, and her husband who had just finished his tour of duty, and Peggy, the common-law widow of the late Dale Tomkins, and her new baby girl. Max even invited several of the local sheriff's deputies and their wives. Later even Buster showed up for his biweekly report of the goings-on with the Ingrate Order MC. It was a rockin' good time for all who attended.

Inside the trailer, Max and Buster sat down, and over numerous beers, Buster related his latest findings. The Ingrate Order was now down to eleven full patch members. Three were in fact killed in a mysterious boat explosion off Hilton Head Island. The club president, Dick, got into a heated argument with Marcella and wound up getting his head blown off, if for no other reason than he was a smart-ass. The club vice president, a dude named Spider, was now president. Napoleon had been promoted to vice president, and the new sergeant at arms was none other than Buster himself. He opened a brown paper shopping bag and pulled out his leather vest, turning it around for Max to see that he was now a full patch member.

Marcella's behavior was becoming more and more unpredictable by the day. She would be laughing and joking with Janie the bartender one minute, then screaming and cursing the next. Marcella cried over the death of a feral cat that lived on the property, then shot and killed the truck driver who ran over it. She frequently smoked joints laced with powdered cocaine and her behavior became even more erratic and bizarre.

At any rate, grizzled full patch members were scared of her and for good reason. She was the one who had bailed them all out of jail, and they owed her for their freedom. She would not think twice about executing one of their own in front of everyone, just as she had done with the former club president, Dick. Nobody liked Dick anyway, he was always ridiculing and berating other club members, hence his presence was not missed by anyone.

Right now, the Ingrate Order was attempting to build their ranks and they now had six prospects, all seeking to become full patch members. But these guys were soft. They were assigned menial duties like painting, scrubbing toilets and bathrooms, and even patching the holes in the clubhouse roof that Marcella had shot up. At one end of the warehouse, there was now a makeshift boxing ring, and when the prospects weren't performing manual labor, they were being "hardened" by regular ass-kickings administered by hard-as-nails full patch members. The order had become a fascist regime with an insane woman handing out discipline as required. Max thanked Buster for his latest report and rejoined the party which was now in full swing.

The next order of business was to reduce the ranks of the order even further. Max had purchased a .50 caliber sniper rifle from a private seller in the newspaper and had it modified with a flash suppresser. Max and Gina rode out to the compound at night and drove back to an abandoned farm behind the compound. Max disconnected the brake lights on his truck and drove back behind the compound with his headlights off. He lowered the tail gate and used it as a platform on which to set the heavy rifle on its bi-pod. Gina stood by with one of the full-auto AKs, which also had been modified with a flash suppressor.

Max peered through the powerful rifle scope, searching for his primary target Marcella De Silva, but any target of opportunity would do. Buster was back in Georgia with Laura, so there was no chance of him knowing about or even getting hurt in the surprise sniper attack. They were approximately one hundred yards from the compound perimeter fence. They waited. It wasn't long before members were outside the clubhouse involved in some sort of altercation. There was a young prospect being "taught a lesson" by having his ass kicked by not one but two full patch members.

Peering through the powerful scope, Max zeroed in on the full patch member conducting the beating, while another held the prospect's arms behind his back. Max flipped off the safety and held his breath. *Ka-bam!* The .50 caliber recoiled hard as the projectile leaving the barrel whizzed through the night air at extreme velocity. The round found its mark striking the dude square in the back and sending blood and tissue out through the front of his body, covering nearby bystanders.

Everyone inside the compound momentary froze and looked in the direction of the shot. They pulled handguns and began firing wildly into the darkness just as Gina let loose with the full-auto AK and sprayed the compound and its occupants with bullets. Everyone inside the compound ran like scared little rabbits as Gina ejected the spent clip and loaded a full one and continued firing. The heavy bullets struck buildings, vehicles, motorbikes, and anything else in the vicinity. She ejected the second spent clip, and loaded another full clip and continued firing.

Satisfied they had accomplished their objective, Max and Gina quickly packed up their gear and sped across the empty field toward the road. "I love you, baby!" Gina said to Max

"I love you too, sweetgrits!" Max said to her.

They drove off into the South Carolina night. Mission accomplished. Max and Gina were filled with adrenaline as they drove right past the compound front gate on their way home. Who knew that killing could be so much fun? Max couldn't wait to hear Buster's latest report when he came back to Max's house two days from now. When they finally got home, they broke out the liquor and celebrated their killing spree. They had wild, passionate sex until daybreak.

Two days later, Buster showed up looking like he'd been beaten to hell and back. He told Max and Gina that another full patch member went ape-shit on him upon his return to the compound, all while Marcella stood by closely and watched the beating. A full patch member named Razor had been killed by a sniper. Three other full patch members were injured, one seriously, and two prospects were also injured. Vehicles and bikes had been damaged, and where was Buster when all this took place?

Buster said after the beating, they tied him up and brought him into the clubhouse and secured him to a chair. Some scary-looking dude had all this electronic equipment set up and connected Buster's fingers to wires. Marcella chased everyone else out of the clubhouse, but she stayed along with this strange dude. Marcella told Buster he was about to be polygraphed. After some initial questions to zero in the polygraph equipment, they started in with the questions that would determine whether he lived or died. Buster said he thought this was going to be his last day on earth.

Was his name really Buster? Was he a welder from Florida? Did he have a girlfriend in Georgia named Laura that he saw every couple of days? Did he know anything about the deaths of three full patch members who died in a fire on board a boat off the coast of Hilton Head Island? And finally, did he know anything about the sniper attack on the compound last night? The strange dude and Marcella disappeared into an office behind the clubhouse bar. It was so quiet in the clubhouse that Buster could hear every word through the office door.

The man said according to the results, this man was telling the truth. Marcella refused to believe it and questioned the polygraph administrator's competence. He raised his voice at her, basically saying that he had been doing this longer that she had been alive, now pay the money she owed him. Buster said Marcella began cursing in a foreign language, but reemerged from the back office with the man, who began disconnecting the wires and packing up his equipment. The only thing that saved Buster's life, he believed, was that they asked all the wrong questions.

Marcella pulled one her guns out of its holster and pointed it directly in Buster's eye, saying she would be watching him. And just like that, they let him go. Buster said that he believed that if Marcella actually thought he was lying, he'd be dead right now. But the Ingrate Order's ranks were shrinking by the day, and so far, Buster had proven himself to be an honest, loyal member. Buster said to Max that he wanted more money, this was getting too dangerous.

Max became irate, saying Buster was already being paid an exorbitant amount of money. Gina added that the hard part was over, he had already proven himself. Max proposed that once Marcella was dead, there would be a bonus for him. Buster said he could set her up and kill her easily. Max said no way to that, saying that he wanted to be the one that killed Marcella De Silva, or whoever the fuck she really was. Max said he didn't want to just kill her, he wanted to watch her die.

Gina began to argue with Max, saying that if Buster could really pull this off, that would be the end of it. Max surprised her by saying that he was having too much fun inflicting the rage and psychological turmoil upon Marcella. He said he wanted this to take as long as possible, and what was Marcella going to do about it? She didn't know where they lived, she didn't have any way of finding them.

Every day she was losing her grip and her edge. She was fucked, and she knew it. Let her stew in her own juices. Fuck Marcella De Silva!

Gina, who had previously trusted Max's judgment beyond measure, began doubting her unwavering belief in Max. He was becoming a sadist. He was letting his hatred for this woman overwhelm his senses. But there was something else. Gina began to notice that Max was not only drinking less, but he had by now all but lost his taste for weed and coke. He was becoming sharper and more focused. His personality was changing, and each day it became a little more intense. He was definitely not the same joking, fun-loving dude she had met three years ago. They were supposed to get married in another five months. Now she wasn't so sure she wanted to go through with it.

The next meeting with Buster was uneventful. The full patch member who was seriously wounded in the sniper attack died of his injuries in an area hospital. As for the other injured dudes, it would be a while before they were able to rejoin the ranks and ride again. Marcella had disappeared without telling anyone where she was going. Buster left Max and Gina's trailer in a hurry. Eager to enjoy the pleasures his girlfriend Laura afforded him.

Business was good. Martin was getting his packages every two weeks, and the money continued to fill in the buckets in their storm shelter. Gina had always wanted a horse, and Max actually went out and bought her one. It was a big black Arabian, and Gina fell in love with it immediately. She named him Midnight. Max had a barn built for him, and every day, Gina rode him on the trails that snaked through the Georgia countryside.

Everything was fine, right up until Buster's next meeting with Max. Buster informed him that Marcella was back and that she was actually paying dudes to prospect for club. They were mostly down-and-out losers, but a couple had the potential to cause real problems for anyone who got in their way. Some of the previous prospects were now full patch members and were on their way to making names for themselves. But the biggest news by far all centered around a man who literally came out of the blue.

It was a day, just like any other, when the sound of helicopter rotors over the compound quickly got everyone's attention. It circled the compound and then, to everyone's surprise, landed right in the middle of it, raising huge clouds of dust into the fall sky. Marcella came out of the clubhouse and shielded her eyes from the dust storm. As the rotors began losing revolutions, she walked over to it. Obviously, she was expecting it and the passengers it carried.

Two black men and one black woman exited the helicopter and followed Marcella into the clubhouse and into the office behind the clubhouse bar. Everyone inside the perimeter didn't know what to make of the visitors, or their unique mode of transportation. Who in the hell were they, and what were they doing here, everyone was asking themselves. After an hour or so, the strangers all climbed back into the helicopter taking Marcella along with them. She never returned that day.

Max asked Buster to describe the black men and the woman. Buster said the woman was a real looker and was neatly dressed in a black business suit. The men also wore black business suits, were both bald, and both wore sunglasses. Buster said they looked like G-men. Max asked Buster about their physical characteristics. Buster told Max that one of the dudes was tall and skinny, the other had a big barrel chest and was very broad shouldered, like a linebacker.

There was only one person that Max figured it might be. From the description given by the late Ray Bangor, that man had to be none other than Otis Williams. Ray had told Max that Marcella never met Otis Williams, but Ray must have given her enough information as to where to find him. Damn it! There could only be one reason why Otis Williams was in South Carolina. He was after the coke. Marcella must have made some kind of deal with Otis. Max could only imagine what that deal was. It probably went something like, "Help me find this coke, help me kill this asshole named Max and his girlfriend, and we'll make a lot of money when it's all said and done!"

The war between him and Marcella had just escalated to a new level. Max silently cursed himself for not seeing this coming. He cursed himself, then upon reflection, apologized to himself. He was going to meet this new threat head-on. Ray had described in detail how vicious this dude was, how he strangled a woman right in front of Ray the first time the two men met. Max had already decided that he hated this Otis Williams, and he'd never even met the man. Otis Williams was going to pay dearly for trying to inject himself into Max's life.

Gina became insanely angry when told of this new turn of events. They had fought so hard to come all this way, and here some total stranger was just going to muscle in and take from them all that they had worked for. She began pleading with Max to just let Buster take them out. Buster was already inside the organization. He was above suspicion. He was the perfect solution to this problem that was becoming more complex by the day. Max told her that he would take it under advisement. He was now actually considering Gina's proposal.

It was a call from Max and Gina's former neighbor across the street that cemented Max's decision. Amy told Max that there was a white helicopter circling in low orbit over the neighborhood where Max and Gina had just moved from. At one point, it hovered directly over the property Max used to own. Marcella knew firsthand how difficult and time consuming it was to move all the coke from one place to another. She probably figured that Max and Gina would move it and themselves someplace close, and much to the annoyance of Max, Marcella had guessed correctly.

Right now, they were probably searching for Max's old truck from the air. Marcella had no way of knowing that she was wasting time, but the more time she wasted, the easier it would become to put Max's plan into motion. Max could not wait for his next meeting with Buster. He was planning to pay Buster one hundred thousand dollars if he could take out Otis and his people and Marcella along with them. Max eagerly awaited his next meeting with Buster which was scheduled for tomorrow.

But tomorrow came and went, and there was no sign of Buster. Max called Laura to see if maybe she had heard anything. She was just as worried as Max. It wasn't like Buster to miss his biweekly visit. Laura and Max had no way of knowing that Buster had been killed the night before during an altercation with one of the new prospects Marcella had hired. Buster had warned Max that a couple of these guys were dangerous, and now Buster was dead as a result. The new prospect had stabbed Buster in the chest with a hidden knife during a bar fight. The Ingrate Order MC had cremated his remains right on the compound, and now nothing but charred bones and ashes remained of Max's old friend.

When Marcella found about the killing, she personally shot the prospect point blank in the chest. There would be no infighting among the ranks. Marcella personally saw to it that the prospect's body was thrown out of the helicopter, owned by Otis Williams, into a swamp. Maybe someday someone would discover the former prospect's watch and rings in a pile of alligator excrement. The killing, which took place in the clubhouse bar, served to remind everyone how dangerous Marcella De Silva was. She would kill anyone she deemed as unworthy of existing.

The Ingrate Order MC had always been a small club, and even at their height, they consisted of no more than thirty hardcore members. They seldom left the state of South Carolina, and even within the state, they kept a low profile. There were a lot of other motorcycle clubs that despised them and would think nothing of taking out the whole organization if they had the chance. Now, the Ingrates were losing members faster than they could recruit. It would not be long before this small disorganized club would disintegrate completely.

The new club president Spider, the club vice president Napoleon, and Marcella sat in the clubhouse office and discussed the future of the organization. Even Marcella agreed that at the rate they were going, the club would soon be history. It was Spider who proposed a solution that if it panned out would solve this problem. In neighboring Georgia, Spider had a brother who belonged to a small ragtag club named the Miscreants MC.

They were as hardcore as they come. They financed their organization by producing and selling methamphetamine. They had their own lab, and even though their product was of mediocre quality, the drug was becoming more and more popular, and demand often outstripped supply. Also, there was the problem of their meth cook, an intravenous user of his own product. So far, he had blown up two labs over the last two years due to carelessness and lack of attention to detail. Just about everyone in the Miscreants MC were hardcore meth addicts. Collectively, they were the most paranoid group of individuals on the planet. Just about everyone who was not part of their organization was suspected of working for the police.

Spider's proposal was that they dissolve the Ingrate Order and patch over with the Miscreants MC, thereby creating a motorcycle club consisting of over fifty members, with chapters in two states.

That would place the former Ingrate Order in proximity to their number one enemy, Max, his girlfriend, and the millions of dollars in cash and cocaine in their possession. Both Marcella and Napoleon thought it was a brilliant plan. Tomorrow, Spider would call his brother in Georgia and set up a meeting.

It was time, Max had decided, to open season on Otis Williams. Together with Gina's help, Max had formulated a plan that would take him out of the picture, but it wasn't going to be easy. Across the main road from the Ingrate Order MC were dense woods on private property. Gina would drive Max out to this location and drop him off in the woods. In full camouflage, Max would set up a tree stand that would give him a clear shot into the compound. There he would wait, for days if necessary, until he had a clear shot at Otis Williams and his associates. Hopefully Marcella would be there also.

The only flaw in the plan was Max's escape plan. Cellular telephones were just starting to become popular, but Max didn't trust them. It would be all too easy for anyone with a scanner to program it to eavesdrop on the wireless conversations. Max proposed a genius level solution to the problem. He would follow Gina out to the compound on Buster's custom bike that he'd left behind at the rental house occupied by Laura. Max would ditch the bike in the same woods down the road from the compound, covering it with a camouflaged tarp. After the assassination of Otis Williams, and hopefully Marcella De Silva as well, Max would simply run down the road, get on the bike, and ride it home to Georgia. Gina, of course, didn't like the plan. It was far too dangerous, and the chances of Max being captured or even picked up by the police were way too high in her estimation. But Max insisted he had to do this. He had to take Otis Williams out of the equation.

And so the next night, Max set up in the woods directly across from the compound. He had enough food, water, and provisions for three days. He scanned the compound with binoculars. His worst fears about Buster were confirmed when he witnessed two members leaving the compound through the security gate. As they turned onto the main road, Max could clearly make out that one of the members was riding Buster's favorite custom bike, there was no mistaking it. There was only one like it on the entire planet.

Sons of bitches, thought Max. He wanted to kill these guys out of sheer principle. But doing so would give away his position and jeopardize the whole mission. His primary objective was to take out Otis Williams. Max spent an extremely uncomfortable night in the aluminum tree stand he had set up. Although he had generously applied insect repellant, it did not stop the mosquitoes and gnats from flying into the only exposed portion of his body, his eyeballs. He rinsed out his eyes with drinking water and put on his riding goggles. But that didn't stop the biting ants that somehow got inside his clothing.

Due to the uncomfortable arrangements, he did not sleep that night. At daybreak, he opened a can of tuna fish. He hadn't even placed the first fork full in his mouth when he heard the unmistakable sound of helicopter rotors. The sound became louder and louder, and soon it flew directly over his position as it began to circle the compound and position itself to land. Max chambered a round into the AK, the very same one they used to shoot up the compound last week. He flipped off the safety. It was game time.

The helicopter hovered, then began its slow descent into the compound. When it did touch down, the pilot slowed the rotors to idle. A minute later, the sliding door opened and three people climbed out. Marcella was not among them. Max braced the weapon against his shoulder and began firing at the helicopter and its passengers. There was so much dust in the air from the landing, Max could not tell if whether his shooting was effective or not. He loaded another clip and began firing again, he continued firing until he had gone through seven, thirty round magazines. When he chambered a round from the eight magazine, it cooked-off inside the receiver, it was so hot from the hundreds of bullets he had sent through the barrel.

There was a powerful explosion. Parts from the helicopter flew across the compound in all directions. A huge fireball, along with clouds of smoke and dust billowed into the early morning sky. It was time for Max to get the hell out of there. He threw the AK into the woods, where the searing-hot barrel tip ignited the dry leaves on the ground, starting a fire. He stripped out of his camouflage and left his provisions and extra ammo in place. He ran down the road to where he had hidden the bike.

Pulling the bike upright, he began to stroke the kick starter, but the engine would not fire. This was bad, realizing that since the bike had been lying on its side, all the fuel must have drained out of the carburetor bowl. He continued to hold the throttle wide open as he stroked the kick starter a dozen or so times, until the engine finally caught. He pulled out onto the main road and went through all five gears, until he was going eighty miles an hour.

There was no traffic on the road this time of day, but nevertheless he slowed down to the posted speed. After about two miles, he saw blue flashing lights on the road ahead, about a mile or so distant. As they closed the distance between them, Max could make out there were four South Carolina State Police cruisers traveling at what seemed like a hundred miles an hour. As they passed each other, the last cruiser spun around one hundred eighty degrees and began to chase him.

The state police cruiser was a three-hundred-horsepower marked Chevrolet Camaro, and Max could see through the rearview mirror that it was closing the distance quickly. He rolled the throttle all the way open, and the powerful custom bike took off. He fought the urge to continue looking in the rearview to focus his attention instead to the road ahead of him. He slowed down so that he could turn west onto the highway that would take him across the state line into Georgia. Looking in the rearview, he found that he had lost his pursuer, who was by now trying to decide on which direction to take, while probably calling in for roadblocks and having a perimeter set up.

Knowing this would happen if he was spotted leaving the scene, and he most definitely was, Max continued to the next small town where he knew there was a small motel on the side of the highway.

As he got within a half mile of the town, he pulled off on the side of the road as he approached a bridge spanning the river. He got off the bike and ran it down the embankment into the river. He walked the half mile into town, right to the front door of the motel.

It was still early in the morning. Max continued to ring the buzzer in the motel office until a man who had obviously just been awakened appeared through the door behind the office. He asked the man if it were possible for an early check-in. Max placed a hundred-dollar bill on the counter and the motel proprietor pushed a key across the counter. Max opened the door to the small room and collapsed on the bed. He took a pull off a flask of whiskey, and within minutes, he was asleep.

It was afternoon when he finally awoke and called Gina, informing her of his location, and that he needed a ride and a change of clothes. Gina was thrilled to hear the sound of his voice. Ninety minutes later, she was knocking on the door. Max took a shower and was about to get dressed before changing his mind and deciding to pick up Gina and throw her on the bed. He pulled off all her clothes and set himself upon her.

Afterwards as they lay side by side on the bed, Max related every detail of the experience. Gina said she had passed roadblocks on the way to the motel, maybe it was a little too hot to leave today. Max told her no problem as he got dressed and went to the office to pay for another night. For the remainder of their stay, all the couple did was eat, sleep and make love. They did turn on the television, and the story was all over the local news. Authorities were calling the brutal attack the work of professional terrorists, leaving out the fact that Zeigler Trucking Industries was really a front for the vicious bike gang known as the Ingrate Order MC.

Over in neighboring Georgia, Spider sat in the clubhouse of the Miscreants, sitting across the table from his older brother, Shovelhead. Spider laid out his proposal for the club merger and how it would be beneficial to both organizations. Shovelhead was not the least bit impressed with the idea, pointing out that that the Ingrates were under a lot of heat from law enforcement right now in the wake of recent events. Jackie, Shovelhead's wife, agreed. She said the Miscreants MC had enough problems already, they didn't need any more.

Spider was persistent. He lied to his older brother, saying all the recent events centered around the sale of Zeigler Trucking Industries to a wealthy Baltimore businessman. After an initial investigation, the authorities determined that the would-be purchaser of Zeigler Trucking was an underworld figure of dubious reputation, who owned businesses in not only in Baltimore, but Richmond, Pittsburg, and Philadelphia as well.

The businessman, known as the late Otis Williams, was good friends with the late former club president Wolf Zeigler. The two men had served in Vietnam together, and the sale of Zeigler Trucking Industries was actually months in the making, prior to Wolf's death. Of course, there was no way for the authorities to authenticate the story, and there was no way the Miscreants could either. All that was known to everyone was that Otis Williams and two associates were assassinated in the Ingrate Order MC compound. The authorities speculated that a man like Otis Williams had developed a lot of enemies over the years and that the case was probably unsolvable.

Shovelhead looked at his wife and asked her what she thought. Jackie was still unconvinced, but thought that it wouldn't hurt for the two clubs to get together and kind of feel each other out. The last thing anyone wanted were any types of personality problems that could cause problems in the future. And so it was decided that the two clubs would meet at the Ingrate Order MC compound this coming Friday night for a blowout. Spider was greatly looking forward to it. As for Shovelhead and his old lady Jackie, they would just have to wait and see what these Ingrate jokers were all about.

Upon hearing the news that Otis Williams and his two associates were dead, Max and Gina were exuberant. Max's bold plan had succeeded. Though Marcella was still alive, her ability to track them down was greatly diminished. She was probably upset beyond measure, blaming members of the Ingrate Order MC for allowing this brazen attack to occur. How could they be so stupid as to allow a sniper to set up in the woods, right across the road from the compound? Max could only imagine the ridiculous reasoning Marcella used to vindicate her anger. It pleased Max just knowing that Marcella would never let this drop and would continue to harp on the members of the Ingrate Order MC.

Over in Georgia, Shovelhead, his wife Jackie, and the entire motorcycle club known as the Miscreants MC were on their way to the Ingrate Order MC compound for a massive party that was scheduled for that night. Shovelhead was initially impressed by the well-lit compound, surrounded by the eight-foot-high fence topped with barbed wire. But all illusions of security vanished when he saw the completely destroyed helicopter surrounded by yellow police tape. The procession of bikes passed right by the wreckage on their way to the back of the compound where the clubhouse was located.

There were barbeque pits, kegs of beer on ice, and a live band just outside the clubhouse where members of the Ingrate Order MC had already started to party down. The Miscreants MC parked their bikes in a neat line behind the mechanic's garage. Thirty-five stock and custom bikes gleamed under the mercury vapor lamps overhead. Spider and his brother Shovelhead shook hands as they introduced their respective vice presidents. Spider got up on the stage and, through the PA system, invited all present to help themselves to as much food and draft beer as they could handle.

Marcella, dressed in black leather pants and a black leather vest, actually took the opportunity to introduce herself to many of the Miscreants and their women. They were collectively highly impressed with this mysterious Hispanic woman, with her striking good looks and hourglass figure. With her twin .44s at her side, she resembled a character out of an apocalyptic science-fiction movie. No one dared to ask what her title was within the Ingrate Order MC.

Biker women danced to the groovy rock and roll sounds of Los Diablos Locos, a Mexican rock band with a groovy twist on American classic rock. Biker dudes from both clubs traded war stories, drank beer, and smoked dope. Some of the Miscreants introduced their fellow bikers from the Ingrates to sample some of their home-cooked meth, which went over really well with dudes who had never tried it before. Spider gave his older brother and his wife a complete tour of the compound. Inside the warehouse terminal, Spider confided to Shovelhead that the trucking business was losing money due mostly to the fact that the late Wolf Zeigler had handled all the business affairs along with Janie, who was by now so strung out on coke, she could not even tell what day it was most of the time.

In the office behind the clubhouse bar, Marcella, Spider, Shovelhead, and Jackie sat in air-conditioned comfort as they sipped liquor drinks and discussed the future of the two biker organizations and the proposed merger. Marcella gave a performance worthy of an Academy Award as she outlined her plan for the future. Somewhere, across the Savannah River in Georgia, lived a couple named Max and Gina. They were sophisticated rednecks who stumbled upon a wrecked sailboat that contained hundreds of kilos of pure cocaine from Colombia, South America.

All they needed to do was combine their resources and find this couple who right now was sitting on millions of dollars in cash and pure coke. Jackie proceeded to tell Marcella that with their manufacturing and street-level sales of meth, they had plenty of coin to live on. Not just that, both their kids went to prestigious private schools. They were doing just fine. Marcella stepped around the desk, sat upon it, and looked both Shovelhead and Jackie in the eyes as she explained further what this all meant.

In Colombia, one kilo of pure cocaine could be purchased for five thousand dollars. Here in the States, that same kilo could be cut and sold at street level for 2 million. Let's say that they were only able to recover one hundred kilos from this redneck couple. At street level, it would be worth 200 million dollars. Marcella now had the complete and total attention of Shovelhead and Jackie, who now sat upright in their chairs.

Jackie was still skeptical. If Marcella knew so much about these people, then why had she not been able to locate them? Marcella's temperament changed instantaneously as she resumed her seat behind the desk. Max and Gina were devils, she explained. She personally witnessed them and their former business partner kill five vicious underworld criminals in the blink of an eye. They were highly intelligent, heavily armed, and completely willing to kill anyone who got in their way. When she first met them, she thought they were a sweet, fun-loving couple just trying to enjoy life. Marcella tried in vain to break their relationship apart by seducing Max, only to find that Max and Gina were swingers. They would fuck anyone they were attracted to, but they always came back to each other. They were anything but a normal young adult couple. They were both swingers, and cold-blooded murderers with no regrets.

Shovelhead said that even if they were willing to work with Marcella, she would have to provide more information, starting with the last names of Max and Gina, their former employers, family members, anything else that could be of value. Marcella went into a ballistic tirade, slamming her fist on the desk while trying to explain that these people were ghosts. Ghost devils! They were not human and should not be treated as such. They would never in a million years disclose the secret of their hidden stash. They would have to be interrogated on a medieval level to break their silence.

Jackie was not all moved by Marcella's sales pitch, but Shovelhead was. If Marcella was right about how much money was at stake, they could live like royalty for the rest of their lives. This offered them a chance at becoming richer than they ever imagined they could. Marcella herself thought she had made a pretty good case, and she invited them along with all the Miscreants MC to make themselves at home in the compound. Inside the safety and security of the warehouse terminal, with its own bathrooms and showers, they were all free to roll out their sleeping bags, relax, and sleep off their hangovers. Tomorrow was another day.

A few days later, Welder, the resident meth cook and hardcore member of the Miscreants MC, would make the mistake that cost him his life, forever changing the course of the club's future. A huge explosion destroyed not only the meth lab, but killed another club member as well. The fire department reported to the police that the explosion was the direct result of methamphetamine manufacturing. But the fire was so hot and burned so violently, all the evidence was destroyed. The police had no case for lack of evidence.

That was all it took for Shovelhead to make his final decision. He called his brother Spider and said that a club merger was a fine idea. Jackie was not on board with the decision, but almost every club member had voted in favor of the merger. They would become a bigger, stronger organization, and besides which, those guys really knew how to throw a party. Shovelhead was actually glad to retire from the crystal meth business. It was just too dangerous, and no one else in the club knew how to cook like Welder. Now all they had to do was help find this couple named Max and Gina, and they would be set up in the cocaine business. It was time to set up another party, this time at the Miscreants MC headquarters in Georgia.

It was a beautiful sunny fall afternoon as Max and Gina drove home from the flea market through the Georgia countryside, only to come up behind a lone biker wearing a patch. As Max got closer, he recognized the patch as belonging to the Miscreats MC, a club based in Georgia, and a club with whom Max had no problem with. But this lone biker was riding the custom-built chopper that once belonged to Max's now-deceased friend Buster. Max pulled up right behind the chopper to make absolutely certain this was Buster's bike. The pin striping on the rear fender confirmed what Max already knew. This was in fact his late friend's custom ride.

The rider, seeing Max right on his rear bumper, flipped his middle finger at the truck that was mere inches away. Max backed off a little, then floored the accelerator striking the chopper and sending both the bike and the rider into a ditch. Max pulled the truck halfway into the ditch, pulled his gun from his waistband holster, and approached the seriously injured rider. The rider had been thrown from the bike and had suffered compound fractures to his lower right leg. Two bloody bones had not only punctured the leg muscles, but through the man's pants leg also.

"Where did you get that bike?" Max asked the severely injured man.

"Fuck you, asshole!" the man yelled up at Max, who now stood over him holding the gun at the man's head.

Max stepped on the broken bones with his boot and leaned hard on the injury. The man screamed as he writhed in pain.

"That chopper belonged to a friend of mine, he built it himself, and would never part with it … I'm going to ask you again, where did you get it?"

The injured rider spit on Max's boot, prompting Max to apply even more pressure, sending the man into the preliminary stages of shock.

"My longtime buddy Buster built that bike in his spare time, it took him two years … how did you get it?"

"Buster was killed in a knife fight weeks ago!"

Max stood over the injured rider and fired a .40 caliber round into his head. Looking down at the now-deceased man, Max recalled the night he set up to snipe the Ingrate Order compound. This was the exact same scraggly-looking bearded man he saw leaving the compound on the stolen bike. Max removed the vest from the dead man as a trophy and, as he did so, noticed an Ingrate Order tattoo on his bicep. Either this guy had defected from the Ingrate Order or the two clubs had possibly merged.

Gina told Max they needed to leave this area immediately. Max agreed and drove his truck out of the ditch leaving the dead rider behind. Max was angry. Here he was trying to dwindle the ranks of the Ingrate Order, and if they had, in fact, merged with this other club, who knows how many adversaries Max and Gina would now be facing? It was time to head to Charleston and retrieve the remaining AK-47 from his boat.

Back in Georgia, Max made it his number one priority to locate the clubhouse of the Miscreants MC. He spent the next day patrolling the Georgia countryside in the hopes of spotting more members and letting them lead him to their hangout, but to no avail. Late at night, he drove into South Carolina to the former Ingrate Order compound. It was a Friday night and it was busy. Music could be heard along with random gunshots. Max pulled up to the gate, and hung the leather vest he has taken off the dead rider on the chain link fence.

A newly ordained full patch member found the vest and brought it to Spider and Marcella. They identified it as belonging to one of the original founding members of the Ingrate Order, a man named

Smokey. Spider was visibly affected by the notion that Smokey was probably dead. Marcella was furious that Smokey let himself get killed. Later, Smokey's sister called the compound and told Janie that she had just gotten off the phone with the Georgia State Police who informed her that her brother was found dead on the side of a back country road.

It was now time to begin decimating the ranks of the Miscreants MC, Max and Gina had decided. Gina suggested they find a rival gang and pay them to go to war with the Miscreants. Max told her that would never work, there had to some type of grievance between the two gangs. That gave Max an idea. If they could kidnap or even kill a rival gang member and somehow let that gang know that the Miscreants MC were the perpetrators, that might actually work. But they didn't know of any other bike gangs operating in South Carolina or Georgia. It's not like they could be found in the phonebook.

Early one Saturday morning, Gina saddled up her horse Midnight and took him for a ride through the Georgia countryside. She returned just an hour later with Midnight, running at full gallop onto Rob's property. She had spotted fifty bikes riding in formation several miles from where they lived. She told Max she was almost positive they were the Miscreants taking a riding event. Max pulled out a map of Georgia and asked her to show him where she had seen them. Gina studied the map and pointed to a highway several miles north of where they lived.

Max wondered if they were having a poker run or some other day-long riding event, and if so, would they be returning the same way that they came. It was worth checking out anyway. Max loaded his truck with the full-auto AKs, as well as an assortment of other firearms and headed out to the location Gina had pointed out on the map. Max told Gina there was no way she was coming on this one. Five minutes later, she was fastening the seatbelt in the passenger seat of Max's truck.

The area they found had little cover. Gina suggested that they set up behind an old billboard, but Max thought it would look suspicious to motorists passing in the other direction. Also, how did they know that this place was not a preferred spot used by police to set up speed traps? With no available cover in the area where the bike gang was last seen, Max opted to cruise the highway in the hopes they might get lucky. It was late in the afternoon when Max and Gina decided that they were just wasting time and decided to return home for the day. They would have to come up with some other type of offensive tactic, some other time, Max decided.

Just as they were about to make the turn onto the highway that would take them home, Max happened to glance in the rearview only to see a procession of motorcycles coming up behind them.

At the first opportunity, Max pulled the truck into a roadside gas station. As the fifty or so bikes rumbled past, Max and Gina could clearly see that it was in fact the Miscreants MC. Giving the riders about fifteen seconds of lead time, Max pulled the truck out onto the highway and began to follow. After several miles, the formation of motorcycles began to slow down and make a right turn onto a dirt road.

Driving past the dirt road, Max and Gina were able to see that it was a private road, with NO TRESPASSING signs clearly posted on either side. Max was willing to bet that somewhere on this private, secluded road, out in the middle of nowhere, was the headquarters for the Miscreants MC. Max asked Gina to circle the area on the map where the private road was located. It was so private, it was not even on the map. Now Max was all but certain, this was what they had been searching for. He would need more time to evaluate this new information and formulate an attack plan.

Out in Los Angeles, Gina's brother Martin continued to receive packages every two weeks. Martin invited Max and Gina to come out and visit him in his new house which he shared with his girlfriend, Vicky. Max was surprised to hear that the couple was engaged to be married. Gina pleaded with Max to consider going out to the West Coast, even if it was only for a couple of days. Martin insisted it would be a great time for everyone. They would get to attend extravagant parties and meet famous people. It would be a chance for Max to unwind and forget all about Marcella and the Miscreants MC, if only for a little while.

As long as Marcella De Silva was alive, there was no way Max would be able to put her out of his mind. Like a bad memory, she would always be there, lurking in his subconscious. Marcella would never stop until she accomplished her objective. Max couldn't just take off and forget that Marcella and her band of outlaw bikers were still out there, searching for Gina and himself. He tried very hard to convince Gina that a vacation at this point was simply not an option. They could take a vacation when Marcella De Silva was dead and the threat posed by the Miscreants MC was neutralized.

Besides, did they really want to leave their bunker loaded with cash, and their safe house loaded with coke, and go to the complete opposite side of the country? At least if they stayed in the area, they could respond to any threat in a matter of hours, not days. Prior to tearing down their old house, Max paid the security systems specialist to remove all salvageable equipment from the condemned house and reinstall it on their single wide, so that it could be remotely monitored along with the rental house.

Of course Gina was pissed off about Max's decision not to visit L.A., nevertheless, she helped him plan their next coordinated attack on their enemies. Friday nights seemed to be a big deal for the club. Either at the compound in South Carolina or the headquarters in Georgia, there always seemed to be a big party at the end of each week. Max and Gina had the distinct advantage in that most if not all of the partygoers were highly intoxicated at these events and ill-prepared to deal with a surprise attack. So far they had killed, maimed, and destroyed property, all with the element of surprise in their favor. Let's just keep a good thing going, Max insisted.

The next Friday night, they set off for the old Ingrate Order compound, only to find it all but deserted, with just a few members left behind to stand guard duty. Max figured correctly that this week, the party was being held over in Georgia. But the following Friday night, they headed back out there, if for no other purpose than to cause as much mayhem as humanly possible. Gina drove past the compound as Max sat ready in the passenger seat, armed with an AK. Gina made initial pass, and they both determined that there was indeed a wild party already in progress.

Gina made a three-point turn and headed back toward the compound, slowing down as they approached the main gate. From the passenger seat, Max began firing full auto into the compound. Not aiming for anything in particular, his purpose now was to "wake them up." Gina brought the truck to a complete stop, and now they waited. The compound gate began to roll open, and the sound of revving motorcycle engines filled the air. Max and Gina were now the little boy who had just poked a stick in the hornet's nest. Max climbed over the seats into the cargo area. Gina waited until she was sure they had been seen and floored the accelerator. Dozens of bikes began pouring out of the compound, chasing the truck as Max sat ready with the AK. When the pack got to within ten yards or so, the lead members opened fire on the truck with handguns. Max returned fire with the AK, watching bikes and riders spilling all over the highway. This was just too easy, Max thought as he loaded another clip and resumed firing.

Any biker that was not killed or seriously injured stopped the pursuit, realizing that it would be suicidal to continue. Gina put the truck in reverse and backed up as Max continued firing at the fleeing members who had escaped the first wave of attack. Yeah, it was a dirty thing to do, thought Max, but this was war. He wanted to not only kill as many members as possible, but to also send a message to their new adversaries, the Miscreants MC. Max and Gina meant business, and killing their enemies had escalated from their favorite hobby to their full time occupation.

Filled with adrenaline, Max and Gina drove back toward Georgia, but not before passing numerous speeding police cruisers headed toward the scene of the shooting. It was still relatively early in the evening, and Max and Gina were not the only vehicle on the road this time of night. As they crossed the state line into Georgia, they assumed correctly, they had just gotten away with murder, again. Back at their single wide, Max couldn't wait to until they were inside, he dropped the tailgate and bent Gina over it, and gave it to her and gave it to her, right there under a mercury vapor lamp in their own front yard.

It was now Saturday morning and Max asked Rob if he could give them a lift to a new car dealership in the greater Savannah area. Max's truck was now easily recognizable to any survivor who saw it, and besides which, it had several bullet holes in it. Max picked out another four-wheel-drive truck, this time a black one. There had to be a thousand black trucks in Savannah, he figured. He now grappled with the decision of what to do about the other truck. For now, he would just leave it at the rental house, along with the weapons. Maybe he could sell the truck to one of Rob's employees after patching the bullet holes and having it repainted of course.

Max actually drove into South Carolina on Sunday morning just to get a newspaper. He was horrified to see crude police sketches of both Gina and himself, both listed as suspects in the vicious attacks on the former Ingrate Order compound. Marcella was getting desperate to locate the couple and now sought the help of law enforcement. It was an extremely bold move on her part, Max thought. Only Marcella herself could have provided the descriptions needed for the police artist to make the sketches.

It now occurred to Max that if Gina and himself were apprehended, Marcella would know exactly where they were being held. She could use contacts within the prison to administer retribution for the brutal slayings that, according to the paper, killed five members and injured another eleven. But that would all but negate her chances of getting her hands on the coke. As for the hidden cash, it would be nearly impossible for her to get her hands on that as well. Max had given the post office an alias. The public records available would only list Max and Gina's former address.

Why would Marcella cooperate with the authorities and subject herself and her counterparts to law enforcement scrutiny? Max could only think of two reasons. First, this had become personal. Many of her underworld cohorts were dead as a direct result of Max and Gina. Second, Marcella was losing her mind. Only an idiot would call attention to themselves and their underworld organization. Marcella was probably consuming illegal drugs at a rate that was undoubtedly clouding her thinking and her judgment.

Marcella was obviously under the influence when she gave the police sketch artist details necessary to produce the drawings. The crude pictures in the paper did not look anything like Max or Gina. It had been a while since Marcella had seen the couple, so her memory was probably a little fuzzy. But her own perception of Max and Gina was altered to the point that the sketches made Max and Gina look like strung-out junkies capable of doing anything just to get that next fix. At least Max hoped the pictures did not bear any resemblance to them. The people depicted in the drawings were just plain ugly.

When Gina saw the pictures in the paper, she busted out laughing. She though it was the funniest thing in the world to see what Marcella and the police artist thought she might look like. But there was nothing funny at all about the police search warrant that was executed the next morning. The only thing the police were able to find in Max and Gina's trailer was a small amount of marijuana. There were no illegal weapons, and there was no evidence linking them to the crime scene. Max had covered the storm shelter door beneath a huge pile of landscaping debris. Anytime he needed access to the bunker, he could use Rob's backhoe and easily push the debris pile aside.

Max and Gina were questioned separately about their whereabouts Friday night. They both said they were at home together. When asked if they were willing to take lie detector tests, they both refused. They both told police investigators that they had seen enough television crime shows to know that polygraph examinations were not reliable. It was not uncommon for an innocent person to fail or a guilty person to pass a polygraph test. That was the whole reason why they were inadmissible in a court of law.

They did ask Max about what he did for a living. He told investigators he ran a charter fishing service out of Charleston. It was so profitable, he did it part time. Max told investigators that he did have a sexual relationship with Marcella in the past, but he broke it off on account of Marcella's usage of hard drugs and her unpredictably violent behavior. Also, he suspected that Marcella was responsible for the disappearance of her former husband. It was just hearsay, but it did give investigators a window into Marcella's personality.

Finally, Max suggested that the police investigate their accuser and the company she kept. Practically all the club members had criminal records. Max went on to say that he wasn't even sure if Marcella De Silva was her real name. Investigators met privately and discussed the case. The former Ingrate Order MC and the Miscreants MC were well-known to authorities. Both clubs were not exactly on good terms with law enforcement. There was obviously more to this case than either side was letting on. They released Max and Gina for lack of evidence.

The next day, Marcella De Silva was arrested for using a false identity to enter the United States illegally. Her plan to enlist the aid of the authorities had back fired. She was immediately deported back to Brazil. A week later, she was back in the States and still in bed with the Miscreants MC. But Marcella De Silva, whose real name was Alicia Anna Perez, had planned in advance for such an eventuality. Flush with cash from her cocaine dealings after meeting Ray, she had sent a significant amount of money back home to aid in her re-entry into the U.S.

Knowing that their identities were compromised, Max and Gina reluctantly abandoned the single wide and moved into the rental house with Laura, taking with them all the cash from the storm shelter. Max told Rob he could keep the rest of the year's rent paid in advance. Rob wished them the best of luck. Max confided that they were moving because of problems they were having with a local bike gang. Max told Rob to be vigilant, these malefactors were capable of anything.

That very night, Rob shot and killed six club members with a perfectly legal AR-15 as they entered his property in a passenger vehicle with the intent of committing a home invasion on the single wide formerly occupied by Max and Gina. Rob was questioned and released and not charged. Inside the vehicle, police found numerous illegal weapons, but also implements of torture, which included handcuffs, ropes, blowtorches, and garden snips.

In a private meeting, Shovelhead and Spider were livid with Marcella. So far since she had been involved with both clubs, over two dozen men were dead as a result. It was obvious the authorities did not give a fuck about the biker clubs. The people responsible were still out there. The club was not only losing men, they were losing money, all because of Marcella and her insane ambitions. Marcella sat back in her chair, rolled her eyes, and basically acted like she did not care one bit about all the trauma she had caused.

Exploding into a drug-induced tirade, Marcella angrily told the two brothers that every man killed so far was dead because of his own stupidity. What kind of idiot rides alone wearing a patch? What kind of idiots chase a vehicle containing people armed with machine guns? What kind of idiots trespass onto property in the middle of the night? What were they expecting? They were all dead because they were all morons. If they hadn't died in this manner, they all would have died from something else because of their own stupidity.

Shovelhead and Spider had two choices. They could track down the persons responsible, punish them severely, and steal their money and their drugs, or they could run like scared little puppies with their tails between their legs. Out there was a fortune, easy money for anyone smart enough to figure out how to get it. What the hell kind of bike gang were they anyway? They were supposed to be bad-asses that didn't take any shit from anyone.

Both men agreed, she did have a point. Shovelhead had heard just about enough, and he now shot Marcella between the eyes with a gun hidden under a newspaper in his lap. The two brothers dragged her outside, and threw her in the back of a pickup truck. If all went according to plan, Marcella De Silva would be a pile of alligator excrement on the bottom of a lake. Spider looked at his older brother, wanting to know what they should do now. Shovelhead suggested they go back inside and have a beer. Spider thought it was a great idea.

The bitch was right about one thing in particular. The people that did this needed to die, slowly. If it were possible to get the cash and the coke, fine, if not, it really didn't matter that much anymore. All they wanted was payback, big-time. The two brothers stripped the body of clothing and jewelry and threw it into a lake on Shovelhead's property. Nature would see to it that nothing remained of this crazy bitch.

They called a meeting of the remaining twenty-five members. Shovelhead called the meeting to order. There was complete silence in the room as Shovelhead arranged his notes on a desk in front of him. He took the opportunity to thank all the surviving members of the club for their bravery and commitment to their cause. He went on to honor their fallen brothers who had given their lives protecting the club and its values and traditions. In furtherance of financial freedom for the club, poor judgment had been used, and he personally felt responsible for everything bad that had happened since the merger of the two clubs. For that, he was very sorry.

Shovelhead produced a stack of papers and handed them to a club member sitting in the front row, instructing him to pass them around until every member had a copy. On the paper were black-and-white photos of Maxwell Earnest Hart and Gina Lidia Rodgers. This couple was suspected of killing and wounding every member who could not be present here tonight. The couple were to be taken alive preferably, but dead if it was required in self-defense. Shovelhead could not stress enough that this seemly innocent-looking young American couple were savage murderers. Extreme caution should be used in any attempt to apprehend or kill them.

On the walls of the Miscreants MC clubhouse were the pictures of every deceased member. It was hard for anyone to believe that two young adults could be responsible for the murder spree that had taken out half the club's members so far. This couple would have to pay, and pay dearly for what they had done. The surviving members collectively vowed to avenge the deaths of their fallen brothers. The perpetrators would pay the ultimate price.

On the other side of the county, Max and Gina discussed their future. Gina was convinced they should move to another state, to another region of the country. Max asked Gina about her horse Midnight. Every day, Max drove Gina to Rob's house so that she could be with, take care of, and ride her horse. Gina would have to sell Midnight if they were planning to move a long distance away.

But Gina had grown so attached to Midnight, she could not imagine the thought of selling him to someone else.

Gina said that Rob could take care of Midnight while they searched for somewhere else to live. But Rob was so busy with his tree service company, he would never have the time to care for Midnight the same way Gina did. And did she even know anyone else that could do the same? Also, Max pointed out there was no way they could just leave Laura alone with the cash and the coke. The temptation would be just too overwhelming. Max kept everything locked up in the basement of the rental house. If there were any intrusion into the basement, Max would be notified by a pager. Of course, that wouldn't do them any good if they were on the other side of the country, would it?

If anyone needed to move, it was those damn Miscreants. They universally despised everyone, including law enforcement, and they themselves were universally despised by just about everyone, including law enforcement. Not all biker organizations were bad people, Max explained. He personally knew of a biker club in Atlanta that was composed entirely of young professionals. They were real gentlemen. But those Miscreants, those boys were bad news. They had a bad reputation and rightfully so.

The surviving members carried the pictures of Max and Gina everywhere they went. The couple were completely unaware of this fact, and they continued to live their lives unbothered by the thought of these malefactors who would take them out at any given opportunity. But Max and Gina were prepared to do the same to their adversaries if their paths crossed. And so the couple went about their normal routines. They were not about to let this group of misfits interfere with their lifestyle or well-being.

After her morning horseback ride, Gina drove to greater Savannah to go shopping. In a pawnshop she frequented, she saw something very unusual in the jewelry display case. It was a very unique gold pendant. Gina asked the owner if she could see it. It was a beautiful solid gold dragon with white diamonds for eyes. The price tag said four hundred fifty dollars, but Gina offered the owner four hundred cash and he agreed. Gina took the pendant to a jewelry store owned by her Uncle Joe.

Uncle Joe examined the piece closely under a magnifying loop. He asked her where she got it from, and how much she paid for it. When she revealed she paid four hundred dollars at a pawnshop, Uncle Joe smiled. Obviously, the owner of the pawnshop was completely unaware of what he had. This piece was handmade, somewhere in Asia, probably China. It was probably over one hundred years old and was in all likelihood one of a kind. Gina asked how much was it worth. Given its age and unique design, probably fifteen hundred to two thousand, Uncle Joe estimated. When she got home, she showed it to Max. Looking at it closely, Max told Gina this was no ordinary piece of jewelry. Gina told him that her uncle had already explained that to her. Max told Gina she was missing the point. The last time he saw something resembling this, it was hanging around the neck of Marcella De Silva. Gina said she thought it looked familiar but couldn't remember where she had seen it. Max and Gina drove back to the same pawnshop. Max wanted more information.

Max asked the pawnshop owner point blank who had sold the dragon pendant. The owner said he couldn't quite remember offhand. Max placed five hundred dollars on the counter and asked the owner to think about it really hard. Suddenly, the owner's memory improved. Some rough-cut-looking biker chick sold it to him a couple of days ago. Max thanked the proprietor for the information as he turned and walked out the door.

Next, they went to see Gina's Uncle Joe. Max asked him what were the chances that this particular pendant was one of a kind. Uncle Joe said that the probability was near one hundred percent. Thanking Uncle Joe, they walked outside to the truck. Max exclaimed that this was in fact the very same pendant worn by Marcella. That could only mean one of two things. The biker chick who sold the piece had either killed Marcella or received it as a gift from the person who did. Max knew Marcella would never part with something like this, especially for the paltry price the pawnshop owner had probably offered her. Max was now convinced that Marcella was dead.

If that were the case, would the Miscreants MC still be seeking to find the cash and the cocaine? Max was inclined to believe that, yes, they would. Also, given the number of members Max and Gina had killed, they probably weren't about to let that drop either. In all likelihood, they were probably out there right now, looking for them. If taken alive, Max was certain the Miscreants MC would do terrible things to them to get them to reveal the location of the money and the cocaine. Max was not about to let that happen. He already knew that Gina would never let herself be taken alive. They would both rather leave this earth in a hail of gunfire than to be subjected to who knows what type of torture.

But there was no use wasting time thinking about what may or may not happen. They drove back to the rental house. Laura told Max that his former neighbor Amy had called and said it was important. Max returned the call and spoke with Amy's husband. Remembering Max from the party, Amy's husband explained that he'd applied for and was offered a high-paying IT job in Atlanta which he accepted. Would Max be interested in buying their farm? Max told him, hell yeah, he was interested and would meet them tomorrow morning.

Amy told Max that the old farm had been in her family for years and she really didn't want to sell it. But circumstances being as they were, they needed the money to start their new life in the big city. All morning, Max and Gina surveyed the ten-acre farm. It had everything they were looking for, and more. There was a really nice three-bedroom country house with a garage, far back on the property away from the main road. There was a small guesthouse as well. The small farm had existing horse stables, with two horses included in the asking price. And most importantly to Max, a thousand and one places to hide things they wanted no other person to find.

Max and Gina were already sold. The only question now was the asking price. Amy said they wanted one hundred sixty-five. Max countered with one hundred fifty, he could have the money this afternoon. Amy looked at her husband. They both thought it strange that Max and Gina would have that amount of money available so quickly. But they needed a buyer, and Max and Gina were good people. They finally settled on one fifty-five. Gina asked if she could bring her horse Midnight over the stable this afternoon. That would be just fine!

They were excited. This was everything they were looking for—privacy, seclusion, and peace of mind. They could farm their own vegetables, harvest eggs from the chicken coup, and maybe even add some livestock later on. When they got settled in, maybe they could get Laura to be their caretaker while they took that vacation to Los Angeles that Gina wanted so badly. Amy told them they could move in thirty days from now. That would be perfect.

Later on in the day, Max brought the five-gallon plastic bucket containing the one hundred fifty-five thousand. Amy's husband said he did not want to appear nosey, but how did Max come up with the money so quickly? Max said he inherited the money from his father who didn't believe in banks. Satisfied with Max's explanation, Amy's husband accepted the money and spent a good part of the afternoon counting it. Tomorrow, they would all meet at the lawyer's office to sign all the documentation. Things were looking pretty good for Max and Gina right about now.

Gina went to get Midnight and was alarmed to see that he was not standing in the barn waiting for her. As she got closer, she could see the animal was lying on his side, dead from a gunshot wound to the head. Gina became hysterical and grabbed on to Midnight and cried and cried. Max felt so badly for her as he stood by, letting Gina say goodbye to her beloved horse. Max could feel the rage building inside of him. He needed to talk to Amy's husband, Mark.

Mark had served his country proudly as a demolitions expert in the Middle East. Max explained what had happened to Gina's horse and went on to explain their ongoing problems with a certain biker organization called the Miscreants MC. Mark was very familiar with the gang, they were suspected of killing one of his brothers a few years ago, but charges were never filed. Max told Mark that he needed his help in building a powerful fertilizer bomb. Mark said he would be more than happy to assist Max in his endeavor.

Two days later, Max and Mark drove out to the private road which Max and Gina had previously identified as being the entrance to the Miscreants MC headquarters. Working with night-vision goggles Mark had provided, they set up the powerful shrapnel bomb Mark had designed and built from scratch. They loaded fifty-pound sandbags on one side of the device, so as to direct the full force of the explosion toward the entrance road. They covered a large area around the device with a heavy application of deer repellant. The final step was for Mark to set up the trip wire which would detonate the two-stage explosive device. It was now 4:30 a.m.

It was the following day when Max learned that Shovelhead; his wife, Jackie; and Shovelhead's brother, Spider, were all killed by the roadside bomb when they left the Miscreants MC headquarters at 8:00 a.m. The bodies were so badly burned and mangled by nails, broken glass, and nuts and bolts, all three were unidentifiable. The device was so powerful, it could be heard from as far as a mile away. The remaining members of the Miscreants MC held a meeting at the former Ingrate Order MC compound after sweeping it for booby traps. They all swore revenge, but solemnly realized they could all be next to be blown to pieces. Their sworn enemies were so sophisticated, cunning, and ruthless, the Miscreants all knew they had stepped on the tail of a sleeping dragon.

There was no sympathy from the community or law enforcement for that matter. Whoever did this had done society a favor, and there was brutal backlash from the community. It was open season on the Miscreants MC, and any patch-wearing member was fair game. Surviving members were rifled, shot-gunned, and beaten to death by a community gone anarchic. Investigators deemed most of the cases unsolvable due to the extreme number of enemies both clubs had created for themselves over the course of many years.

The few surviving members literally disappeared, knowing they were no match for an entire county turned against them. The former Ingrate Order MC compound was sold at auction, as was the land that belonged to Shovelhead and his wife that had served as the Miscreants MC headquarters. The lake on Shovelhead's former property was drained by the authorities, and numerous partial human skeletons were found, along with discarded firearms and the remains of vehicles long since reported stolen. The county had vanquished a long-standing enemy that would terrorize its citizens no more.

Inwardly, Max and Gina both knew they were no angels. They were no heroes. They were every bit as evil as their former enemies, just a little bit smarter and a little bit more cunning, and a lot luckier. When it came down to it, it was pure luck that, in many instances, allowed them to continue their campaign of murder, unmolested by police. They settled into their new life on the farm and continued to do business with Martin out on the West Coast. And business was good.

All would have remained good, and everyone would have lived peacefully, had it not been for the arrest of a former Miscreant member named Bones in Miami, Florida. Bones had gone to Miami, trying to hook up with an old girlfriend. Instead he wound up carjacking a wealthy couple, making off with their 1993 Rolls-Royce Silver Spur, three thousand dollars in cash, and an assortment of expensive jewelry. He forced the couple into the trunk of their own car and released them in Hialeah. Just before ditching the stolen car, he caused a four-car accident at a busy intersection.

He was charged with carjacking, kidnapping, DUI, and possession of narcotics, and, as a repeat offender, was sentenced to life without parole in the Miami Dade Prison. The grizzled biker was placed in general population and was an easy mark for the much younger, much more brazen prison population. Bones would have continued to suffer beatings and harassment on a daily basis had he not made a deal with another prisoner, who was a Cuban gang leader named Rafael. In exchange for protection from other inmates, he would offer Rafael the score of a lifetime.

There was a couple living out in the Georgia countryside who was sitting on millions of dollars in cash and cocaine. This couple had murdered dozens of motorcycle gang members, eventually causing the gangs to disintegrate completely. Rafael said he had heard of the story, but refused to believe it. There was just no way two people had caused the collapse of two hardcore motorcycle gangs. Bones reassured him that not only had they done so, they continued living in the area, viewed as unsung heroes by the community they lived in.

Rafael gathered intel from other prisoners and actually found one originally from Georgia who had heard the same story about the murderous couple. But how could Rafael know that this lowlife prisoner Bones was right about the money and the coke? Bones told him it was rumored that the couple had taken six hundred kilos of pure coke off a wrecked sailboat off the coast of South Carolina. They had a partner who moved the coke and eventually committed suicide when the authorities were about to move in on him.

No one could just make up a story that detailed and farfetched, Rafael decided. And so the two inmates struck a deal. Word spread quickly around the prison not to mess with the skinny former biker known as Bones. The Miami Dade Prison had a considerable number of incarcerated members of the gang known as the Cuban Street Sovereigns, whose undisputed leader was Rafael. The gang had a heavy reputation for the use of extreme violence both in and out of prison.

Rafael obtained a road map of the State of Georgia and asked Bones to identify the area where the couple could be found. Bones studied the map closely and drew a tiny circle on the map, explaining that his former gang were positive the couple were living within this area. If all went well, Rafael would be released from prison in two more months for his narcotics possession charge. He would enlist the aid of some of his more trusted associates and head north into Georgia upon his release.

Life for Max and Gina was picturesque on their new farm. Max had buried close to three million dollars in cash on the property and safely stored the coke in a hidden compartment he built under the kitchen floor. Also, buried on the property was Gina's beloved horse, Midnight. Farming was a simple life that agreed well with Max and Gina. Max built a greenhouse, and they had fresh vegetables growing year round. There were apple trees, pear trees. and peach trees as well as a blueberry field.

When they were all settled in, Gina was finally able to convince Max to take her long-awaited vacation to see her brother Martin out in Los Angeles, leaving Laura to care for the animals while they were gone. Max was very impressed with Martin's home, which boasted an indoor-outdoor swimming pool, but he hated Los Angeles. Max could never understand why anyone in their right mind would want to live in a part of the country where the traffic was so bad, it took all day to reach the other side of town. Not to mention the air pollution was so bad, it could actually be seen.

Martin invited them to concerts with sky box seating, and the couple met more than a few famous rock stars. It was interesting for Max that upon meeting these people, most of them seemed like ordinary everyday folks until they got on stage under the lights and became almost superhuman with their abilities to transfix their audiences with their musical prowess. It was all good fun, but Max eagerly awaited their flight back to Atlanta. Los Angeles was definitely not meant for him.

As the release date neared for Rafael, Bones was warned repeatedly that he'd better not be joking about this treasure hunt up in Georgia. There were plenty of Cuban Street Sovereign members that would still be in prison after Rafael's release. All it would take is a phone call to Florida, and a prison visitor would give the word, and Bones would be taken out. Bones would need some type of insurance policy, and he began to consider what other prison gang may be up to the task of protecting him in the event that Rafael was unable to locate what he was searching for. Bones spoke with the leader of the Black Palisade and offered the same deal as he made with Rafael.

The Miami Dade Prison was such a volatile institution that even rumors were capable of starting a prison riot. The Black Palisade was attacked by the Cuban Street Sovereigns in the exercise yard, and there were casualties on both sides. The leader of the Black Palisade was killed during the attack, leaving Bones without any hope of backup protection. Rafael was not among those present in the exercise yard that day as he was in the process of meeting with his attorney and prison officials going over the conditions of his parole.

The very next day, Rafael was released and was met outside the prison by his mom and his sister.

Part of the conditions of his parole was that he was not allowed to leave the state and he was not allowed to associate with felons. Upon arriving at his mother's house, he picked up the phone and called two Sovereign members who had also been recently released.

The three men made plans to head north into Georgia, for what they hoped would be the score that would make them rich.

Bones had provided an ace in the hole for Rafael by giving him the location of an abandoned farm where Bones had camped out after his gang had been decimated. There, in an abandoned house, Bones had hidden his meager belongings in the attic and never bothered to retrieve them after his bike engine threw a rod. The Sovereign members followed the crude map Bones had drawn, and they arrived at the abandoned farm right at dusk. Just as Bones had promised, they did find the backpack in the attic, which contained mostly useless items such as clothing and the like. But there was one item that made all the difference between success and failure. It was the piece of paper on which were the photos of Maxwell Hart and Gina Rodgers.

The old farm suited the ex-cons just fine, even an old crumbling house was better than prison. Rafael, Javier, and Luis studied the photos of Max and Gina in the hopes that they would be recognizable on sight. The three men still could not believe that such an innocent-looking couple could be responsible for killing and maiming so many men, especially hardcore bike gang members. What had happened to these fresh-faced young adults that turned them into monsters, capable of mass murder? Rafael knew from his own life experience that drugs were capable of making people do things that they would never normally do.

The ex-cons were short on cash, so the next day they planned a bank robbery in Savannah. It was a bold plan. They would drop Luis off at a decoy bank to phone in an armed robbery in progress, while Rafael and Javier would commit the actual robbery at a bank on the other side of town. Luis would hop on a public bus and meet the others at a prearranged destination at a shopping mall. All day was spent planning the robbery and logistics. Tomorrow, they would put their bold plan to the test.

Early the next morning, they synchronized their watches and dropped off Luis in front of the decoy bank downtown. Rafael drove to the target bank which they had carefully chosen due to its location and its perceived vulnerability. At precisely 10:00 a.m., Luis made the call on a public phone and casually walked to a nearby bus stop.

Numerous Savannah City Police cars responded quickly, just as Luis was stepping onto the bus. Meanwhile, Rafael and Javier launched the actual robbery which caught the bank employees completely off guard.

An hour later, Rafael and Javier ditched their stolen car in the parking lot of the shopping mall after wiping it clean of fingerprints. They met Luis and proceeded to steal another car from the mall parking lot. Luis, a former car mechanic, hot-wired an old Chevy Caprice using tools he had brought with him from Miami. On the way out to the abandoned house, they bought beer and groceries and counted the stolen money. They had made off with almost ten thousand dollars.

The three ex-cons joked among themselves that perhaps they should just abandon their pursuit of Max and Gina and become full-time bank robbers instead. It was too easy. Apparently, that part of town was unaccustomed to hardened criminals like themselves committing bold robberies out in the open. They would definitely reconsider when their funds ran low again, but for right now, they had their sights on finding Max and Gina and "persuading them" to reveal the location of the money and the coke. They were optimistic and emboldened by the successful robbery they had just committed. They spent another night in the abandoned house drinking beer, and all the while talking about what they would do with the millions of dollars they had yet to steal.

In recent years, a lot of migrant workers had moved into the county, working on farms for cash money paid to them each day. Rafael decided that these migrant workers would be a good starting place for them to gather intel on their intended targets. After countless unsuccessful interviews, Rafael finally caught a break when one of the migrant workers recognized the picture of Gina. The worker told Rafael that this good-looking blonde woman was often seen riding horseback on a dirt road that passed right by the fields he worked each day, mending fences. She wasn't seen there every day, the worker explained in Spanish, but it was a good starting point, the ex-cons figured. Rafael slipped the worker a twenty-dollar bill.

Next, they set about to finding the farm and locating the dirt road that ran through it. The worker didn't know the area really well, but then again, neither did the three gang members from Miami. After a couple of days searching without success, they finally found what appeared to be the farm they were looking for. The worker had described a lake with dead trees protruding above the lake's surface. This had to be it, thought Rafael!

But there was a problem with the location. Out here in the middle of nowhere, a parked car with three men sitting inside would look highly suspicious. All it would take is a nosey neighbor or a cop, and they were busted. It was Javier, a former cowboy himself, who proposed a genius-level solution to their problem. They would steal horses and ride the area searching for the woman. When they located her, they could surround her and force her at gunpoint to take them back to her home.

What seemed a simple plan on the surface actually turned out to be a lot harder than they thought. They would have to first find a farm where they could steal the horses, and it had to be relatively close. It wouldn't be feasible to steal three horses then have to ride twenty miles to the area they were looking for. Again, it was Javier who proposed a solution. They would look in the phone book for an equestrian farm that offered horseback rides to tourist.

It all sounded good. Approximately six miles west, there was an equestrian farm that offered just what they were looking for. Something a little closer would have been nice, but that was the closest. Rafael, who had been born in the USA to Cuban parents, had no Spanish accent, so it was he who made the reservations to go "riding" the next day. That night at the abandoned house drinking beers, Javier tried to explain to his partners in crime that horseback riding was nothing like riding a bike or driving a car.

Horses were a lot smarter than most people think. When climbing onto a horse, it would immediately sense if the rider were experienced or not. An especially intelligent horse may even decide it would fuck with the inexperienced rider. Rafael and Luis dismissed Javier's comments as nonsense. Horses were just dumb animals. What other creature would let a human get on its back and go wherever the human wanted it to go?

But Javier knew horses well. They could flip the reigns out of an inexperience rider's hands, so the rider would have no control over the animal. It could also buck the rider. It could also kick and stomp the rider it has just bucked. Horseback riding was serious business, Javier insisted. But by this point, Rafael and Luis were drunk and arrogant. They dismissed his advice as total bullshit. Tomorrow, they would see for themselves just how "smart" horses really were. If the horses were able to help them execute their plan, then yes, Rafael would consider them as smart.

Something about the three gang members from Miami didn't sit right with the owner of the equestrian farm. They were dirty, unkempt, and looked as though they had not a cent between them. But they paid the fee and seemed to be excited about taking a tour of the Georgia countryside on horseback. Much to the annoyance of Rafael, they were assigned two guides, one to lead and one to pick up the rear. When asked if anyone of them had ever ridden before, Javier, in his broken English, told the guides that he started riding horses when he was a boy. They handed him the reigns to a huge Appaloosa. Rafael, Luis, and both guides would be riding American Quarter Horses that day.

The lead guide was a woman in her midtwenties, and the rear guide was a man, perhaps a little older. They rode nose to tail on dirt roads alongside fields, then turned onto a trail that led them through the woods. Once they were deep in the woods, the three gang members pulled guns on the surprised guides. The male guide pulled a hidden gun and was subsequently shot and wounded by Rafael, leaving the guide's horse running off into the woods ahead of them without its rider. The female guide, they took hostage.

Fortunately for all of them, the horses were accustomed to gunfire. Rafael pulled the female rider down off her horse at gunpoint and showed her the Georgia State road map, pointing to the area known to be frequented by Gina. The woman, now very frightened by the shooting of the other guide, told them that the area they were looking for was a good two to three hours' ride. Rafael suggested that they had better get going then.

As they rode, Rafael told the woman that if she tipped off any passerby, she would suffer the same fate as her coworker. She promised she would cooperate fully. They did pass several other riders early that morning, but true to her word, the female guide acted as though nothing were wrong, and they merely exchanged greetings as they passed. But they came upon a lone woman with long blonde hair wearing a cowboy hat. Rafael realized that they were looking right at Gina Lidia Rodgers. But the woman guide was obviously known to Gina, and realizing something was wrong, Gina took off on her Mustang, right past them at a high rate of speed.

Javier turned his horse one hundred eighty degrees and took off after Gina. Rafael ordered the woman guide to follow Gina and Javier, but the woman told them there was no way they would ever catch up to the Mustang. Rafael fired a warning shot, and the woman obeyed, leading them in the direction of the two other horses, now well ahead of them. The older American Quarter Horses were no match for the much-younger Mustang and the much-younger and spirited Appaloosa.

Gina looked behind her, realizing at this point she was being followed by a single rider. Although Gina was wearing a gun, she decided that it would be safer to continue, hoping to eventually outpace her pursuer. But the Appaloosa was strong, and Javier's riding skills kept him within sight. Onward they ran past the lake of dead trees. Javier realized they must be getting close to Gina's home and kept right on her tail.

A decision had to be made. Should she continue past her own farm or ride into it in the hopes that Max would see them and realize something was wrong? Knowing that Max would be somewhere out on the property, she opted to head straight for it. Instead of taking the driveway entrance, she jumped the Mustang over a fence into a field. But Javier was a skilled horseman and the Appaloosa jumped over the high fence with no problem.

Screaming for Max as loud as she could, Gina headed straight back onto the property. Max saw them and, realizing Gina was being chased, ran toward the house to grab a firearm, cursing himself for forgetting his gun this morning, leaving it on the kitchen table in its holster. Javier had to end this pursuit here and now. He drew his weapon and began firing, striking Gina's horse in the hindquarters. The startled Mustang bucked and sent Gina to the ground.

Looking up, Gina saw Javier, standing over her with a gun pointed at her head. Max now ran toward them, and seeing Gina at gunpoint, he slowed to a walk with his hands over his head. Javier warned Max he would kill Gina if he made one wrong move. For almost a half hour, Javier held them there, until Rafael, Luis, and the female horse guide came trotting onto the property. Rafael jumped off his horse and immediately relieved Max of his sidearm.

Rafael now stood facing Max, holding Max's own .357 caliber magnum in his face. How ironic would it be, Max thought, to be shot by his own gun? Luis threw the woman horse guide to the ground beside Gina and stood over them with his gun. Luis stood beside Javier and slapped him on the back and, in Spanish, congratulated him on his horse-riding skills. Rafael held the gun in Max's face and cocked the hammer. Max looked directly into the eyes of the Cuban gang leader from Miami. Just by looking at him, Max knew this man would not hesitate to kill him.

Having killed a lot of men, Max thought this what Karma must be all about. He knew these men were not going to just take the loot and run. They would kill everyone, leaving no witnesses to the crime, just as Max had done himself many times before. He felt very badly for Gina and the female horse guide. If it were not for him, none of them would be in this situation right now.

Max could have easily told Ray they were not going to bother the wreck of the *Windsor2,* and called its position in to the Coast Guard, just as he was about to do when Ray stopped him. And what had Ray gotten from their discovery? A self-inflicted gunshot wound to the head. If Max had only listened to his inner voice, right now he would be kicking back with Gina, enjoying the off season from his charter fishing business, as it was now the beginning of winter.

Rafael had come a long way for this, even doubting in his own mind if he would be able to pull this off. Against incredible odds, they had found what it was they were looking for, and now it was within their grasp. There would be no more looking over his shoulder to see if a rival gang member were standing right behind him. There would be no more crimes committed with the fear of going to prison. For the rest of his life, all he would have to do is sit back and enjoy himself, and he was pretty certain he could handle that.

Having not known the pleasure of a woman since he was incarcerated two years prior, Rafael and his two partners in crime were greatly looking forward to spending some "quality time" with these two fine-ass bitches, sitting on the ground right in front of him. But right now, they had business to conduct.

They could do this the easy way or the hard way, Rafael didn't care. All he knew right now was that this was going to be the day that was going to change his life forever. He instructed Luis and Javier to take the two women and tie them up in the barn. Javier would stay in the barn to make sure they didn't try to escape, and Luis would assist Rafael in getting Max to tell them everything they wanted to know.

Max took the opportunity to try to talk to Rafael man-to-man. He told Rafael that he knew exactly why they were here. He knew exactly what they were looking for. But if Rafael were to kill him, they would never, and he did stress never, find the money or the cocaine. Max told Rafael he would show him exactly where to find the money and the drugs if Rafael gave his word man-to-man that they would not torture himself or the women. If they were planning to kill him, and he knew that they would, he just wanted a merciful death, without relentless, agonizing pain.

Rafael released the cocked hammer on the .357, but still held it at arm's length, pointing directly at Max's head. Max told him they would need a shovel. Rafael told him to lead the way. Rafael followed Max into the barn. There, Max saw Gina and the women horse guide tied up tightly, side by side, crying. Javier and Luis held guns on the women, giddy with the excitement of knowing what was to come later. Rafael hollered at Luis to come join them outside. Their new friend Max had something he wished to show them. Max grabbed a shovel from the tool rack.

Luis and Rafael followed Max to an area about twenty-five yards behind the barn. There, beneath an old tractor tire, was a fifty-five-gallon steel drum, buried about a foot below ground. Max told them it contained three million dollars in cash. Rafael pointed the .357 at Max's boot and fired a shot. It missed Max's foot by two inches. Max began to dig. Rafael and Luis watched him closely, making sure Max didn't have some nasty surprise waiting for them.

After a few minutes, the shovel struck the top of the steel drum. Max continued to dig, exposing the top of the steel drum, then began to dig around the edge so that the quick-release handle on the lid would be exposed. Dropping the shovel to the ground, Max began digging with his hands, until it was possible to flip the quick-release handle all the way open. As he grabbed the lever to open the drum, Rafael ordered him to stop. Both men were excited, but still cautious of Max's intentions. How did they know that Max didn't have a weapon in that drum, right underneath the lid? Rafael ordered Max to step away from the drum. Rafael got down on his knees and removed the drum lid as Max turned his face in the other direction and dropped to the ground.

A column of flame erupted five stories into the sky. It completely incinerated the entire front of Rafael's body. Luis suffered severe burns to his face and the entire front of his body, but he was still alive. Max began to roll on the ground, away from the column of flame to extinguish his burning clothing and hair. Screaming could be heard from the women inside the barn as they had no idea what was happening. Javier came running out of the front door of the barn and turned to see what appeared to be a scene out of a science-fiction horror movie, right before being struck on the back of the head with a rock.

Max pulled off his smoldering winter jacket and soaked his head and trousers with water from a garden hose. He stood there watching his handiwork from afar. He had built a petrol bomb similar to the one he used to kill three members of the former Ingrate Order MC, except on a much-larger scale. Standing twenty-five yards away, he could feel the intense heat radiating from the flame. He ran into the barn and cut loose the women who now embraced him tightly. He told them they needed to get out of the barn before it caught fire.

But the petrol bomb was burning itself out by now. When it was safe to do so, Max made sure there were no survivors, but there were. Luis was severely burned but still breathing. Javier was bleeding profusely from the back of his head but was still breathing. Max used Javier's own gun to put him and his buddy Luis out of their misery. Then sun had begun to set as Max escorted the women to the house. The women removed his burned clothing and filled a bathtub full of ice water for him to sit in. The burns were mostly to his head and legs, his heavy winter jacket had protected his torso. But considering the intensity of the flame, he was lucky it was not much, much worse. The women did everything they could to make him as comfortable as possible. They gave him whiskey and narcotic pain pills. They poured cold water over his head. They thanked him repeatedly for saving them from being raped and murdered.

The women, so caring, so nurturing, had completely forgotten the fact that if it were not for Max's greed, his poor judgment, and his stupidity, none of them would have even gone through the hellish experience. He felt especially bad for both women. This poor innocent horseback guide, her life would never be the same after this experience, Max was certain. And his beloved Gina, it was he who introduced her to illegal drugs in the first place. Would she have ever become so wild sexually if she had never used drugs? This Max would never know for certain.

But he did know for certain that Gina would never have become a cold murderess had it not been for him. He had led her by example. When they first started dating, Gina had confided to him she wanted to kill another woman, all because Gina hated the other girl. Max remembered that he told her that if she was, in fact, planning on killing someone, then kill someone who truly deserves it. Since the discovery of the coke aboard the *Winsor2*, Max had convinced her that everyone who got in their way was worthy of being killed. And Gina followed his lead, without questioning whether they "deserved it" or not.

In Max's opinion, they all deserved to die. But who was he to teach an innocent young woman to kill and not feel any remorse? Everyone, once they reach a certain age, carves out their own path in life. But it was Max who held the knife and did the cutting, Gina just followed and destroyed additional tissue along the way. Gina was a promising, good-looking woman as recently as just a few months ago. Today she was still just as beautiful, but willing to kill almost anyone for almost any reason. And it was all because of Max.

The next morning brought it all home for Max. Waking up at the crack of dawn, he surveyed the damage he had caused the day before. Gina's favorite Mustang was not looking so well. The horse had been shot and had lost a lot of blood and was certain to die. Max had to put her out of her misery with a bullet between the eyes. Standing over the body of Javier, Max looked into his deceased, still-open, clouded-over eyes. An expression of total shock frozen on his dead face, he probably died thinking this was going to be the best day of his life. Instead, it was the day he lost it. Luis was a gruesome sight if ever there was one. The entire front of his body had been burned so badly, Max could not believe he had to shoot the man to finally kill him.

But it was the body of Rafael himself that was the most ghastly thing Max had ever seen. It was burned down to a charred skeleton, the arms and legs curled up into a fetal position. There were still wisps of smoke rising into the cool morning air from all that remained of Rafael. Max bent down up to pick up his .357 caliber magnum, but dropped it immediately, it was still hot. The wood grips were burned, and the weapon was destroyed by unspent rounds that cooked off inside the cylinder.

There was heavy lifting to do on this brisk, clear early Georgia Saturday morning. Max called Rob's Tree Service, knowing that Rob, like himself, was an early riser. Rob answered the phone still half asleep, as Max told him he needed to hire Rob's backhoe for the day. Rob told him it was already on a heavy equipment trailer, he could have it there in an hour or so. Max burned a joint in his driveway, and as a new day dawned, Rob arrived and swung the tractor trailer wide to make the turn onto Max's property.

Early on, Rob had always been suspicious of Max, his prowess with women and his seemingly unending supply of cash money. Rob knew better than to ask questions, but on this early winter morning, he didn't have to. Max greeted him as he stepped out of the cab of the Mack tractor. Max offered Rob a fat joint which he had just rolled. Much to Max's surprise, Rob lit the joint and passed it back to Max. Rob knew something really fucked up was going on when Max offered to pour a splash of whiskey into his coffee cup.

After they finished burning the fatty, Max laid it all out. Max told Rob he was a kingpin coke dealer. Yesterday, he had killed three Miami gang members who were trying to rip him off. He needed Rob to help him bury the bodies as well as a dead horse and other evidence as needed. For his services in this matter, Max would pay him twenty-five thousand dollars cash for not even one whole day's work. As the strong weed began to kick in, Rob thought about the risks versus rewards. Rob knew Max to be highly intelligent and slippery as a green eel when it came down to slithering his way out of legal trouble. But something deep in the back of his skull told Rob that Max was being honest, sincere, and he really needed his help right about now. As for the twenty-five thousand, who in the hell need that anyway? Well, Rob did. He reached behind the seat of his Mack tractor and handed Max a hard hat and a safety vest. If they were going to do this, it needed to be done safely.

Following Max to the rear of the ten-acre farm, Max first instructed Rob to dig up the remnants of his homemade petrol bomb behind the barn. The intense heat from the steel drum full of burning gasoline had caused it to melt and collapse in on itself. Where the petrol bomb had been buried, Rob dug a hole as deep as his backhoe would allow. Into the hole went the bodies of Rafael, Javier, and Luis, as well as the steel drum and the .357 caliber. Rob asked Max if they were going to bury Gina's Mustang as well. Max told him yes, but in a separate, proper grave that would be marked, right next to Gina's horse Midnight.

By now, Gina and the female horse guide, whose name was Sharon, joined them outside. Max introduced Rob to Sharon and told him about all that had happened to them the previous day.

Rob offered her a ride back to the equestrian farm and she gratefully accepted. Rob asked if it would be okay to drop his trailer and pick it up later. Max said of course, as he handed Rob two hundred fifty one-hundred-dollar bills.

Before they left, Max pulled Sharon aside and gave her twenty-five thousand as well. That was more than a year's pay, and she refused to accept it. Max told her that it was the very least he could do. He was the whole reason behind her hellish experience the day before. All he asked was that she not mention Gina or himself when she talked to the police about what happened. Sharon agreed, and Max stuffed the fat wad of bills into her winter coat pocket. She gave him a big hug. She gave Gina a big hug as well right before she climbed into the cab of Rob's tractor.

Max and Gina stood in their driveway and waved goodbye. She turned to Max and told him that he looked like hell. He told her that he felt like hell. He apologized for what had happened. Gina apologized for not shooting those lowlife gangbangers on sight. She explained that as she passed Sharon on the horse trail, she knew something was terribly wrong. She knew by the look on Sharon's face that she was in grave danger. The three men following her looked out of place. Gina should have just pulled her gun and shot those bastards. Max put his arm around her and told her not to worry her pretty little head. She had handled herself just fine.

The owner of the equestrian farm had called the sheriff's department and reported the missing riders one hour after they were due to return. The sheriff's department deployed a search party and were able to locate the male guide who had been shot and wounded. They had in fact saved the man's life. In another hour, he would have bled to death. The following day, when asked for the perceived motive behind the shooting and subsequent kidnapping, Sharon told the authorities she suspected the men were desperate horse thieves.

After the questioning, the owner of the equestrian farm and Sharon brought the horse trailer to Max and Gina's farm to pick up the Appaloosa and the three American Quarter Horses. There they found that Gina had cared for the animals well, and they were all uninjured. The owner was quite suspicious about how it was that

Sharon had wound up on Max and Gina's farm. Sharon said she had lied to the three men, telling them she knew a couple that owned a farm and would pay cash money for the stolen animals.

The owner had actually heard stories about Max and Gina and how they were suspected of taking out not just one but two criminally violent bike gangs. Sharon's story seemed to coincide with the owner's beliefs that Max and Gina were not model citizens, but they were in no way buyers of stolen horses. When asked about the fate of the three men who committed the shooting, the kidnapping, and the theft of the horses, Sharon told him bluntly that Maxwell Earnest Hart had mercilessly killed them.

If it were not for Max, the three gangbangers from Miami would have raped and killed her along with Max's woman, Gina. The farm owner lit a cigar and rolled down his truck window. He pulled a whiskey flask from his coat pocket and offered it to Sharon. Sharon was not a whiskey drinker, but took a small sip anyway before handing it back. The equestrian farm owner, now satisfied that Sharon was telling him the truth, asked her for one additional thing. He asked her to remind him to never do anything that may piss off Maxwell Hart or Gina Rodgers. Sharon laughed and said she would, but added, someone had to do something really incredibly stupid to wind up on the wrong side of Max and Gina.

Gina stood over the grave of the Mustang that was shot by Javier, not feeling at all bad about what had happened to him or his other moronic, evil friends. The Mustang was named Bullet, on account of her incredible speed. It was a tragedy that this brave animal was not able to outrun the projectile that ultimately caused her death. Gina asked Max why does God allow the innocent to suffer and die. Max thought about it for a moment and said that perhaps God does not allow the evil that happens down here on earth.

Pointing to the sky, Max said that up there is the realm of God, down here on earth is the realm of Satan. Gina looked at Max and, for the first time in her life, was convinced that this was true. She always knew Max was smart, but she often questioned his wisdom. Now, she was convinced that Max was probably the wisest man she had ever known. Yes, he was a lawbreaker; yes, he was a killer—but so was she. Gina never looked at her fellow human beings the same way again after that day, standing out in the cold, over the graves of her dead horses, Midnight and Bullet.

Max was right. God works through people, and so does Satan. Gina asked Max where they were in the grand scheme of things. Max had to think about that as well. He said that we do not have to know or understand what life is about any more than we have to know and understand the process of breathing in order to breathe. We just have to let it happen. We do not have to understand it. Deeply affected by what Max had just said, Gina looked him in the eyes and asked Max what they should do now. Max grabbed her by the shoulders and looked deep into her eyes and said that she needed to stop asking so many heavy questions. Gina laughed at his response, but Max inwardly knew that he was going to have to face that question directly. Sooner or later, everything Max had done in his life was going to catch up with him.

The following day, Max walked to the mailbox at the end of the driveway, only to find a single white envelope from Los Angeles. Max opened it on his walk back to the house. Inside, he found two first-class round-trip airfare tickets to LAX. They were accompanied by a letter on which a single sentence was printed. It read, "Need to talk, Urgent!" What in the hell could this be all about? He showed it to Gina. She said that obviously Martin wanted to talk with them in person. Max told her that she had a very firm grasp on the obvious.

Max said he would rather jerk off with a handful of broken glass than go to Los Angeles. Gina said it would be fun, besides Martin, she knew, would not have taken the trouble to send them the tickets if it were not really important. And so they packed and drove to the Savannah International Airport for their early flight on Friday morning. They were seated and found themselves in the midst of a group of wild long-haired dudes and very pretty female companions.

This was to be no ordinary airplane ride, Max and Gina decided, when they found themselves surrounded by America's newest rock sensation, ABC Class Morons. Originally from LA, they were returning from a successful US tour back to their homes in California. They had just played the Savannah Civic Center the night before and were looking forward to returning to LA. They were already wasted, and it was only 7:30 a.m.

The airline actually allowed these highly intoxicated individuals aboard the flight, but hey, they were rock stars, for fuck's sake! Max and Gina were amused by their over-the-top antics. They repeatedly fucked with and were subsequently warned by the flight staff to behave themselves even before takeoff. On the climb to cruising altitude, they were on their best behavior. But when the aircraft leveled off at thirty thousand feet, they collectively became the most misbehaved group of people to ever board a passenger plane.

At one point, the pilot stepped out of the cockpit to warn them that he was obligated to call in an emergency landing if they didn't settle down. He said they would all be arrested for disrupting a commercial flight. The tour manager assured the pilot they were just burning off steam, and they would not cause any more problems on the way to their connecting flight. The pilot did not believe him, repeating his warning, that if these "hippies" didn't calm the fuck down, they were all going to be spending the night in jail. Max was a bit concerned, given the fact that he was holding a vial of ten grams of pure coke.

Seated across from Max was the ABC Class Moron's lead guitarist, who introduced himself as Spaz. They began to converse and Max found him witty and funny. Spaz said he was not feeling all that well from booze over top of barbiturates. Max slipped Spaz the ten-gram vial, warning him that it was probably the best coke he'd ever had. Spaz thanked Max graciously and proceeded to snort the contents of the vial. Suddenly, Spaz seemed to feel a lot better, and he shared the coke with his beautiful girlfriend. Max knew this was bad business already.

Spaz didn't heed his warning about the potency. Max had just watched him and his girlfriend snort enough pure cocaine to kill five adults. The guitarist was probably accustomed to coke that was at best fifty percent pure. Spaz now stared at Max and asked him how he got so badly burned. Max mumbled something about an accident when Spaz went into full cardiac arrest. The beautiful curvy brunette seated next to Spaz called for the flight attendant.

Unaccustomed to dealing with in-flight emergencies such as this, the flight attendants attempted to defibrillate Spaz, but were unsuccessful, causing his girlfriend to go into full cardiac arrest as well. The pilot even came out of the cockpit to assist in the in-flight medical emergency. But it was the end of the road to Spaz and his girlfriend. They made an emergency landing at Jackson Mississippi International Airport. The ABC Class Morons were pulled aside for questioning along with Max and Gina.

The police found the vial of coke directly under the seat formerly occupied by Spaz. Max felt as though this was a new low, even for him. This poor dude and his girlfriend were dead because of the coke he had given them. They would still be alive had it not been for him and his self-centered objective of trying to get rid of the coke before the outrageous antics of the ABS Class Morons forced the pilot to make an emergency landing and have the Morons and probably himself arrested.

The Jackson Mississippi Police were suspicious of Max and Gina, if only because they were sitting right next to Spaz and his girlfriend when the in-flight medical emergency occurred. The authorities asked the same questions in a thousand different ways, and Max became visibly annoyed when the questioning stretched on into the afternoon. It now occurred to Max that he could end the relentless questioning at any time, saying that he and Gina were on the way to a wedding in LA. Unless they were planning to charge him with a crime for which he was not guilty, they were obligated to release him.

The police investigator conducting the interview had just one more question for Max. How did Max sustain the burn injuries to his head, which had burned off every hair down to the roots? Max said that if he wanted to eat lead paint chips, why would the investigator even care about that? The officer became combative and told Max that if any further evidence revealed that he knew more than what he was telling them, they would come for him. Max left the police station with Gina not the least bit concerned with the investigator's warning.

Two connecting flights later, Max and Gina finally arrived at LAX. They took a taxi to Martin's house two hours away. By the time they arrived at Martin's house, Max was so pissed off he could not think straight. There was a full-blown party in progress when they arrived and the loud music and the scantily clad female partygoers did not do anything to help Max with his headache. Martin, ever the gracious host, showed them to the guest room where they could relax and unwind after their long and stressful trip.

Max fell onto the bed in the guest bedroom, and Gina excused herself to join the party downstairs. It was an hour later when Max realized that he was not alone in the guest's quarters. In the bathroom attached to the guest room, he found two young women who had just finished melting and were in the process of injecting heroin. Max was annoyed by the intrusion, the two young women had to have passed him sleeping on the bed in order to gain access to the bathroom.

The girls were obviously startled when Max opened the bathroom door without even knocking. He was both pissed off and curious at the same time. He told the girls he wanted to sample what they had. Reaching into his pocket, he threw a wad of cash onto the bathroom sink. One of the girls, a sexy freckled redhead, told Max this was not street-level-quality heroin. It was China White, a very potent variety that was to be used only in moderate amounts. Max said he was fine with that and sat on the edge of the bathtub and proceeded to roll up his sleeve and offer his right forearm to the pretty redhead.

It was now apparent to Max that these two young women knew exactly what they were doing as they prepared to inject him with the potent drug. As blood backed up into the syringe, the redhead pushed the plunger home. Instantaneously, Max was overwhelmed by a sensation like he had never known in his whole life. If there ever was something on this earth better than sex, this was it. He could now fully understand why people became addicted to heroin, it was the ultimate sensation matched by no other.

Gina found him in the bathtub barely responsive. She instantly knew that some of Martin's party guests were responsible for Max's present condition. She was extremely angry at Max, but at the same time concerned about his condition. She ran downstairs to fetch Martin. Looking into Max's pupils, Martin assured Gina her man would be just fine. Gina did not believe her own brother, stating that she had never seen Max in this condition before.

She began striking Martin in the face and head with her fists. Her older brother grabbed her wrists and told her to cut the shit. Whatever had happened to her man was the direct result of something he had initiated himself, Martin was sure. Max was a full-grown man, and Martin told her that neither she nor anyone else could control his actions. Martin knew precisely what had happened and he told his sister to just relax and leave Max right where he was. Gina slapped her brother full force in the face.

Gina was drunk and she was pissed off. She trusted her older brother's instincts, but then again, she didn't. Martin was wild and careless, much like herself. But Martin was very social and had lots of friends, none of whom Gina trusted. Gina resigned herself to falling asleep on the big comfortable bed in the guest room. She was greatly relieved to find Max curled up around her in the bed the next morning. Rather than berate Max for his idiotic behavior, she let it ride. She knew Martin had sent for them for the purpose of something really important. That was all she was concerned with right now.

Beautiful young women in bikinis snorted coke, went swimming in the pool, and helped themselves to the buffet provided by the same catering service Martin had hired for the entire weekend. Over lunch, Martin told Max and Gina they would be having a very special dinner guest this evening. Martin advised Max that he needed to be sober for the meeting which would take place six hours from now. Martin was more than a little annoyed at Max's inattention.

Martin stressed the importance of Max being sober for the planned meeting, but Max grabbed Martin by the throat and shook the skinny cokehead like a ragdoll. Max told Martin face-to-face, man-to-man, that he had always hated Martin from the first time they had met. Gina pleaded with Max to release her brother, but Max continued to strangle him, all the while telling him he was a useless piece of shit human being. Throwing Martin onto a glass table, Max yelled that he was surprised no one had ever blown Martin's head off.

Gina went berserk and began striking Max with her fists and kicking him with her high heels. Max stood there stoically, allowing his own girlfriend to vent her frustrations while the shocked guests all looked at them in disgusted horror. Max now pulled Martin from out of the smashed tabletop frame and held him by his shirt collar. Martin tried to defuse the situation by telling Max that whatever the problem was, this was not the solution.

Regaining his composure, Max released Gina's brother, who now stood awkwardly in front of his guests, embarrassed for what had taken place. Max also felt embarrassed and apologized for his violent behavior. Gina suggested that Max take a walk and calm down. Of all the places in the world he could be right now, Max cursed himself for putting his own self here in this situation. But his mood changed abruptly when he saw the pretty redhead and her friend getting out of a car in Martin's driveway. Of course they remembered Max and asked him how he was doing. Max told the girls he was in the market for the China White heroin he had tried yesterday. They asked him how much he was looking for. Max was unsure of what that particular drug went for at street level and told them simply he wanted two thousand dollars' worth. They invited him to take a ride with them to a house several blocks away. Max handed the redhead a wad of bills.

Max waited in the car with the other girl, while the pretty redhead disappeared inside the house. She came back out fifteen minutes later handing Max a paper bag containing the heroin. That was too easy, thought Max. He suggested that they go somewhere and sample the drug. The redhead suggested that they just go back to Martin's house. Max thought that was a really bad idea, but where else were they going to go?

Sitting in the car in Martin's own driveway, they proceeded to get high, really high. Max gave each of the girls several grams, a finder's fee, he explained. They were all too happy to accept. Max thanked the girls and excused himself. He stretched out on the bed in the guest room and stared at the ceiling. Life was spinning out of control, and he was content with letting that happen. It was only a matter of time, he figured, until all the fucked-up things that he had done were going to come back on him.

Gina aroused him from his stupor and told him he needed to get ready for dinner. Martin had a special guest he wanted Max to meet. Max was annoyed, but figured this was the whole reason they came out here, and he may as well just get it over with. After helping themselves to the dinner buffet, Martin invited Max and Gina into his own private office in the house. Martin was annoyed by the fact that Max was obviously stoned, but didn't want to provoke him again.

Martin introduced the couple to a business associate named Simon. The man explained that he was very impressed with the quality of the cocaine he'd been getting from Martin and was interested to know if Max were willing to make a bulk sale. Max asked the well-dressed and well-groomed man in his forties how much the man was looking to purchase. Simon asked Max how much product he had available for sale. Max asked that he be excused to speak with Gina privately.

They sat down in the living room, and Max asked Gina how much inventory they still had. It was Gina who kept the books and told Max they had exactly three hundred ten kilos remaining. This was their chance, Max figured, to finally get out of the cocaine business for good. Gina was concerned that they didn't even know this man, how did they not know he was working for the police? Max said it was her brother's associate. Would Martin actually be that stupid to try to set up this deal if he didn't trust the man one hundred percent?

Martin was a lot of things, but he wasn't stupid. Gina knew her brother well enough to know that he would never put himself in a situation that could jeopardize his future. He had a good thing going on. He had a successful career and he had money. She knew he would never throw all that away in a risky business deal with a man he didn't know or trust. The couple agreed, this was their ticket out of the coke business. And it could not come any sooner.

The couple rejoined the men in Martin's study. Max told the associate he would sell off all the remaining product, three hundred ten kilos for three million one hundred thousand, cash. There was only one condition of the sale, however, the associate along with Martin would have to come to Georgia and personally pick up the coke themselves. That was the deal, take it or leave it. Simon commented that it was an unusual arrangement, he was a busy man and would just assume to let his own people handle the transaction.

There was no way Max was going to allow people unknown to him to carry out this transaction. Those were his conditions of the sale, there was no negotiation. Max explained that if he wanted this deal bad enough, Simon would have to make it happen on Max's terms. Simon told Max he was a shrewd businessman and agreed to Max's terms. Simon and Martin would fly to Georgia, purchase an RV, and use it to transport the load back across the country. Max said that sounded like a good plan.

So this was it. This would be the deal that ended Max and Gina's careers as kingpin drug dealers. Max could not be happier with the way things had worked out. They could spend the rest of their lives not having to worry about the possibility of getting busted with enough coke that would send them away to prison for life. This would be an entirely fresh start for Max and Gina. If it all worked out, Max was looking forward to not ever having to deal with Martin's brother ever again.

By now, Max had a new problem. He had become a daily user of the heroin that he'd brought back from LA. It was bad business, he knew, but as much as he tried to care, he could not. Embedded in his mind were the memories of everything that had happened over the last few months. As much as he tried not to think about it, something would jar his memory, and he found himself replaying the bad experiences in his mind over and over again. Heroin became a release mechanism that freed his mind.

Now it was all up to Martin and Simon to make good on the deal they had set up. Max didn't really trust either man, but in the interest of their own self-preservation, Max figured they would do the utmost not to screw this up. They had everything to gain and everything to lose, but so did Max and Gina for that matter. Max had two choices right now. He could either keep on worrying about this one last deal, or he could get a fix. The choice for him was obvious.

Finally, the day came when Martin and Simon showed up as promised. They had just come from an RV dealership in Savannah, and Simon was proud of his new acquisition. It was a luxury hotel room on wheels, and they had brought guests along with them. Two young women had made the flight with them from LA and would be returning with them on their long drive back across the country. Martin tried to explain that two traveling couples would look less suspicious. Max wasn't fooled, nor was Gina.

When the opportunity presented itself, Max asked Martin if the two female traveling companions were aware of their purpose for being here in Georgia. Martin explained that the women were both employed by Simon. Max asked him again if the women knew they would be traveling back across the country with almost seven hundred pounds of cocaine stashed in the RV. Martin told him yes, they were aware of their purpose but did not know exact details. Martin asked Max if he could please not mention anything to Vicky about the women. Max responded by saying he didn't care at all about that, he just wanted this deal over and done with as soon as possible.

This was going to be a problem. Max needed Gina's help counting the money and he needed Martin and Simon to help load the product. How were they supposed to accomplish this with these two other women present? Martin asked Max how he thought it should be handled. Max suggested that Martin take the women to the guesthouse and help them get settled in. After nightfall, they would bring the money to the main house and load the RV with the coke.

Martin asked Max why it was so important that this all be done tonight. This was business, explained Max. They were free to spend the night here, but tomorrow they needed to be gone. Martin seemed upset by the fact that they were being rushed. What was the big hurry? Max told Martin that ever since the coke became part of their lives, things have never been the same. All he wanted was the coke off his property and out of his life, forever.

When nightfall came, Simon personally brought the suitcases containing the cash into the living room of Max's house. Gina would count the money while the three men transferred the coke from the hidden compartment in the kitchen floor out to the RV. All would have been fine except that Martin and Simon's traveling companions happened to find them loading the three hundred and ten kilos into the storage compartment under the RV. Simon, who had so far been a pretty cool customer, became a little nervous when the women saw what they were doing. The woman knew that they were transporting narcotics on the way home, they just didn't know that it would be almost seven hundred pounds worth.

Martin offered one of the kilos to the women and told them to take it back to the guesthouse and enjoy themselves. The women were fine with that, but as they turned to leave, Max stopped them. Cautioning the women about the potency of the coke they held in their hands, Max explained that a lot of people died so far because of it. Some had died using it, and others had died for reasons he'd rather not mention. The women seemed uneasy and a little scared. Just be careful with it, Max explained to them. It's very pure and very powerful.

The three men resumed loading, but Martin was mad with Max for upsetting the women. Max felt the urge to knock Martin out. But instead, Max regained his composure, telling Martin that dozens of people had died because of this particular batch of pure cocaine. Max told them that he'd personally lost count of how many people had either died or were killed because of it. He did not want to see the two pretty women that Martin and Simon brought with them fall victim to it.

Simon tried to smooth things over, telling Max this was not their first rodeo. People get killed in the drug business all the time. This was nothing new to either himself or even Martin here. Those two women, Simon told Max, may look all sweet and innocent, but they are anything but. They both knew the business. Simon told Max not to worry about the women, they were full-grown adults and knew what they were doing. On through the night they worked until the last kilo was stowed and the last bill was counted.

Gina said goodbye to her brother the next day, right before he stepped onto the RV. Simon shook hands with Max and thanked him for the opportunity to conduct business with him. Max in turn thanked Simon. Because of this deal, Max was out of the business for good. Gina and Max stood in the driveway as the huge RV turned onto the main road in front of their house and was gone. She turned to Max and asked what they were going to do now.

They were not completely out of the woods yet, Max told her. It was possible that people still believed they were sitting on the drugs. They would need to move somewhere people would never suspect. Max proposed that they drive to Charleston and take *The REEL OPPORTUNITY* to Hilton Head Island. There they could buy a nice house, and Max could set up his charter fishing business. They could still keep the farm and use it as a vacation home.

Gina liked the idea, but was not happy about having to get rid of the other Mustang they had bought with the farm. Max said she had a choice, she could either board it at the equestrian farm or bring it to Hilton Head Island and board it there. On the island, there were limited places where she could ride, but out here, she could pretty well ride it wherever she chose, just like she had done many times before. Gina decided that for now the Mustang would stay in Georgia.

Taking one last walk around the property, Max locked up the main house and climbed into the truck beside Gina. It was time for them to move on with their lives. They said goodbye to Laura at the rental house on the way out of town, then onward toward Charleston they drove. Just for kicks, they drove past the old Ingrate Order MC compound. The property had been auctioned off and the new owners were a trucking firm that actually used the property for that purpose. The place was busy. On this cold winter morning, there were tractor trailers backed into every available bay and there were even a couple waiting to either load or off-load. If the new owners only knew what had happened there, Max wondered if they still would have bought it.

It conjured up bad memories for Max, and he regretted his decision to drive past it. He suggested that they drive to the next town and have lunch. There in the bathroom of the restaurant, Max shot up a dose. He wondered how long it would be until Gina figured out he was on his way to becoming a full-blown heroin addict. How would she react? In another few seconds, it was the furthest thing from his mind.

Upon arriving in Charleston, they first stopped at the marina to check on *The REEL OPPORTUNITY.* It sat high and proud in the water. They drove on into downtown and checked into a fancy hotel. They ordered room service and went to bed early. The next morning, they ordered a big breakfast before checking out and heading to the marina. It would be a cold ride on the bridge for the cruise to Hilton Head Island.

But all was not well with the boat when Max tried to start the engines. The starboard engine refused to start due to a dead battery. Max decided that the quickest way to remedy the problem was to simply fix it himself. But halfway through the project, he wished he had called a marine service company. The engine room of the sport fisher was cramped and difficult to work in. It was freezing cold, and the 8-D engine batteries probably weighed one hundred and fifty pounds each. Max strained his back lifting out the dead battery through the engine hatch.

After loading the heavy battery into the back of his truck, they drove to an auto parts store. The man behind the counter offered to help Max bring in the old battery with a hand truck. Max was grateful for his help. As the man behind the counter printed out Max's receipt for the new battery, Max saw something that made him cringe. On the man's forearm was a tattoo of the former Ingrate Order MC.

The man didn't recognize Max. How could he? The two men had never met. Unbeknownst to Max, however, was that the man had seen his picture and just didn't recognize him, perhaps because of his burn injuries. If this man only knew who Max was and his role in bringing down the former motorcycle club, Max was certain the man would try to kill him on the spot where he now stood.

As he got in the truck, Max was about to share the chance encounter with Gina but thought better of it. There was no sense in worrying Gina if he didn't have to. Max spent the remainder of the day transporting the replacement battery from the marina parking lot to the pier, getting it on board, and lowering it down into the engine hatch. After terminating the battery cables, Max looked at his watch. What he initially though would take a couple hours had taken all day. And he messed up his back.

Early the next morning, they casted off and motored down the Ashly River. Inside the cabin, it was toasty warm with the aid of an electric space heater, but up on the bridge, it was freezing cold. The sky was the color of slate gray and the winds began to pick up as the headed out into the Atlantic. It was probably the coldest day of the year, and once again Max cursed himself for his poor judgment. He took breaks to come down into the cabin to thaw out his hands and fingers, then it was back up to the bridge to continue their cruise. *The REEL OPPORTUNITY* was not designed for cold weather voyages.

They anchored off the coast of Kiawah Island, and Max left the generator running all night. Really they should have made marina and hotel arrangements, and Max found himself questioning his poor judgment again. He was more concerned with Gina. Though Gina was a tough chick and never complained, he still felt bad about making her go through this, especially given the fact that it was avoidable. It was the heroin, Max decided, that was making him lose his edge.

The next morning the weather was even worse. Now there was a cold rain on top of the wind and the cold. This trip just keeps getting better and better, Max thought right after his morning fix. Climbing up to the bridge and now sitting at the helm, it was hard to tell where the dark gray sky ended and the sea began. The ocean swells were much more intense today making for a very uncomfortable cruise down the South Carolina coast.

The REEL OPPORTUNITY rolled from side to side the entire day as they cruised parallel to the coast and parallel to the ocean swells. The entire trip they never did see another craft out on the water. By late afternoon, they were passing the Joyner Banks, where their odyssey all began five months ago. It looked different now with large waves crashing onto it, but it still made Max recall everything that had happened since they passed this very spot.

Ray and Marcella appeared to be a happy couple, and now they were both dead. Diego Ortiz and his associates were dead. Orlando Rodrigues and his people were dead. Esmeralda and her husband were dead. Dozens of men from two motorcycle clubs were dead.

Dale Tomkins, the guy that tried to steal the coke and make off for Chicago, was dead. Ten gang members trying to protect their own turf in furtherance of trying to steal the coke were dead. Otis Williams and his associates were dead. Spaz and his beautiful girlfriend were dead from an overdose. The three gangbangers from Miami were dead, all suffering greatly as they perished.

It wasn't Max's place to judge any of these people. All he knew was that if it had not been for his decision to anchor his boat, right where they were, right now, none of those things would have ever happened. Down in the salon, he opened a compartment and found the original kilo Ray had brought aboard after his discovery. Max would have probably have forgotten it was even there, but right now, all the memories of that day's events had brought it all home.

Gina woke from her nap and asked why they were stopped. Max told her he had something important to do. Gina saw the package in his hand and followed him out to the rear deck. This was where it all started five months ago, this was where it would all end. He slit the package open with his knife and poured the contents into the sea. Sure, they could have held on to it, shared it with friends at special occasions. Or they could have even cut its purity and sold it at street level and made over two million dollars. But Max decided that it needed to be destroyed, and this was a fitting place to do so.

Max docked *The REEL OPPORTUNITY* at his reserved slot at the marina on Hilton Head Island. It was just getting dark as they loaded their suitcases into the taxi cab and headed for their hotel. Tomorrow they would go house shopping, but right now, in the hotel bathroom, Max needed a fix. He'd forgotten to lock the door and Gina found him there, sitting on the john and injecting himself with the China White. Max would never forget the look on her face when she realized what he was doing.

Gina slammed the bathroom door behind her as well as the hotel room door on the way out. Max stumbled out into the room and saw her suitcases were still there. She would be back later, he figured. They could talk about it then. He woke the next morning to find her sleeping on the couch. He gave himself a fix and ordered room service. Gina woke up still wearing her clothes from the day before.

She sat at the table and stared at Max, ignoring her hot breakfast. Max stared right back at her. He told her that if she needed to say something, now would be a good time. She said nothing at first, a cold blank stare on her face. Finally, she asked how he could do this to himself. How could he do this to her?

Max said that in the wake of everything that had happened, he could no longer stand how he felt inside. Anything that was capable of changing the way he felt, well, he was all for it. Two of Martin's party guest had introduced him to it, and he knew this was a drug unlike anything he'd ever experienced. Gina felt a twinge of guilt. If it were not for Martin's fucked-up friends, she wouldn't have a man who was now a heroin addict. She pleaded with Max. There was help available, he could kick this thing, and she would be right there to support him. There was only one problem, he now explained. Anyone in any drug rehab will say that unless they really want to quit using, they will not. Such was the case with him right now. Maybe someday he might lose his taste for the heroin, but it was not going to be today. Gina said she couldn't live with a heroin user.

But she was just fine living with a kingpin drug dealer and mass murderer? Shooting dope was a far cry from killing people, he explained. She was right there beside him when together they killed Diego Ortiz and his four goons. She helped him do it. And what about sniping into the Ingrate Order MC compound? She was right there beside him. When he shot Esmeralda's husband in their own backyard, she was there right beside him. And what about the gangbangers in Chicago? How about all the Ingrates and Miscreants they wasted? Now, here she was sitting beside him, the only difference being that now he was shooting dope, not other human beings.

A lot of bad mistakes had been made. A lot of poor judgment used. All Max wanted to do right now was forget about the past and try to move on with his life. And he just wanted to enjoy himself. Today for example, Gina could spend it sulking about Max using heroin or accompany him looking for a new house. They had all day. They could have a nice lunch and a nice dinner later to discuss which properties they liked. It was all up to Gina to decide how they wanted to spend it.

As much as she wanted to stay mad at Max, she couldn't. Max had always been there for her every step of the way. Now it was her turn to be there for him. Maybe there was some way she could convince him that the path he was taking led straight down. Just as Max realized that he'd made a huge mistake entering the cocaine business, he might just do the same with his heroin addiction. There was no way Gina was going to control Max or his actions.

It was going to be a fun day, Gina decided as she got ready to go out and look at properties. Max could struggle with his inner demons all he wanted, but it was not going to stand in the way of Gina enjoying herself today. She loved the prospect of picking out a new house. Max looked in the hotel phone book for a realtor whom he thought would not just work with them, but also cut through the bullshit of trying to show them properties that were way out of their price range.

Even though they were sitting on almost 5.7 million, that money would have to last them the rest of their lives. The charter fishing service would be a good source of income, but it came with a high overhead cost. It would be perfect for laundering the coke money, however. Max told Gina they should look at houses in the half million range. In 1993, that could buy a really nice house for the two of them, with room for a family later if they wanted.

There was an ad in the yellow pages that stood out from the rest of the realtors. This firm boasted personal service and attention to detail and client needs. The realtor's name was Lester Price. Lester's schedule was wide open today, he would be more than happy to show them properties in the price range they were looking for. As they drove to the first property, Lester asked them if they were at all familiar with the island. Max told him he used to have a friend that lived here named Ray Bangor. Lester's mood changed dramatically.

Not knowing exactly what to say, Lester gave his condolences for the loss of Max's friend. Max seemed more annoyed than distraught as he told Lester that Ray was a ticking time bomb waiting to go off. Lester knew all about Ray and his subsequent suicide right before the authorities were preparing to raid the house he rented. Lester knew of the illegal drugs and weapons found in the house and silently wondered exactly what Max's take on what had happened. Was Max involved in illegal activities along with Ray?

The fact that Lester had known Ray completely caught Max off guard. So as not to be assumed guilty by association, Max attempted to downplay their relationship. Ray was an all right guy, Max told Lester, until he met up with this wild Brazilian chick who called herself Marcella. Again, Lester was shocked by what he was hearing. Marcella did some appraisals for him before disappearing without a trace. Lester often wondered whatever became of her. Lester asked Max and Gina if they knew whatever happened to Marcella. Max was becoming annoyed by the invasive questioning and decided to answer truthfully, in the hopes that it would scare this weasel real estate agent into not asking any more questions. Max told Lester bluntly that he heard Marcella was killed by a motorcycle gang in Georgia. She was heavily involved in narcotics trafficking and was a suspect in the disappearance of her former husband.

Shocked by the allegations, Lester decided to let the subject drop for now. Suicides, narcotics trafficking, and murder were not things he wanted to know about, or in any way be associated with. Lester had bought coke from Marcella in the past. He knew she was trouble from the first day they met. Lester had even tried to initiate an affair with Marcella, but they both knew she was way out of his league. Could Lester handle the wild Brazilian fox? Marcella didn't think so.

Deciding to just let the subject drop, Lester showed the couple the first property. The asking price was six hundred fifty thousand. Max was pissed. He had told this guy they were interested in properties in the half million range, and just like a typical scumbag salesman, he was trying to show them something over and above what they budgeted. Lester must have some type of hearing problem, Max decided, but they looked at the property anyway.

When asked what they thought of it, Gina said she liked it. Of course she would say that. The pretentious real estate agent began spewing gobbledygook, informing them that the seller was highly motivated and would probably accept an offer of six hundred forty. Max said he was sure that they would accept the lower offer for the overpriced property. Lester took offense to Max's statement and asked the couple if they already been approved for financing. Max was getting more pissed off by the second and told Lester it was none of his business.

It was now obvious to Gina that the two men were becoming highly agitated with one another.

She tried to settle things down by saying that they were serious buyers, not lookers, and would just like to view some more properties, please. The next property Lester showed them had an asking price of five ninety-five. Which part of one half million does Lester not understand? Max told the agent to please take them back to the real estate office. He was through with Lester Price. They drove back to the real estate office in complete silence.

Lester, ever the high-pressure salesman, handed Gina his business card and told her to call him when her husband was in a better mood. Max said that this was as good as it gets and took the business card out of Gina's hand and tore it in half, throwing the pieces in the real estate agent's face. Part of being a real estate agent was pretending to be nice to people, but Lester decided that this Maxwell Hart was the biggest asshole he'd ever met. No one had ever spoken to him that way before.

Gina berated Max for his outlandish behavior. This guy was just trying to do his job. Max countered with the fact that he thought Lester absolutely sucked at his job. When Lester asked if they had been approved for financing, Max felt as though the agent had overstepped his bounds. It was the most insulting thing to say to a wealthy, prospective buyer. Max was unwilling to do business with anyone he did not respect.

Unbeknownst to Max and Gina, Lester was now on the phone with the South Carolina State Police, stating that he had just shown properties to Maxwell Hart. This individual had admitted ties to a known criminal underworld figure named Ray Bangor, who committed suicide as the authorities were preparing to raid the house Lester had rented Mr. Bangor. This was in fact the same residence where two illegal fully auto AK-47s were confiscated, along with two kilograms of pure cocaine. Lester was certain that Maxwell Hart had been criminally involved with Ray Bangor.

The state police investigator asked Lester where this individual was at this moment. Lester could not answer that, but said the initial call came to his office and was identified by caller ID as coming from a local hotel. Lester went on to say that Maxwell Hart may have information regarding the disappearance and presumed murder of one of his associates, one Marcella De Silva. The investigator thanked Lester Price for the information and said that they would follow up on the matter. Lester hung up the phone and smiled.

At 6:00 a.m. there was a loud knock on the door of Max and Gina's hotel room. Gina answered the door in her nightgown and was surprised to see two plainclothes policemen presenting their badges and asking to speak with Maxwell Earnest Hart about an ongoing narcotics and missing person's case. Gina was shocked, but not really. She turned to wake up Max but found he was now fully awake. They asked that for their own safety, they wished to search the room for weapons and narcotics. Knowing that there were neither of those present in the room, Max invited the police to search all they wanted to.

Satisfied now that the room was cleared, the investigators began asking Max a series of questions about his relationship with the now-deceased Ray Bangor and the missing Marcella De Silva. Max knew he could have said no to the search without a warrant, but they would have detained him and called in one anyway. Max knew he could have refused to answer any questions without his attorney, but he waved that right also. Max was a genius level liar, and today he was going to prove it beyond all doubt to himself.

Yes, Max knew Ray Bangor, they were fishing buddies. Yes, he also knew Marcella, she was Ray's girlfriend. As for narcotics, Ray and Marcella were both heavy users and probably sold narcotics to support their addictions. Yes, he'd actually seen Ray and Marcella use narcotics in his presence, and he wasn't pleased with his friend's careless behavior. Max said he knew that eventually something was going to happen to both of them based on their reckless disregard for the law and the dangerous criminal elements that Ray considered his friends.

The investigators took notes and asked Max if the address in Georgia was still current. Max told them that no, it was not, they were looking for a new place to live right this very week. The investigators said they would appreciate it if Max gave them a call if there was any other information he had inadvertently left out. Max said he would do just that. As the two investigators drove away from the hotel, they discussed the case. Both agreed that Maxwell Ernest Hart was indeed telling the truth, or he was the best liar they had ever interviewed.

Instructing Gina to carry on with the house search, Max handed her some money along with the keys to the rental car. Gina asked where he was going. Max told her the truth, he was taking a cab to the marina to check on his boat, his guns, and his dope. What he neglected to mention was that he was going to make Lester Price his new hobby. Max was certain that Price had tried to set him up for an arrest. All rats are vermin, thought Max, and they all needed to be exterminated.

The weather had warmed up considerably since they had arrived. One thing that Max did enjoy about the Low Country and Coastal Empire was that even though it did get a little cold sometimes in the winter, it never stayed cold. Max spent the morning aboard his sport fisher. After a good fix, he relaxed in the sun, catching rays in the fighting chair, all the while thinking of how he was going to take care of this Lester Price. Max knew where Lester's office was. A rental car and a good disguise was all Max would need to start his surveillance of the man who was going to die, he just didn't know it yet.

Lester arrived at work right at 9:00 a.m., stepping out of his black Mercedes-Benz, and into the building where he kept his office. Max sat across the parking lot in a plain white economy class rental car, where he had a good view of the entire office complex. His chosen disguise that morning was cheap and effective, aviator-style sunglasses and a wool cap, pulled down over his burned ears. He sipped coffee and read the newspaper and was annoyed to see a private security guard knocking on his window, Max produced a fake badge and

ID card saying he was a licensed private investigator performing a marital infidelity investigation.

Right about 11:30 a.m., Lester held open the front door of the office building allowing a pretty young woman with glasses to step outside. Max thought the woman resembled a naughty librarian in a pornographic movie. Max followed Lester's Mercedes, but instead of going to lunch, Lester went to one of the more inexpensive hotels on the island and was met by none other than the naughty librarian in the hotel parking lot. Max was next to certain that the woman was not Lester's wife. She was way too young and way too pretty.

Max had a plan. On a hunch, he would stake out the hotel in the hopes that this was a regular lunchtime occurrence for Lester and his coworker. Damn, if he was not right. Two days later they were back at the same hotel, in the same room no less. Max had taken notice that the woman always left the hotel a little earlier. Presumably so that it would not look suspicious when they arrived back at the office at separate times. Also, this would give Lester the opportunity to take a shower and wash off the scent of the other woman, so as not to tip off his wife.

Each morning, a hotel employee would push linen carts down to the hotel laundry, leaving them just outside until the workers in the laundry could get to them. Max walked by and noticed that some of the carts actually contained the uniforms of hotel employees. Max stole a pair of black pants and a white shirt, the very same type of uniform worn by the laundry workers. When the naughty librarian emerged from the room ahead of Lester Price, Max stole one of the laundry carts and waited outside Lester's room.

As soon as the door opened, Max pushed the cart forward, causing the room door to strike Lester in the face, knocking him backward onto the floor of the room. Max pounced upon him and stunned him into submission with an electric stun gun, before injecting him in the neck with a moderate dose of the China White. It was a waste of good heroin, Max thought, but hey, it would all be worth it in the end. Max bound Lester's wrist with a wire tie and loaded him into the laundry cart and covered him with dirty linens.

It was the off season, and back in those days, the island was all but deserted. Max loaded the wasted Lester Price into the back of his truck and returned the laundry cart. Lester began mumbling incoherently as Max drove to the marina. It was midafternoon, and the marina was nearly deserted. Using a very large cooler he had bought just for this purpose, he loaded the completely wasted real estate agent into it. Lifting the front end of the cooler and pulling it on its rear wheels, Max wheeled the heavy cooler down to his slip and manhandled it aboard the rear deck of his boat. He started the engines and let them warm up as he cast off. He motored out into the Calibogue Sound and out into the Atlantic Ocean. Once the sport fisher hit the open ocean, Max pushed the throttles wide open. Lester Price lay sprawled out on the rear deck, still comatose from the heroin dose.

About twenty miles out at sea, Max attached *The REEL OPPORTUNITY'S* spare anchor to Lester's ankles with chain and padlocks. The sport fisher bobbed over the ocean swells and Max prepared to send Lester Price over the side. Now regaining his senses, Lester pleaded with Max to spare his life. Max opened a cold beer and sat in the fighting chair as Lester went on and on about his wife and his kids and how this would be so devastating to them.

Max asked Lester Price if he was finished whining like a scared little puppy. Apparently, he was not and continued to plead for his life. Sitting back, drinking cold beer, Max let Lester ramble on about why Max should spare his life. Max even felt a little sorry for the guy who somehow thought he could talk his way out of this one. But Lester would not shut up. Max became annoyed and told him to just shut the fuck up for one minute.

Grabbing Lester by his business suit collar, Max hauled him up into a sitting position against the stern. Man-to-man and eye-to-eye, Max told the real estate agent about the entire experience, starting with the discovery of the *Winsor2*, right up to the present moment. Max was not born a sociopath, he explained. He became one over the course of five months. He had personally killed so many men, he'd lost count. Most, if not all of the deceased, suffered from an artificially high sense of self-esteem and a highly exaggerated level of self-confidence.

Every dead man so far had made the same exact mistake. Each one had mistaken Max's boyish looks as a sign of vulnerability and weakness. They never suspected that someone who looked as though they could never harm anyone would become such a formidable adversary. One can never tell what someone is capable of, until that man is pushed over the edge. In Max's case, he'd been pushed over the edge so many times, he was still in a free fall.

Now here they were, out in the ocean with no witnesses. Max had just confessed to just about every crime he had committed in the last five months. He couldn't just let Lester go now, could he? Lester had made the ultimate mistake anyone could ever make. He made the mistake that would cost him his life. He had not taken his enemy seriously, and now he was going to have to pay for it.

Lester Price now realized that this was going to be his last day and asked Max for a favor. Would he please shoot him in the head and spare him the agony of drowning? Max said to Lester that was the bravest thing he had said all day. Max pulled his gun and held it to Lester's skull, then thought better of it. He picked up Lester and held his head over the side of the boat so as not to mess up the rear deck with blood and bone and brain tissue. Max pulled back the hammer on the .40 caliber and held it against the back of Lester's skull. Lester began to whimper and cry out loud. Something inside of Max made him stop. He could not just kill a defenseless man. Max pulled Lester back, letting him fall onto the deck.

Every single man Max had killed thus far was a vicious dude in his own right, who would have thought nothing of killing Gina or himself if they could. But this was not some bad-ass biker gang-banger or organized crime thug. This was just some completely helpless schmuck, who just happened to piss off the wrong guy by reporting his suspicions to the police. It was still an offense worthy of death. Max just could not bring himself to do it.

What to do now? Max reached into his coat pocket and pulled out his works, laying the implements out carefully on the bait table. Tapping out a dose of the potent China White from a small glass vial onto a spoon, Max melted the powder with a butane torch. He placed a cotton ball into the spoon and drew the liquid into a syringe, using the cotton to filter out any impurities. He tied a tourniquet around his left bicep and smacked his forearm until the blood vessels became visible. Sitting in the fighting chair, he steadied himself as best he could and mainlined the dose.

Lester watched in disbelief, realizing he had been kidnapped by a junkie. There was a glimmer of hope. Perhaps that under the influence of the powerful narcotic, Max would have a change of heart. But all sense of hope vanished when Lester realized that Max was probably high when he developed and executed the kidnapping plot in the first place. Lester knew right at this moment that this would be his very last day on earth.

The two men stared at each other for several minutes. Finally, Max broke the silence by asking Lester about his wife. What did she do? Lester explained that his wife, Miranda, was a black belt taekwondo instructor at a martial arts studio. They had been married for sixteen years. Max went inside the salon and reappeared with a folder. He produced a glossy eight-by-ten black-and-white photo and held it in front of Lester's face. In the photo, Lester could clearly be seen opening the hotel room door for his mistress, while grabbing her ass as he did so. What would Miranda think about this? Max wanted to know. Was this supposed to be some type of psychological torture? Miranda would probably kill him. She had already killed one man in self-defense and was exonerated. She would probably kill him and be given probation from some liberal judge. If Max really was intent on killing him, then why didn't he just do it and get it over with already? Max laughed. What would be the fun in that?

As far as Max was concerned, there were but three options available. Option number one, he could offer Lester a relatively quick and painless death by shooting him in the head. Option number two, they could cruise back toward the island and Max could drop him off on the Joyner Banks. Lester could swim the remaining two miles or so to the island before the high tide covered the sandbar completely. Or there was option number three, Max's favorite. Lester could just tell his wife about his affair with the naughty librarian.

Of course, he would have to show her the photographic evidence in Max's presence.

Would Lester care for a nice cold beer to think it over? Max turned his back on Lester and reached into the cooler and pulled out two cans of beer, handing one to Lester. With his wrist bound in front of him, Lester popped the top and drank the beer with both hands. It was an extremely difficult decision, he was going to need another beer. Max was happy to oblige him. After nine beers, Lester made his choice. He would just have to tell Miranda about the affair. Good choice, thought Max.

If Lester would just take a seat in the fighting chair, Max could remove the anchor from the chain and secure the chain with a padlock around a cleat on the stern. Turning the sport fisher around one hundred eighty degrees, Max pushed the throttles forward and they cruised toward the coast of Hilton Head Island. It would be well after dark before they arrived at the marina. Periodically, Max turned around to see that Lester was where he was supposed to be. There was no other place for him to go, except over the side.

Upon reaching the marina, Max was happy to see that Lester was passed out. The marina was all but deserted this time of night. Max expertly reversed the 46' sport fisher into his rented slip. After tying off the boat, it was time to remove the restraints from Lester and wake him up. Lester said he needed to use the restroom, and Max cautioned him that if he tried anything, he would be shot. Max joined Lester inside the men's room. Lester had a lot of time to think about how he was going to handle the disclosure with his wife, Miranda. Max wanted to know if he was ready for this. Lester said that yes, he was, right before he bolted out the door.

Son of a bitch, thought Max. Try to give a guy an even break, and he pulls something like this. Max ran out after Lester who by now had a five-second head start. Lester began screaming that he was being chased and needed help. But it was late, and the area was deserted. Nevertheless, Max would have to catch up with him quickly. Lester continued to run, yelling as he did so, turning around to see if Max was gaining on him, right before running into a tree trunk. Max caught up to Lester and found him unconscious.

This was a big problem, one that Max hadn't counted on. Lester lay on his back, bleeding profusely from the head. Max took off his windbreaker and ripped off his shirt. He applied direct pressure to the head wound. Max felt for a pulse. There was none. Not wanting to believe what was happening, Max checked for a pulse again. Nothing. Max attempted CPR, but found that every chest compression forced more blood out of the head wound. There was nothing more that Max could do for Lester Price. Then it occurred to Max, why was he even trying to help this guy who had tried to rat him out?

Max ran back to the marina and called 911 on a pay phone. He told the dispatcher there was a medical emergency on Harbor Town Club Road. Hanging up the phone, he realized his fingerprints were all over the handset. Just as he was about to wipe the handset clean, the phone started ringing. Picking up the handset, and wiping it clean, he placed it back in the receiver. Max needed to get the hell out of here before someone came along and arrested him. Thinking fast, he decided the only safe place to go was back to his yacht. He could here sirens in the distance as he ran back to the marina. He slowed down to a walk, so as not to attract any attention.

Once aboard *The REEL OPPORTUNITY*, Max opened a fifth of scotch and started guzzling. He sat in complete darkness inside the salon, while one block away sheriff's deputies and an ambulance were arriving on scene. This was not how it was supposed to go down at all. Max prepared a fix. Just as he injected himself, he realized that the heroin was the root cause of what had happened here tonight. Every bad decision made was a direct result of it. In another five seconds, it would not mean anything.

Early the next morning found Max on the floor of the salon. It was daybreak. Gina was probably worried sick right about now. Max prepared a fix which knocked him out till about noon. He changed clothes and walked to a marina pay phone and called for a taxi to take him back to his hotel. There he found Gina in the room, very pissed off, but very happy to see him. She told him she had been waiting by the phone all night and had not slept.

Gina demanded that Max tell her what had happened the night before. He said it was a long story that he would get into later. Right now, she needed to rest. Max made her a strong drink and handed it to her. She didn't even finish half of it before she was asleep. Max climbed into bed with her after shooting up again. He finished Gina's drink for her before passing out on the bed next to her. They slept until 5:00 p.m.

They took a cab to a nice place for dinner. It was quiet on a Sunday night. Max explained to Gina all that had happened since they last saw each other. Gina was livid. She looked as though she was going to explode with rage. How could Max be so stupid? How could he be so careless? How could he be so sadistic to Lester Price? Max told her how he tried to help the guy, but couldn't. Gina didn't want to hear it. If it were not for Max, none of this would have happened. It was right then that Max understood why Ray had shot himself. He just couldn't live with the guilt anymore.

While he did feel bad about what had happened to Lester Price, he also felt angry about the fact that Lester had called the police on him. It was that incident that pushed Max over the edge and made him do things he would never normally do to someone. Just because someone was a condescending, arrogant person did not give Max the green light to get down in the gutter with them. There was a time when he would have just bitten down on it and kept his mouth shut. But lately, the way things were going, it didn't take much to set Max off. The heroin was not helping his judgment either.

Arriving back at their hotel, they were greeted in the lobby by another couple. The woman introduced herself as Miranda Price. The man with her was her attorney Richard Cohen. Miranda wanted to speak with Max about the death of her husband, Lester. How in the hell did this woman not only know exactly who Max was, but also where he could be found? Max suggested that they meet in the hotel cocktail lounge.

Miranda Price was not at all what Max had expected her to be, not that he ever even expected to ever have to meet her. She was very athletic, very attractive, and had a very cool, calm demeanor. How could Lester cheat on a woman with such natural beauty? They ordered drinks, and Miranda surprised everyone by asking Richard and Gina if she could speak with Max alone for a while. Richard and

Gina excused themselves to another table close by out of hearing distance.

Miranda got right to the point. What did Max know about the death of her husband? Max was caught completely off guard and found himself stammering while he tried to turn the question back around on her. What made her think that he had anything to do with her late husband? Miranda disclosed that Lester kept a daily journal. When Lester never returned home, Miranda started reading it and found that Max and Gina were the last clients Lester had met. There was a description of Lester's failed attempts to show them properties. There were also some not so flattering comments about Max.

"I know that you had something to do with Lester's death … I can see it in your eyes!" Miranda's piercing blue eyes bore into Max.

"I don't know what the fuck you are talking about, woman!"

"Listen to me … it's all right. Lester had made a lot of enemies over the years. Most men thought he was an asshole … most women thought he was a creep. It was only a matter of time before he pissed off the wrong person … that person is you … isn't it?"

Max began to realize that in addition to being beautiful and talented, Miranda possessed some type of ability to read people as well. There was no sense in continuing to lie to this woman. "You know, for a woman who just lost her husband, you don't seem to be the least bit distraught by it!"

"That would be because I'm not the least bit distraught."

"Then what exactly is your purpose here tonight?" Max wanted to know.

"I just want to know why … that's all? When you're married to someone for sixteen years, and they turn up dead, it really makes a person wonder what it was that caused their death."

"You seem like a really nice woman … the very type of woman who deserves better than Lester Price! This is your chance to move on with your life … find your soul mate."

"I already have," Miranda confided. "He's right over there talking with your fiancée. I know all about Lester's infidelity. I stayed with him for the sake of our children. Now he's gone, and I'm going to receive a two-million-dollar life insurance claim. I just wanted to know why you killed him, that's all? If you don't tell me, I'll spend the rest of my life thinking about it."

"Arrogance killed Lester Price! His death was ultimately an accident, but it all started with arrogance! We had a common associate who committed suicide. We had another common associate that's still part of an ongoing missing person's case. Lester took it upon himself to associate me with these two individuals by contacting the authorities. They questioned me, and that's all you need to know!"

"Thank you, Maxwell Earnest Hart, for taking the time to talk to me tonight." Miranda rose from the table and was joined by Richard. They left the bar arm in arm.

Did that really just happen? Max asked himself. What if Miranda was wearing a wire? But there was something deep down inside of Max that made him think that was highly unlikely. It was now obvious to Max that Miranda hated Lester, and she was more or less celebrating his death. She just wanted to know more about it, that's all. Max realized that he had just about confessed to Lester's demise. If there were more to it than Miranda had let on, the cops would be busting him right now.

Seated over at the next table was Gina, having a very animated conversation with a male bar patron. Max very calmly asked Gina if she was ready to go. Gina said she'd been waiting for like an hour already, yes, she was ready to go. Gina pressed Max to reveal all that was said between him and the widow of Lester Price. Max told her she would hear all about it in the privacy of their room. When it was all laid out before her, Gina's response was, "That's it?"

The body of Lester Price was sent to a forensic laboratory for analysis. The autopsy revealed ligature marks on the deceased, and foul play was determined to be the official cause of death. An investigation revealed that the deceased had no known connections to organized crime, however, the incident had occurred in exactly the same area as the homicides committed aboard the pleasure yacht *PRINCESS* almost five months earlier. Were the cases connected? The authorities were not so sure. More information would be obtained when the toxicology report was completed.

In the meantime, detectives reviewed the case and determined that Maxwell Earnest Hart was a person of interest in not only the ongoing missing person's case of Alicia Anna Perez, a.k.a. Marcella De Silva, but also the death of Lester Price as well. A public records search revealed that Maxwell Hart did not own any properties in South Carolina on which he paid taxes. In neighboring Georgia, however, he was found to be the former owner of a condemned house which had been torn down months ago, following an unsolved drive by shooting.

It was all too coincidental for this one individual to be connected with so many as yet unsolved cases. If the man did possess any assets, they were registered in someone else's name. It was a common tactic used by drug traffickers that authorities were all too familiar with. The very same investigators who interviewed Max four days ago were sent back to his hotel, only to find that he had checked in under an alias and had already checked out. At least one thing was certain in the minds of both investigators. Maxwell Hart was the missing link in Operation Kingsnake. Once in custody, investigators were certain that the unsolved criminal rampage that had affected Hilton Head Island over the last five months would come to an abrupt halt.

But Max and Gina were already three steps ahead of the law. On their journey back up the South Carolina Coast aboard *The REEL OPPORTUNITY*, Gina told Max all about the fantastic female real estate agent she had met with and all the beautiful properties she had looked at on the island. There were incredible houses well within their price range. Max attempted to let her down gently. Hilton Head Island was just too hot for them right now, maybe they could come back in the near future and try again. Gina, while being very disappointed, was at least looking forward to riding her horse in the unspoiled Georgia countryside in winter.

The weather had turned cold once again, and their trip up the coastline in midwinter was unpleasant. It was further complicated by the loss of the port engine which shut down and failed to restart about halfway through their voyage back to Charleston. Despite his best efforts, Max could not produce a solution, and they were forced to continue their journey with just one engine. It was times such as these that Max wished that Ray were still alive and with them right now. Despite his personality problems and drinking and drugging, Ray was by far the best diesel mechanic Max had ever known.

If they were to lose the remaining engine, Max would have no choice but to call the Coast Guard for assistance. This was a worst-case scenario that Max didn't even want to consider. There were two full-auto AK-47s, as well as numerous other unregistered weapons aboard. There were narcotics, including about one and three quarters of a pound of high-grade marijuana remaining, taken off the *Winsor2*. There was also Max's personal heroin stash. There was also a five-gallon bucket with two hundred thousand cash stuffed inside.

All that on top of the fact that *The REEL OPPORTUNITY* was registered in Gina's name, she just didn't know it yet. Unbeknownst to Gina, Max's deceased father had a very crooked lawyer. After they found the *Winsor2*, Max anticipated the worst and had the vessel's ownership transferred over to Gina without her knowledge. He later did the very same thing with the recently acquired farm house property. With Gina aboard, this could be real trouble if they lost the starboard engine. Max had to come up with a solution that would prevent the Coast Guard, or anyone else becoming involved if they ran into further propulsion problems.

Max decided he would "hug" the coastline. If the need arose, he could simply drop anchor and row the dinghy ashore and summon for help. But this plan, like all things in life, was risky. The coastline was always in a state of flux. A sandbar that did not exist one month ago could abruptly halt their forward progress with little or no warning. They could be in ten feet of water, and in a matter of seconds, two feet, which would ground the vessel and stall their remaining engine.

If Max did have to go ashore, he would have to leave Gina behind or take her with him. There was no proper course of action. Decisions would have to be made, and that decision would determine whatever else followed. Right now, right at this moment, Max was high, really, really high. But it somehow all made sense to him now. Life is about making decisions. The better a person is able to make decisions, the more successful that person is inclined to be. Max had been lucky so far, and he knew it.

The "fear" began to strangle his thought processes. There were just too many "what-ifs." He slowed the starboard engine down to idle. There were just too many things that could go wrong right now. They would drop anchor right here. Gina climbed up to the bridge. Why were they stopping? There were plenty of daylight hours left for cruising. Max told her to go below, where at least it was warm. He would join her there directly. Max stared at the South Carolina coastline. He stared at the ocean. For the very first time in his life, fear was making decisions for him.

Gina made supper down in the galley while Max tried to maintain a sense of normalcy. But Gina was not fooled, she knew something was wrong with Max. Probably what he needed right now was a good, slow blowjob to help him relax. But Max did the unthinkable. He stopped her before she even got started. No man in their right mind refuses a blowjob. Right then, Gina knew there was something seriously wrong with her man. Gina asked him if he was okay. No, he was definitely not okay. Maybe they could just cuddle for a little while. Really, Max! Are you kidding?

It now occurred to Gina that Max was flipping out. This was bad. For the last three and a half years, Max exuded confidence in all that he did. Whether it was just driving a motor vehicle or just plain killing some asshole who definitely deserved it, Max did what he had to do. Nothing in the world prepared Gina for this moment in which Max was losing his edge and his grip. Was it the drugs? If so, then why was it never a problem before? Why now, out here in the ocean? Max tried to reassure her, saying it would all be all right. But she knew just by looking in his eyes that even he didn't believe that. Max was always good at lying under pressure, but he had never, as far as she knew, lied to her. She needed Max. She needed Max to be strong for her. This was not the time nor the place to be freaking out. Max needed to pull his shit together now.

They left the generator to run all night. This would serve to keep the cabin warm, but also they could play music or watch videos. When they first acquired the sport fisher, Max explained that generators needed to be run under load. Gina took it upon herself to turn on almost every electrical fixture on the yacht and leave it on through the night. From a distance, *The REEL OPPORTUNITY* must have looked like a yellow star in the blackness of the universe.

Gina put on some spacey British rock on the stereo and fired up a joint. But this only severed to lull Max to sleep. That's fine, thought Gina. Max had been under a lot of stress and had not been keeping regular hours. Maybe he just needed to sleep right now. It was not going to stand in the way of Gina amusing herself, however. She perused through the videotape collection and found a raunchy XXX-rated adult film made in Brazil. She popped it in the VCR.

Having seen raunchy triple X–rated films made in the States, Gina was more than a little aroused by the hardcore antics of Brazilian porno stars. Brazilian women, it seems, come in all shapes and sizes, just like here in the US. Some of them were blond-haired, blue-eyed, some were dark-skinned and appeared to have African ancestry, just like here in the US. But pretty much all of the men were dark-skinned and looked like they actually came from South America. Gina watched, smoked weed, drank beer, and was becoming very aroused. She could not take her eyes off the screen.

Then she saw something that stunned her back to reality. Max was snoring beside her, and she nudged him awake with her elbow. "Max … it's Marcella!"

Max woke up from his drug and alcohol-induced stupor. "Huh?"

"There, on the screen is Marcella De Silva!"

"You have to be fucking kidding me!" Max said, not fully awake.

But there she was. Much younger, but every bit as pretty. It was unmistakably Marcella. Even if there was some wild Brazilian chick with a dragon tattoo in exactly the same place, there was no mistaking Marcella's voice. Although neither Max nor Gina could speak or understand Portuguese, there was no mistaking the tone and inflection of her voice as Marcella chided her male Brazilian co-star. She was teasing him, just like she teased everyone else while she was alive.

Gina decided she would try her hand at translating. "So … chu think chu are man enough to handle theeese?"

"I don't know … I don't know?"

"Well … chu better theeenk hard, man!"

Max could not contain himself. He burst out laughing as hard as he ever had in his entire life. He actually laughed all the air out of his lungs until they collapsed. He continued laughing, until he started coughing. When the coughing fit subsided, he began laughing again. Of all the women on the entire planet, only Marcella De Silva could keep a straight face while teasing her co-star.

Then it all came home. This woman was every bit as funny and sexy and uninhibited as she was vicious and crude. On the cathode-ray television screen before him was a ghost. Max could not believe he was looking at the very same woman who called him one day, out of the blue, and told him to come to Ray's villa "queeeek!" Upon opening the front door, Marcella pulled him inside and began to fellate him. The rest, well the rest is what it is, or was. Max felt the fear grabbing a hold of him again. He began to shake.

"Max … cut the shit already!" Gina yelled.

Gina hit the stop button. For just a few minutes, she had actually believed that Max had somehow snapped out of his depression. But she was dead ass wrong on that. It was perhaps the first time she could ever remember being so wrong about something. She silently cursed herself. But it was not her fault. Thus far, she had done everything she could for her man. If that was not good enough, then it was his problem.

Out in the ocean surrounding them, the droning and droning of engines could be heard. It became louder and louder. This was not the sound of some sport fisher or other large oceangoing pleasure craft. This was the sound of speedboat engines. Gina was now unable to contain her curiosity and made her way to the salon. Peering through the salon windows, she saw an oceangoing speedboat making circles around *The REEL OPPORTUNITY.* Gina went below and retrieved one of the AK-47s.

"Max, what the fuck is wrong with you?" Gina snapped.

"They are probably just kids trying to fuck with us," Max reasoned.

"Really, Max … kids?"

The speedboat continued to make ever tightening circles around the sport fisher. Max began to realize he had better do something. He shut off all the lights in the salon. Gina stepped out onto the rear deck and chambered a live round. She had already decided that if they come any closer, she was going to blow their assess to kingdom come. Max joined her outside and peered through binoculars. He handed the spyglasses to Gina and she in turn handed him the loaded rifle.

"They are just kids, I'm telling you. They're probably drunk and in the mood to fuck with somebody!"

"Well now … that's a problem!" Gina responded. "Because I've been drinking and I feel the same way!"

Handing the binoculars back to Max, Gina now grabbed the rifle and shouldered it. "I'm going to give them ten more seconds to quit fucking around!"

Ten seconds came and went, and the speedboat made the closest pass yet. Gina pulled the trigger and emptied the thirty-round magazine in the direction of the other vessel. Gina loaded another clip and did the exact same thing. There was a huge explosion and fireball which lit up the night for all of three seconds. If there was anyone else awake at this hour, Max was sure the explosion could be seen for miles. "We need to get the fuck out of here, now!" Gina yelled, handing the rifle to Max.

"Yeah … no shit!" Max agreed.

Max climbed up to the bridge and gave the single remaining engine the command to start. As the engine warmed, he went around the boat and turned off every single light. Max gave the winch the command to weigh anchor, and just like that, they were heading northeast into the night. Max turned around in his seat to watch the burning vessel. What was Gina thinking? This could possibly become a huge problem.

In their crippled running condition, they were an easy mark for the authorities if anyone happened to have seen the blast. Max took a long pull off the whiskey bottle he had brought up to the bridge with him. What was the worst that could happen? He could be arrested for operating a vessel while impaired while leaving the scene of an act of piracy with illegal drugs and weapons on board. No worries here! He briefly thought about putting the vessel on autopilot and going below to bust Gina out for her reckless behavior. He then thought better of it.

On through the night they cruised up the coastline. Gina put on a winter jacket and joined Max up on the bridge. She grabbed the whiskey bottle and took a healthy swig. She put her arm around Max. She was proud of him. When it came down to it, he had bitten down on it and accepted their precarious circumstances. Not only that, he took decisive action. They both had no idea what was in store for them, but they did not let that fact interfere with their actions with regard to self-preservation.

One hour later, they were about eight miles north of the scene. Two-way radio traffic informed them that the burning wreck had been spotted, a Coast Guard helicopter was on the way. They had a choice. They could either continue on their present course and risk being spotted from the air, or duck behind one of the barrier islands, at least until daybreak. Max guessed that right now they were off the coast of Seabrook Island. Using the radar, they could find anchorage between Seabrook Island and the Deveaux Bank. Gina agreed, it was too risky to continue their forward progress.

The second choice came with a significant amount of risk as well. Max didn't know these waters at all. They would have to rely completely on radar and GPS, but they could still run right over a submerged wreck and not know it till it was too late. It was a risk they would have to take. They found anchorage close to the shore in about fifteen feet of water. They dropped anchor and returned below decks for the cozy warmth of the salon and master stateroom.

Gina made breakfast, even though it was 4:00 a.m. It just seemed like the thing to do, besides they were both starving. They were already drunk and stoned as they cuddled up under the sheets. They were both exhausted but too wired for sleep. Eventually, Gina fell asleep, leaving Max to struggle with his inner demons all over again. Ever since they entered the coke business, life for them had been all about killing. Now they were out of the business for good.

But killing had become such a way of life, they could not just turn off a switch and become normal human beings again.

When Max finally did awake, it was noon. The temperature had dropped even lower. It was freezing outside and a stiff wind blew in from the ocean. After a fix, Max fired the engine and burned a joint on the rear deck. Back up on the freezing bridge, they continued on their journey. It gave Max a chance to think about where they were in life right now and where were they headed. They were rich. They should not have a care in the world.

People create their own misery sometimes, they really do. Max recalled a time in his youth when he knew a girl who did nothing but complain about her abusive boyfriend and her minimum-wage job. For Max the answer was simple. Get rid of the abusive boyfriend. There are plenty of decent men in the world who actually know how to treat a lady. Then quit the minimum-wage job. A person cannot do any worse than minimum wage. But what seemed like obvious choices for Max were alien concepts to this person. There was no doubt in Max's mind that he had made his choices, and they were incredibly bad. Even if he could somehow straighten out his life, nothing would erase the memories of the last five months.

Gina was a sport. She was wild and carefree. She didn't let things bother her. But she had become a completely different person as a result of Max. Gina would not think twice about killing someone she didn't even know. Last night was a perfect example. Whoever was aboard that other vessel was definitely asking for trouble. They obviously overlooked the fact that when someone looks for trouble, they almost always find it. Max was willing to bet that those individuals aboard that speedboat were oblivious to the fact that people like Gina and himself, for that matter, exist. Monsters do exist, and they don't always look like what people expect them to look like.

Who in their right mind would look at Gina and think that she was a sociopathic murderess? With her long blond hair and incredibly womanly figure, no one would ever suspect that this young woman was not only capable of murder, but an accomplished murderer at that. Add to that the fact that Gina did not feel the least bit bad about any person she had ever wasted. To Gina, every victim was someone who deserved to die. Max felt the same way. The only difference being that Gina would have never turned out like this had it not been for Max. Max had no one else to blame but himself for the way things turned out.

At any rate, they were both freezing. They would have to stop again for the night, if only to thaw out. Why did Max have to pick the coldest days of the year to make this voyage? But it was all good. Gina was feeling feisty, and when she felt feisty, she felt like wrestling. And she was good at it. Yeah, she fought dirty, but that was part of the fun. Max had long ago lost count of how many times he'd been bitten by Gina while wrestling. An hour later, they were both sweating profusely from the effort. They had completely forgotten how cold they were just a short time ago.

The simple pleasures of life. On this cold winter's afternoon, it was all that any man could want—booze, heroin, marijuana, and a sexy girlfriend willing to do anything without even being asked to. Most men would kill to be in the position in life that Max was in now. But it was all a ruse. Max knew that anything could happen to them once they resumed their voyage, and anything could be waiting for them on the other end. As much as he tried to let loose, the fear was always there, right outside their little world.

This boat was just a warm, cozy speck on the surface of the ocean. Out there were demons. Out there was the unknown. Out there were other human beings that would kill him if they only knew what he had done to their brothers. The only proper thing to do at this time was to enjoy the pleasures afforded by his sexy girlfriend. Here, they were invisible to the outside world. No one else on the entire planet knew exactly where they were right now.

On the south shore of Folly Island, a teenage couple stood in the cold winter sun, passing a joint back and forth. Their attention was drawn to a yellow hulled sport fisher anchored just a hundred yards or so from shore. Now these were people who had it all figured out. They had obviously made their money, now they were free to enjoy it. How was it that they accomplished that? How was it that they were able to make enough money to buy this yacht and take it cruising wherever they wanted to? Now that was freedom.

Gina screamed curses down in the galley. She had just burned her hand for the second time making supper tonight. Too much weed and too much wine makes for a careless chef. However, that would not stand in the way of her perfectly grilled mahi-mahi fillets. It was delicious, as always. Max asked Gina if she had ever entertained the idea of being an executive chef in a restaurant that she owned. The thought had never even occurred to her. Gina knew she could prepare restaurant-quality dishes, and she did so all the time. She could not possibly imagine doing so under a time limit on a much-larger scale. She would much rather marry a retired coke kingpin and never have to worry about money ever again. She was kidding, of course, or was she? Max knew that without him, Gina was capable of doing whatever it was in life that she set her mind to. He felt bad that he had fucked it all up for her. Max knew that if something were to happen to him, Gina would be just fine. He felt bad for anyone who made the mistake of pissing her off, however.

After dinner, Gina surprised Max by telling him that he was getting fat. Max used to be lean and strong and ripped, and now he was soft and weak and pudgy. Gina had the perfect solution—dance!

Over Max's initial objections, Gina persuaded him to get up and dance to the music. Gina had a lot of black friends who introduced her to black music, and she liked it a lot, the funkier the better. Max insisted that dancing was a lot like sex, one had to be in the mood for it. Gina countered by saying that if Max wanted sex later, he was going to have to get up and dance now.

It was now early evening, and the same teenage boy who had earlier in the day looked upon the mysterious sport fisher and its owners had returned with a pair of binoculars. They were dancing, for fuck's sake! They must not have a care in the world, the young man thought. What had this couple done in life to achieve such greatness and have so much freedom? Maybe they had done nothing at all. Maybe everything in life had been handed to them.

Collapsing on the sofa in the salon, Max was completely out of breath from the dancing. He looked out the window only to see the teenage boy standing on the shoreline, watching them through binoculars. Max felt a pang of jealousy in his heart. Oh, what he would give to turn back time and be a teenager again. Those were the best years of his life, and he missed the much simpler time when all he had to worry about was school.

The winter sun dipped below the horizon. Max dreaded the thought of having to resume their voyage tomorrow morning, but right now, all was good with the world. The weed, the wine, the heroin, and the company of his woman made for a peaceful winter night aboard their floating hotel room on the sea. Max wished they could just share this moment forever. Right now, he decided he would enjoy this night as though it were his last on earth.

Early the next morning, they continued their final leg of the trip to Charleston with just one engine. When they finally arrived at the marina, Max felt a sense of relief like he'd never known before. Tonight, they would stay in a fine hotel and eat dinner in a fine restaurant. Tomorrow, he would call a marine engine service company to produce a solution for the port engine which would crank but wouldn't start. But right now, he needed a fix and a strong liquor drink.

In the hotel room, the local news was still covering the story of the stolen speed boat found shot up and burning off the coast. As it turns out, some rich kid had taken the vessel without permission from the owner, and now he along with his girlfriend were dead as a result of automatic weapons fire. The deceased man had prior felony convictions for narcotics and grand larceny. Gina sat on the bed and watched the news story with Max. She confided that she knew the operator of the other vessel was looking for trouble. How did she know for sure? She did not. It was something she felt inside.

What would have happened if they were unable to defend themselves out on the ocean? Max did not even want to think about it. This deceased young man and his girlfriend probably never saw their fate coming. They were probably just fucking with Max and Gina, but that's exactly how people get killed. When a person decides to fuck with a complete stranger, they are taking their life in their own hands. These two young folks found that out the hard way. But on the bright side of things, at least they would never do it again.

The marine mechanic found the problem with the port engine almost immediately. A bad fuel solenoid had prevented the engine from starting. Max told the mechanic to order an extra so it could be kept aboard as a spare. The total cost for diagnosis and repairs was twelve hundred. Max thought it was a little steep, but paid the bill without complaint. He was just glad to have the vessel fully operational again. Maybe they would return to Hilton Head in a couple of weeks, but right now, they loaded up the truck and headed to their farm over in Georgia.

The old two-story farmhouse had fared just fine while they were away. Max surveyed the property and found everything in order. He called Rob, Amy, and her husband Mark just to let them know they were in town and invite them to dinner tomorrow night. Gina called the equestrian farm and made arrangements to pick up her Mustang. She was greatly looking forward to riding in the Georgia winter, free of all the biting insects and the oppressive heat. Max lit a fire in both fireplaces. It was good to be home.

But over dinner the following night, both Rob and Amy had some bad news. There was a rookie sheriff's deputy who was out to make a name for himself by reinvestigating all cases as they pertained to Max. The rookie asked a lot of questions about Max and Gina, including where they could be found right now. The young deputy was convinced that Max and Gina were not ordinary citizens and that they knew much more than they were letting on in earlier police interviews. That's just great, thought Max. This was the very last thing in the world that he needed right now.

It didn't take the rookie deputy very long to find out Max was in town. Max was splitting firewood out by the barn when the deputy pulled into the driveway. The deputy introduced himself and asked Max if he could spare a few minutes to answer some questions. Max said sure, why not. The deputy produced three photographs, courtesy of the Miami Dade Correctional Institution. Max immediately recognized them as the gangbangers from Florida who tried to steal his money and coke.

The deputy explained they were all suspects in a Savannah Bank robbery. This Max did not know. They were also suspects in the shooting of a horse guide who worked on an equestrian farm in the area. Max asked why would he know anything about these three men he'd never seen before. The deputy explained that he was just trying to gather information on cases that were starting to turn cold. The deputy switched gears. He now asked if Max had ever had any run-ins with the Miscreants MC. Max responded by saying no, he'd never even knew they existed.

Was Max absolutely sure about his facts? The deputy wanted to know. Max was starting to become more than a little annoyed by the line of questioning. What in the world would make the authorities think that Max had anything to do with these people? The deputy put it all out in front of Max. People, especially bad people on the wrong side of the law, had a habit of either dying or going missing whenever Max was in town. Max apologized for not being able to help the authorities with these cases. The apology was not required. The cases would remain open until they were solved, and they would be solved at some point. The young deputy told Max to have a nice day.

Did that just really happen? Max asked himself. This rookie obviously knew Max was being evasive. Was he just fucking with Max just because he could? All Max knew was that if they had any real evidence against him, they would be arresting him, not just coming by to fuck with him. Maybe that was their whole purpose anyway. Maybe they were just trying to let Max know that any form of vigilante justice would not be tolerated. Maybe they were already onto him and just letting him know that he was being watched.

At any rate, Max was still a little unnerved by the fact that the missing gangbangers were buried behind the barn, a mere fifty yards or so from where the deputy questioned him. Max decided that this was never going to end as long as he was alive. Even if he could move to some obscure part of the world, he knew he'd always be looking over his shoulder. At least if he stayed close, he would never be lulled into a false sense of well-being that could come to a screeching halt at any moment.

That cop was just trying to bust his balls, Max decided. He went inside and told Gina about what had just happened, Gina, felt pretty much the same way. If they had something, they would be doing more than just poking around. It was as if the deputy wasn't even trying to scare him. He was just letting Max know that he'd better mind his Ps and Qs from here on out. And they meant it this time. Max decided to take a drive and clear his head.

He decided that he would ride over to the rental house and see how Laura was making out. Max would have called first, except for the fact that he'd lost her number. He was happy to see Laura's little red sports car in the driveway when he pulled up. Laura answered the door and was genuinely happy to see Max. She asked how he had gotten so badly burned. Max told her it was an accident and a long story that he didn't feel like reliving at the moment. Laura said she understood and let it drop. She confided in Max that she missed Buster. Max told her that he missed his friend too. They gave each other hugs and said goodbye.

This gave Max an idea. He decided to drive to the area where he had abandoned Buster's prized custom bike after shooting up the Ingrate Order MC compound. It was a long drive, but if he were somehow able to retrieve the bike, maybe he could have it restored and it would always be there to remind Max of what a good friend Buster had been. Buster was just another example of someone who would still be alive if Max had never entered the coke business.

Max found the custom-built motorcycle in the river, just where he had abandoned it, but it was obvious to him that the bike was beyond salvageable. Having been immersed in water for several months, it was beyond any restoration attempt. He should have known this already and not even bothered to waste time driving all the way out here to find it. Staring at the custom bike, just below the water's surface, only severed to bring up bad memories. It was just another bad idea resulting from the boredom he felt most days. He began driving all the way back to the farm dejected and depressed.

It was as if Max had created his own prison. It was bad enough that the authorities were looking to send him there, but here out in the free world, he felt as though he could not enjoy life. The prospect of being sent to prison was always there in the back of his mind. He even considered just turning himself in, but that was insane thinking. If he thought he was miserable now, he could only imagine life behind bars, devoid of female company. He would have to soldier on and just wait to see what life ultimately had in store for him.

Something caught his eye on the way back to the farm. On the side of the road, parked at the end of someone's driveway, was a 1988 Harley-Davidson XLH 1200, with a For Sale sign attached to the handlebars. Max pulled into the driveway to have a closer look. It looked mean. An old grizzled-looking biker dude came out and met Max at the end of the driveway. The two men exchanged greetings. Max wanted to know why the man was selling the bike. The man explained that he had fallen on hard times and was doing so reluctantly, besides which he could no longer ride it. Increasing back problems kept the old biker home most of the time, he explained.

For some reason, Max just wanted it. He paid the man the full asking price after taking it for a short test drive. It looked and sounded good. Ten minutes later they were loading it onto the bed of Max's pickup. Max asked the man how much he wanted for the steel loading ramp. The man said he could take it home with him no additional charge. Max thanked the man and set off on his way home with his newly acquired toy.

Gina, who had been horseback riding all day, was shocked to see Max offloading the motorcycle in their driveway. Max had always commented to her about how dangerous they were, and here he was bringing one home. Did he have some sort of death wish? Gina wanted to know. Max couldn't really explain why he went ahead and bought it. He just did. It felt like the right thing to do. Gina was now convinced that Max was losing his mind.

Maybe he was, he just didn't know it yet. All he knew was that out on the open road, all his thoughts and actions were devoted to riding. Riding a motorcycle, especially around here in the Georgia countryside, required complete focus. There was no room for daydreaming or not paying complete attention to the road while riding. There were a lot of things worse than death, and taking a spill on a bike could have life-changing consequences.

Next Max did the unthinkable. He began prospecting for a motorcycle club in Savannah called the River Dogs. They were the real deal. They were mostly comprised of young professionals who did weekend riding events. Every Saturday was a day long outing that usually ran into Sunday. They were a good group of guys. Many took their wives or girlfriends with them when on their weekend excursions.

Of course, Gina was upset when she found out. How could Max do such a thing? Joining a bike gang. Really, Max? Max told her they were taking a riding event this weekend out to Tybee Island, Georgia. Max assumed that Gina would not want to ride along. He had assumed correctly. It was going to be freezing again this weekend, were they all nuts? Was this some sort of premature midlife crisis Max was going through? It was all good fun, Max insisted. These were good guys, really. Gina would not be so easily convinced.

Saturday morning, the twenty or so members of the River Dogs MC met at their downtown Savannah clubhouse. They drank coffee, and more than a few joints were smoked. The club president, Zeke, explained to Max that in winter, they took short rides like the one they were taking today. It would probably take them about one half hour to ride out to Tybee Island where they had hotel reservations for that night. This would be a stag event with all the wives and girlfriends opting out on account of the freezing cold weather.

Tybee was a great place to go this time of year. It was practically deserted, and the rooms were cheap. With Zeke riding front row left, the procession of bikes pulled out onto Bay Street. Max, in the very last row, rode alongside another prospect named Sparky. Sparky was a cool dude and was a motorcycle mechanic by profession. Max was unaccustomed to riding in formation, but he quickly learned how to keep pace with the pack, while maintaining a safe distance from the guys in front and alongside.

It was cold. Max couldn't blame the women for not wanting to go. On the ride out to Tybee Island on Highway 80, Zeke kept to the posted speed. There was no sense in adding to the wind chill factor. When they finally arrived, it took a few minutes for everyone just to thaw out. It felt like the coldest day of the year so far. They parked their bikes in a neat line and went inside a pool hall, sympathetic to their cause.

Inside they were greeted warmly by the bartender who must have been expecting them on this day. Max thought it a bit strange that the female bartender did not even appear old enough to drink herself let alone serve alcohol. Zeke warned Max that whatever he did today, do not under any circumstances do anything to piss off Cindy, the bartender. At first, Max thought he was kidding. Later on, he would find out Zeke's warning was shit serious. The place was pretty nice sized, and Max was surprised to see more than a few locals on this Saturday morning.

The locals present that day were the town drunks and drug addicts who loved this place. In most drinking establishments, once a patron exhibited signs of intoxication, they were immediately cut off. In this place, however, a drunk could fall off his barstool and be helped back up to a sitting position so that he could get another beer in him. The River Dogs MC had all day to drink beer, play pool, and even mess with some of the local women if they were so inclined.

Max thought he had died and gone to heaven. What a perfect way to spend a blustery cold winter day. The bartender, Cindy, was obviously known to Zeke and informed him that in the event of any trouble today, she might need his help. Her doorman had called in sick with the flu. The River Dogs MC had games going at five of the six pool table with money riding on every game. The only remaining table was being used by a couple of locals, who Max could somehow sense would be the cause of some type of trouble in the very near future.

One of the locals was a truly obnoxious redneck from hell. After repeated warnings in which he was chastised for putting his beer bottle on the pool table, Cindy took it upon herself to throw the man's beer in the trash when he went to use the restroom. When the redneck came back out and found his beer missing, Cindy told him right to his face that he'd been warned not to put his fricking beer bottle on the fricking poll table.

The drunken fool told Cindy that he wasn't going to buy any more beer in this establishment. Cindy told the man that he would have to leave. The man responded by saying that if he left, he was not coming back. *Oh, please, mister, please stick around and cause more trouble, don't leave.* Max could not get over the thought processes of this idiot.

Zeke came over to where Max was sitting at the bar. Zeke told Max that the drunken fool was fucking with Zeke's kid sister and would Max be so kind to show this gentleman the front door. *Okay, tiger, it's time to earn your stripes.* Max went over to the drunk and told him that he'd been asked nicely to leave, please do so peacefully. The man wanted to know who in the fuck was Max and what right did he have in asking him to leave. Max explained that it was not a right, but a privilege.

But now the attention of every single River Dog present, along with everyone else in the bar, was on Max and this man, who was obviously hell bent on causing as much trouble as possible. Cindy even turned down the house music, just so that everyone in the bar could hear what was being said. Max knew that whatever he did or said from here on out would be forever engraved in the minds of all those present. He decided he was going to let this joker make the first move.

The drunk man grabbed a pool cue and swung full force at Max's head. The man's movements were clumsy and predictable, and Max grabbed the business end of the cue and pulled it out of the man's hands. Max used the cue to poke the man in the chest, not hard enough to seriously injure him, just hard enough to let him know who owned the situation. Max handed off the pool cue and grabbed the drunk in a headlock and dragged him outside, opening the door with the man's head.

Max came back inside to the sound of applause, just as the man he'd just thrown out came back in through the door and tried to jump Max from behind. Max delivered a well-placed elbow to the man's nose, breaking it. Again, there was hearty applause all around. Max grabbed a wrist and twisted it up behind the man's back, and this time used the man's whole body to open the front door. Outside, Max kicked the dude in the torso for good measure.

Max resumed his seat, only to find a patch that read PROSPECT on the bar in front of him. He was not expecting this at all, and he was honored. Cindy, behind the bar, told Max to take off his leather vest, and she would be happy to sew it on for him. Max did just that. Zeke sat down on a stool next to Max and asked him how he felt right now. Pretty damn good was Max's answer. Zeke instructed Cindy that all Max's drinks were on Zeke's tab from here on out.

Fifteen minutes later, a sheriff's deputy came in through the door of the bar and, after shaking hands with Zeke, began to speak with Cindy. The deputy asked Cindy if he could view the bar surveillance video of the beating. Cindy invited the deputy back to the office. The deputy, now satisfied this was clearly a case of self-defense, told Zeke that the River Dogs MC had all better behave themselves while they were in town. And one more thing, no patches! Zeke instructed every River Dog to remove his vest, that order stands.

The deputy, now satisfied that he had done his job, left the bar and subsequently placed the local in the backseat of the patrol car under arrest for public intoxication. It was turning out to be a great day so far, and they hadn't even been there an hour. As the afternoon wore on, even more local drunks and drug addicts began to file in, and soon the place was pretty packed. Apparently, this particular bar was the place to be on a Saturday afternoon.

They played pool and drank heavily. Groups of guys periodically stepped outside to burn one or two, before being chased back inside by the same deputy who was making this bar his new hobby this afternoon. On an island that's only three miles long, there wasn't much else going on today that required the deputy's attention. The young deputy was cool about everything though, and he let the rag-tag group of bikers have their fun. As long as there weren't any more altercations between the bikers and the locals, it was all good.

A very pretty brunette sat down next to Max and asked him how much fun he was having today. Max told her he was having a great time hanging out with his new friends, the River Dogs MC. The woman explained that she was here on vacation with her friend. Really? A vacation on Tybee Island, Georgia, in the middle of winter? She said that she came here every year, but had never come in the winter. She just wanted to see what it was like. She introduced herself as Jessica. Max said he was glad to meet her.

But Max had been watching Jessica all afternoon. She was an expert-level pool player and had won hundreds of dollars thus far this afternoon, playing various locals as well as members of the River Dogs MC. Jessica asked Max if he was with the bike gang. Max said that he'd just been made an official prospect earlier in the day. How about that now! Jessica was very forward and asked Max if he had a woman waiting for him at home. Max said that yes, he did. He was engaged to be married.

But the relative tranquility of the afternoon was shattered by a loud argument at one of the pool tables. Apparently, one of the locals was accused of stealing fifty cents off a pool table. Zeke got up from his barstool and went over to the men to try and settle things down. It was only fifty cents, for fuck's sake! Zeke threw some bills on the table and told the men to enjoy a couple of games on him. Max could easily see why Zeke was the leader of the River Dogs MC. He was as cool as they come.

This did not go unnoticed by Jessica, and she asked Max who that dude with the ponytail was. Max told her that Zeke was the club president, and he didn't take any shit from anyone. Jessica was impressed and asked Max if he were willing to introduce her to Zeke. A bit regretful of his earlier decision, Max introduced Jessica saying that she had come all the way from Atlanta just to meet Zeke. Zeke turned to his club vice president, Floyd, and told him to make room for Jessica. Floyd reluctantly surrendered his barstool, while Jessica sat down and began having a conversation with Zeke.

They didn't even get a chance to talk for thirty seconds before there was yet another altercation. This time the combatants had skipped the verbal argument and went straight to fighting. Soon every River Dog and every local male patron was involved, including Max. Fist were flying, as well as billiard balls and pool cues. Someone is going to get killed, Cindy decided, and she picked up the phone and called the police. But the bar was getting trashed. Furniture and light fixtures were being broken. The owner would not be happy about this at all.

Cindy reached under the bar and pulled out a large frame revolver and, pointing it at the ceiling, fired it. Everyone stopped fighting for a moment. When they saw Cindy standing behind the bar, holding the firearm above her head, everyone resumed fighting. But the local drunks were no match for the seasoned and drunk River Dogs, and within a minute, just about every single River Dog stood over an opponent, lying on the floor. Zeke yelled out to all his buddies that when the police come, no lipping off and no resisting.

This time there were five deputies who entered the bar with their hands on the grips of their side arms. They made every single River Dog form a line up against the wall. The shift supervisor talked to Cindy, while the remaining deputies searched every River Dog for illegal drugs and weapons. But no drugs or weapons were found on any bike gang member. There were, however, plenty of both lying all about the floor of the bar.

The shift supervisor went back into the bar office to review the videotape evidence, while the remaining deputies held the River Dogs up against the wall at gunpoint. After reviewing the surveillance footage, the shift supervisor determined that this was clearly a case of provocation on behalf of one of the locals, who felt like striking the club VP in the back with a pool cue, if for no other reason than to lay him the fuck out.

In the interest of justice, the shift supervisor said to the disbelieving deputies that the River Dogs were free to go, but would have to pay for all damages caused to the bar during the altercation. Also, they were barred from every drinking establishment in town for life. Zeke said that they had all been drinking heavily and that they had hotel reservations just a couple of blocks away. If they could just check into their hotel, Zeke promised there would not be any more problems.

That was fine with the supervisor, but what about the restitution to the bar owner? Max came forward and produced a stack of hundreds and set it on the bar. The supervisor asked Max if he were some sort of drug kingpin. Max said that he was a wealthy businessman. By this time, the bar owner had showed up, and he was pissed, until he was made aware that the River Dogs were not at fault in this instance and had offered to pay for the damages. The bar owner picked up the stack of bills and said that would do nicely. The bar is closed until further notice.

Several ambulances had arrived by this time, but every single conscious victim refused medical treatment. The River Dogs all got on their bikes and started the engines. Jessica got on the back of Zeke's bike, and her friend got on the back of the club VP's bike. Cindy got on the back of Max's bike and grabbed him tightly around the waist. Max straddled the bike allowing the engine to warm up before their short ride to the hotel. And just like that, they all rode in formation to their destination for the night. They parked their bikes in a neat line in front of the hotel entrance, there seemed to be no other guests staying there that night.

Every full patch member got their own room, but the two prospects, Sparky and Max, would have to share. Max offered to pay for Sparky's own room without objection. Cindy had loaded her backpack full of cold beers and asked Max if she could stay with him tonight. Max said okay. He had just stretched out on the king-sized bed when there was a knock at the door. Much to Max's surprise, it was Jessica, informing him that his presence was required in Zeke's room. What in the hell was this all about? Max wondered as he put his riding boots back on.

In the hotel hallway, there was a party already in progress, they had the whole floor to themselves. Max found Zeke's room with the door already open. Zeke motioned for Max to come inside. Zeke tossed what appeared to be a collapsible Frisbee at Max who caught it, only to realize it was a beautifully embroidered patch of the River Dogs MC. Max couldn't believe it! He'd only been a prospect for not even one whole day.

Zeke told Max to take a seat. Also present were the club VP, Floyd, and the club sergeant at arms, Bear. The club president congratulated Max on his full patch member status. Max said that he was honored and shook hands with all three men. Max asked Zeke man-to-man what really happened back there at the bar. Max was certain they were all going to jail. Zeke explained that there were several factors at stake in such regard, the first being that Max offered to pay for all the damages.

Second, the River Dogs had been patronizing that particular establishment for years. None of the River Dog members had felony criminal convictions whereas most of the locals who caused all the problems today did. They ranged from felony drug convictions to convicted sex offenders. Third, and most importantly, the shift supervisor was his uncle Tony. Down here, they call it the good-ole-boy system.

Zeke invited Max to have to a liquor drink with them. Max accepted, all the while not fully believing he was a full patch member already. He had not even known these guys for one whole week, and now he was one of them. Max attributed their collectively laidback attitudes to the fact that none of the River Dogs used meth or coke. As for Max, they all somehow sensed that he was in no way a threat to their way of life. Max thanked the men and headed back to his room.

There he found Cindy getting out of the shower and drying herself off. She had a great body, but Max just couldn't do this to Gina. Also, he was concerned about Cindy's age. Also, he was concerned about the fact that she was Zeke's sister. He'd just been made a full patch member, for crying out loud. He tried to explain his concerns to Cindy as she sat on the bed next to him, wearing nothing else but a bath towel.

Cindy tried to put his mind at ease. First of all, she was twenty-three, she just looked a lot younger. Second, she was not in any way related to Zeke, he just said that as a joke. Third, as for Max's woman, did she really have to know? Cindy made an impressive case, still Max found himself struggling with his inner demons once again. There was a time when he would not have thought twice about it, but in the wake of all that had happened, he somehow didn't want to tempt fate.

Max decided to call Gina, who did not answer the phone. Strange, Max thought, where could she be on a Saturday night? He decided he would try again later. Right now, he asked Cindy if she wanted to smoke some pot. Cindy said sure, why not. Max twisted up a doobie, lit it, and handed it to Cindy. She puffed heavily, inhaled deeply, and coughed profusely. Max warned her it was pretty strong ganja. They passed the joint back and forth while they watched television together.

When Max finally snuffed out the joint, Cindy asked if they could smoke another. Max was surprised by the request and told her to wait a few minutes and see how she felt. In the meantime, Max tried to call Gina again. This time she did answer the phone, out of breath and wheezing. In the background, Max could hear the television and a man's laughter. It sounded a lot like Rob. All this time, Max assumed that Gina didn't even like Rob. Max asked Gina if she was okay. She said she was fine. Max got straight to the point. Was that Rob he heard in the background? Gina said that yes, it was, she didn't feel safe in the house all by herself. Really, Gina? In a house full of firearms and she didn't feel safe? Max just put two and two together, and it added up to the fact that his fiancée had just finished fucking Rob. Max told her good night, he just wanted to make sure that she was okay. Gina assured him that she was just fine. Yeah, Max thought. He was sure Gina was just fine, right at the moment.

Max now turned his attention to his female hotel room guest, but there was something wrong. Cindy said she was having heart palpitations, she needed to be taken to the hospital. This is precisely why marijuana will never be legalized, thought Max. Max told her that she would be just fine, it was really good weed, he told her. Cindy was not convinced, and she accused Max of giving her weed laced with PCP. Max couldn't believe this turn of events. Max had to think fast.

He called Zeke's room. The phone rang seven times before Zeke picked it up. Zeke sounded out of breath and he was annoyed, saying this had better be important. Max explained that he had just smoked a joint with Cindy and now she was freaking out, she wanted to go to the hospital. Zeke hung up the phone. In less than a minute, Zeke was knocking on Max's hotel room door wearing nothing but a towel. With him was Jessica, also dressed in nothing but a towel.

Zeke tried to assure Cindy she would be just fine. Jessica meanwhile picked up the half-burned joint and lit up. Jessica told Cindy that was some good weed. Zeke said he would be the judge of that. Zeke agreed that it was, in fact good weed, spiked with PCP. Max angrily told Zeke he wasn't helping matters any. Zeke apologized and told Cindy that it was just good ganja, from the good earth. He asked Max if he had any he could spare. Max told Zeke, sure he did.

Jessica spilled the weed out onto the table and began rolling joints. Zeke admonished Max for interrupting an especially erotic moment. Max apologized and thanked Zeke for his help, although he really didn't help the situation out at all. Jessica, for her part, was at least trying to be convincing about the purity of the weed in question by puffing on a joint while she rolled several more. When Zeke and Jessica were convinced that Cindy would be all right, they left the room. Max offered Cindy a beer, saying that it would help calm her down. Cindy took a big gulp and said it didn't taste right. Max was just trying to get some nooky, but the weed had ruined everything.

Sitting on the edge of the bed, Max drank the beer that Cindy said "didn't taste right." He drank another. He asked Cindy if there was anything at all he could do for her. Cindy told him no. She got in the bed and pulled the covers up to her face. Max turned to her and said that everything would be all right. Cindy would be all right, the beer was all right, and the weed, well, the weed was all right too. Max told her he was going to step outside for a few minutes.

In the hallway, he found Floyd and asked him how he was feeling after being struck from behind with the pool cue earlier in the day. Floyd said he was all right, but it was obvious the guy was still in a lot of pain. Max asked him why that guy just decided to haul off and hit him. Floyd said he wasn't sure, the guy was just some asshole looking for a fight, he guessed. Floyd seemed like a good guy. It just figures that some moron would try to pick a fight with the totally laidback dude.

Other gang members came and approached Max to congratulate him on his full patch member status. Max said he was completely surprised and very honored. They all agreed that if it were not for Max offering to make restitution for the damages, they would all be in jail right now. He definitely deserved full patch status. Bear asked Max how he had become so financially successful. Max said it was luck mostly, just being in the right place at the right time.

Back inside the room, Max found Cindy sitting upright in the bed, watching television. She apologized for freaking out earlier. Max told her no worries, he'd seen the very same reaction before in others unaccustomed to the extra strong weed. Max fell asleep, and sometime later, so did Cindy. Tomorrow they would say goodbye and probably never see each other again.

The sky was slate gray the next morning when the River Dogs mounted their bikes and prepared to leave Tybee Island. It was cold, but not quite as cold as yesterday. They stopped by a gas station on their way out of town. After some hot coffee and breakfast sandwiches, they mounted their bikes and made the long ride on Highway 80, back toward Savannah. It was still early on a Sunday morning, and not much was going on downtown. They were all shocked to see that their clubhouse downtown had been broken into probably last night.

Anything that was not stolen was purposefully destroyed. What a cowardly chicken-shit thing to do, thought Max. Whoever had done this knew the River Dogs MC were all going to be away last night. Zeke tried to keep his cool as always, but he was finding it hard to control his emotions. He had an important choice to make. Should he report the break-in to the authorities, or seek justice on their own terms? Zeke asked Max what he would do in a situation such as this. Max told Zeke he would keep the authorities out of the loop, but definitely go after those responsible. However, Max suggested that they might want to let things simmer down for a while.

Zeke told Max he was a fucking genius. That was precisely what they would do. They would lay low for a week and go after their adversaries and beat their brains out. Who were the people that did this? Max wanted to know. Zeke said it could only be the Hornets MC. Was there any provocation that had let up to this? Absolutely not! The two clubs were bitter enemies and always had been. Max said he had some automatic weapons stashed if they would be any help. Zeke said no, shooting was just plain too good for these guys. They all need to be beaten to death.

Riding out to his farm, Max wondered if the normally cool Zeke was serious about the beatings. He sure did seem serious. This was just another of life's examples of what happens when a man or group of men get pushed over the edge. Max wondered what was in store for the River Dogs. He had just become one of them, and he didn't want to see the club go down in flames, or anyone wind up in jail. Maybe he could be of help to these guys, having gone up against vicious bike gangs before. Of course, he could never reveal his actual involvement in the previous killings.

Upon arriving back at the farm, Max was frozen stiff. Where was the good weather they had forecast for this week? Gina grabbed him by the neck and gave him a big hug and offered to make him lunch. Max told her that wasn't going to work, he figured out what she was up to last night. But why Rob of all people? Gina knew she was busted out but played it down. Max hadn't exactly been perfectly behaved during their relationship, so he couldn't fault her or stay mad at her for very long.

The next day Max got a call from Zeke. There was a club meeting Wednesday night, mandatory for all full patch members. Max told Zeke that he would definitely be there. As he hung up the phone, Max wondered what this was all about. Had Zeke developed a plan so soon after the fact? If so, he had to give the guy credit. Either that, or Zeke knew much more about the Hornets MC than he had let on.

Wednesday night Max showed up as promised at the destroyed downtown clubhouse. He found Sparky outside, packing a sidearm. Sparky explained he had been assigned to watch the bikes while the meeting took place. Max went inside and found the other eighteen members milling about. On the floor, in the middle of the room was a plastic baby pool filled with beer and ice. Max grabbed a cold brew and stood around with the other guys waiting for Zeke to call the meeting to order.

All the smashed-up furniture had been piled up against the wall. The entire bar had been smashed apart with axes and sledgehammers. All the tables, chairs, and barstools had suffered a similar fate. Even the old jukebox was completely destroyed. Zeke estimated that about two thousand dollars' worth of liquor had been stolen. Even the sinks and commodes had been smashed, causing flood damage. Obscene graffiti covered every wall.

All eighteen patch members stood in a semicircle around Zeke. It was time to begin the meeting.

"This is not about vandals destroying our clubhouse!" Zeke began. "This is about people in society that do not know how to act civilized! We didn't do anything to provoke this! Nothing! We always kept a safe distance from our enemies, for a reason … so that we could coexist. They have their turf and we have ours, but they took it upon themselves to invade our turf, and completely destroy it! Now as you all know, we rent this place. So we're all going to have to bite down on it and fix this place up ourselves.

"As for the stolen liquor and smashed-up furniture, we're gonna have to eat it! Now, you all might be asking yourselves … why bother? Why should we all go through the trouble of fixing this place back up if there is even a remote chance this could happen again? We're gonna do this because this will never happen again! The animals that did this without provocation or cause are all gonna pay! Try not to think of them as rivals or enemies or even humans! The people that did this are vermin, plain and simple!

"And like all vermin they need to be exterminated!" Zeke stopped to catch his breath, while cheers and applause filled the room.

"Now … if there is any man here tonight who doesn't feel up to the task, please, by all means, feel free to walk out that door, now! No one will hold it against you! All we ask is that you forever keep your mouth shut about what you heard here tonight! There is no shame in opting out! Some of you have promising careers, some of you have families. We understand if you decide you don't want any part of this!" Zeke turned his back on the assembly. "There is no shame, here is your chance to opt out now!"

Zeke faced the rear wall and waited sixty seconds before turning back around. Not one man had left. "The law calls what we're about to do conspiracy to commit murder! I submit to you that we are doing the rest of the world a favor!" There were cheers and applause.

Zeke had clearly gone off the rails, and everyone was okay with it. Hatred can be a powerful motivator. Why would every man present here tonight, risk everything they have, everything they ever worked for, in the name of vengeance? There could only be one answer. They all had complete and total faith in their leader. Zeke had obviously developed a plan that was foolproof. None of them would ever have to worry about getting busted for this.

At the farm, Gina was none too pleased that her presence was required Saturday night for a club meeting at a restaurant named Ismael's Pub and Pasta. Max explained to her that all wives and girlfriends were required to attend. Zeke had booked a private dining room, and every full patch member and every patch member's woman was required to attend. Gina asked Max what would happen if she were to just refuse. Max told her he wasn't sure exactly what would happen, he just knew it wouldn't be good.

The weather had warmed up considerably, and Saturday saw a daytime high of seventy-two degrees. This was a welcome change, and it would make it easier to convince Gina to ride with Max on his bike, rather than to meet him there. Gina had purchased a black leather outfit, complete with spiky high-heeled boots. Max had even gotten her a sleek matching black helmet with a darkened face shield. Max admired her from across the room as they prepared to leave. She looked hot as hell.

This would be the first time Gina had ever even ridden on a motorcycle. Max told her to just hang on tight and lean in to the turns along with him. Gina was a little nervous, but she tried not to let it show. It was up to Max to get them safely to their destination and back again in one piece. Gina trusted him, but the ride was scary for her. The powerful motorcycle and the vibrations it produced made her a little wet not even five minutes into the ride.

They pulled up to the entrance of Ishmael's Pub and Pasta, and Max expertly backed the bike in a line alongside all the others. He greeted Sparky, who would be standing outside all night, just to keep an eye on the bikes. It was part of Sparky's prospecting duties. Max was so glad he did not have to perform any menial or mindless task to become a member. But then again, Max was not Sparky, and Sparky was not Max. Max had bought his way into the River Dogs MC.

Inside the private dining room, Zeke greeted Max and Gina. Zeke was genuinely pleased to meet Gina for the first time, but then again, so was every other man she met. She was striking in her black leather pants and jacket. Zeke introduced his woman Robin to the couple. She was not at all what Max had expected her to be. She was pretty, but in a natural, down to earth sort of way. Both Gina and Robin looked as though they had purchased their outfits at the same retailer, but then again, so did all the other women present.

Everyone took their seats, and the waiters and waitresses began to uncork bottles of wine. When everyone's glass was full, Zeke, seated at the head of the table, proposed a toast. "To the Brotherhood of the River Dogs Motorcycle Club!" Everyone raised their glasses. Hors d'oeuvre and baskets of hot fresh-baked Italian bread were served. Then came the magnificent main course, all laid out buffet style. During dinner, Max asked Zeke how he was able to nail down private reservations at such an exclusive dining establishment. Zeke told Max that the owner was a friend of the family and was sympathetic to their cause. Zeke encouraged all the women to eat and drink as much as they could handle.

It was time. Zeke stood at the head of the table and announced there was a private ceremony tonight, for full patch members only. The women needed to stay here and help themselves to whatever they needed or wanted. The men would return in an hour, maybe two. Zeke instructed Robin that once the men left, the women could do whatever they wanted, just don't let any wait staff in the private dining room. Robin agreed, she had a plan to keep the girls busy.

One by one, the full patch members kissed their women and exited to the very back of the building. In an alley, behind the restaurant, was an old school bus. One by one, the River Dogs stepped aboard. In the first rows were piles of black coveralls, from which every man took a pair. In the second row were boxes of night-vision goggles. Again, everyman took a pair. In the third rows were a collection of weapons that would clearly have an impact on their adversaries. There were bats, pipes, and ax handles. Each man grabbed whatever it was that felt comfortable in their leather gloved hands.

Every man was ordered to change into the black coveralls. Floyd got behind the wheel and they drove off into the night. Floyd expertly wheeled the bus through town and they soon found themselves crossing over the newly constructed Talmadge Bridge which would take them over the Savannah River into South Carolina. Zeke sat in the first row and told Floyd to go ahead and cross into South Carolina. On the right, he would find some vacant roadside lots. Floyd was to pull into one of these lots and wait for the bridge traffic to clear.

"Go for it!" Zeke yelled at Floyd who turned the bus around one hundred eighty degrees and got back on the highway. But they didn't cross the bridge over the Savannah River. Instead they made a left turn onto the no-man's-land known as Hutchinson Island. In 1993, there was nothing on Hutchison Island, absolutely nothing. But tonight, Zeke knew for a fact there was something on the very south end. It was an induction ceremony for prospects to be awarded full patch member status for the Hornets MC. Zeke told Floyd to put on his night-vision goggles and kill the bus headlights. Floyd climbed under the driver's seat and removed the fuse for the brake lights as well. When they were within on quarter mile of the southern tip of the island, Zeke instructed Floyd to do a three-point turn and parked the bus so that it faced the Talmadge Bridge.

Every River Dog disembarked carrying his weapon of choice. They walked another two hundred yards or so until they could see the Hornets MC induction ceremony. Instead of a bonfire which could attract unwanted attention, the Hornets used gas lanterns to illuminate the area where the ceremony was taking place. In the distance, the Hornets club president could be seen presenting two new prospective members their full patch member status. With their patches awarded, the newly ordained members turned around to face the assembly. Every Hornet present produced a gun and fired it over their heads simultaneously. Then there were cheers.

The Hornets put out their gas lanterns and climbed onto their bikes. They were probably headed back to their clubhouse to celebrate. But Max knew, along with every other River Dog, they would never make it to their final destination that night. The River Dogs had staggered themselves on either side of the road and hid in the tall grass as the first bikes approached. The bike engines growled at idle as the procession made its way toward the Talmadge Bridge off in the distance.

Zeke hid in the high grass, waiting for the procession of bikes to advance on his position. When the first rider approached, he was struck full force with an ax handle to the throat, knocking the rider off his bike and onto the ground. And so started a chain reaction down the line. Every River Dog hiding in the grass sprang from his position and began swinging their weapons wildly at the completely unsuspecting victims, who never saw it coming.

Bats, pipes, and ax handles came crashing down upon the skulls and bodies of the Hornets MC. Some were killed quickly, with a single blow to the head or throat. Others rolled off their bikes and produced guns, firing into the darkness. But it was the night-vision goggles that made all the difference between life and death. The Hornets were essentially blind, and as each attempted to pull a gun on their attackers, it was struck out of their hands, breaking fingers, wrists, and arms in the process. Screams of pain echoed across the barren island.

Some of the Hornets tried to run for it, firing their weapons at the men following them into the high grass. Zeke grabbed Max by the collar and told him to follow. Two of the Hornets had ditched their bikes and were running off into the high grass toward the south end of Hutchinson Island. Once they reached the south shore, there was no place else for them to go, unless they wanted to swim for it. One of the fleeing Hornets held an Uzi at arm's length and began firing in the direction of Max and Zeke.

Zeke could clearly see his adversary firing his weapon randomly into the darkness. Zeke waited until the clip was emptied, then motioned for Max to follow him, while the enemy attempted to reload. They now stood on opposite sides of the man. Zeke smacked the weapon out of the man's hands with the ax handle. The two men stood, facing each other. Zeke removed his night-vision goggles and threw his ax handle to the ground. He sprang forward, tackling his adversary around the waist and pulling him to the ground.

Having grown up in downtown Savannah, Zeke was a street fighter without equal. As his adversary attempted to regain his footing, Zeke delivered a roundhouse kick to the torso, sending the man face down into the sand. The man produced a knife and stabbed the air, only to have a fist full of sand thrown in his face. Zeke delivered another kick, this time to the side of the knee, once again causing the man to collapse. Picking up his ax handle, Zeke stood over his opponent now, bringing the weapon down upon the man's skull, crushing it.

Max had followed the other fleeing man until there was no other place left for him to go. The man produced a revolver and scanned the darkness for his pursuer. Max crouched in the high grass. He threw his baseball bat several yards away, striking a piece of driftwood. Max's adversary turned in the direction of the noise and squeezed off five shots randomly. Max used the diversion to pounce on the man knocking him to the ground. Max produced a five-inch double-edged knife and stabbed the man in the chest, causing a sucking chest wound. The man began spitting and coughing blood. Retrieving his bat, Max stood over the man and brought the bat down upon his head, splitting it apart.

Zeke began blowing a lifeguard's whistle, which was their prearranged signal to meet back at the area where the ambush started. There could be no survivors, he explained. Every single member of the Hornets MC had to be accounted for. Zeke told everyone to fan out, count up the number of bikes, and account for all the deceased. Zeke personally went around and shot each fallen Hornet in the head, just to make sure there would be no witnesses. After ten minutes, they all met back in the same spot. There were twenty-three motorcycles lying on their sides, and twenty-three dead members of the bike gang formerly known as the Hornets MC. Zeke congratulated everyone. Their work here was finished. They all hiked back in the direction of the school bus.

On the bus ride back downtown, the River Dogs MC began their celebration. Max could not get over how well Zeke had executed his plan. How was Zeke able to acquire the night-vision gear, Max wanted to know. They were stolen, Zeke explained, from a warehouse about a year ago. Zeke knew they would come in handy one day. What about the school bus? That actually belonged to the club for events like family day. Max was so glad that he himself did not have a family from which he would have to hide the terrible secret of what they had all done this night.

Floyd parked the bus in the alley behind Ishmael's Pub and Pasta. All the members of the River Dogs MC removed their black coveralls and tossed them, along with all the weapons into a heap at the very back of the bus. Tomorrow, Floyd would take the bus to his family-owned junkyard, and the bus along with all the other evidence would be destroyed. As they approached the back door to the private dining room, raucous female laughter could be heard on the other side of the door. What the hell were they doing in there?

Zeke grabbed the doorknob and found it locked. Zeke beat on the door with his fist. A female voice shouted to go away. Max stepped forward and produced his pick gun and proceeded to unlock the door. Upon entering the room, Max, along with all the others, could not believe what they were seeing. In their absence, the women had all decided to engage in a lesbian orgy. Max found Gina and grabbed her by the hair and proceeded to bend her over the table. Soon, every other River Dog was doing the same thing to their women. It was all great fun, right up to the point where the restaurant owner beat on the front door, informing them all it was time for the restaurant to shut down for the night. Bummer!

Everyone it seemed was exhausted as they made their way out the front doors of the restaurant. Zeke was shocked to see two city policemen standing out in front of the restaurant. But they were merely admiring the neat line of stock and custom motorcycles. The River Dogs MC and their women mounted the bikes and left the restaurant riding in formation to their hotel several blocks away. It was there that the party resumed, until the early morning hours.

They had done it. They had carried out their plan and left no survivors, and they had rock-solid alibis for where they were that night. It's not often that a gang of bikers has the opportunity to take out an entire rival organization. For Max, of course, it was different, but for the rest of the River Dogs MC, it was a memory they would cherish for the rest of their lives. As far as they were all concerned, the men that were killed tonight all deserved what they had gotten. Hatred was indeed a powerful motivator.

The next day, they all rode in formation out to Max and Gina's farm for a cookout Max had planned to celebrate their success. Max had a keg of beer delivered, and all afternoon, he burned steaks on the grill. The rest of the club members were highly impressed with Max and Gina's farm. They all secretly wondered how Max and his woman had achieved such success at such a young age. To anyone who asked, Max just said he had been very lucky in life, very lucky indeed.

There was a front-page newspaper article about the murders of the entire biker organization formerly known as the Hornets MC. It seemed that motorists crossing the Talmadge Bridge from Georgia into South Carolina were amazed to see hundreds of vultures flying over the southern end of Hutchinson Island. There the authorities found the remains of twenty-three murdered men, along with their bikes.

Rumors started like wildfire. The police commissioner held a press conference where he said that his department would do everything in their power to find out who was responsible. He also added the fact that when people go through life making as many enemies as the Hornets MC had done while they were alive, cases such as this become next to impossible to solve.

As for the River Dogs, their asses were covered. Floyd had destroyed the bus along with all the evidence, and for his efforts, he was awarded a specially made patch for his club vest. It was a very nicely embroidered black vulture. The patch was presented at a special ceremony to honor Floyd's as well as Sparky's efforts. During the ceremony, Sparky was awarded full patch member status. Sparky could not have been more pleased.

The following weekend, Max invited Zeke and his wife, Robin, to Charleston to go deep-sea fishing in the Gulf Stream. Once again, Zeke and his woman could not get over how rich Max and Gina actually were. Sitting up on the bridge with Max, Zeke asked Max how he had become so rich by age thirty. The two men had already shared a life-and-death experience together. Max figured that they already shared secrets they would have to keep until their deaths, so what was one more?

On the long cruise out to the Gulf Stream, Zeke listened with total fascination about everything that had happened, starting with the discovery of the *Winsor2* six months ago. Zeke absolutely could not believe what he was hearing, but he listened to every word without interruption. Max detailed the falling out with both bike gangs formerly known as the Ingrate Order MC and the Miscreants MC. Zeke could not believe he was sitting here talking to the man responsible for their demise. Zeke had heard rumors, but as of right now, they were all ridiculously false.

Zeke hated the bike gangs Max had taken out, every bit as much as he hated the Hornets MC when they were alive. Still, Zeke could not believe he was hearing firsthand from the man who practically singlehandedly toppled both organizations. Unbelievable! Zeke told Max that his story would make for a great Hollywood movie. Max laughed at that. It probably would have, but it would also incriminate Max in dozens of as yet unsolved homicides.

Max confided in Zeke that the only thing in life he was afraid of was Karma. Max was somehow convinced that everything he had done since the discovery of the coke was going to catch up with him one way or another. Zeke told Max there was no sense in worrying about something which may or may not happen. What if there is an afterlife? What would be the fate of Max's soul then? Zeke didn't have an answer for that, but he did remind Max that every man that had died thus far would have probably been killed in similar fashion.

Around the time of Ronald "Wolf" Zeigler's death, the River Dogs MC were actually planning to attack the Ingrate Order MC compound. Wolf had ordered the gang rape of a woman who was the old lady of a prospect named Rooster who later disappeared without a trace. Rooster's woman was a distant relative of Zeke's. She managed to escape when the compound was later raided by the police. Ronald "Wolf" Zeigler was already a dead man, he just didn't know it, before he ultimately was killed in the accident.

As for the rest of the Ingrate Order MC, they were all dead men as well. Zeke's relative couldn't live with the memory of her ordeal, and she committed suicide. The River Dogs were actually planning very cruel deaths for all involved, which meant all of them.

The police actually did the Ingrates a huge favor by busting them when they did. Otherwise, they would have all suffered greatly. It's funny how things have a way of working out.

What about the Miscreants MC, did Zeke have any problems with them? Of course. Everyone who ever knew any man connected to either organization had a problem with them. But the Miscreants MC, they were a special breed all their own. They were so wired on meth all the time, anyone who was not a member was suspected of working for the police. They were all that paranoid as a result of their drug usage. One of the reasons that their ranks continued to shrink in recent years was directly because every single prospect was thought to be working for law enforcement.

Zeke fetched a couple of cold beers from below and returned to the bridge, handing one to Max. All this time, the two men had shared a special hatred for both the Ingrates and the Miscreants, yet neither man even knew of the other's existence, let alone their mutual disdain for their common enemies. For the first time in months, Max felt vindicated for the killings. It really did not matter what Max had thought at the time. What really mattered was how many other people felt the same way. All the guilt he had felt melted away that afternoon as they motored over the ocean swells on their way out to the Gulf Stream.

Down below in the salon, Gina and Robin listened to music, smoked weed, and drank beers. The two women had become fast friends, and the lesbian party last week only served to make their bond tighter. They knew that their men were responsible for the demise of the Hornets MC, but neither one cared about that. They did what they had to do for a reason. They would never betray their men, no matter what.

The further they went offshore, the larger the waves became, until they were as tall as houses. Wave after wave, the sport fisher bobbed over them like a cork. As far as the eye could see, from horizon to horizon, the huge waves made Zeke realize how small they were in the world. Max puffed on a joint as he adjusted the throttles to match the sea conditions. It was then that Zeke decided that his new buddy Max was one of the bravest men he'd ever known.

Hours later, when they finally arrived at the Gulf Stream, Gina took the helm with Robin sitting alongside her. Max and Zeke went below and set hooks. The two men sat on the rear deck as *The REEL OPPORTUNITY* trolled over the ocean swells. Max had seen seas like this many times before, fishing with his father. It was not conducive to catching big game fish, Max knew from his own experience. The skies were overcast and both the sea and sky were gray. Maybe they would get lucky anyway, thought Max. He really wanted this to be a memorable experience for his new friends.

Up on the bridge, Robin was greatly impressed with Gina's skills as a boat handler. Gina showed not the least bit amount of fear as she expertly motored the sport fisher over the swells that went on for miles and miles. Most people, Gina knew, would have already gotten seasick. But not Robin. She stoically sat by her friend, never taking her eyes off the horizon. That was Gina's advice to avoiding seasickness.

Aside from a couple of nice-sized mahi-mahi, nothing else was caught that day. But it was the sheer thrill of the voyage to and from the fishing grounds that would forever leave an indelible impression on Zeke and his wife, Robin. Gina grilled some of the fish they had caught, and they all enjoyed a splendid meal with white wine. While they were eating the freshest fish they ever had, it began to rain. Max charted a course that would take them back to Charleston.

It had been a great day. When they arrived back at the marina, it was nighttime. Zeke said he was too tired to make the drive all the way back to Savannah and so was Max for that matter. Tomorrow, they would all head home, back to their normal lives, but tonight was meant for relaxation. Zeke sat up on the bridge with Max as they burned a joint and admired the nighttime view of the harbor. They all slept aboard *The REEL OPPORTUNITY* that night.

The following week found Max along with the other members of the River Dogs MC cleaning and repairing their destroyed clubhouse. All the smashed furniture was loaded on trucks and taken away. New flooring and new bathroom fixtures were installed. A new bar was constructed and new tables, chairs, and barstools were ordered. Neon beer signs hung on the walls and everyone had to admit, the place looked better than any clubhouse any of them had ever seen. Max paid for everything. Zeke insisted that the new clubhouse be dedicated to Maxwell Ernest Hart.

With their clubhouse now fully restored, they threw a party in honor of Max and Gina. A beautifully painted portrait of the couple was unveiled, and it hung proudly on the wall as a reminder to all club members of the unparalleled generosity of Max and Gina. Max gave a short speech thanking everyone for making them part of their way of life. Every single full patch member made it a point to personally thank Max for all he had done. Max said he was honored.

It was Gina who became the official club DJ, spinning funky techno music over the initial objections of some of the members. Their objections soon subsided, however, when every single female present was on the dance floor, shaking their booties to the red-hot dance music. Zeke sat on a barstool by himself and just shook his head. His motorcycle club had been completely transformed by this mysterious couple, who seemed to come out of nowhere. Their zest for life was infectious. On some level, they had managed to affect every other club member in some way.

The time had come for Max and Gina to do what they had always wanted to do. It was time to return to Hilton Head Island to resume looking for their dream house. They met with the same female real estate agent Gina had met with the last time. This time, however, they found exactly what they had been looking for all along. It was a beautiful old four-bedroom house at the very end of a dead-end street.

A title search revealed that the old house had changed owners five times over the last ten years. Max thought this was a little odd, but not outside of the norm for Hilton Head. People were always coming or always leaving.

They bought all new furniture for the house, and they settled into the quiet neighborhood where most all of the neighbors kept to themselves. Max liked it that way. But there was something odd about the house that neither Max nor Gina could explain. There were strange noises in the middle of the night. There were apparitions that could be seen out of the corner of one's eye that would disappear when they were looked upon directly. Max thought he was losing his mind until Gina began to reveal similar experiences.

The couple figured that as long as whatever it was did not interfere with their lives, they could live with the strange entities. But that's when things started getting really weird. Every night, something would wake up Max at exactly 3:00 a.m. Max could swear it was a woman's voice whispering in his ear, but not in English. Max would wake up, only to find Gina asleep beside him. He now began to understand why all the previous owners had relocated. Like everything else in the last six months, their dream house was turning out to be a nightmare.

Gina was affected on some level, but it was Max that the ghosts enjoyed messing with the most. Then came the night when Max awoke to find a vaporous, smoky pair of eyes, hovering just over his face. He closed his eyes tightly, but the eyes remained fixed in his mind. He sat upright in the bed, sweating profusely. Had he been dreaming? He certainly hoped that he was and he dared not share the experience with anyone, even Gina. Anyone who heard his story would think that he was insane.

He carried the secret with him everywhere, to the point where it affected his daily routine. There were times when he would be preoccupied with some mindless task, like paying bills, for example, when he would just stop and stare at the wall. Looking at his watch, he would find that he'd been sitting like this for over an hour. Was this the punishment due for all that he'd done wrong in his life? he wondered. Or was it just him? Was he actually going insane and just didn't know it yet?

There was a riding event scheduled for the upcoming weekend, and Max was really looking forward to not having to deal with his "problem." The River Dogs MC all met at their newly restored clubhouse on Friday night. Even though it was still winter, the weather was unseasonably mild, and practically all of the women would be along for the ride including Gina. Their destination was Jacksonville Beach, just a couple hours' ride south.

After dinner, in the comfort of their hotel room, Gina asked Max what he thought they should do about the house on Hilton

Head. Gina confided that she no longer felt comfortable there. Max agreed. Yet he was uncertain about the paranormal activity they had experienced there. How did they know for certain that what they were experiencing were not just bad dreams? At any rate, things were getting all too weird for them as of late.

The next day was beautiful, not a cloud in the sky. The River Dogs MC and their women spent the entire day at the beach. Some were even so brave as to swim in the cold ocean, it was after all still February. Watching Zeke and his wife, Robin, swim in the ocean gave Max an idea. Zeke and his woman were fearless. As the club president stretched out on his beach blanket and relaxed in the sun, he was approached by Max.

Max confided in Zeke about the strange experiences that had plagued the couple since they had moved into their new house. Would Zeke be willing to stay there with Robin by themselves for a week? Zeke's initial response was hell yeah. When he asked his wife what she thought, Robin was all for it also. Robin said she was fascinated by paranormal activity, she couldn't wait. It was exactly the response Max had been hoping for.

When told that Zeke and Robin would be staying at the house on Hilton Head, Gina was pleased. She just had to know for herself if what they had experienced was real or imaginary. Zeke and Robin were straight shooters, and Gina was confident that if the couple experienced anything out of the ordinary, they would be straightforward about it. Gina also knew that the club president and his wife would be discreet about their experience.

And so it was arranged that the two couples would essentially switch places for a week. Zeke and Robin would stay in the house on Hilton Head, and Max and Gina would stay in Zeke and Robin's townhouse in Savannah. Also, Max would have to oversee the motorcycle repair and custom build shop that Zeke owned and operated. This was a bit of a concern for Max. He knew nothing about the business at all. What if something were to happen?

Zeke explained that it was only for a week. Besides, all Max had to do was show up and look authoritative. Heck, Max already knew most of Zeke's employees. They were all club members and they all respected Max. They all had projects they were already working on. All Max had to do was show up and not take on any new customers for just this one week. As far as hours and payroll were concerned, Zeke's secretary handled all of that stuff, as well as answering the phones and closing out work orders.

But as soon as Max saw Zeke's secretary for the first time, he knew there would be trouble. She was a biker chick as hardcore as they come. But underneath all her tattoos, she was very attractive. Her name was Luna, and she basically ran the day-to-day operations of Zeke's business. She also never missed an opportunity to mess with Max. She somehow sensed that Max was highly uncomfortable in his new role, she did the utmost to make him feel even more so.

On Tuesday morning, a very large black man came into the shop demanding to speak with the owner. Luna directed the man to Zeke's office where Max was sitting behind the desk, flipping through biker magazines. Max had watched the huge man pull into the shop riding a tiny 100 cc off-rode bike. The large man took off his riding helmet and proceeded to chew Max's ass. The man explained that he had just taken possession of one of Zeke's 1000 cc custom creations. The bike had thrown a rod and was now out at the man's house in Pooler, Georgia. The bike was supposed to appear in a custom bike show this upcoming weekend, and in the meantime, he was forced to ride the tiny 100 cc bike back and forth to work and it was embarrassing.

What was Max going to do about it? Max said he would call a wrecker service and have the bike delivered to the garage. The angry black man became even more agitated. He explained that he just paid twenty-five thousand dollars for the bike, and this was totally unacceptable. The man said he wanted a "loner." He brazenly walked over to a custom bike that Zeke had designed and built himself. The man told Max that this one would do just fine. Max stammered and said he would have to personally contact Zeke to get approval.

This would not do, the large man explained. He was already late for work, and any further delays might cost him his job. Max told the man to just relax, he would see what he could do. The man began to swear, but could not contain himself any longer, and he burst into laughter, as did everyone else in the shop. It was a setup contrived by Luna to unnerve Max, and it had worked. Luna said it was a training exercise to help Max deal with potential problem customers, and Max had failed miserably.

Max didn't know what was worse, the unknown entities in his house in Hilton Head, or this ill-conceived practical joke that was not the least bit funny. Max was not sure that he could handle any more pranks like this. He told Luna he would not say anything to Zeke on the condition that she cease and desist all practical jokes from here on out. Luna burst into laughter, saying that the whole thing was Zeke's idea in the first place. Max had no idea whether to believe her or not.

The following day, Luna said she was having some sort of problem with her desktop computer. She asked Max if he could help her. Reluctantly, Max agreed to take a look at it. He found the hard drive on, but the screen had been turned off. When he turned it on, there was a close-up image of a woman's vagina. Luna thought it was the funniest thing in the world. Max didn't think so. To make matters worse, one of Zeke's longtime clients just happened to walk into the office and was clearly able to see the image on the computer screen. It didn't help that this client was female. Was she part of the joke? Max would never know. Luna was having way too much fun at Max's expense.

Reluctantly, Max called Zeke at the house on Hilton Head. There was no answer. Max confided in Gina about the problems he was having with a certain female prankster at Zeke's bike shop. Gina's reply was simple. There were only three work days left. Max was on Luna's turf, and the best thing to do was let her have her fun. Let Zeke deal with her when he got back. Max decided that a lot could happen in three days.

The next day Max was in the bathroom when Luna knocked on the door frantically. She said there was an emergency in the mechanic's bay. Max was not amused, until he smelled smoke. He opened the door to the bathroom, only to find that Luna had detonated a smoke bomb right outside the door. Max reprimanded Luna, who hung her head sheepishly and rolled her eyes. But as the smoke bellowed out of the garage door, a neighboring business owner called the fire department.

Max explained to the fire chief that this was just someone's idea of a joke. Max explained that he was filling in for his friend Zeke, and someone took it upon themselves to play a joke on him. Max said he had no idea who would do such a thing. It could have been a customer or an employee, he had no clue. Gina laughed her head off when told of Luna's latest prank. She thought it especially funny when she learned that the fire department responded with no less than two fire trucks and an ambulance. The police even responded and wanted to know who was responsible. Things were getting out of hand quickly.

That night, Max and Gina lay awake in the upstairs bedroom of Zeke and Robin's townhouse. A powerful line of thunderstorms swept across the Coastal Empire and the Low Country. It was unusual because it was February, but not unheard of with the extreme change in temperatures lately. Then came the call. At 2:30 a.m., Zeke called his own house and told Max that their house on Hilton Head had been struck by lightning. Max couldn't believe what he was hearing. Zeke told Max he needed to come quick.

It was an hour's drive from Zeke's house in downtown Savannah to the southern end of Hilton Head Island. When they arrived, Max and Gina found that Zeke was not kidding, the house and all its contents were a total loss. Zeke and Robin were okay, but the old house had practically burned to the ground. There was nothing to salvage, everything was destroyed. Zeke apologized repeatedly. Max told him there was nothing to be sorry about, it's just one of those things. Besides which, the insurance would pay out, and Max and Gina would no longer have to deal with this house.

Zeke agreed that he would return to his business in the morning. Max and Gina checked into a hotel. They would call the insurance company tomorrow. Before parting ways, Max asked Zeke if anything unusual happened while they were staying in the house. Zeke said they would have to discuss the matter further some other time. The suspense was killing Max and he could not sleep.

When Max finally met with the insurance adjuster the next day, he told the adjuster he had just bought the property and just had it furnished with all new furniture and electronics. The adjuster asked Max if he had the receipts for all the items purchased. Max explained that they were all in an office desk on the first floor. The adjuster became suspicious and said that further investigation would be required. Max felt this was insult on top of injury.

Was it not bad enough that he just lost a house and tens of thousands of dollars' worth of furnishings, only to have the insurance adjuster all but question the legitimacy of the claim? Max angrily told the adjuster that his attorney would be in touch. Gina added that they would call the attorney right after making a formal complaint to the South Carolina State Director of Insurance. The last remark seemed to upset the adjuster as he got in his car and left the scene. Serves him right, thought Gina.

The next day was Friday, and Max and Gina showed up at Zeke's Custom Creations in Savannah.

Zeke still felt bad about what had happened. Again, Max told him not to worry, everything would be okay. Luna stood in the doorway of Zeke's office, when Zeke asked Max if he had any problems while running the shop. Max replied that he did not, everything was as smooth as glass. Zeke leaned across the desk and asked Max once again if he was sure there were no problems, before glancing in the direction of Luna. Max said that it was all good in the hood.

Changing the subject, Max asked Zeke if either he or his wife experienced anything unusual in the house on Hilton Head. Zeke responded by saying that he could not answer that question with a simple yes or no. His wife, Robin, fancied herself as a paranormal investigator, and they had brought video cameras and tape recorders and set them up at strategic locations throughout the house. Yes, there were some unexplained phenomenon, but it was just that, unexplained. Nothing too weird. But they never had a chance to review any of the audio or video tapes. Everything was destroyed in the fire.

As they left the shop, Max made eye contact with Luna, who mouthed the words "Thank you" to Max as he passed by.

Max mouthed the words "Fuck you, bitch!" before walking out the front door.

From Zeke's downtown shop, Max drove straight to the methadone clinic. He had somehow been able to reduce his daily heroin intake gradually, but he now decided he needed to kick this thing once and for all. Things had gotten so weird that Max decided that heroin was the last thing in the world he needed right now. When Gina realized what Max was now doing, she was overcome with joy. She hated the fact that her man had become a heroin user. This was to be a new start for both her and Max. In Max's own mind, he knew he was circling the drain. The last thing in the world he wanted was to drag Gina down with him, owing to his poor judgment.

Back on their farm in rural Georgia, life began to take on new meaning as each day Max used the methadone in increasingly smaller amounts. Gina was there for him every step of the way, and she offered sex as a way of keeping Max feeling good. Then came the day when Max woke up and told himself he would not be going to the clinic this week. He had managed to kick his heroin addiction without any type of counseling or rehab, and he was proud of his accomplishment. Everything in his life became sharper, more in focus. He felt good. He could not remember the last time he felt so good.

One morning, after his daily regime of log splitting, Max walked into the farmhouse to find Gina doing her nails on the couch. He sat down next to her, turned to her, and asked her if she wanted to get married this coming weekend. Gina was completely shocked. Where did this come from? At first, she did not know how to respond. Yes, she wanted marriage, but in a week? That would hardly allow for any proper preparation. Why did it have to be so soon?

With all that had happened recently, with all the crazy things that had happened over the last six months, now just seemed like the right time. They had shared the last three and a half years together, and they were both lucky to be alive, and they both knew it. This was the chance to add some normalcy to their lives. Both had lost touch with their families. All they really had right now were each other. A small private ceremony was all they needed.

Gina had always wanted a large elaborate wedding. She wanted her parents to be there along with her brother, Martin. But she knew that Max couldn't stand her brother. Her parents she knew would never warm up to Max. It wasn't that they thought Max was a bad person, which in some respects, he was. No one on the planet would ever be good enough for their daughter. Gina would never be able to explain how they had acquired 5.7 million dollars in six months. She could never explain the fact that Max was a member of a bike gang. Maybe Max was right on this one.

And so it was agreed. The next Saturday, they were married in their own backyard by a Justice of the Peace. The only other people in attendance were Zeke and his wife, Robin. After the brief ceremony, they had dinner. The two couples now sat on the back porch and enjoyed the mild late winter weather. Zeke and Robin discussed how their own marriage had made them more whole, how they had more to show for it. It had made them better people, especially to each other. But as the sun started to dip below the horizon, Zeke and Robin excused themselves, wishing Max and Gina the best of luck.

What now? Max asked Gina if she'd ever been to the Bahamas. When she replied that she had not, Max revealed that he'd never been there either, but it just seemed like the perfect place to take their honeymoon. Max was just full of surprises lately. It sounded like a fine idea to Gina. They made preparations for their trip. After securing their farm, they made the drive to Charleston. There, they provisioned *The REEL OPPORTUNITY* for the long voyage. Their last stop before heading down the Ashly River was the fueling pier

Stowed aboard, they had hundreds of canned goods and a hundred gallons of drinking water. They had weapons and ammunition. They had two sealed five-gallon buckets stuffed to the brim with American currency. There were books, videos, and music to keep them occupied during their long voyage. And of course, they had weed, wine, and liquor. Ever since Max had kicked his heroin habit, his taste for weed and alcohol had returned with a fury.

Gina sat up on the bridge with her husband. The cruising conditions were ideal. Now this is the ultimate freedom, Gina thought as she lit up a joint and passed it to her partner at the helm. Max was already working on his third Bloody Mary, extra spicy, and he was feeling no pain. He felt no pressures either, they were in international waters a hundred miles offshore. The only thing in the world they had to concern themselves with were modern-day pirates. But Max and Gina were not even the least bit concerned by that. They had automatic weapons aboard, and they both felt they could easily thwart a pirate attack.

The first stop on their journey would be St. Augustine, Florida, where they would refuel and spend the night at a marina before proceeding on their next leg of the journey to Miami. After refueling in Miami, they would head straight for the Bahamas. Max and Gina were both excited. This was to be a vacation dream of a lifetime. All the stress they had endured over the last several months was finally wearing off, and they were free to enjoy life on their own terms.

Max thought about everything that had happened to them up until this point. If he had it to do all over again, would he make the same choices? Probably not, he thought. He was convinced that his ordeal had taken years off his life. The stress, combined with his unhealthy lifestyle choices, made for a bad combination, not conducive to longevity. All he needed to do now, he decided, was to relax and enjoy the remainder of his life. This adventure they were undertaking was something he never thought he would be able to achieve even in his wildest dreams.

Out here, there were no authorities breathing down his neck. There was no one out here looking for them, trying to rip them off. The only people on the entire planet who even knew of their travel plans were Zeke and his wife, Robin, and they had both promised to keep it a secret. Right now, there was not one person on the entire surface of the earth who knew their exact location, and Max liked it that way. Out here, there were no schedules, no time limits, and no deadlines. They could pretty much do whatever they wanted. They ate when they were hungry, slept when they were tired, and made love whenever they felt like it.

Life has a funny way of working out sometimes, Max thought to himself. It could have easily gone the other way. It was a miracle they were both still alive, a little banged up and traumatized maybe, but they were alive and breathing. What more could anyone ask for? They had provisions, they had money, and they had the zest for adventure. Anything could be waiting for them over the horizon, and they were ready for it.

Two days into their voyage, they were still well offshore. All the drinking, weed, and sex were making them tired, and Max struggled to stay awake while at the helm. Gina would relieve him for a few hours, and the process would start all over again. Still, it was better than any life he had ever known before. Gina was his soul mate. Despite her wildness, and the infidelities on both sides, they had settled into married life content with each other's company. They were a perfect match.

Max silently wondered what lay in store for them once they reached the Bahamas. It would be a totally alien culture for them. He'd read books about the Bahamas. Three hundred years ago, it was a headquarters for pirates, who used it as a base of operations as they preyed upon merchant shipping, as well as warships and treasure ships from Spain, France, and England. In the 1980s, it was a stopover point for smugglers on their way from Colombia, South America, to the United States.

For Max and Gina, it was an escape from the real world and the heinous things they had done building their cocaine business. Now all that was behind them, and Max had to often struggle not to think about what had happened that led up to this point in their lives. It would always be there in the back of his mind. He would just have to force himself to think of something else whenever the bad memories slipped through the cracks of his consciousness. All he needed to do from here on out was to focus on the here and now, and everything else would fall into place.

But the relative tranquility of their new life was shattered by a violent collision with an object just below the water's surface. The port engine went into overspeed alarm and shut down. Whatever they had struck had either severely damaged or sheared off the port propeller. Gina was asleep in the master stateroom room and was thrown against the forward bulkhead by the collision. This is bad, she thought, really bad, as she scrambled through the salon.

On the bridge she found Max, who had been thrown against the ship's wheel, striking his chest against it. He struggled to catch his breath as he realized they had a very, very big problem. A moment later, the starboard engine shut down as well. Max reached overhead for the two-way radio to broadcast an SOS signal. But the radio was dead. All the electronics were dead. Max was sure he'd cracked a couple of ribs, and the pain was overwhelming as he climbed down the ladder from the bridge to the main deck.

He pulled open one of the engine hatches and was engulfed by thick, acrid black smoke. There was an electrical fire in the engine room. Max quickly let go of the hatch in the hope that the fire would put itself out from oxygen starvation. But that was the least of their problems at the moment. The sport fisher had begun listing forward. They were taking on water. They were sinking. Max climbed around the outside of the cabin forward to release the survival raft from its stowed position. He yelled for Gina to start throwing provisions and bottled water out of the salon onto the rear deck.

Gina wanted to know what it was they had struck. Max wanted to know as well but realized that didn't even matter right now, they were going under. Max pulled the ripcord on the survival raft, which self-inflated in an instant. He walked it around the cabin to the stern where it could be loaded with provisions. Tying the raft off to a stern cleat, he saw what they had struck. It was a steel container lost off of a container ship. But how could it be there floating just below the ocean's surface? Max guessed that it could, if it was filled with cork or Styrofoam or empty containers, but none of that mattered right now. The only thing that did matter right now was loading as many provisions as the life raft would allow, leaving room for two adults.

But the life raft's rubber bottom wasn't designed to hold a large amount of dead weight. At some point, they would have to decide exactly how much they could bring. The reality of their predicament began to set in. Max calculated that they had twenty to thirty minutes to get what they needed before *The REEL OPPORTUNITY* sank out from under them. Right then, it occurred to Max that they still had the dinghy, which could be loaded with additional provisions and tied off alongside the survival raft.

They now threw additional canned food, bottled water, fishing gear, weapons, and even the five-gallon buckets full of cash into the dinghy. Max closed all the hatches, windows, and the salon door in the hopes that it would slow the process of sinking. All that would do was prolong the agony, but at least they could stay aboard until the very last second. What had started out as a perfectly good day had become a nightmare in which they were having to make decisions that could mean the difference between life and death.

As the rear deck became awash with seawater, they knew they were going to have to abandon their vessel. Climbing into the rubber survival raft, they immediately became aware of how uncomfortable it was. But Max and Gina both knew it was not designed for comfort, it was designed for survival. It was nothing more than a rubber ring with a rubber bottom and a tent-like dome cover to protect the occupants from the elements.

Through the folding entrance flap, they watched in disbelief as *The REEL OPPORTUNITY* slipped beneath the ocean surface, never to be seen again. Max guessed that they were probably one hundred miles offshore, in ten thousand feet of water, somewhere off the coast of Brunswick, Georgia. Gina began to cry. Max felt so badly for her. If it were not for him, they both would not be in this situation right now. They faced the prospect of a very slow, agonizing death.

Max was beside himself with grief and guilt. Just when he thought he had it all figured out, his sorry little world turned upside down. What were the odds of striking that submerged container out here with hundreds of miles of ocean on either side? But this was to be his unluckiest day ever. The only thing he truly regretted now was dragging Gina into all of this. She would have followed him anywhere. Max was a fool for ever thinking he could just pack up and sail away from his past.

Taking a long pull off a bottle of vodka, he handed it to Gina who did the same. He twisted up a joint, lit it, and handed it to her. He looked at his watch. A mere thirty minutes had passed since the sinking. Using a dinghy paddle, he rotated the survival raft three hundred sixty degrees, while scanning the horizon for any sign of another vessel. All that could be seen was empty ocean in all directions.

Even if they were to spot another vessel, it would have to be relatively close in order to spot them. They had six shells for the flare gun. They would have to be used at precisely the right moment if they stood any chance of being spotted. A ship or another vessel would have to be almost right on top of them in order to see the flares in daylight. And what about the night? A ship could easily run over them and they would never know it. There were a thousand and one things that could go wrong out here.

They continued drinking and smoking weed throughout the day and into the night. They were completely wasted by nightfall, but too wired to sleep. Overhead, a million stars shone in the blackness of the universe. It was such a shame they could not enjoy the spectacle under different circumstances. It just made them realize how small they actually were in the grand scheme of things. They were nothing more than a speck, floating on the surface of the ocean, on a planet eight thousand miles in diameter.

The following morning was cold. They were drifting north in the deep, dark, clear blue waters of the Gulf Stream. They could have drifted fifty miles overnight, they would have no way of knowing. This could possibly be to their benefit. Eventually, they would cross shipping lanes to and from large American East Coast cities. There was at least a glimmer of hope, knowing that it was not outside the realm of possibility to be seen and rescued.

Something nudged their raft. Max paddled the raft in a circle, only to see a large gray dorsal fin protruding above the water. It was a shark, and a pretty damn big one. They watched it circling the raft again and again. It was obviously curious of this strange object floating on the ocean surface. Max could not make out the species, but it was a magnificent animal, much larger than the raft they were floating in. This could be a problem. If it decided it wanted to bite the raft, there was nothing they could do about it.

Gina asked Max what they should do. Max said he was just going to have to wait for the right opportunity and shoot the damn thing. Max fished one of the AK-47s out of the dinghy and chambered a round. But this was not like the helpless, played-out black tip Max had shot between the eyes six months earlier in the Savannah

River Shipping Channel. This was a man-eater, every bit of fifteen feet in length. The animal swam on its side past the raft, just below the surface. It was a great white, and Max could swear that its black eye was looking directly at him.

Why hadn't Max taken the shot? Gina wanted to know. Max told her that it just didn't feel right.

And with that, the animal was gone, never to be seen again. Sometimes in life, not doing certain things was every bit as important as doing certain things. Max's reasoning didn't make much sense to Gina right at the moment, she was just glad the shark had lost interest. An animal that size could have easily eaten both of them.

They opened a couple of cans of fruit cocktail for breakfast. Max poured a splash of vodka into his, and Gina held out her can for him to do the same for her. They passed a joint back and forth. Gina climbed on top of Max and they made love, finding the rubber floor of the raft being similar to a water bed. It was time well spent. They continued the drinking, smoking, and lovemaking, until Gina spotted a ship. Max pulled the dinghy in closer so that he could find the binoculars.

It was definitely a large ship, but it was probably ten miles away. There was no way anyone on board could have seen them, even if they were actively looking for them. The ship was just too far away. They watched it disappear over the horizon. For Max, it was a sign of hope, and he tried to lift his wife's spirits. Right now, there were probably hundreds of ships out there plying the ocean. All they had to do is cross paths with one.

But as the Gulf Stream carried them further north, each day got a little colder. They made more ship sightings, but they were all during the day, and they were all way too far away. They decided they would search for ships during the night, reasoning that a signal flare could be more easily seen, but that night, no ships were spotted. They slept all through the day and repeated the tactic the next night. They spotted a ship in the middle of the night, and Max fired three flares into the sky above their raft, hoping to attract the attention of someone on board. But once again, it was too far away. Even if they had miraculously spotted the flares, finding the tiny raft in complete darkness would be next to impossible.

Early the next morning, they spotted a US Navy warship. Max guessed that it was on its way to Norfolk, Virginia. Through the binoculars, Max was able to identify it as a Ticonderoga-class cruiser. It was probably six or seven miles away. Max and Gina decided to fire one of the three remaining flares. But these types of ships were fast, capable of traveling at thirty-two knots. By the time Max fired the flare, it was already past their position. If only they had seen it just a little earlier, they might have stood a chance.

They decided they were in the area where they were most likely to spot ships, so they rotated shifts. The trouble was that the ships could only be seen through the single opening, requiring the lookout to keep rotating the raft every so often. By now, however, the outside air temperature had dropped considerably, it was still late February. The only protection the couple had against hypothermia were some wool blankets and each other. It never occurred to them to pack heavy clothing or jackets as their original destination was the Caribbean.

The strong ocean currents continued to carry them north and the ship sightings became less and less frequent. They both were suffering from hypothermia and exhaustion, and they were finding it difficult to stay awake and search for ships. This was it, Gina said to her man, seriously. They were going to die out here, weren't they? Max told her not to give up hope just yet. They were still alive. Yes, but for how much longer?

The days came and went, and as their raft drifted even farther north, the cold became unbearable. Then came the day Gina woke Max and asked him what that thing far off in the distance was. It was an iceberg! It was right then that Max and Gina abandoned all hope of being rescued. They both knew this was the end of the line for them. Max tried to stay strong for his wife, but he became visibly upset, cursing himself repeatedly. He stammered, on and on about his life, and the fact that he never listened to his own conscience.

Every decision in life he had ever made, every course of action he had ever taken, was based on impulse. Right or wrong, righteous or evil, it was all based on impulsive decisions that came straight from the gut. Sure, there were instances that required careful consideration, but they were a rarity. Rather than base a decision on pros and cons, for Maxwell Ernest Hart, it was always his gut instinct that guided his every move throughout the course of his entire life.

Sometimes his choices were dead-nuts-on, like his decision to marry Gina. Sometimes his decisions were horrific, such as the way he had tormented the real estate agent Lester Price just prior to his death. But Max knew the worst decision he'd ever made was to listen to his friend Ray Bangor the day they found the *Winsor2* wrecked on the Joyner Banks. That single decision was not only his downfall, but the downfall of countless others as well, Gina Lydia Rodgers most tragically.

Deep within the conscience of Maxwell Earnest Hart was a voice that was always there, always urging him to relax, always urging him to reconsider, always urging him to have a change of heart. But he never listened. He never even tried to listen, it was too much of an effort. In order to listen to the voice, he would have had to silence all the other thoughts racing through his head. If he were able to do that, he would have been able to hear the voice which was never more than a whisper.